A Devilish Element

MADELYNNE ELLIS

Cover Design by Madelynne Ellis
Cover images from Depositphotos.com
& Periodimages.com
Edited by Dayna Hart of Heart to Hart Edits

First Published in 2024 by Incantatrix Press.

ISBN- 978-1-917284004

www.madelynne-ellis.com

Join my newsletter!

A Devilish Element

Can a bluestocking and mathematician admit the truth of their feelings, or will a certain devilish element end a love that's just begun?

Remote Cedarton Castle is haunted. That's what Eliza Wakefield's sisters say before she sets off to visit. Somehow, the crumbling ruin is even more isolated and foreboding than expected. Its inhabitants are a small cluster of Lord Linfield's closest allies. Moreover, all is not well with the Linfield's marriage, leading Eliza to fear for her friend's safety and her mind.

Mathematician Jem Whistler is owned by a lord who demands things he'd rather not give. Unexpectedly reunited with the woman who holds his heart, he struggles to keep his attachment hidden. When the threat from Cedarton's white lady increases, Jem and Eliza must work together to uncover the true nature of the spectre haunting Cedarton's shadowy halls. That's if they can keep their hands off one another long enough to investigate.

Scandalous Seductions
A Gentleman's Wager
Indiscretions
Phantasmagoria
Three Times the Scandal
The Viscount, His Lover & I
The Ghosts of Christmas Past
The Serpent's Kiss

Romps & Rakehells
Capturing Cora
Seducing Sophia
Taming Taylor

Forbidden Loves
The Kissing Bough
Pure Folly

The Black Halo Books
Come Undone
All Night Long
Off the Record
Come Together
All Fired Up
Come Alive
Reflex
Replay
Refrain
Toxic
Reckless Beat

Anything But...
Anything But Vanilla
Anything But Ordinary

Stirred Passions
Cherry Bomb
Black Velvet
Soul Kiss
Mint to Be
Screw Driver

Standalone titles:
Tempted
You, Him, & Me
Passion of Isis
Sharing Adam
Gabriel's Naughty Game
Confessions of a Greedy Girl
Crazy Love

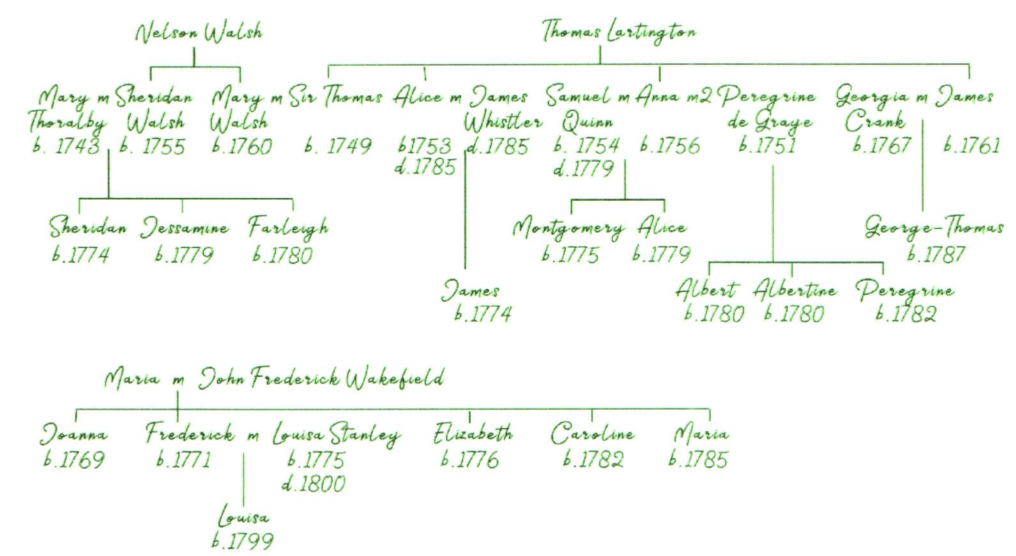

Nelson Walsh
Thomas Lartington
Mary m Sheridan
Thoralby Walsh
b. 1743 b. 1755
Mary m Sir Thomas
Walsh
b.1760 b. 1749
Alice m James
Whistler
b1753 d.1785
d.1785
Samuel m Anna m2 Peregrine
Quinn de Graye
b. 1754 b.1756 b.1751
d.1779
Georgia m James
Crank
b.1767 b.1761
Sheridan Jessamine Farleigh
b.1774 b.1779 b.1780
James
b.1774
Montgomery Alice
b.1775 b.1779
Albert Albertine Peregrine
b.1780 b.1780 b.1782
George-Thomas
b.1787
Maria m John Frederick Wakefield
Joanna Frederick m Louisa Stanley Elizabeth Caroline Maria
b.1769 b.1771 b.1775 b.1776 b.1782 b.1785
d.1800
Louisa
b.1799

-PROLOGUE-

Eliza

October 1801, London.

The impact of the horse and phaeton had shattered the woman's collarbone, leaving her neck with a sideward tilt that James Whistler reached out to straighten, only to have his hand stayed by the bark of his acquaintance, Dr Ludlow Bell.

"Don't touch her. That is my task. Have you a paper, a pencil about you? Good, then please record what I bid you record, and nothing else."

"It is only that her head—"

"The matter of appearances are beyond her now. We need not concern ourselves with bodily comforts or the crease of a dress, nor a muddy hemline."

"Of course." Jem nodded his understanding. It wasn't as if he wished to poke at the woman's broken body, only that she lay in such an uncomfortable and ungainly pose. Head crookedly set, and both legs stuck out at unnatural angles, like they were the edges of two set-squares and not the limbs of someone who had been a living, breathing person only a moment ago. The only positive thing one could say about the death was that it had been mercifully quick. Lord Linfield's phaeton had been mid-race. Where she had come from, no one could say.

Linfield was miraculously unscathed, but two horses had been shot.

"Record, please: a woman of some twenty to thirty years of age, of stouter proportions and"—Bell felt about his pockets for a measuring tape—"statuesque height. You may record that as five feet, nine inches. Impact has splintered the left collarbone and broken both shinbones... and the left wrist. The lady is married, if the ring on her finger is to be believed. The ring is gold." This Bell slipped into his waistcoat pocket. "That will suffice for observations in situ." He waved over a pair of grooms ready with a stretcher and a cart. "You will deliver her to this address. My housekeeper will show you where to put her."

No sooner had they doffed their hats than Bell's hand extended to Jem.

"My notes, Mr Whistler. I thank you for your assistance."

Jem tore the page from his pocketbook, glad that he'd had the foresight to mark the observations on a fresh page, and hence was not forced to sacrifice his algebraic formula. The matter of steam, resulting pressure, of pistons and volume had consumed him these last few days. He was sure he was on the verge of something, might have already grasped it had Lord Linfield not insisted that Jem accompany him to the race. How he wished he'd remained at his desk, with his thoughts and his scribblings. The vision of death, the permutations of angles and trajectories and resulting impacts would surely haunt him for nights to come. Linfield, however, was not easily gainsaid, and so Jem frequently found that despite his best intentions, he ended up someplace he never intended to be.

"Bell," he remarked. "Will you not check on the viscount before you leave?"

The physician was already rolling down his sleeves. He raised his chin and peered down his hooked nose with raven-black eyes. "I would say that Linfield is in remarkably sound health given that I can hear him from here, a distance of some considerable yards. I'd be surprised to learn he sustained more than a bruise, and therefore the services of an anatomist are not required. No, I will attend to the lady instead, and leave the company of Lord Linfield to yourself. An arrangement I think he will vastly prefer. Now, good day to you, sir. Thank you again for these. Please assure the viscount that I will attend to any matters that might arise with the magistrate, and the notification of any kin."

-1-

Eliza

December 1801, Yorkshire.

If Eliza Wakefield was certain of one thing, it was that only the foolhardy or truly stubborn willingly undertook carriage journeys in the month of December. Though she dearly loved the moors of her beloved Yorkshire, she was the first to admit that they were prone to trying fits of pique, especially in the grey months of the year. Today was such an occasion.

The dark clouds had folded themselves around the hilltops like a smothering shroud sometime after two and were now inching into the valleys. Soon the entire landscape would be nothing but mist so thick one could barely see one's own hands held before them.

"I don't know how wise it is to press on, Miss," Martins, the coachman, advised in his throaty drawl. The poor man had been injured in battle fighting in the Americas, and since, had always sounded rather strangled. "Even with the lantern lit, Posey can barely see the way, and I don't know these parts well enough to be sure of them in this wuthering nonsense. Perhaps…"

"Perhaps?" Eliza prompted, allowing the coachman a moment to gather his thoughts. Martins was prone to rather woolly thinking. After a rather lengthy pause, when he seemed unlikely to reply, she added, "I agree that it's not ideal weather, but our destination is surely closer now than home, so it would be illogical to turn back. Nor will I sit here in this damp in the hopes of it clearing. No, Martins, we must be almost at Cedarton by now. We will press on."

"If you think it's best, Miss, I won't gainsay you, but Posey ain't too fond of this. She's getting twitchy, so she is."

Posey, being perhaps the mildest mannered mare ever to have pulled a gig, was enjoying the moment of relative idleness to feast on the surrounding vegetation. If she was twitchy, she wasn't displaying it in any way Eliza could discern.

"There's the worry of boggarts, too, if we stray from the path."

"Boggarts?" Eliza heaved an inward sigh. "Yes, I suppose that is a concern, but I put it to you, Martins, I'd rather risk an enchantment than huddle in this rickety vehicle for an indeterminate amount of time. Why, it doesn't even have the luxury of multiple walls to shelter us, merely this rather inadequate hood."

A fat bead of moisture dropped from said hood

at that very moment and worked its way inside the collar of her pelisse. "Come, get Posey to trot on. We'll all be happier once we arrive."

~Ж~

Cedarton was not what Eliza expected. To be fair, she'd had little to go on beyond the name, which had conjured in her mind a vision of autumn: bright days, blue skies, fresh breezes, and leaves swirling around in a rainbow of golds and bronzes. Built of stately grey stone, Cedarton Castle ought to have impressed one with a sense of solidity. Instead, it squatted like a fat moggy about to pounce. To Eliza, gazing on it for the first time as the gig came to a jerky halt, it inspired a sense of menace. This was no cosy manor, rather a weather-beaten, battle-scarred fortress, complete with iron-pinned doors and soot-stained ramparts.

"Seen some troubles in its history, I should say," Martins muttered under his breath. "I'm not well acquainted with the folks or lore of this stretch, but I'll hold to my earlier warning: you're to be on the lookout for boggarts, spectres, and the likes, Miss Wakefield."

"I shall certainly keep your words in mind, Martins." Eliza slipped from the high seat. The moment her feet touched the gravel, the great door opened, revealing dear, Silent Jane. It seemed quite a feat for her to have captured a viscount.

"Eliza...Oh! It is so very good to see you."

"And you also," Eliza accepted her swaddling

embrace with a degree of perplexed amusement.

"I can hardly believe you are here. When the fog came down, I was certain you'd about turn, but bless my heart, I am joyful that you did not. It has been so, so long." She grasped Eliza's hands tight and led her towards the entrance. "We are a small party for the week. Friends of Linfield's. I should be quite lost if you were not here too. You must tell me all that has happened since we last saw one another in... was it really April? But first, come inside. I am forgetting myself. You must be half perished after your journey. I'll have Mrs Honeyfield draw you a bath."

"No, indeed," Eliza waved away the offer. "A fire and your company will soon ward off the chill. Although I will not say no to a saucer of tea."

"Which you shall have at once."

Martins had handed down her trunk to the footmen and was all set to turn the gig about. He doffed his hat at Eliza by way of goodbye.

"Your manservant's not staying?" Jane enquired. "Oh, but he must, at least until the fog clears."

"They're expecting him back home. You'll be quite all right, won't you, Martins?"

"Aw reckon the moon'll be peeping out afore long, Miss. Don't see no sense in lingering. I'd rather be tucked up snug afore the witching hour comes around, so seeing as you're all square, I'll be gannin, though I do thank yers kindly, Lady Linfield, fer ya offer of warmth and victuals. Alls be back at end of ah week t' get ya, Miss Wakefield, as arranged." He touched his cap again and was off, the mist swallowing him within a couple of feet.

"Not your man, then?" Jane observed.

"The cobbler's. Desperately superstitious, the whole family is, but Freddy's of a mind to train him for better things. I'm not sure what will come of it."

"Your brother is well?"

"Aye, and all my sisters, and my niece too, but what of you, Jane? I was most surprised, I must confess, when you wrote at Michaelmas to say you were wed, and to an earl's son, no less. 'Jane has married a viscount!' Caroline was positively astonished. 'How did such a mouse capture such a man?' she said, but it is perfectly obvious, for what man could not look at you and stumble. You have grown lovely, my friend. I believe your hair was still in plaits, with no hint of curl papers last we met. I think marriage suits you."

Jane tapped her hand in gratitude at the compliment, but there was a strain to her smile that showed plainly in her eyes. "I don't know that it has entirely sunk in. It has all been rather... overwhelming. A veritable whirlwind, what with the marriage and the move. We've only settled here these last two weeks, and you will surely know it when you see what I have invited you to."

"I'm sure I will be very comfortable, and very much at home. The fire is delightful."

Seeming to recall her friend's recent arrival, Jane nudged Eliza closer to the hearth. The entrance hall was a large square space, blessed with an enormous fireplace, and oak-panelled walls, over which were draped a series of ancient tapestries. It created a welcoming feeling, but it was true too that a certain mustiness sat in the air, and cobwebs still clung to the ceiling rafters, conjuring a sense of abandonment and crawling decay.

"I'm afraid Cedarton has not been a home for a good many years, and no amount of fires can quite take away the chill in its bones. I hope you will not find it too uncomfortable."

Eliza bore Jane's fussing a moment, before warding her off by handing her the shawl from her shoulders. Prior to the visit, her middle sister, Caroline, had been only too eager to relate all the gossip and rumours about Cedarton and its unhappy history that she could muster. Most of it had no business outside of a novel. All of it was overblown and fanciful.

"Don't fret so, Jane," she squeezed her friend's hand. "I'm certain I'll find it very pleasant indeed. Besides, once Cedarton has seen your touch, it will be transformed into the very warmest of homes. But, let us not talk of property. You must tell me of your adventures. How came you to be Lady Linfield?"

"Oh, there is little enough to tell. We met a time or two, and now we are wed, and that's really all there is to say of the matter. I wish you would tell me of your doings instead."

"And so I will, but you will not divert me so quickly. Is this to be your main abode? Are there grounds to explore? How many rooms? Have you other guests? And of course, both Caroline and Maria beg me to ask for a full account of your romance with Lord Linfield."

"Perhaps if we head to your room and take that tea." Jane shooed a footman off to see to a tray and drew Eliza through a doorway towards a grand carved staircase. "I will show you around as best I can once you are properly warmed and settled, but I hardly have a proper sense of the place myself. It is rather vast and sprawling, too large really, for two people alone, but the housekeeper is very good, and has everything in hand. I thought we would stay in London, but"—she shook her head sadly—"there is some... I don't know. A difficulty that Linfield prefers to avoid, and so we are here, tucked away in the countryside, away from everyone and everything. I confess, I had no idea Cedarton was so remote. I supposed when he said it was on the moors I ought to have realised, but Yorkshire always brings to mind your quaint little cottage, or the cobbled streets of Harrogate, or the seaside at Scarborough."

"What sort of difficulty?"

"Scarborough was so glorious this last summer," Jane replied, as if she hadn't heard Eliza's question. "I had such fun chasing waves and paddling in the sea. It was thoroughly delightful." Her expression took on a wistfulness that Eliza couldn't fail to notice. Something about her seaside stay had obviously made a lasting impression, and she didn't think it likely it'd been the North Sea pounding the shore. Matter of fact, she'd hazard it was a person— a man—responsible for that glow in Jane's eyes, and not the one to whom she was now wed.

"It was right after that Linfield and I were engaged," she said, practically confirming Eliza's supposition.

"You said there was some difficulty in London," Eliza prompted.

Jane tipped her head from shoulder to shoulder. "Oh, don't ask me about it, for I don't know a thing. It's a trivial matter. He says we can return in the Spring."

"You must miss your family," Eliza hazarded, seeing her friend's smile fade. "And here I am glad to have a break from mine, but are Linfield's family not here? Is there no sister or cousin you might strike up a friendship with? No company?"

"I have you."

"Indeed, you do." Eliza linked their arms, eager to see off the gloom cobwebbing her friend's shoulders. "But surely there are more than ourselves in residence? Linfield's family?"

"Some of his friends, but the family are all at Bellingbrook."

Eliza shook her head, the name being unfamiliar.

"Bellingbrook Hall in Lincolnshire. You've not heard of it? I'm told it's preposterously grand, but I haven't seen it, and we weren't invited. Linfield and the earl are," —she chewed her lip— "well... They're father and son, and Linfield doesn't care to be ordered about, you see, and here at Cedarton he can entirely please himself. It's not part of the Earldom."

"It isn't?"

"No, it came to him via his mother's people. That's why it's been abandoned so long. Linfield's had no need of it while he's been engaged with his studies, but—"

"Oxford?"

"Yes."

"And did he?" It seemed hideously unfair to studious Eliza that she was excluded from the halls of England's universities simply for being a woman, when a man might be awarded a Bachelor's degree without once opening a book or attending a single lecture, providing he was of sufficiently privileged birth. Equally confounding to her was that anyone would waste such an opportunity.

"He has a tutor," Jane blurted. "So, you mustn't brand him a shirker. He'll take the examination in the new year."

"Of course," Eliza said, still choked by the unfairness of the system. Linfield would sail through life, never once thinking about the privilege his rank granted him, never once considering how another life may have benefited from the education he paid for, but never engaged with. If she could learn, then she would listen to every lecture, read every book.

"You're in the Grey Room, close to me." Jane coaxed her across the upper gallery and then wound a path through a horrendously disorientating series of poorly lit and increasingly spider-filled corridors. The deeper they went, the more the taint of dust and mildew battled with the scent of the beeswax candles.

"This is you," Jane announced at the end of a corridor thick with shadows. She turned the handle of a near invisible door, only for a shadow to bolt across the runner. She shrieked, as if something mightier than a mouse had startled her. One pale hand clutched to her chest.

"Jane, are you—"

"Darned vermin. I'm sorry, Eliza. I'll have Mrs Honeyfield set more traps and see if we can't acquire a decent mouser. If you wish to leave in the morning, I'll completely understand."

Leave? "Don't be absurd." It would take more than a single mouse to scare her away, especially one so eager to make itself scarce. "I'm not going anywhere. But tell me, Jane, what necessitates that?"

Her attention, initially drawn by the mouse, had travelled along the runner and discovered a door hidden amidst the gloom, and not just any door, but an iron-pinned monster, secured with a wooden bar and a series of heavy bolts. "Are we expecting invaders?"

"Of course not." Jane clasped Eliza's elbow and began to steer her into the Grey room, but Eliza turned away from the unlatched door in favour of the bolted one.

"Another wing?" She claimed the candlestick from Jane's hand and raised it to make a closer inspection of the iron-pinned monster. It was the strangest of doors to find at the end of an upper wing corridor, its strength more suited to an entrance one wished to defend. The wainscoting ended short of its position, and the grey stone wall in which it sat was unadorned by painting or tapestry, but streaked with light-stealing stripes, leading to the impression that a squid-like entity was attempting to squeeze its bulk around the frame.

"Don't you wish to change out of those travel clothes?"

"Momentarily. Whatever is beyond here?"

Jane stayed by the door to the Grey Room as Eliza inched forwards. Now she was level with the strange door, its proportions were more clearly defined. Eight feet tall, at least, and almost the same across. She touched the brickwork, and her fingers came away stained.

"Soot?"

"There was a fire in the past. There's nothing beyond now."

"So many bolts, there is something."

"Ruins. That is all. It was the Lady Tower, but now it's only a shell. Throw back the bolts if you must. They're a safety measure, as the key is lost, and there's a sheer drop on the other side."

Far too intrigued to pass up the invitation, Eliza drew back the bolts, even though it was clear the door predated any fire, and thus its purpose remained obscured. The ancient hinges protested with a whine as she drew the door open, revealing a vast abyss that snuffed the candlelight.

Her breath caught, and Jane hurried to her side. "See, there's nothing of interest here. Please come away."

Nothing of interest, and yet Jane's fear was palpable.

Also, not strictly true. As Eliza's eyes adjusted to the murk, the shadows yielded the shell of what must once have been the grandest and tallest of Cedarton's towers. Further sooty tendrils reached towards the absent roof, while several storeys below, weeds poked up in inky thickets, and between her and them, the remains of floorboards and charred furniture hung suspended like the tiers of an off-centre wedding cake.

"What happened?" Having drunk her fill of the view, Eliza took a step back from the edge.

"A fire, some fifty years back. You'll have to ask Linfield if you desire the full particulars. I don't know them and don't care to. I believe the last Lady to live here died in the inferno." She shivered and drew her shawl more tightly around her shoulders.

So Caroline's tales of Cedarton's terrible past weren't entirely unfounded. "It must have been an inferno indeed. It's a wonder the rest of the castle was spared."

Jane shrugged, as if she'd given it no thought, which was practically confirmation that it had weighed on her mind, but Eliza saw no sense in pressing her. Jane would reveal her thoughts in her own time, at her own pace, as had always been her way. She'd never been one to bleat about a matter until it suited her to do so. "It won't give you sleepless nights, will it? I would spare you that at least, given Cedarton's lack of comforts."

"Jane, you are being too hard on the place. It's a little gloomy, but far less bleak than you're making out. In any case, I'm not given to flights of fantasy. A dark history will not disturb my rest. Come now, show me my room." She refastened the bolts, then let Jane lead her into the bedchamber. "See, this is quite delightful."

The room was large, with a low ceiling fashioned with plasterwork embellishments. A large, open hearth dominated the centre of one wall. The fire was lit and cast a pleasing glow over the room. There was an armoire, and a grandly dressed window with a sill wide enough to be used as a seat, and a writing bureau beside it that she might use to write to her sisters as promised. The bed, an old-fashioned canopied affair, sat square and central, its drapes of grey and green Kidderminster stuff, which also covered the lower half of all four walls. If the house had been more recently occupied, the Kidderminster would surely have been banished to the room of a minor servant by now and replaced with more fashionable paper hangings. Still, it had been thoroughly aired, and was to Eliza, so used to doubling up, both pleasant and expansive.

"So much space," she observed.

Jane drew her attention to a door she had presently overlooked, presuming it to be a closet. "Look, through here is where I am. We shall have ever so much fun. It will be like school all over again."

School had not always been a particularly pleasant affair.

"Linfield?" she enquired. Surely the adjoining rooms were intended for husband and wife.

Jane knotted her hands and dragged her teeth over her lower lip. "His rooms are in the other wing."

A knock prevented her from saying more.

"The tea you asked for, milady."

"Good, yes. Bring it in."

Two plainly dressed servants carried in a tray, along with the smaller valise Eliza had brought.

"This is Mrs Honeyfield," Jane introduced the older of the two women before she could make her escape, "Who has been so good to us in seeing that Cedarton was made ready."

The housekeeper appeared to be barely a year or two Eliza's senior, making her far younger than was typical for a housekeeper for a house of this size. She bobbed a curtsy, prompting the maid, who wasn't above thirteen if she was a day, beside her to do the same. "Eliza, you must ask Mrs Honeyfield if you need anything, for I know she will find it. Now, Mrs Honeyfield, this is my very dear friend, Miss Wakefield whom I've been telling you about. I wish her to stay as long as possible, so we must do everything we can to make her stay perfect and not frighten her away with Cedarton folktales and its eternal draughtiness."

"Good day, Miss Wakefield. There's warming pans aplenty, an' we'll keep fires stoked. If you want owt, be sure to ring and we'll be reet on it."

"Mrs Honeyfield is very efficient. Whereas you, my dear friend, are being overly dramatic. I'm sure I'll be very comfortable without any sort of fuss being made."

The housekeeper winced.

"I'm sorry, are you all right, Mrs Honeyfield?"

The housekeeper cupped her cheek. "Aye, Miss. It's nowt. A spot of toothache, that's all. If you don't need owt else, milady, we'll be off."

"I think we're all set," Jane said.

"Perhaps I might look at it, if it's painful." Eliza's offer stopped the servant before she'd taken more than a step. "I have some skills in that regard. You've a still room, haven't you, Jane? It won't take me a minute to mix a remedy."

Jane, who had already settled at the tea table, paused, teapot in hand. "I quite forgot about you and your potions. You were forever patching us up at school. There is a still room, and very impressively stocked if you can believe it, though I can't take any credit for it. It's not my doing. It's Linfield's. Leastways, it's a benefit of him having his personal physician in attendance."

"Linfield employs a personal physician?" Eliza said at the same time Mrs Honeyfield made another anguished gasp. "I suppose he is too high and mighty to see to a servant's comfort, or is it that he doesn't see teeth as a necessity to a body?"

"Eliza, you are so hard on men of learning. I'm sure if Doctor Bell is made aware of the matter, he can prescribe something."

"I shall be very surprised if it's for anything with any efficacy," Eliza retorted. "My remedy, on the other hand, works a treat."

"Old family recipe?" Jane enquired.

"The basis of it, but I've modernised it some. I never found that the honey helped do anything other than sweeten the patient's temper. Tell me the way to the still room, and I'll make it up right away."

"Eliza, truly? You've not been here five minutes. If you really must, then can it at least wait until after we've taken tea? It will be cold if we have to wait until you've attended your patient, and I'm sure Mrs Honeyfield can soldier on a little while."

"Aye, milady. It's kind of ya to think of us, Miss Wakefield. It's much appreciated. Me John knowed about such stuff. It's times like this I don't half miss 'im."

"Oh, you lost your husband recently?" Eliza asked, more eager to explore Cedarton's still room now than she was to take tea, but when Jane waved her towards a chair, she nevertheless sat.

"Aye, a wee bit back, Miss. I should get back t' kitchen now. Cooky'll be havin' conniptions over t' feast his Lordship asked for. But I'll be mighty grateful for that tooth remedy if you've time to mix it." She winced again but followed it with a tight little smile before departing.

"Honestly, Eliza, your things aren't even in your room and you're already meddling," Jane admonished as she poured. "I'll tell you right now that I doubt Bell will let you through the door of the still room, so you might as well forget any thoughts of potion making. He's very protective of his domain."

"His?"

Jane nodded. "It's not a mere still room he's set up. He's taken over three whole rooms on the ground floor and furnished them as a consulting room and surgery."

"Is he setting up practice? I thought you said he was Linfield's personal physician."

"That's right," Jane confirmed. She thrust a plate of parkin at Eliza. Jane, herself, was already biting into a second square. "Though it confounds me as to why it's necessary. Linfield's the picture of health. You don't mind that it's parkin, do you? I've had a proper hankering for it of late, and the only other thing on offer is some marmalade that Linfield's mother sent. It's horridly bitter, but apparently Linfield loves it. I daren't say that I've not the same love of it in case it gets back to the Countess."

"Yes, probably best not to slight your mother-in-law's marmalade afore you've met."

She accepted the offered piece of parkin and tucked in.

"As for Bell," Jane continued. "Well... I suppose I had better tell you now, that he's no ordinary physician, before you go rattling on about his sort never sullying their hands. He's very well respected, but rather eccentric. Mixes his own potions like an apothecary and he's performed for the Royal College of Surgeons in Lincoln's Inn Fields and studied at the Anatomy School in Oxford."

"I see." He didn't sound much like any physician she'd had the pleasure of meeting, more like a—

"Don't, don't say it."

Ginger exploded fiery on Eliza's tongue. "—body thief."

Jane sighed into her teacup. "Please don't say that to his face. It's not at all accurate."

"I know," Eliza thoughtfully chewed on her cake. "He dissects corpses. Resurrectionists only dig them up. Although, one has to wonder which is worse. Personally, I thought the role of the physician was to keep people alive."

"You know as well as I that's the whole point of… of chopping people up. Can we talk of something pleasanter? I hope when I go, I'm left peacefully in my grave, not relieved of my organs and pickled in a jar. The whole idea makes me feel nauseous." She pressed the back of her hand to her mouth as if she might gag.

"You were always squeamish." At school, Jane could be relied on to faint dead away at the sight of the merest scratch. Eliza was made of hardier stuff. Delivering babies required it, as did the recent forays into anatomy she'd made for herself, not that she was about to tell Jane of them. Her friend was already gulping tea as if her life depended on it.

"I'll be scrupulously pleasant to your Doctor Bell, I promise—"

"I'm pleased to hear it."

"—for how else will I get him to share all his tricks?"

Jane put her head in her hands. "You ought to have been born a man." She sighed.

There was much Eliza could have said about that too, but Jane looked too pale to handle it. She'd seemed the picture of health when Eliza arrived, but on closer examination it was plain there were dark smudges beneath her eyes, and a pallor to her skin not manifested with powder. Eliza stretched across the table and squeezed her friend's hand. "Tell me about Linfield. I can still hardly believe that you're wed. How long have you known one another? It must have been a whirlwind match."

When her friend remained silent, Eliza said, "I could tell you about the pistol ball I removed from a man's leg."

Jane raised her hand. "Stop. I will tell you everything you could ever want to know about Linfield, if you'll only spare me your love of blood and guts."

-2-

Jem

"Dear God, are you really going to let him assault you with those things?" James Whistler declared, watching with rapt fascination as Ludlow Bell extracted a coterie of leeches from a glass jar in which he had them stored and set them on a saucer.

Linfield, idly sprawled across the chaise Bell had procured from the attic a few days ago to serve as a consulting couch, turned his head, only to recoil from the plate of invertebrates. "I don't see that I have much of a damned choice. Having been coerced into marrying the wench, I'm now expected to produce a brace of tailfruit." He gulped and shot an imploring glance at Jem.

"There's no use looking at me. I'm not the medical man, and if I were, I'm not sure I'd ever prescribe anything quite so revolting."

"Bodies are revolting," Bell intoned, his expression sepulchral. Jem hadn't yet decided whether it was an affectation intended to add gravitas or if the doctor spent so much time around corpses that he had one foot in the grave himself. "Diseased and injured bodies, particularly so."

Linfield wriggled backward as if he could escape into the ghastly pattern on the upholstery. "Would this be the time to point out that I'm neither?"

"Yet you are, by your own admission, afflicted by a debilitating malady."

"Acutely debilitating," Jem droned. It was hard not to feel a smattering of sympathy for the sod, though Jem was finding it equally difficult not to laugh at his lordship's predicament. It was, after all, a pickle of his own making. He could have refused to marry the girl his family had picked out. Lord knows why he hadn't. Linfield wasn't usually one to docilely bow to pressure. If he had one strength, it was that he was rarely galled or swayed, and while his opinions weren't always based on sound rhetoric, they were always his own.

Bell's shadow fell across the chaise. "You'll need to lower your falls."

Linfield reached for the fastening but showed a deal of hesitation over slipping the buttons. "You're sure this will work?" He gave doctor and the saucer both sickly glances, and rightly so, given the delicate part of his anatomy they were headed for.

Bell captured one of the wrigglers between a pair of forceps. "There are no guarantees in this life of anything other than eventual death. However, this treatment is based on firm scientific principles. Erections depend on blood flow, and one thing leeches are very good at is drawing blood."

"That's because they bite, with teeth." Jem flashed his own pearly whites. "Up to sixty of them so I've heard." It wasn't that he'd made a study of leeches, but he knew a fellow who had.

"You're not helping," Linfield whined.

"If you prefer, we can forgo the treatment, and go back to playing cards or whatever other vice you might care to entertain us with." Bell said.

Relief released the tension from his lordships jaw. His eyes lost their nervous squint. Hope blazed like a sentinel beacon.

"That is, if you don't mind remaining a bungler."

And was snuffed out.

Jem snorted. The situation was positively ridiculous, albeit unfortunate, given the entire point of marriage was procreation, and Linfield's prick had evidently lost all its vigour the moment he said I do.

Bell, too, was fighting off a smirk and catastrophically failing. Linfield swung a fist at one then the other of them.

"Oh, yes, it's hilarious. Let's laugh at the man who was doing no more than minding his own business, and had a lass thrust on him without so much as an opinion asked and is now stuck in fumbler's hall because of it."

"Had his arm twisted right up his back, he did," Jem said to Bell over the top of Linfield's head.

"I know, I had to treat the sprain."

"You're devils, both of you. I should dismiss you both." He smacked them both, Jem on the wrist and Bell the thigh. It did nothing to kill their humour. They both knew he wouldn't send them away. He couldn't afford to. They were his only hope, albeit for ostensibly different reasons.

"You didn't have to wed the woman," Jem said.

"You say that, but you've no papa breathing down your neck, threatening to disinherit you if you don't comply."

Jem, whose parents had both departed this life when he was a boy of eight, took this statement with the sort of stoicism necessitated by an acquaintance with Linfield. The young viscount was an entitled, indolent rogue, and he said that with as much affection in his heart as he could muster, but truly, he was the sort Jem had ruthlessly avoided throughout his own studies, and regularly had nightmares about being allowed to run the country. The man had barely a bean of sense, no head for numbers, only a smattering of Latin, no Greek and maintained a mien of complete lassitude, stirring only when there was mischief to manage or a wager to make. How they had come to be acquaintances was a lengthy tale, but reduced to its simplest form, Jem had been employed by Linfield's papa, the earl of Bellingbrook, as a tutor for his wayward eldest son. Five years of Oxford education was deemed quite sufficient. It was time he shouldered the burden of responsibility, passed the confounded exam, produced an heir, and got on with learning the ropes of managing the ancestral estate. Not necessarily in that order, but now, while the earl still had wits enough about him to set his son right. Jem couldn't fault Bellingbrook's logic. If left unsupervised, Linfield would reduce the earldom to penury inside a decade, which would be an accomplishment indeed given that the family owned half of Lincolnshire and stretches of Rutland and Yorkshire too.

If not for the tutoring, they would never have met. Jem wouldn't have got sucked into Linfield's set, or come to be wintering in the wilds, or endured a host of other questionable activities which took him away from his studies. Still, he couldn't deny there were benefits to the association too. Trailing after Linfield reminded him of his younger years, constantly surrounded by his cousins and being embroiled in endless adventures and escapades. It'd reminded him that life didn't always have to be serious, and that joy could be found in unlooked-for places.

His gaze fell on Linfield's face again. He was hardly the handsomest man he'd seen, being somewhat weak of chin, but he had eyes that were forest green and flashed like the summer peeking through leafy bowers, and hair that stood out from his head like puffs of smoke. Jem curled his hand over Linfield's shoulder, whereupon the other man clasped his fingers tight.

"Ready?" Bell lowered the first of the leeches.

They were some of the most disgusting creatures Jem had ever come across, right up there with slugs, centipedes, and weevils. Likely, there were more repulsive creatures on this Earth, but fortuitously, he'd avoided encountering them.

"Jem," Linfield moaned. He squeezed Jem's fingers tight while he loosened his front fall with the other hand. "Say something. Distract me."

"Like what? This is making my eyes water, and I've the good sense not to let one near bare skin." He continued to squint and clench his thighs as Bell positioned the beast. Truly, one had to wonder if it was worth it. There had to be other means, a kinder means of curing impotency, or performance anxiety, or whatever affliction it was Linfield claimed to be suffering. Maybe if he drank a little less, or a little more, or thought of his wife as something other than a shackle, then he could fix his tallywhacker and make this whole procedure entirely unnecessary.

"Oh!" Linfield turned his head to look at the leech sitting on his cock. "I thought it would hurt, but there wasn't even a pinch."

"It's still disgusting, and I remain unconvinced as to the efficacy," Jem said.

"Are you a physician?" Bell placed the remaining leeches. Four... five of them in total, which seemed unduly excessive considering Linfield wasn't especially well endowed, and he was currently as limp as a wet stocking.

"I prefer to stick to the mechanics of iron and steel to that of flesh," Jem retorted. Numbers were a deal less messy and rarely drew blood.

"Then I'll thank you not to persist in offering your opinions."

Bell could be a soulless killjoy.

While Jem might not care for flesh-tailoring, that didn't mean he wasn't intrigued by the mechanics of it. That said, he wasn't desperate for a lesson on leeches. Actually, he was rather surprised to find them in Bell's repository, given his reputation as a proponent of modernised medicine. Leeches were the province of quacks, along with old theories of imbalanced humours and cupping.

"I suppose the theory is that the little devils draw out the bad blood, allowing the good to flow and produce a rise, or is it just a matter of sucking fluid into his cock? If it's the latter, I have to say there are more pleasant ways—"

"No," Linfield released his grip on Jem's hand in order to hold up his own, thus stopping Bell before he replied and got into the guts of the theory, and Jem from expanding on alternative means of creating inflation. "I don't care to know. It doesn't matter how it works, as long as it does. The pair of you are dull enough with your constant scientific blathering without it involving my cock." He flicked a glance up at Bell. "I don't feel it doing anything."

"They've not been on you a minute."

Linfield huffed, then settled himself more comfortably. He closed his eyes.

Jem used the moment of quiet to rub the residual ache from his fingers. They'd been crushed almost to numbness by Linfield's grip. "I've one question," he said to Bell.

Go on, the doctor nodded.

"I can't help wondering... Assuming this here treatment works, surely... Well, is it a temporary fix?"

"Erections are by their nature temporary. The aim isn't to give him permanent priapism."

"No, no... of course. But... if it's temporary, then

how does it help him to get it up for his wife?"

It seemed Bell didn't have a straight answer for that, given he found a sudden interest in rearranging the shelves of pills and potions he'd accumulated since they'd set up at Cedarton. "It'll... um, well, it'll unblock the mechanism."

"Assuming it was blocked?"

"It was blocked," Bell said, and Linfield waggled his noggin in agreement.

"Couldn't get it to half-mast, never mind full tilt. Bloody disaster of a wedding night. Had hoped I could be done with the whole thing by now, duty done and all that."

"I feel that was a tad optimistic," Jem said. "I think it's more usual for it to take a couple of attempts, or in some cases, many."

"And what would you know of such matters?" Linfield's jade-green gaze pinned him with an inquisitor's zeal. "Proper studious little saint weren't you before we got our hands on you? Where would your knowledge of such carnal matter come from?"

Jem surrendered, offering no explanation and no resistance. It was a topic fraught with peril, and he had no desire to quarrel or linger on the matter. The fact that he knew he was right, helped immensely. He might not have spent his Oxford days roistering and frequenting whore-houses, but he wasn't wholly unacquainted with womenkind. The same could not be said of his lordship.

~Ж~

Jem had been tottering on the edge of a doze when a knock on the door brought him to. Watching leeches suck blood had turned out to be as dreary dull as watching paint dry. Bell turned to answer, but Jem leapt up. "I'll get it." He hobbled across the room, thighs stiffly protesting having been tensed for so long. Usually, he'd have thrown the door wide as was his fashion, but with Linfield prone upon the couch with his tallywhacker out, he strove for a less boisterous approach.

"Lady Linfield," he enunciated, throwing a glance back into the room, before slipping out and pulling the door too, so that only the presence of his fingers kept it from shutting. "Are you looking for Linfield? He's a tad indisposed right now."

"Oh!" Her ladyship, a demure, strawberry-blonde with a thousand freckles, clasped her hands together and blinked at him owlishly for a moment. "No, we weren't looking for anyone, but the door was closed, and I know Doctor Bell is so particular, so it seemed prudent to knock. Eliza wanted some things, you see. For a remedy. Mrs Honeyfield has the most awful toothache, and—"

"Eliza?"

Jem's attention slid past Lady Linfield to the turn of the corridor. He had not seen the other figure initially, her form concealed by the thickness of the shadows in this part of the house. Bell's suite occupied a stretch of the lower floor accessed only via a servant's tunnel beneath the wreckage of the old drawing room. The physician had chosen the location precisely because of its separation from the main body of the house. Servants, he'd observed, did not fare well with the notion of corpses being stored and dissected in the places of their employment, and given Cedarton's whispered-about history, not alarming the few servants they'd managed to secure was rather a priority. On that basis alone, he had not thought to look for another figure. It was surprising enough to find Lady Linfield before him. He'd especially not imagined he'd find this particular woman blinking at him in reciprocal wonder.

"Eliza Wakefield. What are you—? This is quite the last place I expected to see you."

"Mr Whistler." She came forward to him, holding out her hands so that he might take hold of them, while they both looked one another over. The contact sent a frisson of heat straight to his groin, and with it an entanglement of memories and daydreams. She smiled impishly, "You know, that rather implies that you were expecting to see me someplace else."

"Having made your acquaintance, I freely admit I wasn't averse to the idea of doing so again."

Jem dropped a bow over her hands, a broad smile stretching his cheeks into aches. Rakishly, he planted a kiss on her bare knuckles and his pulse quickened at her gasp. He'd thought of her often, probably too often for his own good. Their acquaintance over the summer had sadly been too short-lived for him to have made anything of it, but that didn't stop him imagining how things might have been if time and circumstances had been on their side. The haze, the passion of those summer days made his heart swell, and wakened parts shrivelled by fear at what was going on in the room beyond. His gaze lingered on her fingers, and finding no wedding band, muscles he hardly knew he'd held clenched, relaxed. It seemed his friend and rival had not pipped him to the post. He'd not forgotten the kiss she'd granted. First he, then Joshua, thus ensuring complete fairness.

"Mr Whistler, if that is so"—Eliza said, a merry old glint dancing in her eyes—"you might stoop to replying to the correspondence I sent you."

"Ah." He offered up a sheepish grin. "I confess my laxity in such matters. I am a dreadful correspondent."

"Letters," Jane interjected. "What is this?" Her lips quirked into a pursed smile before she levelled a meaningful stare in Eliza's direction. "How exactly come you to be acquainted with my husband's tutor?"

"His tutor?"

"As you see me," Jem replied, making another bow. "And allow me to enlighten you, Lady Linfield. My aunt and uncle, Sir Thomas and Lady Lartington, were good enough to introduce us at Stags Fell last summer."

"And Jem was good enough to show me both his work sheds and to converse with me about mathematics," Eliza added. "He's fanatical about steam engines. Did you know that, Jane?"

"I confess I didn't. Nor did I realise it was something that interested you."

"I'm woefully ignorant about them."

The statement prompted a cough from Jem. "Not so very woefully. I recall you being a willing and very able student." He looked her over, failing to take in the details of her appearance, instead seeing her as she'd been, with a borrowed leather apron tied over her skirts, and a smudge of soot on her nose, side by side with him and Joshua in the workshop at Stags Fell. Her delicate hands had been covered in grease that day, and her rose-scent entwined by the tang of metal filings. They'd both been utterly smitten.

"Well, I confess I was sorry to leave for I did have half a mind to petition for membership of the Puffing Devils. Did you ever solve the conundrum you were working on?"

"Hm, not as yet."

"The Puffing whats?" Jane interjected.

"His society of gentlemen engineers," Eliza replied, without breaking eye contact with him.

"Forgive me," he mouthed. "How did I not know that you were to join us here?"

"Eliza, should I be the one to point out that you are neither a gentleman nor an engineer?" Jane remarked, though neither other party paid her any heed.

Eliza's attention was raptly fastened on Jem. "I had no notion of your presence either, but it's a joyous surprise."

"Aye, it is that. But tell me how? How comes it to be?" He looked back and forth betwixt the two ladies, seeking answers.

"Jane and I were at school together. You're

looking at the co-founders of the Women's Natural Philosophical Fellowship."

Jane swished aside the remark. "More like the founder and her simpering devotee. I never could get my head around most of your arguments, even though I was thoroughly bewitched by them."

Eliza jeed her head, dismissing her friend's remarks as poppycock.

"You know it's the truth. I've not looked at a sum nor read anything that wasn't a novel or attached to a fashion plate since we left school, Eliza. But I see that Mr Whistler falls prey to the gravitational effect you exert. She is so very engaging, is she not?"

"What? Oh." Jem relinquished his grip upon Eliza's hands, which he had clung to far too vigorously and for far too long, judging by Lady Linfield's remarks. While Jem mourned the loss of contact, Eliza clapped her hands together, glee painting a fresh glow across her cheeks as she turned to her friend.

"See, you say that, yet you still recall Mr Newton's theory."

Jane rolled her eyes toward the ceiling before casting her attention to the door once more. "Only in the vaguest sense. I couldn't scrounge together the details no matter how hard I tried."

"It relates force and mass," Jem elaborated.

The lady only shook her head at his explanation.

"The one is directly proportional to the mass of the other and inversely proportional to the square of the distances between their centres."

Bewilderment swept across his hostess's face,

while Eliza clapped again in delight. "Oh, how I have missed you, and I know I shouldn't say it, but there it is, and I shall very much look forward to hearing about all your progress and new theorems, but we did come with a purpose. I wonder, if we might..." She cast a meaningful look towards the door at his rear.

"Ah, yes, you wished to see Bell. You're in good health? No—you already said you require a remedy."

"Not for myself. I'm very well, thank you. It's for the housekeeper."

Jem supposed there must be one but couldn't rightly recall having met her. If he was quite honest, he couldn't recall much at present. That was the effect of Eliza Wakefield's luminescence. He quite forgot himself. "I'll fetch Bell."

He turned, only for Eliza to grasp his arm, stilling him instantly. A touch through clothing should not affect him so greatly, but his innards turned loops.

"No-no don't bother him. I simply need a few ingredients. I can easily gather them and mix it myself."

She took a step forward, leading him, her hand outstretched to raise the latch.

"Ah!" Reality burst through his lovelorn haze. He moved with all speed, inserting himself between Eliza and the door, acutely cognisant of what was occurring on the other side. Even ignoring the fact that Linfield was stretched on a couch with his privates on display, that there were issues with his lordship's knob wasn't something he'd want getting out, particularly to his bride. Additionally, there was the fact that Jem was wretchedly ill prepared to have the hereto unconnected parts of his life collide. "You know, now isn't really a good time. Do you have a list? Maybe I could gather—"

"It really will only take a moment." She patted his hand, clearly expecting him to move aside.

Jem stood firm.

"The thing is—" He chewed on the words. "Bell, he's—well, he's in the middle of an experiment. Vital that it's not disturbed."

"Experiment?"

Of course, her eyes lit.

"What manner of experiment?"

Lady Linfield groaned. "Eliza!" She clasped her by the hand and tried to turn her about. "You're not to tell her, Mr Whistler. I invited her here to be my companion, not to lose her to whatever nonsense it is you gentlemen find to do down here. I've heard enough talk of fish heads and entrails this last week. I had hoped additional female company might make for a little less of it."

"Entrails?" Eliza hadn't budged an inch despite Jane's continued tugging. "And fish heads."

"I did tell you he was an anatomist."

"Yes, and you know that I'm positively enthralled. I must say that Cedarton is far exceeding my expectations. Jane, you implied I would be quite sorry to visit such a place, but why if it isn't filled with the most intriguing and engaging characters." She turned her smiles on him. "Jem, you can't think me the least bit squeamish. Let me in at once."

"Definitely not, on both counts."

Eliza was brimming with so much barely contained joy, one might assume she'd just received a proposal from the man she'd hoped would marry her.

The matter was made moot by Bell wrenching the door open from the inside. His lanky form filled the space and swept over the assembled persons. "Is there some issue here?"

"Doctor Bell, I assume," Eliza said, peering around Jem and offering her hand to the cadaverous brute. "Miss Wakefield. Pleased to make your acquaintance. I was wondering if I might bother you for a few things—supplies to make up a remedy, and Jem says you are in the midst of an experiment. I should be honoured if you'd allow me to observe, I'm most fascinated by such things."

The luscious curls of Bell's full-bottomed wig trembled, though whether in horror at the thought of a woman entering his surgery or mirth over the suggestion that she might relish looking at Linfield's leech dotted cock was uncertain.

"Most assuredly not, madam," he replied. "If on the other hand, someone is ill, and you require my—"

Jem raised a warning hand. "It's the housekeeper, a minor ailment, nothing that can't wait."

"I'm perfectly able," Eliza stuck her nose in the air. "If you'll just allow me—"

"No." Bell rasped.

"—I can have the remedy mixed in a matter of

minutes."

"That really won't be possible, Miss Wakefield, was it? You see, I don't allow women in my surgery. And I certainly don't allow them to meddle with the preparations I put a great deal of effort into assembling. If Mrs Honeyfield requires any treatment, I will see to it myself. Good day now." He closed the door in her face.

"Well of all the rude..." She slapped her hand against the door.

"Eliza," Jane beseeched.

"How dare he treat me...us...you like that? This is your house."

"And my husband has given Bell these rooms. We should leave him to whatever it is that he's about. Eliza, I did warn you that this would be the likely outcome."

In other circumstances, Jem would gallantly have risen to Eliza's assistance. Bell, like many a man of learning, could be hopelessly backwards over the matter of female intelligence, seeing them as inferior creatures, mentally and constitutionally suited only to child-rearing and housekeeping tasks, and on par with domestic pets. When Jem had raised the notion of there being lady physicians in the future, the phlegm explosion had necessitated three clean shirts. However, presently, it seemed wiser to let his bullishness stand for the sake of expediency and Linfield's dignity.

"Let us go now. It can't be far off time we changed for dinner. It was most kind of you to offer to help Mrs Honeyfield, but I'm sure Doctor Bell has it in hand, and I didn't mean for you to come here to Cedarton to administer treatments to my staff. I desired your company. Your friendship. And you to have a restful break."

"Of course. Forgive me." Eliza turned to Jane with a bright smile plastered across her face, and they looped their arms together. "You know I never did have the knack of idleness."

"I know it. I know it well, my friend."

-3-

Jem

Jem watched them go, while sucking on his teeth. He'd make a point of finding out what Eliza needed and gathering the ingredients for her when Bell was otherwise engaged. "Did you have to be so frightfully condescending?" he muttered as he pushed past Bell, ignoring his blustering defence.

Eliza, with the same formal training he or Bell had received, would have changed the world by now. She would certainly pass the Oxford exam with a fraction of the trouble Linfield was making of it.

Jem wasn't certain of it, but he'd heard a whisper that his lordship had already attempted and failed it twice, and one of those times, he'd bought the damned answers. Linfield's particular talents didn't run to Greek, Latin, mathematics, or theology—not unless you counted ecstatic screams of 'Oh God!'. Which was not to say that he was a complete pigwidgeon either. Only that his true forte sat outside of the realms of classical study. Sadly, what he ought to be doing, if one ought to devote themselves to that which they truly excelled, was parting others from their morals and cash.

"What the devil was all that about?" Linfield demanded before Bell even jammed the latch.

"Visitors," Bell replied.

"Your wife, and her guest," Jem elaborated, trying to maintain a neutral countenance, and evidently failing judging by the deep furrow that rooted in the centre of Linfield's brow.

"What did she want?"

"Nothing important." Jem crossed back to where he'd been earlier perched. He noted a couple of the bloodsuckers had so gorged themselves they'd detached and were now fouling the upholstery.

Linfield seeing his line of sight, bellowed, "Bell! Get these confounded things off me. They're not doing a damned thing besides bleeding me dry."

"A few more minutes," Bell responded, prompting Linfield's elastic features to contort into something vicious enough to make Jem jerk his chair back.

"Now, Bell."

Jem winced. Ludlow Bell muttered something indelicate under his breath, then tucked his hands behind his back and said, "Very well, if you insist upon disregarding my advice, but know this, my lord, it could be that even one extra minute is the difference between a cockstand and misery."

"Misery has been a given since I was forced into matrimony. Now, get the bastard things off me. I have had quite enough of your demonic pets. I can say wholeheartedly that they are without a doubt the worst cocksuckers I've ever had the misfortune to encounter. They cannot live up to the best," he caught Jem's eye, "nor even the mediocre."

The doctor sighed. "Of course, my lord. As is your whim, so I shall make it."

Removal proved a trickier feat than positioning. The beasts couldn't be pulled off but instead had to be coaxed into releasing their jaws by sliding a nail under the head end. It was altogether disgusting, made worse by the fact that their hideous, mottled bodies were now bloated with blood. Bell carefully set them on the saucer like delicacies, before wrinkling his nose at Linfield's still entirely flaccid cock.

"It may take more than one tre—"

Linfield waved him away. The doctor took that as his cue to return his bloodsuckers to their jar in the adjoining room.

"I've heard nitrous oxide can—"

Linfield pressed a finger to Jem's lips, then slid his caress over Jem's chin and down his throat, causing Jem to stumble over his words.

"—it can throw one into a theatrical attitude. That is… I've heard it said it makes you tingle in every fingertip, every toe."

Linfield huffed. He touched Jem's lips. "We both know you can do that to me without the assistance of some recently cooked-up noxious emission."

"Could," Jem corrected him, and moved out of reach of his touch.

Linfield sank dramatically into the chaise, allowing his head to loll. "Anatomists, chemists, scholars, what do any of you actually know? I may as well hire a whore and be done with it."

"And where do you propose to find one of those in this godforsaken place?" Jem asked. Batting words back and forth was easier on his brain than attempting a reasoned defence that would fall on deaf ears, anyway.

His lordship merely chuckled. "James... Jem... I invited accordingly."

Their party numbered but half a dozen... seven, with the addition of Miss Wakefield, and none among them prostitutes. Accordingly, he bristled, shoulders lifting.

"Ha!" Linfield slapped the chaise. "You baulk at the label. It is all right, dear Jem, I did not mean you."

Then unless there was a hereto unknown brothel located on their doorstop, he had no idea to whom Linfield attributed the label. Not Bell, or George, or Lady Linfield...

"Did you really think I'd give the serious matter of my cock no thought?"

"On the contrary, I imagine the matter consumes you. As indeed is this beast." Jem pointed down, drawing his friend's attention to the leech half-shadowed by his shirt tails. "It seems the good doctor left one of his pets behind."

"Goddammit! Get it off me."

Jem traced a fingertip along the length of Linfield's thigh to where the leech sat near the root of his bruised and sullen prick. "I'm not certain I know the technique—"

Linfield grabbed his wrist. "Don't play games. Get it off."

It or you? The thought flashed, lightning fast through Jem's brain. Despite Linfield's counter, he still bristled at the implication that he was employed as his lordship's plaything. Jem instead drew a circle around the sanguisuge. "Look at its plump little body. It's thoroughly gorged on your essence. One might even venture tumescent with it." He gave a slow, almost flirtatious blink, then slipped his fingernail beneath the sucker, releasing it. He flicked it away, so that it landed with a splat upon the tea tray between the sugar bowl and a spray of cake crumbs.

Such marks it had left behind; a vibrant mottling of black, blue and red. It was a cruel sight and a barbaric treatment. His anger dispersed, as he reflected on Linfield's dilemma. Would he too, be willing to endure such torture if he found himself in similar straits? Consumed by a sudden wave of guilt, Jem applied his handkerchief to the wound and gently wiped away the smear of blood. "All these marks in such tender places. It seems an extreme measure."

"What choice have I?"

"There must be other ways, the nitrous—"

Linfield clenched his fist around Jem's coat front. "Stuff your science experiments. You and I both know there's one tried-and-true way, and if you cared even half as much as you once professed—"

Love words had never fallen from his lips. "Linfield, no amount of cajoling will change the facts. I told you when you wed, that we were done with all that."

"I'm not done with it. I need you. You've abandoned me when I need you most." His nostrils flared. Then he sucked in a jagged breath. "I... Goddamn you, James. Seriously, just, goddamn you. This is your fault. The whole situation. 'I can't'," Linfield imitated in a whiny voice. "'Not with a married man.' Why in hell's name should that make any difference? It's hardly a love match."

"Nevertheless, you made a vow to her." Jem replied, tempted to point out that it had never been a love match between them either. "To love... to keep her... forsaking all others. Swore it before God and in Christ's name, if you recall."

"You speak as if I had any free will in the matter when I had none. Thus, now having been coerced, you abandon me. You condemn me to be a fumbler forever. To feel no more joy, experience no more pleasure—"

"Your wife, I'm sure will provide those—"

"My cobs shrivel at the sight of her, my prick wilts, so that I am forced into this," he gestured at his bruised member. "And it is grossly unfair. And you... you who claim to be my friend, can fix this, but you will not."

They had never been friends. Their relationship was far too lopsided for that. He was the hired help. The man coaxed into performing additional acts through the dangling of carrots.

"Linfield, I cannot. It's not right."

Linfield clasped him tight about the wrist and

wrenched his hand over so that it sat firm against his prick.

The effect was instantaneous.

Jem snatched his hand away. "I said I can't. Moreover, I won't."

Linfield's eyes lit with a challenge. His thin mouth puckered into a nasty expression before turning sly. "You don't mean it, though, Jamie. 'Tis only to appease your conscience. But you must put that aside. This is a serious business, and there's no place for squeamishness. I must do my duty, and you, you must perform yours."

"My duty is to teach you equations and languages."

"*Te Iuppiter dique omnes perdent! Quaeso, melius discerem si mentula tua in me exercitio usus es.* Please, Jem. You want me to pass the exam, don't you? And somehow it all sticks in the old noggin better when you use non-standard methods."

Jem was saved the effort of articulating a response by Ludlow's return. "Is that a cockstand I see before me?" The physician's smile was utterly conceited and equally undeserved. "Did I not promise?" He took a bow, only for Linfield to fling a wine glass at him. It flew wide and smashed against the wall, sending the good doctor diving for cover.

"Evidently, you need a moment." He scurried off into the depths of the suite he'd carved out for himself, probably to prod at a pickled eyeball or some other grotesque.

"That was a little overdramatic," Jem remarked.

Linfield levelled his gaze at Jem. When it came

to emotions, the viscount wore them like a child's first artwork. Happy, sad, angry, bitter. There was no mask, no artifice. "Don't you dare criticise. If you were less squeamish, then I wouldn't be suffering the indignity of having leeches sucking my cock. I could have gone from thee to she, and it could all have been done and over with. As soon as there's a seed planted, I needn't be bothered with her ever again."

It wasn't squeamishness that had prompted Jem to make the decisions he had, rather a notion of fair play coupled with a desire to extract himself from Linfield's clutches. To Linfield he remarked, "I like Lady Linfield." Jane was a sweet girl. A little timid, yes, but oh so very desperate to please.

"Well, that makes one of us."

She didn't deserve the hand she'd been dealt. She and Linfield were hopelessly ill-suited. But, as much as she seemed determined to make a go of it, Linfield seemed equally determined to compound the matter. As for the wedding night, Jem knew exactly how that had gone, for Linfield had burst into his chambers white as a sheet and given him a blow-by-blow recounting of it, before passing into a total stupor.

One might, if they were not as intimately acquainted with the viscount as Jem, have ventured that a little less drink was the obvious solution. While a little abstinence wouldn't have hurt, the source of the issue was far more problematic.

"So go be done with it now," he advised, unable to take his gaze off his lordship's now prominent erection.

He received a petulant sneer in return. "One can't go charging through the house and throw one's wife over the nearest piece of furniture. It's not the done thing, you know. It must be arranged...negotiated."

Stuff and nonsense! Jem turned away from the man. "I wouldn't know," he remarked. He also didn't see why marriage had to preclude passion. "If the purpose of this... interlude, wasn't to make use of," he waved a hand directly over Linfield's groin. "Then what was?"

"To establish that I'm still capable, of course."

Unbelievable. "As if you ever required Bell's pets to do that. You know perfectly well how to achieve a rise."

"Yes. Yes," Linfield repeated himself more softly. "You're right, I do. The solution is right before me. But out of reach, resistant, recalcitrant. Would you have me beg, dear Jamie? I'll prostrate myself if it pleases you."

Brow troubled by a frown; Jem shook his head, leaving them staring hotly at one another again. Honestly, Linfield's marriage had been a godsend. It'd given him a reason to extract himself from a situation that ought never to have even existed.

The problem... and it was a problem, was that Linfield... well... he was fun. And he had a charm, a way about him... He could be ridiculous, mercurial, oft times, mad as a box of frogs. Linfield reminded him of freedom, of pleasures that couldn't be bought, like sunshine and dandelion clocks, and of secrets, the sort that you could taste, and that were sworn over with pricked thumbs, then guarded like precious gems.

He told himself he was here at Cedarton because he was employed to do a job. One, God willing, that would end soon. But really, he hadn't been ready to let go of that precious last breath of adventure. He'd imagined that he'd lost Eliza, not that she'd truly ever been his. He'd seen no reason to truly bank on the possibility of it. He might be smitten, but she... she would not be. Not when she learned what sort of man he really was.

No woman in her right mind wanted a man who also happened to relish the affections of other men.

He shifted uncomfortably. What could he possibly offer?

He was not, thank the Lord, like Linfield, so cursed as to find the feminine form repulsive, quite the opposite, he... He felt desire the same as any red-blooded fellow. He liked bosoms and hips, and the clench of a woman's cunt around his cock. He just also liked pricks and arses, and buggery.

Linfield still hadn't bothered to cover up. In fact, seeing Jem's gaze slide over his cock, he made a fist around it.

"This is the first rise it's seen since... since we... I've missed you, Jem. Is it so wrong to want it, to want to feel something? Why should all our fun end?"

He was stroking himself now, drawing his palm from root to tip and back.

"It's not wrong to want it," Jem conceded.

Linfield reached out to him.

"Only to act on it. It's not simply a matter of thee and me anymore. There are others to think of. Jane did not ask for this, and I won't indulge in something that will inevitably hurt her. It isn't fair."

"It seems to me you care more for her feelings than mine or your own. Are we to sacrifice all joy? What is the point of life if not to enjoy it? Jamie, listen to me, please. I know you're determined to be a saint, but be merciful, and keep your wits. Ask yourself truly, what difference will one more poke make in the grand scheme of things, when we're both already condemned to hell's furnaces?"

"Don't pretend. You don't mean it to be one last time."

One moment of madness had never been enough and never would be. If it had, then they'd have been done with each other after the first time. There would always be a next last time. Always. Into Eternity. Dammit, this was his way out. He didn't want to be Linfield's pawn for the rest of his days. He ought never to have fallen into his clutches in the first place.

If he'd never met Eliza... But he had, and he couldn't regret it. She'd turned his world upside down.

Why wasn't she wed to Rushdale? He'd fled south to avoid heartbreak. Telling himself it was all futile; she wouldn't want him if she knew, and he couldn't offer for her without first letting her know. It had just seemed easier, simpler to concede to the other man. No wonder he'd fallen straight into Linfield's trap.

After no more than a week of study, Linfield had shoved the arithmetic texts aside, and baring his arse as if to receive some schoolboy punishment, given him a sly wink and crooned, "You want to, don't you?"

He ought to have run from that golden imp. Instead, he'd stood there, tension building like a knot in his stomach and his cock swollen and all too eager to divest him of his dignity.

Linfield's breeches weren't around his ankles ready to receive five smart whacks for his badly calculated sums, though Jem had delivered them anyway prior to them fucking all afternoon and into the evening. Linfield had an arse like a peach, and a pucker that seemed designed for no other purpose than to be stretched around Jem's cock.

He couldn't deny he'd enjoyed his abuse of that tightly wrinkled hole. That he enjoyed filling Linfield's arse down to his cobs and spending load after glorious load there.

Linfield wasn't his first. That had been a guest of his aunt and uncle. The man had bent him over a water trough and buggered him. Had practically drowned him too. He'd cast up his assets the moment the deed was done, and then spent three days shivering in bed expecting to be struck by lightning or drop-kicked to the fiery pits of hell for not only allowing it to happen, but enjoying it too.

When that hadn't happened, well... he'd made subsequent forays into madness. It had all been very shifty and clandestine until Linfield. Then he'd pursued the act as if sodomy were neither a crime nor a mortal sin. Again, and again… until there was no pretending he was anything other than a deviant who derived supreme pleasure from swiving other fellow's arses, sucking their pricks or having them do the same unto him.

Tossing himself off in place of nightly prayers wasn't nearly as satisfying.

"I'm desperate, James." Linfield irritably sunk his teeth into his lower lip. "What am I supposed to do if you won't help me? Look at my cock, I'm black and blue. I'm trying." He pouted with his chin bowed towards his chest. "I just know that nothing is going to work, nothing but your hand, your touch."

He clasped Jem's hand and drew it to him, formed around his shaft. "It's been damn lonely without you. I've missed you. Missed us. I'm not cut out for marriage."

"This is madness." Yet even as he said it, Jem's palm covered Linfield curled fist and began to move it in a steady rhythm, causing his lordship's cock stand to thicken further. "Tell me you've missed it too." Linfield leaned into him, not quite close enough for his lips to brush Jem's cheek, but close enough so that his breath warmed the skin and sent anticipatory shivers through Jem's body.

He had missed it—the fucking. Not any other part. Certainly not Linfield's company. Nor his petulance, temper, or general lack of intellect. "It doesn't mean we should—" He pulled his hand away.

"We should." There was no doubt in Linfield's voice. "We should, James. What's the point of being prissy about it? If I'm ever going to tup my wife, then

I'm going to need your cock in my hole first. It's a simple fact. Truth is, my prick doesn't care for her. Shrivels to nothing at the mere thought. Yes, she's sweet. Yes, I should be grateful she's no harpy, but if there's nothing there, there's nothing there. And the family demands an heir. Jem, all hell will break loose if I don't provide one. Why do you think we're rusticating here, and not partaking of the comforts of Bellingbrook? A nagging mama is not going to help my situation."

"I thought it over the carriage incident."

Linfield huffed and rolled his eyes. "As if anyone cares about that. No, it is my punishment for my failings. I disappoint. I am not the son my father desires me to be, and no attempt to make me over in his image by providing me with a wife will change that. He desires that I produce a brace of bairns, but..." He took to shaking his head solemnly. "It is not in me, Jem. It's not just her. I've been this way since I emerged from boyhood. Dames can't get a rise out of him."

"But you said—"

Linfield pressed his fingers to Jem's lips, quietening him.

"I'm giving you the facts, Jem. I didn't say I wasn't willing to give it another go. Happens I know of a certain lady with a reputation for being able to secure a rise and release from even the most stubborn of members. I'm willing to put the old tallywhacker in her hands, but I've no more faith in that experiment than I have in Bell's daily leechings."

"Daily?" Jem gulped.

Linfield cupped his hand around Jem's cheek and forced him to meet his piteous gaze. "You see why I seek your mercy. Will you not help me?"

"How?" he asked, against his better judgement. "I won't consent to any scheme that sees you going from my arms to hers."

"Jem...Jem," Linfield sing-songed while swiping his thumb across Jem's lips. "It would only be until the seed was planted. And think on it. If there's no child, who will be blamed? They'll say she's barren. She'll be ridiculed."

"I can't. This is just... It is wrong." He kicked the chair backwards thus jerking himself clear of Linfield's reach, then stumbled to his feet. His lordship followed, clinging to his open breeches.

"Can't you, Jem?"

God, that purr. He hated how much it coiled itself around his being and addled his head. He had to keep a clear mind about this. Realistically, how could it ever work? Even supposing he did as he was asked and fucked Linfield until his cock was iron-hard and weeping, and supposing they managed to disengage in the middle of it... Truly, how far down the corridor would Linfield make it before he turned limp and about turned to Jem's bed?

"It won't work."

"You say that as if you're sure, but how will we know if we don't try?"

"Because everything you have just said tells me so."

His lordship's eyes narrowed. "Perhaps you

need time to think on what the consequences of refusing me might be."

Oh, how the spoiled boy hated to be thwarted.

"Are you...? Good God, man. Are you truly threatening me? Because that's so likely to endear me to you."

"Now see here, James. You're looking at this all wrong. Am I not paying you for your services?"

Incredible.

"You're paying me to tutor you through your exam, not to... not to..."

"Go on, say it. Not to bugger me senseless. Weigh it up now, Jem. How much studying and how much fucking have we done? Then tell me what I'm paying you for. Oh, don't look at me like that. What is so very wrong with acknowledging the truth? It's something you've enjoyed without qualms until recently."

"Hardly without qualms." He gasped and cupped hands over his mouth and nose forming a confined space in which to master his outrage. Allowing the lid to fly off his temper would only make him easier to manipulate, and if Linfield was good at anything, it was that.

"Jem... James... Jamie." Linfield's eyes gleamed, and his narrow lips turned upwards into an appeasing smirk. "We both know I learn best when incentivised, but all the knowledge in the world won't matter if I can't provide an heir. Is it really so very great an ask?" He put his hands together as if in prayer. Knelt. "The other options are mere wishes, borne of desperation. Please don't abandon me to

Bell's quackery or worse. I'm not asking for anything you haven't given a dozen times before. And it's not as if I'm asking you to bugger me while I'm poised between her thighs.... Although, you know, thinking on it—"

"No!" Jem growled. That suggestion was so ludicrous it ought to have put an end to the appeal.

"No?"

"Most assuredly."

"Perhaps, just outside her door then?"

An equally farcical suggestion. And yet...

There was a certain thrill to be had from pushing one's luck. What sort of euphoria might one achieve from fucking a swain outside his wife's door?

It was madness. Madness to even think on it.

Jem took another pace away from his lordship. "You've a silver tongue, Linfield, I'll not deny it, but—"

"Spare me your rebuttals. James Whistler, are you not always telling me how desperately in need of a sponsor you are? That engine work is an expensive business, quite beyond the funds of one genteel scholar. Do you not think I might be favourably inclined towards the passions of the man who saved me from unimaginable shame?"

Damn him and his thumbscrews.

"You would fund my endeavours?" he said through gritted teeth.

One fair brow arched up Linfield's brow. "Indeed, why not? Should we all not be looking to the future? You've told me, oh so very many times now that steam mechanics is the way forwards. That it's the future, and engineering is set to change things in ways I can hardly imagine. Are you not then the most sensible of investments? Think of the assets at my disposal once I assume the family title."

Jem bit his thumbnail. This was bribery, pure and simple. "I don't care to be manipulated."

Linfield snorted. "Oh, it's hardly that. Come now, this is a business arrangement, one that'll see us both flush." He turned about and draped himself artfully over the chaise. "There's some butter left on the tray."

Jem stared at the arse presented to him. It was a nice arse, beautifully shaped, and he knew the delights of the delicate pink pucker cradled between those two globes only too well. He was tempted. Even knowing Bell was still lurking about, and that Eliza was here in the castle, he was tempted.

With the Bellingbrook resources at his disposal, what scientific wonders could he discover?

He let the dream envelop him a moment, then dismissed it.

"Find yourself a different fool. This discussion is done. I'm going to change for dinner."

Linfield turned his head, his eyes flashing with ire, but then his annoyance melted into a puckish pout. "So cruel. You're a cruel swain, James Whistler."

"Very well, I'm cruel," he agreed, not imagining for a moment this would settle the matter.

Out in the corridor, he found Ludlow Bell leaning against the wall a few feet from the door, arms folded, long legs outstretched. How he had come to be there was a puzzle, though one Jem didn't care to worry over at the present time.

"I suppose you heard all of that," he said.

"It sounds as though the third-floor corridor is the place to be tonight."

Jem kept on walking, only for Bell to fall in beside him.

"You realise that what he says is true. You really are his best option."

Jem pulled up sharp. "Did you not just put leeches on his pizzle? If it wasn't to cure him, what the devil was the purpose of it?"

Bell shrugged. "One needs to act the part if one aspires to remain on retainer. He demanded a treatment; I gave him one. It's a well-documented method. Maybe it even works. We're unlikely to find out, since his lordship isn't impotent."

"He's unable to fuck his wife. Is that not the very definition?"

Bell pursed his lips as though he were sucking eggs. "Technically, it describes an inability to get a rise or spend. Something I believe he manages very well every time you molly him. You may claim it isn't so, but I know what my eyes have seen."

"They've seen nothing."

Bell gave a surprising laugh, then set two fingers to his lips. "Not this time. Past times. Linfield appreciates an audience."

Jem had no words. He'd believed if they had not been entirely discreet then they'd at least been circumspect. But this was... this was... wholly unsurprising, if he was honest.

"Before you imagine me some peeping Tom, it was entirely of Linfield's arranging. His Oxford rooms have more than a few interesting holes in their walls. For my part, I assure you, it is an entirely academic interest. It's fascinating to me. I've never felt that pull for such connection myself, but the parade, the parlays of others...well, so much can be discerned. I wonder, do you ever?" He made a series of intricate and crude gestures with his fingers.

"What business is it of yours?"

"I'm a scholar. Some believe aspects of our personality are reflected in the body. That has not been my experience in those I've examined, though the providence of one's cadavers cannot always be relied upon. Do you think it an anomaly of the brain, or a flaw in the mechanics of the genitalia?"

"I cannot believe you would even ask me such."

"And you call yourself a man of science. The brain, I believe. There are those, men who consider themselves great thinkers, who would have us all believe that it is entirely a matter of choice, a wilful rejection of God's intent, obstinate perversion."

"Whereas you, I suppose, believe it something that can be cut out of one much like a tumour."

"What a fascinating notion. I wonder, James Whistler, if it was, would you,"—he made a scissor like motion with his fingers—"snip it out?"

Jem didn't grace him with a reply, choosing instead to continue his journey to his room. Of all the preposterous notions. He was no fool, he realised he could no more cut that part of himself from his body than he could remove his intellect, compassion, or —

God help him—his soul. And why in heaven's name was his capacity to love both sexes equally so vilified? Surely, it was a boon. Didn't the church preach love for one's fellow man?

Love, a little voice in the back of his mind said, *not fornication.*

-4-

Eliza

They were to gather in the drawing room ready for dinner. Fashionably late. Linfield insisted on London hours. No one seemed to have mentioned that dinner was served earlier in the countryside. It made Eliza glad of all the parkin Jane had plied her with earlier, for she was so famished her stomach was engaged in some unladylike gurgling. If not for that, she might have taken the opportunity of being ready a little early in order to return to the still room. Doctor Bell would surely be elsewhere. Even quacksalvers were expected to dress for dinner.

She shook, trying to dislodge the feeling of irritation he'd wrought, so arrogant, so dismissive. Her intellect was in no way diminished by virtue of being a woman, only less-honed, as she had been largely deprived of tuition and barred entry into the seats of learning he was welcomed into.

All at once, she missed her still room and garden at Bluebell Lane with its pungent aromas and seas of blooms that flourished from March to November. Within its confines were so many miracles of nature. After dinner, she would make time, find an opportunity to slip away and mix that powder for Mrs Honeyfield. The poor woman probably already imagined herself forgotten by the gentry she served.

For too much of her life, the Wakefield's had only been one step away from destitution themselves, and the fact that Freddy had changed that did not always feel like a boon. Now, her tolerated foibles—bookishness, healing, and the vindication of women—were no longer considered accomplishments. All anyone cared about was whether she could embroider, sing, paint, and produce something delicate on the ear upon the harp or pianoforte. As it happened, she could not.

Next door, she could still hear Jane bustling about with her toilette. Feeling stifled, Eliza determined to make her own way down to dinner. The castle's layout was really not so very confusing as it had first seemed. She found the red drawing room with ease and entered to find a couple already present: a young buck with sandy hair and a ruddy complexion, round of face, but long-limbed, and a lady—a relation, if twin snub noses were to be relied upon. Her hair was bound beneath a brightly striped turban and dressed with a plume of feathers Eliza thought probably better suited their original owner.

The buck leapt from his seat at once on spying her and darted forward all, courtly charm. He dipped into a bow.

"Good evening, you must be Lady Linfield's

friend."

Eliza allowed him to brush his lips against her knuckles. The stock he wore was so large that it almost swallowed his head as he bowed. "Excuse the presumption, but as our hosts are not yet down, allow me to introduce myself. I'm George Cluett. Linfield and I are old school chums. I'm told that is how you and Lady Linfield are acquainted. What a hoot! And this lady here is my mother, Mrs Cluett."

Her suspicions were correct.

The lady rose, graceful as a ballet dancer though she was plump as a French hen, with cheeks a cherub would have envied. There was a bloom about her that maturity hadn't stolen. If Eliza had not just had it confirmed, she would not have believed her old enough to have an adult son. "Henrietta, please dear," she chastened in good humour. "I can't abide pointless formality. We are thrust here together in the wilds, and such a cosy party, I expect we will all know one another very well soon enough." To Eliza she added. "You are Miss Wakefield, I believe."

"Eliza."

Henrietta swaddled her in a bosomy embrace. "It is very good to make your acquaintance, Eliza. Come in, you must take the other fireside seat. George can stand. I confess I'm quite astonished to find you among us. I believed we were quite cut off by this ghastly mist. I cannot think how you managed to find your way. It is worse than when the fog rolls in off the Thames. Did I not just say that to you, George? Of course, at least then, one has a source of navigation, a lamplighter, coachman... Out here, simply miles upon miles of desolation."

"I had both a coachman and lamp," Eliza assured her, not wishing her to labour under the supposition she'd arrived alone on foot. "Truly it was not so very bad, other than the very last stretch when we dipped in and out of the dells."

"Ha—the wind whistles across those moors," George said, planting himself between the two armchairs with his back to the fire. He made a spectacularly efficient fire guard.

Henrietta returned to her chair and pulled a blanket over her skirts. She waved Eliza towards the other. "A local girl, are you? Hardy, I expect, not comfort born like George here. Doesn't know the price of coal, he doesn't. What do you think of Cedarton?" She did not give Eliza the opportunity to answer but dived headlong into an opinion of her own. "It's not what I was led to believe. Not a jot. Mice always scampering about. Dead birds on the window ledges." She sniffed and cast a beady glance at her son, making it plain that she blamed him for the discrepancy.

"Mother," George whispered a chastisement under his breath, that his mother seemed likely to ignore. "It's good of Linfield to invite us."

"It would have been a bigger mercy to have been spurned in this instance." She snapped her gaze back to Eliza. "Come, dear." She patted the cushion, indicating once again that Eliza should sit. Eliza drifted closer but found she did not care to sit. It was all she'd done since leaving Bluebell Lane that morning, and it was not in her nature to idle. "You must forgive me my grumbling, Eliza dear. Like my son, I am a creature of comfort, and this ruin, it is like something out of a nightmare. Have you seen that half the rooms are exposed to the elements? Holes in the roof, experiments in the basement, mice scurrying about as they please—there were a whole litter of them on the canopy of my bed that the housekeeper had to remove—and there's barely a soul to speak to. Just two maids, for a house of this size? It's unthinkable. Only a trio of male staff, too, and no butler. Oh, well I suppose there's the grizzled groundsman too, but he hardly counts. Do you think he counts, dear?"

George cast an exasperated sigh toward the ceiling.

"I shouldn't hope for any decent conversation from the gentlemen, either, they are too preoccupied with their sports and science experiments."

"Mother, please."

"I was promised music, George. The cream of the local gentry. I'm told there's many an aged squire about these parts, past his prime and secured of an heir, but still desirous of an amenable companion, although like as not, they're all smugglers. And what was the other thing? That's right, scenery that would melt my heart. Freeze it more like. If there is beauty to be found out there, it is well hidden. There aren't even any gardens one might perambulate about, just thickets. I shall be glad to return to London when this house party concludes."

"I rather like it," Eliza said. To her, Cedarton possessed a bleak sort of beauty. She was looking forward to the fog lifting so that they might ramble across the moors, and explore the very thickets that Henrietta despaired over. It was too cold for a picnic, but she was not the fondest of those, anyway. Really, they were the delight of Maria and Caroline. Her youngest two siblings found inordinate amounts of joy in eating *al fresco* sat upon an old blanket or shawl. "I'd quite like to take a good look at the tower ruins too. The shell of the gallery was rather fascinating."

"The ruins? Good gracious, I can't imagine how anyone could find anything appealing about such decay." Henrietta rubbed her hands together, as if to confirm they were soft and smooth, not cracked like the abandoned furnishings in the destroyed rooms.

George lifted his coat-tails to better warm his rear. Eliza ambled over to one of the long windows and peered out, only to find her reflection obscuring the view, and straight after, Mr Cluett's too. "Forgive my mother, Miss Wakefield. She has quite the imagination, and I fear we weren't as circumspect as we ought to have been last night with our storytelling."

"Now you have me intrigued, Mr Cluett."

"Must you, George? I beg you, don't encourage him, Eliza. Last night was quite bad enough, between your talk of fires and apparitions, and Doctor Bell's obsession with morbidity."

Eliza clapped her hands. "You were telling the tale of the Cedarton fire, perhaps? I am sorry to have missed that. The ruined tower is quite close to my room. Such damage, I'm quite fascinated."

"Fire is not a good thing to be fascinated by," Henrietta muttered.

"Perhaps you haven't heard. Cedarton has its very own ghost," George confessed, a dimple winking in his cheek. "No mere story intended to thrill, either, it's been sighted, and recently, I might add." He tapped his nose. "Very recently."

Intrigued, Eliza bowed her head towards his.

"Not a week gone, the scullery maid saw it on the upper floor. 'Twas a lady, handsomely dressed, but chilled as if frozen. Didn't make a whisper, and translucent as glass. The maid near expired on the spot. Bell had to tend to her. Have you met Doctor Bell? I think he scared her twice over. Pretty cadaverous himself, an absolute twig, and eyes like a blanket burned through. And not a clue how to speak to a woman, let alone one scared out of her wits. Dosed her up on laudanum, he did. It was the only way to quiet her shrieking. Anyway, next day she was gone when everyone woke. Butcher's boy brought a note yesterday morning, asking for her wages. She's got the whole village stirred up, so she has. Course, Linfield's not happy about it. Had a devil of a time finding staff to open the place up, and now this has got tongues and fingers wagging all the more."

"But she didn't really encounter a spectre."

"You don't believe in such things, Miss Wakefield?" George seemed intrigued by that possibility. "You are a confirmed sceptic?"

"I prefer to rule out rational explanation first, and there surely is one. It's an old building, with many dingy corridors."

George conceded this point with a nod. "It was up on the third floor, near that great oak door to the Lady Tower when she saw it. You've seen it, I suppose? A door with that many bolts is there for a purpose, don't you think?"

"I thought it was commonly accepted that spectres were not confined by walls."

"Ah—she has you there, Georgie," Henrietta piped up.

The gentleman didn't seem the slightest bit perturbed. He returned to the fireside. "There have been rumours about this place for years. Heard most of them direct from Linfield himself right in the schoolroom. Frightful business, was quite surprised when he said he meant to open the old place up again." He patted the mantlepiece affectionately, as if the building were possessed of sentience, and he wished to mitigate any offence it might take at being spoken of in such a manner.

Henrietta gave a theatrical sigh and fanned her bosom. "George, really, you and your gossipy superstitions. Cedarton's nothing more than bricks and mortar that ought to have been pulled down in favour of a modern building long ago. Is that Linfield's intention, do you think? A generous modern house."

"I'm not aware of such a plan, mother. Perhaps it would also be better to keep such a suggestion to yourself, rather than seed any ideas that he might not wish to take root. You wouldn't want to be the source of any potential discord between him and his new bride."

"Oh, I'm sure Jane has no fancies in that regard."

"A new wife often wishes to redecorate."

"That is hardly the same as tearing the place down to its foundations and rebuilding it anew."

The Cluetts exchanged tight-lipped expressions, the sort that were a form of silent shortcut between familiar persons. Eliza had enjoyed many such conversations with her siblings. Some sort of accord was evidently reached, for George harrumphed, and Henrietta, hand settled across the top of her bosom said, "Perhaps dear Jane hasn't told you that she's also seen the ghost."

-5-
Eliza

Jane soon arrived, along with everyone else, so there was no opportunity for Eliza to take her aside and grill her over her apparent sighting. They were not many in number; Eliza was surprised to find she had met all Cedarton's inhabitants. They were uneasy bedfellows, which was obvious enough from observing the various figures around the table: Jane steeled herself before every interaction with Linfield, then there was the calculating joviality of both Cluetts, coupled with a thread of obsequiousness from George. He rattled on at length about fishing and past wagers, all of which seemed to involve Linfield's ultimate triumph. Lady Luck evidently smiled upon his lordship.

For her part, she found Linfield an unremarkable sort. Sandy fine hair that fell over his brow in delinquent waves. He was, as many a young man she'd met, possessed of an old bloodline and an indecent allowance, an indolent wastrel. Perhaps in time he would make something of himself, many did, but at present he was still firmly entrenched in making as many of the errors of youth as seemingly possible. Starting—and she was desperately sorry to observe it—by marrying a woman he had not an iota of regard for. It wasn't just affection that was lacking between Jane and her earl's son. She was like an object come into his possession—one that would fall from his memory were it not for her unfortunate presence at his dining table.

Eliza swallowed her soup, hardly tasting it so sick did she feel for her friend. No wonder Jane hadn't wanted to speak of him. She could only wonder why Jane had ever consented to the match. It had to be a result of family meddling on both their parts.

Across the table from her, Doctor Bell cut his fish into flakes and stirred them around his plate. Eliza tried to recall if she'd seen him eat anything at all. He could do with a good meal. There wasn't much to him, though his height rather added to the appearance of slenderness. She would have liked to talk to Jem some more, but he was at the other end of the table. His presence remained such a pleasant surprise that the unexpected fizz of it still sang in her innards.

Linfield caught the line of her gaze. "How are you finding Cedarton so far, Miss Wakefield?"

Instantly the table gave Linfield their whole attention, leaving Eliza with a wary sensation crawling up her spine as if she was being led into a trap. They were probably simply affording their host the courtesy he deserved.

"It's been very agreeable, so far, and of course it is a delight to see dear Jane again."

"Jane—yes, Jane." He threw a sidelong glance at his wife. Jane in turn blushed and lowered her gaze to her plate. "I suppose it's good that you'll keep one another busy."

"I had observed the numbers were a little uneven before," Henrietta remarked. She shot a glance at her son, as if expecting an explanation from him, then hunched inwards when he failed to provide one.

"I'm sure that's always how you've claimed you prefer it," George shot her a constipated look across the table. "What is it you say? Ladies chatter like birds, and you can't abide their constant shilling?"

"I'm certain I never said such a thing in my life." Henrietta produced a fan and wafted away the very notion. "Yes, ladies like to chatter, but they aren't fishwives. They are graceful, unlike you gentlemen with your slovenly ways and determination to appear as if you've just fallen from bed. In my youth, the mark of a true gentleman was that he was impeccably turned out. Oh, the balls I could tell you of from when I was a girl...."

Eliza remained convinced, despite such proselytising, that Henrietta was not a day over thirty-five, even with a grown son beside her to suggest otherwise.

"Eliza? You are the acclaimed Miss Eliza Wakefield?"

The speaker this time was Doctor Bell. They had already been introduced, so it struck her a rather odd query. Jem seemed to think so too, judging by the glare he shot along the table.

"Is that significant?" Cluett regarded her through a squint.

"Really, George, must you glower like that? It's most unbecoming. How will you ever attract the right sort of young lady if you insist on glowering at them like that?"

George, ignoring his mother's complaints, continued to regard Eliza like a suspiciously undercooked vegetable. Only after a painfully long appraisal, did some penny or other drop, whereupon so did his jaw. "Not the Eliza Wakefield responsible for saving the Marquis of Pennerley's leg?"

"Ah!" Heat rushed to Eliza's cheeks.

"You? But you're just a slip of a girl."

"George."

Henrietta's admonishment again fell on deaf ears.

"It's said he insisted on you over any other surgeon, and that you dug the ball from his leg yourself."

"Well, yes. That is true, in a sense, but—"

"Your father was a ship's surgeon or some such," Bell remarked drily, and far too dismissively for Eliza not to take it as the slight it was clearly intended to be.

"No, indeed. He did not work. He was a gentleman."

This resulted in a tense silence, followed by several uncomfortable coughs. "Maybe you could give us a full account of it after dinner," Linfield suggested.

More dismissal. "I'm afraid it would make for a very brief story, my lord. I was on hand, and able to attend to the wound, which healed in time. Though it is true, I dug the pistol ball from his thigh. I did not, however, attend him during his convalescence as he had removed himself to one of his estates some miles from where I was staying."

"It's true," Jem confirmed, offering her an encouraging smile. His smile, unlike the garrulous ones of the other men, did reach his eyes. "Witnessed the whole thing. It was most extraordinary. She patched the other blood's finger too, that Pennerley had shot right off." Eliza raised her napkin to hide her own bemusement at Jem's referring to Joshua Rushdale as a blood. He was more accurately a sparrow. Small amongst the aristocracy he associated with, dressed in his nankeen breeches and brown and buff coats and waistkits. Not that she minded his drab plumage, for it was born of practicality. Joshua, like Eliza, was a worker not an idler. Those around her last summer had laughed over her willingness to engage with him, but actually, he was fascinating. He hadn't Jem's sparkling intellect, but he was good humoured and passionate about progress, learned, kind, and... lonely. That latter point had been all too obvious.

She still had his finger bone. She wasn't sure why she'd kept it. As a reminder, she supposed, back when she thought he would write. It had both perplexed and disappointed her when he hadn't. Perhaps he felt sheepish about his actions. It'd been he who'd demanded satisfaction from Pennerley. He who'd shot a marquis over his sister's involvement with the man. It had all been poorly done, with ghastly performances made on all fronts, but Joshua she at least understood. He was no villain, simply a man put in an impossible situation, trying to do the right thing. She wondered if he and Jem still maintained correspondence. Bella, his sister, the now Marchioness of Pennerley, often wrote to Eliza's sister Caroline, but she rarely mentioned Joshua in her epistles. They were focused on merrymaking, lasciviousness, and derring-do.

"You never mentioned Pennerley's leg," Jane accused, as they retreated into the drawing room after the meal was through, leaving the gentlemen to their snuff and port.

"I did, but you balked at hearing the details of it." She did not point out that Jane had kept back secrets of her own, not with Henrietta within hearing distance. It wasn't that she mistrusted the other woman, only that she wanted to drag the whole story out of Jane, and she didn't think she'd do so with extra ears listening in.

"Yes, but you saved a man's leg with your doctoring. And not just any man's."

"'Twas a leg like any other, not different by virtue of being attached to a marquis."

It continued to astonish her that Pennerley's leg afforded her such notoriety. His wasn't the only leg wound she'd ever treated, nor the only pistol ball wound, but to the high born of the land, the leg of a marquis was far more precious than an ordinary person's, which was wholly back to front if you thought about it. A marquis could function perfectly without his appendages. He had servants to do his bidding, and means with which to sustain such help.

Not that she begrudged Pennerley his leg. It was only that the farmers, the miners, and village folk she went among, they depended on their mobility. If they didn't work, they didn't eat. The loss of a limb to them was far more devastating. Consequently, they were far more likely to crow about the fevers she'd spared their children, the crooked limbs she'd straightened with splints, or the sight she'd helped return to their ancients, rather than the miraculous recovery of some nob who'd got into a pointless argument and hence shot as a result.

"If you are going to converse about such things, I will say goodnight. Since, if the previous ghastly cold nights are anything to go by, the men will be at their drinking forever and a day." Henrietta shot a backwards glance at the dining room, then beckoned one of the footmen to light her way.

"We can take the teapot up to my sitting room, if you'd prefer," Jane suggested. The drawing room was mostly shadows, save for the glow around the fireplace. The two lit candelabras were wholly inadequate for such a large, and drafty room.

"Let's just drink up quickly and then retire." Eliza had the sense that the gentlemen wouldn't miss them, even if they arrived in a timely fashion. Moreover, she had questions aplenty, now that she'd encountered Linfield. He and Jane... Well, it all seemed... It seemed very untoward and awkward if she was being wholly honest. They were distinctly uncomfortable in one another's presence, and as like as chalk and cheese in every regard that one could think might make them a suitable match. Their families—for that's who had to be behind the pairing—surely weren't blind to that fact. What had persuaded them to pursue such a wretchedly ill-suited match?

Money, she supposed. Was that not always the heart of such matters?

"I thought," Jane said, looking as if she might carry off the teapot. "That it might be fun if we bedded together tonight. Exactly as we were wont to do at school."

Fun was not precisely how Eliza recalled those times, stuck within the cold confines of the school's heartless, echoic chambers. They had clung together then for warmth, for what meagre comfort they could scrounge from one another, but it seemed Jane's memories had become frayed at the edges. "'Tis a sweet notion, but will Linfield not object to having his bride stolen away from him?"

All the lightness in Jane vanished with a hiss. She folded in on herself, hands settling primly on her lap, gaze frosting over. Eliza stretched an arm out to reach her, shocked by the transformation. Jane's hand was icy, like she'd wandered for hours in the bitterest wind, or spent an afternoon moulding snowballs with un-gloved hands. Immediately, Eliza set to rubbing some life back into her flesh. "I think you had better tell me how you came to be married," she said.

Jane's gaze shifted to the fireplace, so that the flames danced in the ink of her pupils. Un-spilled tears clung to her eyelashes.

"Jane?"

She scrunched her skirt in her fist. "There's nothing to say. One wedding is the same as any other."

"That is clearly untrue. Jane...please. I'm no fool. What possessed you? You implied it was a choice, not forced upon you. But it's plain as day that you're hopelessly ill-suited—"

She tore her hand away from Eliza's hold. "Don't say that. How can you or anyone else know that? You don't know him. You barely know anything of my life these last years."

"Then tell me! I know that your letters seemed full of joy. You seemed happy. Are you saying it has all been make-believe, that these last years have been wretched?"

"Not wretched, no." Jane clasped her hands tightly and brought them to her brow, shaking her head as if to deny all that had passed. "I was happy." She looked up, eyes alight. "My time in Scarborough was pure joy. I would not undo it, but it has left me pitiful, Eliza. I have left my heart there, and this place... It makes all seem so gloomy."

Cedarton certainly seemed weighed by its history.

"Then why so hasty a marriage? Why not wait and become better acquainted?"

There was no disguising Jane's wince, though she attempted to hide it by pouring tea, and fussing over milk and sugar. Eliza had almost lost hope of receiving a reply when Jane lowered her cup into its saucer with a decisive clatter. "A delay wouldn't have suited either of us. It was all rather now or never, and anyway, it is done now, so there's no point in chewing it over. I'm sure once we're better acquainted, we'll learn to rattle along together well enough. It's early days. We've yet to reach a quarter."

Eliza steepled her fingers before her lips. None of that sounded remotely appealing. "He's not the sort of man I expected you to marry." She had always imagined mousy Jane Morley would settle for a quiet, studious fellow, perhaps a parson or a country squire, not an aristocratic scapegrace. Many was the man who had a few boisterous incidents in his past. It allegedly added colour to their characters, but it was not the sum of who they were. From what she'd observed of Linfield so far, profligate and Corinthian manners was all that existed, hence there was little to recommend him as a lifelong companion, and surely Jane saw that too. Although, either way, the marriage was made. It would have to be borne. "Does he make any attempt to better get to know you, Jane?"

Jane cradled her cup, then made a performance of taking multiple sips of hot tea, but she couldn't quite maintain her poise, and slumped into melancholic misery. "It would be an outright lie to say he tries. We spend no time at all together. Not during the day, or the evening. It is only at dinner that we eat together. He either takes breakfast in his rooms or rises with the crows. Luncheon," She shook her head. "I don't even know if he eats such a thing, or if he's content to subsist on merely liquid sustenance."

"But, at night—?" Eliza broke off, prickled by the delicacy of what she meant to ask. "I realise you have separate rooms." That was hardly unusual in a residence of this size, though it was curious that their rooms were situated so far apart. "But does he...does he visit you?"

Jane's brow puckered. "You mean, does he demand his conjugal rights?" Her teacup rattled so much from the shaking of her hand that Jane was obliged to put it down. "Not since we arrived at Cedarton." She sighed heavily. "And to be truthful, only the once afore, on our wedding night. I suppose it was expected. Everyone wished to know that the matter was done. I expect his mother examined the sheets and was duly disappointed. There was a terrible row the following morn."

"Was it horrible?" Eliza asked, clutching her friend's hand, she knew how comforting a friendly touch could be in trying situations.

"Ghastly," Jane agreed, though she didn't elaborate.

Eliza sat with her lips pinned. The marriage bed was hardly her area of expertise, though she wasn't oblivious to what occurred there. Birthing babies rather inevitably led to knowledge of such matters. Nor was she blind to what happened in the fields around her.

What she had discerned was that there ought to be some measure of pleasure involved for the participants, else why would the church need to lecture so doggedly upon wantonness and vice, and why did brothels exist, and men take mistresses? "Did it hurt?" She'd heard mention of pain the first time. Anything that resulted in blood-stained sheets surely involved some manner of trauma.

"Hurt?" Jane goggled at her.

"When he?" Eliza wove her hands into some sort of vague entanglement that only made Jane's eyes grow even wider. Then, her sour pout returned this time accompanied by a closing of her eyes. She covered her face. Eliza settled her hand on her bent shoulder. "Is that why you—why you said you'd seen the white lady?"

Up her friend's head popped like a burn blister. "Who told you about that? Oh, no, don't bother to answer, it's obvious enough. It was George, I suppose. Eliza, what I saw—it has nothing to do with Linfield. Leastways, nothing relevant to his performance in the marital bed." She sighed again, weary to her toes, and overburdened with sadness. "I'm not even sure what I saw. Do you think impressions of past events can be left behind on a building? I saw a woman in her nightrail or her chemise. It was hard to make out the details. Everything else around me was black, but her hair was loose, and I think she was holding something. Whatever it was, it burst into flames in her hand. I suppose I must have screamed, because George and Mr Whistler came tearing out of their rooms... It was nothing really, probably an overtired mind and fanciful thoughts inspired by finding myself mistress of such a monstrous place as this. It's all been very..." Her hands filled in her meaning where her words tumbled away.

What was clear to Eliza was that Jane had wholly avoided answering the bedding question. Might she then conjecture the worst case? While she believed pleasure was possible, she'd seen too often the counter of that—it was not always welcomed on the woman's part. Increasingly to her, it seemed marriage had little to recommend it. Rather it was a burden of numerous laying-ins.

She could not remain still and think of it. It bore her to her feet and set her pacing. The injustice of it all. The hours she'd spent scrubbing, pacing, and mending in attempts to dampen the furore she felt over her lot and those of her fellow maidens. At one point, she had thought change could be achieved through letters, that the vindication of women merely required that they opened the eyes of learned men. How foolish she had been. She'd since witnessed the attacks on the characters of those women who argued for such rights and observed their subsequent descent into ruin. But she was allowing herself to become distracted. What mattered in the here and now was how she could support Jane.

"Was it very...very horrid? You must tell him if it was, ask if he might not be more considerate of you. I know it's his legal right, but... but I cannot believe him to be such a wretch as to inflict such heartless discomfort—"

"Eliza, did you not hear me? I said he'd only

come to me the once."

"But?"

"You have it all wrong, Eliza. Dammit! You mustn't think ill of me, but I have some prior knowledge of such things and how...how very distracting they can be. I can only think that Linfield knows and despises me for it."

"No one could ever despise you." Eliza cocooned her in her embrace, resting her head on Jane's shoulder.

She broke away at Jane's humourless laughter, fearing hysteria, but there was no trace of insanity in her friend's visage.

"I thought," Jane began. "I believed that even though we hardly knew one another, that sharing such pleasures would help us grow together. That we'd find a way to love one another, but... Oh, Eliza, I've made such a dreadful mistake. There is no chance of it, for Linfield is entirely indifferent to me. He won't notice if I'm absent from my bed and sleeping with you, any more than he'd notice if I bedded down in the stables with the hounds and horses, and it is entirely my fault. I have scared him off with my unmaidenly ways. I presumed to know best, you see. I acted contrary to his wishes, when he bade me do nothing other than to be still."

"I'm afraid I do not entirely follow," Eliza said, resettling herself in the armchair. "We are speaking of your wedding night? He asked you to lie still?"

"That's right. Stay quiet and still as a board, and turned away from him so that I could hardly breathe for having my face buried in the pillows. 'Don't turn about or raise your head,' he says. 'Don't try to touch me. Don't speak. In a moment it will be done, and thereafter, I won't trouble you above once month, and not at all once the line is secure.' But I didn't do it, Eliza. I couldn't do as he asked. I think he meant for us to rut like beasts, and I couldn't bear the thought of it being so... so utterly impersonal and devoid of love when I know... I know so very well how it can be. So, I didn't stay still, or quiet, or anything. I wanted his touch, you see. Why is it so bad that I wanted his hands on me—all over me? His mouth too. I longed for his kisses, the taste of his breath, his weight over me. So much, I wanted him to lose himself in his desire for me, for then, surely, certainly, it would all work out. We would be happy." She paused, a hand covering her mouth, then began again, voice cracking. "I said to him. I said... 'I'm certain it would be better if we were face to face.' Well, I might as well have cracked his head open with a vase if you could have seen his reaction. Twere as if I'd asked the unimaginable. He up and left and has not returned. So, you see, I have quite spoiled everything."

She set to sniffling into her sleeve. Eliza gazed at her utterly perplexed. That he should behave in such a way made no sense at all. However, the foibles of young Corinthians would have to wait. "Jane," — she swaddled her in a tender embrace— "I'm sure that's not true."

"Then why has he not returned?" her friend mumbled into her clothing. "Why does he avoid my company? Ignore me? Gaze at me with such utter distaste."

"I'm sure it's all just a misunderstanding. Perhaps... perhaps, he is waiting for some cue from you to say that you might begin again, since the first time went so badly." Linfield did not strike her as the sort to think of anyone's feelings but his own, but she was loathe to condemn him after such a short acquaintance.

"Oh, to think I considered him my salvation." Jane screeched with surprising vigour. "The proposal was so timely."

She shook her head, then pulled at the pins securing her coif, releasing the strands of her hair in a tumbling cascade, before making thorough use of her handkerchief.

"I have heard," Eliza said tiptoeing into the subject. "That some men imagine their wives too delicate for such pleasures, and that they feel quite unable to demand of them what they seek without remorse from a mistress."

"You think he has a mistress?"

"That is not..." This was ridiculous. Of course the man had a mistress. Probably more than one along with a score of bastards to his name too. He'd be a funny sort of rakehell if he didn't. But there was no sense in disturbing Jane's mind with such thoughts, since there was clearly no mistress residing at Cedarton to provide Linfield with the satisfaction he ought to be seeking from his new wife.

"Eliza, I fear he means to leave me here." Jane wrung her hands. She looked up, eyes red, and skin ashen. "Once whatever this matter is that has brought us here is resolved, he'll gallop back into town with his barnacles, and I'll be left here to wither with only the housekeeper and a maid for company." Her lip trembled, and hot tears spilled.

"Now you are being far-fetched. I'm sure that's not true. His family will expect an heir at the very least."

She believed that, even if she couldn't entirely depend upon Linfield himself. Like any man, he could not be relied on to do anything that wasn't in his own self-interest. Even though it would be utterly wrong to abandon Jane to the isolation of Cedarton, she had no trouble imagining him doing it. Moreover, what could she or Jane do to prevent it? Men had all the power, both in and outside of marriage.

"Then you must do whatever you can to ensure he doesn't."

Jane worried her swollen lips with her front teeth. "Do you think?" she began hesitantly. "What if I... went to him. Do you think that would make this better or worse? I fear if I wait for him to make the next move I shall expire before our marriage is ever consummated. And it must be, Eliza...must. It's God's will. The very point of forming such a bond."

"I thought you feared he thought you too forward?" Eliza said.

"I don't really know. 'Tis only a theory. Perhaps if I promise to lie as stiff as he likes and not make a single murmur."

"As long as you realise—." Eliza stilled her tongue. If she primed Jane to be ready for rejection, then it would be even more likely to materialise. In any case, Jane was already on her feet, and pulling her shawl around her shoulders. "You mean to go to him this minute?"

Her friend confirmed it with a vigorous nod. "I shall lose my nerve if I don't act now."

"He may still be entertaining." Surely, Jane did not mean to barge into the gentlemen's after dinner conversation and proposition Linfield? That would be most extraordinary.

"If he is at his port, then I will wait in his chamber. Goodnight, Eliza. I hope you will not mind that I'm not right next door when you choose to turn in, but I must do this to secure my future."

"I quite understand," Eliza said, not understanding at all. Jane kissed her goodnight and left. The hall was echoic and lonely without a companion to share the fireside with, so Eliza banked the coals and took up a candle. She would not turn in just yet, but she would retire to her room. She had a feeling that Jane might yet need her again before the night was through.

-6-

Jem

"How exactly is it you're acquainted with the Wakefield woman?" Linfield asked, only to wander over to the side table, apparently disinterested in the answer. Jem wasn't fooled. He knew his lordship too well for that. Understood the nuances of his tone, knew how he tried to disguise his emotions. When he was feigning indifference, he always stuck his head out and pulled his shoulders back, a pose that inevitably resulted in back-ache, of which he would complain. Jem had been expecting the question ever since the ladies departed. It had been foolish of him to draw attention to their prior relationship, but he'd been swept up in the joy of her company.

"Bell?" Linfield waved a decanter at Bell, before pouring a third glass of claret. Cluett had already scurried off, probably afeared, having muttered something about bellyache, that Bell would prescribe a course of purgatives or insist on him swapping wine for milk for a week.

In fact, Bell remained too preoccupied with stoking the fire to have paid George any heed. Linfield put his drink within arm's reach, then came towards Jem. Their fingers brushed more than necessary as the claret was handed over. Foreplay of sorts, Jem supposed it. He was half tempted to run off to his bed, but likely as not Linfield would only see that as an invitation and follow him. There was a definite air of expectation about him this night that Jem found prickled him in a way he intensely disliked.

He'd never actually agreed to Linfield's foolishness. The whole idea that it was all right to fornicate with a wedded man because it was the only means by which he could tup his wife was no more acceptable to him now than it had before he'd understood Linfield's reasoning. And to do so outside the woman's door... Of course, he wasn't going to do that. He'd only entertained the notion because Linfield had this way of addling this thought. In any case, he would not risk Eliza seeing him behaving in such a manner. If Linfield needed a prick up his arse to tup his wife, he could secure some other fellow's.

"Well, what is she to you?" Linfield asked lightly, as if he wasn't about to scratch someone's eyes out to learn every detail.

"Who? Oh, Miss Wakefield," Jem responded, mastering indifference.

That was an altogether more difficult question, particularly so if he wanted to avoid raising his lordship's ire. Who was Eliza Wakefield to him?

Why, nothing and everything. A vague acquaintance, but also the fantastical creature who'd stolen his thoughts right through August and September. Usually, the sort of intense pull he felt towards Eliza Wakefield, he only felt towards the great figures in his field. But Eliza... Eliza had felled him without even trying. She'd stolen his breath when she'd looked up at him, a soot-stain upon her pert nose, and set his pulse alight.

There'd never been a woman like Eliza Wakefield before. Not for him. Not a woman he could converse with as an equal, whose mind leapt and landed, who could pull pieces of the universal puzzle together in her mind and assemble them in new and fascinating ways. She reasoned. She spoke his language. He lost his heart to her over a diagram of one of Richard Trevithick's Puffer Whims.

Yet, if not for Eliza, he would never have found himself ensorcelled by Linfield's wiles.

The fact of the matter was, for all that he was besotted, he couldn't have her. He hadn't a bean of his own. He'd lived entirely off his uncle's good will for most of his life, and he wasn't even his uncle's heir. That was his youngest cousin, George-Thomas. Nor had Eliza given him any indication that she'd be amenable to the idea, even if he felt able to ask. What woman wanted a penniless scholar as a life mate? Especially one who sought the attentions of other men as readily as those of women. No woman, that's who. He could not believe Jane Linfield would have made that choice if she'd been aware, and now she was suffering the consequences of it. Besides, even if

Eliza were able to reconcile herself to that quirk of his, he was a poor choice for one so brilliant. B'gad he was as astonished as hell to find her still unwed. His head had not been the only one turned that summer, and the other fellow was now the brother-in-law of a marquis and had the funds to keep her in the fashion she deserved.

"Well?" Linfield prompted, his eyes bulging a little. Jem was seriously trying his patience.

He shook off the cobwebs of thought. "We were introduced over the summer. She was among the guests at the house party my aunt and uncle held to celebrate Stephen Crakehall's engagement."

"Who?"

Of course, his lordship knew little of anything outside his own narrow circle of interest, which consisted of racing, pugilism —watching not participating—and dancing Sallinger's round. Crakehall, determined to make his mark, had been rousing the Grenvillite Whigs into a froth in the House over Catholic emancipation.

"No one important," Jem said with a sigh. "Just the fellow who occupies my uncle's second parliamentary seat."

"She's kin?"

"A vague acquaintance."

"And that's the only time you've met? One would have thought you the very best of friends, you were so intimately acquainted with her pursuits."

No one who had seen her after Pennerley fell to that pistol ball could have anything but the utmost admiration for her, and he'd been wholly besotted before that.

"Eliza has an enquiring mind. She likes to study natural philosophy among other things."

Jem shot a glance towards the fireside, anticipating Bell's eyebrow raise and perhaps a bleat of blatant misogyny. Sure enough, there was, the eyebrow arch, though what he said was, "Eliza?"

They were acquainted enough for such permissions, yes, but he chose not to elaborate on the fact.

"We share a mutual love of such things."

"So, you're a natural historian now, are you?" Linfield downed his drink and poured another. "And here I was thinking you were a mathematician. Or was it an engineer? An architect? I find, I'm growing quite confused as to which it is."

"A trug?" Bell ventured under his breath.

"Says the man who always gets his hands dirty," Jem replied, shooting the doctor a thinly veiled scowl. If Bell was going to spit insults, then Jem would trade them with equal currency. After all, who ever heard of a physician who mixed his own medicines and soiled his person with viscera?

"So?" Linfield leaned in, encroaching on Jem's space just enough to be irritating, and to prohibit any further discourse between him and Bell. Linfield steepled his fingers over the top of Jem's glass. "Which is it, Jamie, dear?"

"My skills are many, as too my areas of interest."

Perhaps that hadn't been the wisest response, given what skill he knew his lordship was itching to experience in action.

"Well, I suppose there can be no harm in it, providing you recall whose mind it is you're here to expand."

"Mind," Bell guffawed.

Linfield shot him a look of pure malice along the length of his narrow nose.

Bell shrugged it off as if it were nothing. "What? Is there a problem with my speaking plainly? I wouldn't be a very good doctor if I couldn't discern my patient's mien. I believe—do correct me if I'm wrong—that we are all here at Cedarton, except for the Cluetts, for the same purpose. Fixing your broken prick."

"What *is* the purpose of the Cluetts?" Jem asked.

"Entertainment," Linfield replied. "Torture cannot be ones whole provenance, and George can always be relied on in such matters. The question I ask myself is, can I say the same of you two? You have both failed me utterly so far."

There was nothing to do but mutter affirmatives. Though, in truth it was questionable if George filled his role quite so perfectly as Linfield implied. Everyone knew he'd been peevish since the day of the race, having lost a fortune when Linfield swooped to triumph. There'd even been speculation that Georgie had paid the lady who'd been run down to deliberately dive into the path of Linfield's phaeton. The tactic hadn't worked. Linfield had neither swerved nor stopped, and George had limped across the finish line in third place down to a magnificent piece of cornering by Wattlesborough.

"Come and sit by me, Jem." Linfield beckoned

him over to the fireside. Bell remained on the floor, his long legs stretched out before him, his back to the chaise, full-bottomed wig still artfully curling over his shoulders. Jem settled onto the opposite side of him to Linfield, a move that earned him an instant scowl. He was in no mood to be picked at or provide entertainment, and if he was honest, he was a little afraid of Linfield's intention. He'd hoped to use Bell as a sort of hobble, but after the fellow's earlier remarks, his presence might be as much a stimulus to Linfield chicanery as a means of thwarting it.

"How fairs your prick this evening, my lord?" Bell asked.

"It looks like I've been fellated by a pack of harpies."

"Is that why you haven't bounded straight off to nub your wife? I would have thought you'd be keen to prove yourself now that functionality is restored."

Jem watched his lordship's jaw churn.

"There's time enough for that yet. The hour is young. In any case, it strikes me she may have an opinion on the current appearance of my parts, and as I have no desire to discuss my appendage with her—"

"Snuff the candle." Bell's remark was so dry and condescending in tone that it shocked a snort from Jem. Linfield shot him a death glare. The sort he usually reserved for those he was about to cut, ridicule, or crush.

They were both in his employ and would be wise to remember it.

Linfield sacrificed another wine glass to his

temper. "Nothing about this damn marriage is appealing. I said as much before it damned took place, but would the old codger listen? Of course not. My opinion is valueless. It's his will, therefore I must endure."

'Twas a fact that when an earl gave you an ultimatum, you knuckled down to it regardless of how badly it smarted to do so. Perhaps, he was being unkind to judge Linfield so harshly. The situation was not entirely of his making. He was as trapped by circumstances as the rest of them.

Jem was about to mutter something to aid them out of the current quagmire when a shrill scream set all their teeth on edge. A kind of rictus besieged them all, so that they didn't move and barely breathed until the siren's wail ended.

Bell came to first. He flipped onto his feet in a show of athleticism Jem would never have attributed him. "What the devil?"

He had to give the physician his due, Bell never shirked his duty if circumstances arose where it seemed his services would be in demand. Jem had not forgotten that woman's death, the way Bell had handled everything with effortless efficiency. There'd been nothing he could do to save her—she'd been dead by the time he reached her—but the fact that he'd made it his duty to take care of her said much for him, where some of his mannerisms and foibles might have given an opposite impression.

"That is Lady Linfield, if I am not mistaken."

Jem and Linfield caught up with him on the main staircase. A footman was hurrying downwards.

"Her ladyship," he gasped. "She's... she's upstairs, by the ... Dropped into a dead faint—"

"And you left her?" Jem asked, still on the move.

"Mr Cluett's there."

"With my wife?" Linfield's brows knotted.

"He came out of his room," the footman explained. "And was swift enough to catch her when she swooned."

"Well, I'll be damned. It's not like Georgie to be so quick off the mark. But that must mean she's on the second floor. What the devil is she doing there?"

"Perhaps the questions might wait." Bell was already halfway up the stairs. "You," he pointed at the footman. "Fetch my bag."

By the time Jem reached the upper landing, Bell was already skidding onto his knees. He pushed George aside and took up her ladyship's wrist to feel for a pulse.

"Is she all right?" Linfield had followed him up the stairs, though he seemed keen to maintain some distance.

"A faint. Smelling salts will set her to rights." Bell produced a glass vial from his pocket and uncapped it beneath her nose. Lady Linfield awoke with a start, followed by some flailing and another anguished cry. "Get away. No... no, you shan't have me."

"Lady Linfield... Jane, calm yourself, there's nothing to be alarmed about."

"I saw it. Right there." She pointed dead ahead to where Cluett stood. "Clear as day she was. Oh, she wants me. She means to kill me, I know it. We should not have come to Cedarton. It is cursed...cursed! Such utter folly. Linfield. Tell him we need to leave. Right now, this very moment. We have to leave."

"What the devil is she babbling about? Ghosts and nonsense. Utter tripe," Linfield muttered, prompting Jem to chastise him with a stare. While Lady Linfield was clearly overwrought, there was no need to be so impolite about it. The woman had clearly suffered a major shock, and Jem for one believed there was something to it. No one wound up this terrified without cause.

Linfield was barely cowed.

"What did you see?" George demanded, getting in on the huddle.

Jane didn't respond, her mind seemingly unable to fasten on any one of them for more than a moment, and her body continued to judder in a most unnatural way.

"What I'd like to know is why you were wandering about the second floor in the dark?" Linfield said. "What business led you here? Your rooms are upstairs, madam."

She gaped at him, then clamped her mouth closed, and a furious blush spread over her décolletage. Linfield chewed on his littlest fingernail.

The footman came running, carrying Bell's bag, which the doctor immediately rummaged through, and thus produced a vial of reddish-brown liquid and dropper.

"Perhaps we might move her to some place more comfortable before you administer that." Bell returned a nod, and so Jem lifted her. She was light as a child and easily settled in his arms. "Where to?"

Linfield cleared the way and ushered him towards the stairs. "Her chamber would be best." They all followed in his wake, chittering and speculating as to the cause of her malaise as if she couldn't hear them. He wasn't sure when Henrietta joined them, only that it was her who first raised the notion of dear Jane having seen an apparition, and which set Jane off babbling madness again.

Up until this point, Jem had not taken the notion of a spectral presence at Cedarton remotely seriously. The maid's story could easily be reasoned away, so too Lady Linfield's supposed earlier sighting of the ghoul. They'd attributed it to an overactive imagination, without any attempt to dig into the matter. Jane herself had said she'd not been at all certain of what she'd seen. This time around, that was clearly not the case. The woman in his arms was bleached of colour and quaking so her limbs twitched seemingly of their own volition.

Eliza burst from her room with her hand cupped around a candle flame as he waited for someone to open the door to Jane's chamber. "What happened?" she demanded. "Jem, is she hurt? I heard a cry, but it didn't seem wise to run toward it in the thick of night. Where was she? Did you find her? Jane... Jane, dear, are you all right?"

"Eliza." Jane clasped her friend's hand fast and pulled her closer, making it almost impossible for Jem to move. "I saw it...her, old Lady Cedarton. Oh, Eliza, it was no mistake last time. No hallucination. She was right there before me as plain as you are to me now, yet insubstantial as the breeze. I could see right through her to the other side. Oh, Eliza. She means us harm, I know it, right here in my soul." She tugged her friend's hand to her breast. "We mustn't stay here. You have to convince them. Tell Linfield. I know he won't listen to me. We ought to return to town at once. All of us. Oh, Eliza, I'm so sorry. I should never have brought you here."

"Nonsense, Jane. You need me, and right now you are overwrought. Darling, I know what you think you have seen, but ghosts are not real. They are stories we make up to teach one another the lessons of the past. I'm sure there's a rational explanation for whatever it was you saw. You believe that too, don't you, Jem? And Doctor Bell?"

Their nods of agreement did little to calm Jane's panic. Her eyes were wide as saucers, and her skin so milk pale as to be almost translucent. Nor did Henrietta's sudden cry— "It will wreak bloody vengeance on us all and harvest our souls,"—do anything to soothe matters.

"Cluett," Bell swore through clenched teeth. "I've no desire to attend two patients at once. If you could return your mother to her chamber and stay with her until she's settled. I'm sure a dash of brandy and a well-stoked fire will set her to rights."

"Of course." Cluett gave a bow, then snapped to attention as if he were a solider brought to attention by a senior officer. "Come, mother. There is nothing we can assist with here." He led her away, supporting her against his arm.

Eliza flung wide the door to Jane's chamber.

Jem settled her on the bed, then stood back to give Bell the space to do his work.

"Is she deranged?" Linfield remained on the threshold and did not cross it.

"Her heart's racing," Eliza said, which Bell confirmed with the press of his fingers to the pulse point in her throat. Although, it was clear enough that the rise and fall of her chest was unnaturally rapid. A sheen of perspiration peppered her brow and upper lip.

"It's to be expected after a shock. But you must endeavour to gather your wits, Lady Linfield. Such dramatics are undignified in one of your standing."

"She was here, I'm telling you," Jane beseeched him. "Her face...it was." She grasped his coat, though it was not clear if it was to pull him closer or to raise herself up. "Cruel. Hideous, cruel. She wants us gone, all of us, but me especially. This is her house. She means us ill, dreadful ill. You must believe me, doctor...Eliza...husband. Please."

Linfield remained stoically distant. "Might you not sedate her? She's clearly of unsound mind."

Eliza shot Linfield such a look of horror the viscount actually took a step back into the corridor.

"Fetch a glass," Bell instructed. Wine was procured, and added to it, a dropperful of sweet delirium. "Drink this, Lady Linfield. It will help rest your mind." She did so meekly, then fell almost instantly limp against the pillows.

"You really believe an opiate the best recourse?" Eliza snapped, her hand coming to her hips as she faced Bell across the bed. "But then I suppose you're inclined towards your master's viewpoint. Willing to dismiss her alarm as the frailty of her mind, rather than making any attempt to discern the truth of the matter."

"I've a bloodletting knife, if you'd prefer more invasive means. And pray, do not attribute to me views I have in no way expressed. Being in Lord Linfield's employ does not grant him mastery of my mind. I am certain Lady Linfield did see something. As to the nature of that something, as you yourself implied, there is most likely a rational and completely ordinary explanation for it."

Jem could not be certain of it, but he thought he saw a flicker of amusement about the doctor's lips, as if he found in Miss Wakefield some merit where he had not supposed to find it. But didn't he know that all too well himself? Eliza had never been an ordinary miss. Simpering ways and embroidery, warbling like a lark, they were as much of an anathema to her as to the two men of science she currently stood between. "Perhaps we ought to investigate," he remarked. "See if there isn't a simple explanation for whatever she saw." He sought Eliza's gaze, and her approval, but she was busy smoothing the covers over her friend's still form. "If you are done here, Bell?"

"Will you sit with her?" Bell enquired of Eliza. "Or should I have the housekeeper send someone up? It's unlikely she'll stir, but it's best if someone remains with her just in case."

Eliza took a wary perch upon a nearby chair. "I'll stay. I'm not certain there's help enough at Cedarton for any of the maids to be spared."

"But nor can you be expected to tend her the whole night through," Jem said.

"I'll speak to Mrs Honeyfield." Bell asserted. "If her mind is still tender come daybreak, additional help will have to be found, though I'm sure she will wake quite herself again."

"More likely with a head as thick as a woolly mammoth hide, and thoughts like treacle," Eliza huffed under her breath.

Jem found he couldn't disagree with her. He greatly disliked any concoction that meddled with his ability to reason properly. It was why he'd stayed clear of the parties held by Davy and his ilk, who made utter tits of themselves breathing nitrous oxide vapours from a green silk bag. Well, not so much Davy himself; he was far too busy recording the nonsense his experimental gas caused—euphoria, laughter, priapism. "Bell, a word." He followed the doctor out into the corridor. "Did you read Davy's pamphlet on nitrous oxide?"

Ludlow Bell stopped and turned towards him, his gaunt face pulled into a form of rigidity that might be down to derision or fascination, and which caused Jem to hesitate for fear of discovering which. "You're not about to suggest I treat Lady Linfield's malaise with such an analgesic?"

"God no! I was thinking of Linfield's issue. I did mention it to him, and while I don't know if Davy specifically mentions it, I've heard from others that one of the pleasures of the gas comes from the raising of one's flagpole."

His observation was met with a dry chuckle from Bell. "You've a strange mind to think of such things at a moment like this. Are you truly suggesting that I have Linfield inhale and then mount his wife?"

"Is it any more ludicrous an idea than treating him with leeches? Or his suggestions?"

"Indeed not. But your timing is... interesting. Though, I suppose it would also get you out of a tight spot, or should I say from sliding into one. Very well, I will investigate this gas, but as previously discussed, we both know there are simpler methods."

"Out of the question," Jem replied.

"He'd be a happier man for it, and we'd all get away from this place sooner. It's going to be devilish cold once the snow falls."

"Let me state this bluntly, if it's a prick up his arse he needs, it need not be mine. Perhaps as his physician..."

Bell waved aside the notion. "You're the fellow he has on retainer for that purpose."

Jem rounded on him, hand planted flat across the physician's chest. "I'm his tutor. My purpose is to teach him Greek and algebra. You're the one who's employed to keep him in merry health."

Bell remained quiet a moment before releasing a snort. "You're an intriguing case, Mr Whistler. I don't believe you were quite so mired in moral quandaries before today. I'd take care if I were you. A wise man in your situation might choose to downplay their partiality for a certain recent arrival to Cedarton."

Jem shot a look back down the corridor. Jane's door was now closed, but it was the other occupant of that room that his thoughts turned to. He might dislike Bell for it, but the man was right. He would never exchange matrimonial oaths with Eliza, he had nothing to offer her but friendship, and Linfield was already spitting jealous.

"He's a cur, but he's a cur with a near bottomless purse."

"Is he paying you to cajole me?"

The doctor wafted such a suggestion away. "I just fear the consequences for those of us around him if his issue persists."

"What the devil do you mean by that? What consequences?"

"Would you not agree that prior to her arrival here, Lady Linfield was of sound mind and body? Yet now she screams and faints and bleats of apparitions."

An entirely uneasy thought settled in Jem's gullet. The thought had not occurred to him so fully formed before this point, but it loomed large into life now. Linfield's unwillingness to engage, his revulsion. How far would Linfield go to free himself of his current bind and unwanted wife?

"I trust that you'll not stoop so low as to taking part in such a plot?"

Bell halted his long-legged stride. "What is clear to me is that she saw something. As for what that was... We are both men of science, Mr Whistler, I for one cannot entertain the notion that the dead walk abroad, and that leads to the uncomfortable conclusion that this abomination currently hounding our hostess is man-made."

"You think Linfield means to scare his wife out of her wits? Good God, man. You're under his roof. I know he's a cad, but..."

Dammit, the more Jem churned the matter over in his head, the more events seemed to point towards some manner of manipulation.

Bell's pupils blazed black in the poor light. He tore off his wig, revealing hair as black as ebon, shorn short and describing a marked widows peak. "All I'm saying is that it would suit Linfield extraordinarily well if his wife was found to be mentally deficient. She could be removed from his vicinity, and moreover the demands of his family would cease. He would never have to worry over getting a rise to prove himself by planting his seed, and his family would never need to know his true nature as a champion of the windward passage."

Jem sagged from his shoulders to his knees, suddenly weighted by the expulsion of dark thoughts. "You truly think him capable of it?"

"More than. As do you."

"And you'd willingly condemn her."

The man gave him a thin smile. "It may surprise you to learn that I have my own code of morals. I will have no part in such a diagnosis, but if he seeks it, he will secure the necessary evidence. I am but one physician. This country has many, and most will value the tinkle of coins in their pockets over a woman's fate."

"We can't let it happen."

"We can't stop it."

"If it's shown to be a trick, we can. She was nigh to the door of George's chamber when we found her. What if we poked around?"

Bell nodded his consent and followed Jem downstairs to the lower corridor, which stood in the same inky gloom as the rest of Cedarton's environs, and not helped by the dark bowling green hue of the walls, coupled with an excessive array of ancestral portraiture.

"There's nothing here that I can see," Bell remarked, as they pulled back rugs and patted around various picture frames.

"What's in these rooms? The Cluetts are opposite, but where do these other doors lead? And what was she doing along here, anyway?" Jem asked.

"That is a very good question. One must assume some business with the Cluetts, but it's curious that neither made mention of it, nor gave any indication of having seen her before her screech alerted them—"

"We can ask her when she awakens."

Jem turned the handle of the nearest door, which opened on curiously silent hinges. Every other door in the place wailed and groaned like an arthritic old roué bemoaning his inability to function as he had in his youth so, it was a novelty not to hear a screech. "Good lord, there's a whole unused suite of rooms here."

"Two suites, I should say." Bell let himself into the room a little further along the corridor. "Nothing but shrouded furniture."

And little of that, judging by the echoic ring of his voice.

"Likewise, here." The room Jem had entered had been stripped of comforts, retaining only a couple of larger pieces of furniture too cumbersome to remove. Jem peeked beneath one shroud and discovered an old settee, the seat now tattered and wriggling with baby mice. He dropped the cover again and took an idle stroll to the window. It was black out, the clouds sitting low on the moors obscuring anything beyond a few feet. There was no moon.

"Anything?" Bell joined him in the room, swinging the door to behind him after he passed, and thus revealing a second glass-panelled door set at an angle behind the first. He opened it at once and stuck his head inside. "Nothing," he said, emerging immediately. "The same miasma of neglect as the rest, only accompanied this time by the most godawful ox blood stain on the walls. Whoever was responsible for decorating this place had morbid tastes."

"And that coming from an anatomist."

"The body is a fascinating instrument, but I don't endeavour to smear its fluids across the walls of my abode like some sort of demonic slaughterer."

Jem joined the physician in the doorway. The side-chamber was as Bell described it. Devoid of contents except for an old, overturned box, and the stub of a candle in a jar. There was a faint current of something honeyed entwined with the general miasma of neglect in the room, beeswax, perhaps?

"Whatever she saw, there's no sign of it here," Bell remarked. "Perhaps it is that Lady Linfield is simply highly strung and prone to fanciful imaginings."

Jem refused to accept that explanation. Jane had struck him as meek, but hardly of a flighty nature, and certainly not one of the preposterous wailing sirens that society liked to pander to, who absolutely thrived on discord and the attention even the slightest upset could provide them. She was not the type to declare an attack of the nerves and the necessity of a quiet moment with the most amenable of young men to attend her. Still, there seemed little point in arguing the case with Bell, who for all he knew held a similar opinion. He was beginning to think the doctor cultivated a persona, which was not entirely in accord with his inner being. "Let's turn in, there doesn't seem to be anything to be gained by lingering." Except perhaps the prospect of a spider landing on his head, or a mouse scurrying up his leg.

-7-
Eliza

Eliza couldn't settle after the men left. She watched the uneasy rise and fall of Jane's chest, wishing that Jem had lingered. She wanted to ask him what he thought of the Linfield's marriage. He was apparently as well acquainted with his lordship as she was with Jane, and hence was the obvious source of insight. She was not one for idle gossip or poking into other's business, but the marriage was clearly ill conceived and had been arranged so swiftly with little to no communication between the two parties that she couldn't fail to wonder how it had ever come about. Everything about it spoke to the notion that it never ought to have been. One only had to look at this room to see that. It was masculine in every detail, and Jane's scattered possessions could not disguise that. This tired room, with its dark wood furniture and domineering bed was clearly intended to be the master's suite, and the adjoining room the mistress's boudoir. Why therefore was Jane occupying it, and

Linfield quartered in some far-flung area of the castle? Had the events of their wedding night truly afflicted him so much that he was determined to put as much space between them as possible to prevent a repeat? What sort of marriage did he intend it to be if they were never to bed together?

Linfield did not strike one as the sort to eschew pleasures. And even a man ambivalent to his wife surely entered into the arrangement with the intention of siring offspring. Her mind turned to Jane's recollection of the wedding night and Linfield's curious demands. They made not a ha'porth of sense. Also, whatever had Jane meant when she said she had some experience of such matters? Had her friend engaged in some unfortunate liaison? Was that the reason for the hasty and unexpected marriage?

How foolish of her to have arrived expecting a love match.

Still, it concerned her more that Linfield had been so ready to dismiss Jane's terror as the frailties of a female mind. Jane was no society miss, versed in the art of a theatrical swoon. Nor was she a devotee of Monk Lewis or Mrs Carver that delighted in reading intrigue into the ordinary and concocting macabre flights of fancy. Her faint had been genuine. Her terror equally so.

If Jane persisted in saying that she'd seen a ghost when she woke, what would Linfield do? Throw her into one of the castle dungeons and mislay the key, thrilled to be so easily rid of a wife he apparently didn't wish for.

Only a beast would contemplate such a thing, though of course it was every husband's right.

Was that then, what she thought of him after such a small acquaintance? That he was a monster?

Where was her evidence?

A sneer at dinner, a sullenness of disposition when engaged with his wife, his somewhat combative reaction to her. None of these things constituted evidence of maliciousness.

Perhaps she ought to avoid giving in to flights of fancy herself.

But returning to the heart of the matter, what—if the notion of it being a genuine apparition were discounted—had Jane seen?

A play of light? A reflection? She had heard tell of a special lantern, that when pointed at a silk screen could create the appearance of an apparition. Had one of the gentlemen come by such a device?

Was this then, a prank?

Were they even now huddled together somewhere, laughing over glasses of port and brandy about the glorious jape they'd played? Oh, she would have their very guts for garters. Why did men have to be such inhuman creatures?

No...no, she could not believe it, not of Jem, or Doctor Bell, or even jovial Mr Cluett. Linfield... Well, truthfully, he struck her as exactly the type to engage in such behaviour and show not an iota of remorse. Wasn't the very reason he was mouldering at Cedarton because of some unpleasantness in town? She would have to remember to ask Jem about that. See if he could shed any light on things.

Eliza was half out of her chair, ready to track him down at once before she recalled her charge. Bell had administered a dose large enough to render a full-grown man comatose and Jane was but a wisp of a person, elfin, delicate, half the size of a man. It would be a miracle if she stirred before halfway through tomorrow. And opiates left one with such a ghastly sense of disconnectedness.

She settled back down and rested her head against the chair's leather wing. The room was stuffy and overly warm, making her lids grow increasingly heavy. She would write home tomorrow, explain that she needed to stay longer than anticipated. Maria would protest, but only because her natural inclination was to embroil herself in mischief, rather than shun it. She would have to take care not to allude to the 'ghost' or her youngest sibling would be here in a trice.

I'm sure you're all enjoying having one less body in the place, she'd write, and maybe that would remind Freddy to apply himself to the matter of finding them a new home. As beloved as their cottage on Bluebell Lane remained, they had quite outgrown it.

She thought of the acres of mattress she had all to herself next door and tried to elbow the armchair into a more comfortable support. It remained rigidly unyielding. "You'd laugh, Jo," she said to her absent elder sister. "Here I am in a castle with a bed fit for a queen next door, sleeping in a chair, and you having never left the comfort of home, have a bed entirely to yourself."

She must have drifted off, for Eliza woke to a soft knock upon the door and found the fire burned down to nothing but embers. "Come," she bade.

The young maid who'd delivered the tea tray earlier entered and bobbed her a curtsy. "Begging your pardon, Miss, but Mrs Honeyfield said I was t' come and sit with t' mistress so that you can get ya bed."

How topsy-turvy the world was, that her rest should be of concern when she had nothing at all to do, whereas this maid would be up before the sun setting fires, and exterminating intruders of the creepy crawly kind.

"I'm sure you would equally enjoy yours."

The girl cocked her head like Eliza's neighbour's spaniel, listening, but not quite comprehending. "Aw, that's kind a ya, but I'll be fine here. I reckon that chair's less lumpy than me bed, and Lady Linfield a lot less twiney than Betsy Cooper who I normally top to toe with."

"Are Cedarton's servant's quarters that cramped? Surely there must have been a staff of dozens upon dozens in the past."

"I don't reet know about that, Miss. It's not that there ain't beds, only..." She screwed her pretty, freckled nose up clearly seeking the right descriptor, "They're not all that nice, and what with it being so nitherin' out...."

"You mean it's freezing and the roof leaks."

The girl laughed. "That's where there's a roof to be had, Miss. Gordy, he's the groundsman, and me cousin on me mam's side. He allus says the roofs were bad when 'is pa were an apprentice to 'is grandpa, and nuffin's been done to reet them since. 'Tis a miracle there're any roofs left at all."

"It did stand empty for a long while, so I understand."

"Aye, true. Near fifty years accordin' t' Gordy. But here's me blathering on when I'm suppose ta be helpin' ya get t' bed. Will ya need my help with that? Mrs Honeyfield said I was ta ask. Though, ah said t' her, I said, she's one who can do it thisen."

Her forthrightness startled a laugh from Eliza. "Yes, you're right about that. I shall manage just fine."

The maid gave a nod. "It's like ah said, a lady what turns up without a maid is a lady what knows how to do buttons. Though lord knows, Miss, we were all of us praying you'd bring one. We're in a right tither downstairs."

"Ah, yes, I'd heard there'd been problems acquiring help, what with all the local superstitions about the place."

The girl gave another frown. "I don't rightly knows about that, Miss. There are always folks eager for work, and no boggarts ever stopped 'em. Leastways, not until that bit of nonsense Jenny Pickhall up and oft and started wagging her tongue." Her gaze ventured across the eiderdown to where Jane's head rested upon the pillows. "I suppose it's true then, that t' mistress has seen the old hag too?"

"Hag?"

"Sorry. Begging ya pardon, the old mistress... Lady Cedarton. She weren't really old, but they say she had an awful temper. Least that's what folks hereabouts say."

"Gordy?"

"Not him, Miss. I reckon he's too afraid of 'er hearing him to risk it. I suppose I ought t' mind my tongue too, but I've never managed the trick of it. Me mam's been saying as much since I was a bairn."

"Well, I'm certain that Lady Linfield's fright was down to something perfectly ordinary that will no doubt reveal itself come daylight."

"Do ya really, Miss?"

"Absolutely." She shot the girl an encouraging smile. Cedarton needed its servants. "It's such an old ruinous building, dark, disorientating, I'm certain she saw nothing more than a reflection in a mirror."

"I expect so, Miss. Though Betsy did go on so about 'er while we was seeing t' the dishes. Said the old mistress sees her ladyship as an intruder and means t' drive her out. That she means t' devour all our souls if we linger."

"Codswallop. Lady Cedarton's not in a position to have thoughts about anyone anymore. She's long dead and buried."

"You don't think there's any truth t' her spirit being restless?"

"None whatsoever. It's a story meant only to scare you. It's a wonder that Mrs Honeyfield lets Betsy blether on like that."

"Ah don't know that Mrs Honeyfield's been paying much accord to Betsy Cooper and her to-ing and fro-ings. She's frightful poorly with her tooth. I shouldn't say, Miss, but you were kind enough t' offer her that tincture earlier, 'av seen her spittin' blood up more than once a day."

Eliza sighed. It was a promise she'd yet to fulfil. Surely Bell would have retired by now, and she might slip into the still room undisturbed. "Thank you for the reminder..."

"Edith, Miss."

"Edith. Although, I'm not sure how much good my remedy will do if the problem is that severe. It sounds very much like the tooth ought to be pulled."

"Mebee. It's what lordship's valet said, but Mrs Honeyfield wouldn't have it. She says it hurts so bad she's feared half her jaw'll pop out with the tooth. But anyways, I'm keeping ya from ya rest."

Eliza pushed to her feet and watched the girl settle into the groove she'd left behind. "I'll be right next door if you need help with Lady Linfield at all."

"As ya say. Goodnight, Miss."

"Goodnight, Edith."

~Ж~

The connecting door did not lead directly between their rooms as Eliza had anticipated, but to a small dressing room, where her clothing had been hung alongside Jane's, which did seem odd, given the enormous armoire in the corner of her chamber. Perhaps it was locked, and the key lost—not such a far-fetched notion in a house as old as this. However, this proved not to be the case. The key sat squarely in the lock of the oak wardrobe. Eliza peered inside. It was quite empty all the way to the top, which scraped the stucco work on the ceiling, apart from one small, aged lavender bag.

Curious. Quite curious. Whyever had her things not been placed in here where they'd be more convenient?

Rot?

There was no smell of it, nor signs of woodworm or moths. She rapped her knuckles against the back panel. It didn't make sense, but then so little about Cedarton did. There was a knot hole near the base that resembled a keyhole in shape. Eliza traced her finger over it, and there was a sharp click. She leapt back, alarmed, fearing she'd find her finger pricked, but there was no ruby bead on her fingertip. Instead, the back of the armoire swung into the space where the wall ought to have been.

A door in the back of a wardrobe? Whatever was the purpose in that?

Oh, Eliza, she could hear Maria's voice in her head, as if she were right by her in the room. *I'm most terribly vexed with you. As if it weren't bad enough that you are off enjoying ghastly adventures without me, now you have stumbled on a secret passage and haven't the nous to recognise it. I am delirious with envy.*

Was it lucky to discover a disguised entrance to your room that anyone might come and go by without your knowledge? That was also dark and dismal and smelled strongly of mice?

If you even think of sealing it up and leaving it unexplored, I shall disown you as my sister. Maria was so loud inside her head; it was a wonder Eliza could hear her own thoughts. *Really, sister, you are so trying. I'm simply beyond myself. How can I be stuck at home and you in a castle riddled with secrets? It is dismally unfair. And you're still hesitating over finding them. Freddy ought to have let me visit Jane.*

"You don't even know her."

Nor do you anymore, not really. You don't even know why she married Linfield.

He's a viscount. Really did there need to be any more reason for it than that?

Eliza shot a glance over her shoulder. All was quiet in the adjoining room. Perhaps, she could just take a peep at where this led.

Armed with the nearest candelabrum, and the armoire key stowed safely in her pocket, Eliza stepped into the hidden passage. The space was narrow, barely the width of a person, and as far as she could ascertain, wove a path between the internal and external castle walls. One presumed it was intended to be used by the servants, enabling them to pass unseen, its existence now forgotten. Cedarton's layout was confusing, but she thought she was heading towards the burned portions of the castle. Would this then take her beyond the black door? The darkness, and the lack of reference points made it difficult to gauge how far she'd travelled. The passage bent and meandered, seemed to curve back on itself more than once, so that before long she wasn't sure of her direction at all. The only blessing was that there were no side tunnels, so that she had only to retrace her steps to find her way out.

Eventually, she came upon a tight spiral stair that led down into even inkier darkness. Perhaps she might find her way to the portion of the castle that housed the still room, and hence finally be able to make good on her promise to Mrs Honeyfield.

Down and down, she delved, collecting cobwebs, and stirring up long settled dust, before a small landing branched off to one side, bringing with it a gust of air that almost puffed her candle out.

This new passageway was far wider than the first, enabling her to walk easily without fear of scraping her elbows. A few sharp turns soon presented her with an exit. Faint light seeped around the edges of the frame. Quite uncertain of her location, Eliza put her ear to the grain. It wouldn't do to burst in on Lord Linfield, or Mr Cluett, or even Jem, though he at least might see the humour in her emerging from behind a bookcase or one of the grim ancestral portraits. And while she didn't consider herself the sort of woman who would usually be tempted to a gentleman's bedchamber, how much fun might they have, if she could do so unseen?

Eliza found the latch by touch alone. She couldn't hear a thing and did so desperately want to know where she had ended up. She raised the latch carefully, anticipating the squeal of rusted metal, but it lifted as if recently oiled, allowing her to inch open the door just far enough to peep around the gap. The room beyond was shrouded in darkness, with only a faint orange glow from below. She appeared to be on some sort of gallery. A wooden rail surrounded a narrow walkway. She reached out to her right—

books. Row upon row of them. This then must be the library, and she in the upper level of it.

Keeping low and to the shadows, she was able to creep forward and peer down at the central portion of the room.

A single figure, too portly to be Lord Linfield, stood hunched over a gargantuan desk, sorting through a bundle of papers. Several of the desk drawers were pulled open, but the room's numerous lamps were unlit, including the large one on the corner of the desk. The fire had burned low, so that the fellow had to raise each paper to his single candle.

"Drat and damn you for the cur you are, Linfield," he swore.

It was Mr Cluett.

But what manner of mischief was he about?

"It has to be here somewhere. What have you done with it, you monster?" He shoved the sheaf of papers back into the topmost drawer, then turned his attention to the central drawer, rattling it in anger when it failed to open. Petulantly, he cast himself into the desk chair and dug his knuckles into his eyes, only to rise a moment later and snatch a small box off the desktop. The tinkling of notes revealed it to be a music box. George turned it over in his hands, then slid a side panel free and hissed a triumphant "Yes!" through his teeth.

He had recovered the key, which he applied at once to the locked drawer. Another folio was set on the desktop. George licked his fingertips and began to fan through the documents.

Not that one, nor this, she could almost hear his thoughts growing more frantic as the stack thinned, until the last page was turned, and still not having found whatever he sought, he slammed his fist down on the blotter.

Eliza flinched. George too seemed to shrink back over his actions. His gaze darted from one shadowy corner to the next, but never turned upwards to the gallery where she hid.

Satisfied he'd not alerted anyone to his presence, he began a second pass through the papers. "I don't understand. It has to be here. Everything else of import is."

George pulled the drawer free of its housing and turned it over. Only one item remained within. It drifted softly to the hearth rug, from which it was snatched immediately and as swiftly discarded. "That makes no sense." He picked it up again, this time looking at it with considerably more interest. "Linfield, what the devil?"

"You know, desperation is most unbecoming, George."

Cluett started, Lord Linfield stood in the doorway, a glass of spirits in his hand. He came forward revealing himself to be swaddled in his banyan. He sniffed at the disorder wrought upon his personal correspondence, not seeming overly concerned by the intrusion. "You won't find anything of note in there."

"Will I not?" Cluett replied. "It seems to me I've found a puzzle most curious."

"Which was hardly what you were looking for."

"Yet perplexing enough to be noteworthy."

"It is not here, I should add. I made a point of leaving it with my notary, knowing how light-fingered certain of my acquaintances can be."

"No matter, you can retrieve it."

"And why would I ever do that, George?"

"Why?" Mr Cluett's jovial round face twisted itself into an insufferable smirk. "So that we might affect an exchange, of course. Your folly for mine."

"For what? For that?" Linfield stepped closer so that he could see the document over his friend's shoulder. His expression turned saucer-eyed. "Give me that." He made a grab for the paper, but George twisted out of his reach.

"Oh, no. No, I think I shall hold on to this. It's quite the enlightening read. If you wish its return, then you need only restore to me what is by rights mine."

"But it is not yours by rights. When one gambles with the future, one should always be prepared for the consequences should it not pay off."

"I ought to have won."

"But you didn't. Hand over the paper, George." Linfield stretched out his hand, only to have it slapped away.

"I wonder what she would make of this, your poor sweet bride.... What her family...? What *your* family would make of it? They are unaware, aren't they? Remind me, what did she bring to your coffers, a princely sum? Eighteen thousand, weren't it?"

"Around that, not that it's any of your concern."

George seemed not to hear him, for he

continued, "A sum, a blessed sum that would surely evaporate should certain parties happen upon this." He flicked the edge of the paper in his hand. "Goodness knows how many lives could be wrecked, the size of the scandal that would erupt."

"Don't be a fool, George."

"Oh, you don't think it would cause an upset? I think it likely to cause both heartbreak and embarrassment. Let me see, should I read it to you in case you've mislaid the facts? It states that before God and witnesses, Lord Eustace Lionel Linfield, is married to one Miss Ja—"

"You give me that, George, or by God I will throttle the life from you, and then turn your mother out into the streets she grew up on in nothing but her stays."

"It seems to me that is already your intent. And I don't care for your insinuations, my lord."

"I insinuate nothing. Do you even know whose brat you are?"

George lashed out, catching Linfield sharp across the nose. They fell into a wrestle on the tabletop, sending ornaments and papers flying perilously close to the hearth. Then their bodies too, as they smashed down into the chair, sending it skidding across the boards into the bookcase. George had Linfield by the throat. Linfield his thumbs gouging George's eyes. Ought she to intervene? Raise the alarm? She was too slow for either, as the men crashed into one of the many bookcases, causing it to rain its contents down on their heads in an avalanche of leather-bound volumes.

Linfield put his hand to his temple and gazed at his blood-stained fingers in alarm.

"It's just a scratch." George stood and tucked the stolen paper into his coat pocket. He minced closer and offered Linfield his kerchief, only for the viscount to spit and hiss at him like an angry swan.

"Get out of my sight and begone from my property."

George rolled back his shoulders, then straightened his waistcoat, coat, and cravat, transforming himself back into a gentleman. "I leave when the papers are in my hands, and not before. If you're wise, you'll make that soon, or I'll be sure to deliver notarized copies of this to your father and your father-in-law. Men ought to be held accountable for their indiscretions, don't you think?"

Lord Linfield put his hand on a nearby book and hurled it. "Leave." The missile hit George on the knee, leaving him limping towards the exit.

"We'll discuss it after breakfast, shall we?"

"If I don't feed you to the white lady."

Cheeks bloodless, save for the scarlet smear across his temple, and with his hair forming a halo of dandelion fluff around his head, Linfield hobbled over to the desk chair. He sank into it with a hollow moan and rested his head against the desk blotter. "Why this? Why me?" he complained, while drumming out an angry metre with his clenched fist.

Was it quite safe to leave him injured and unattended? Eliza didn't quite know, but nor did it seem a clever point to reveal herself. She was relieved when one of the footmen arrived.

"I heard a commotion. Is everything well, my lord?"

"Get out!" Linfield snarled.

"My lord, you're—" Linfield hurled the nearest object to hand at the servant, which happened to be the small music box. It fell short of its target and smashed into a myriad of pieces.

"Out. If you want to be useful, fetch Bell."

Eliza sensibly took that as her cue too and slipped quietly back into the tunnel between the walls.

-8-

Eliza

Jane's breathing had eased, and the colour returned to her cheeks when Eliza stepped in to check on her the next morning. Edith was dozing, making endearing snuffling snores, her head lolling towards to her chest. She roused when Eliza's shadow cast across her.

"Miss—'ave I overslept?"

"It's early yet." Eliza reassured her, but the maid shook her head at the light pouring through the window and gave a cry of alarm. "Nah, I should have been up ages ago."

"Nonsense, your duties here override all else until someone specifically tells you otherwise." The reassurance did nothing to calm the maid, who danced about trying to right herself, and pinch life into her cheeks. "How has she been? Any disturbances."

Edith pushed several unruly curls back beneath her mob-cap. "She's been quiet as a lamb. Too quiet. Slept right through with nary a whisper, and me too."

It was a joy to hear that the sedative had given her peace, not mired her in disturbing dreams. Eliza leaned over to smooth the hair back from Jane's brow and press a kiss to her skin. "I'm sure the rest has done you both the world of good. Now, make sure there's tea for when she wakes and have her take her breakfast on a tray. Even if she's not hungry, you should encourage her to eat, even if it's just toasted bread."

"I'll do that, Miss."

The little maid continued to yawn and stretch. She had only just made it into some semblance of liveliness when Mrs Honeyfield came in, bearing a tray. "I thought I'd bring this up, rather than 'ave it go cold. Tothers are already at the table, Miss Wakefield, if you'd care t' go down and join them. There's pigeon pie and eggs, and a nice seed cake, as well as bergamot marmalade his lordship's mam's sent. It's said to be Lincolnshire's finest."

"It sounds delightful." She did enjoy a good marmalade, though she'd never encountered a bergamot. "I'll head down right away now that I've reassured myself." She brushed Jane's hand affectionately, but then left off aware of Mrs Honeyfield's scrutiny.

"You as well, lass." The housekeeper ushered Edith towards the door. "Too much to be done for tha to be idling. And don't be listening to none of Betsy Cooper's nonsense now either. I've had to 'ave words with that 'un this morning already. Stirring up a reet storm she is with her tattle, and tellin' all and sundry about her ladyship's turn."

"Word would reach the village soon enough anyway," Eliza said. It was the way of things; news travelled on the wind, and the castle and its monsters would already be on everyone's minds thanks to his lordship's arrival in the area.

"Aye, maybe," Mrs Honeyfield conceded. "Still, if we weren't so rushed ragged ah'd send her on her way. She's a sly piece, an no mistaking. Ah don't want ya pickin' up her windbag ways or any of her other habits, yer hear me, Edith. It shan't be a surprise if I have ta count the spoons afore her next 'alf day."

"She just likes to chatter," Edith said in the other maid's defence.

"Blather and idle, tha's true enough. And sneak off t' who knows where at drop of a 'at. But she's what we hav', so wil't 'ave t' make do. Off with ya, now. You too, Miss."

Eliza was along the corridor and down the stairs before she recalled the need to apologise for her tardiness in getting Mrs Honeyfield her potion. No matter, she would go down to the still room after breakfast and make it up, whether Doctor Bell approved or not. Perhaps she'd encourage him to take a peep in on Jane to get him out of the way for a while. Although, that was a risky prospect. The last thing she wanted was for the doctor to administer another dose of opiates.

It appeared she'd arrived late, for the dining room stood empty.

"Hoo there, through here."

She turned at the sound of Henrietta's greeting and found her seated alongside Mr Cluett and Jem at a large circular table in what one assumed to be a breakfast room.

"There you are dear. Do come and join us, and you must fill us in on how our dear hostess is this morning."

George pushed a chair out for her with his foot.

"We were just saying that you might choose to take a tray upstairs, weren't we, George?"

"The pigeon pie's very good," that fellow muttered. Eliza noted that the corners of his eyes closest to his nose were bloodshot this morning, and the surrounding skin mottled purple. "Seed cake was better yesterday. This one's a bit dry."

Henrietta thrust her elbow into her son's ribs. "Oh, George, she doesn't care about that."

"Well, I am rather ravenous." Eliza settled between the two gentlemen and helped herself to a slice of the pie. It had a gloriously golden crust, which was more than could be said of the disappointing cake, which appeared to have been browned with treacle. Jem raised the teapot and waggled it meaningfully. He looked glorious this morning, turned out in a smart blue coat and paisley waistcoat. He nudged a cup and saucer in her direction, then poured a third for Doctor Bell as he entered.

"Miss Wakefield was just about to tell us how the patient fares this morning," Henrietta said.

Bell cocked an eyebrow.

Eliza indulged in a good swallow of tea, before

indulging Henrietta's curiosity. "She's proving herself a terrible stay abed." She paused, cleared her throat. "She's yet to wake, but all has been calm overnight. I'm sure she'll be quite herself again once she does rise."

"I suppose Lord Linfield has gone up to greet her?" Henrietta proposed.

Truly the woman was a very determined busybody, but then with so little to entertain her, it was hardly a surprise that she'd wish to turn over every aspect of last night's drama. Truthfully, there was plenty about it that Eliza wished to dissect too. She exchanged a meaningful glance with Jem, who nudged some marmalade towards her. Bell cracked an egg into his tea and added a splash of milk.

"Are you not going to eat, Doctor Bell?"

"What I have is quite sufficient, thank you, Mistress Cluett."

"Oh, pish! It's Henrietta, haven't I said so since the first night? But you didn't answer my question about his lordship, either."

"I believe he is abroad on an early morning ramble."

Henrietta gaped at him aghast, while Eliza took to her feet and crossed to the window. "Has it cleared out, then?" It had not, based on what little she could see of the gardens. Mist lingered just yards away, so all that was visible was a small square of terrace and the faint outlines of a couple of big trees. It was certainly not the right weather to be tramping the moors, but a glance at the doctor suggested that his answer may not have been entirely truthful. Perhaps

Linfield was about business he wouldn't wish to be discussed, or Bell simply considered Henrietta too nosy to be indulged.

"Will you check on Jane?" Eliza asked him.

"If you deem it necessary."

"I didn't say that. I'm sure she'll be quite well."

Jem leaned closer. "Don't let him goad you. He has every intention of checking on his patient. It's just he's not adequately fortified himself yet. He functions entirely on tea. That, and he usually only deals with the deceased; I fear he finds the living rather more taxing."

"They are certainly a deal less predictable, but to put all your minds at rest I'll attend to Lady Linfield at once." He took his cup and saucer and left.

"What a dreadfully unsociable man," Henrietta complained.

While Bell was engaged, she could enter his domain without fear of disturbance. Eliza pushed her plate aside half-eaten. "I think I'll just go and tag along."

"Oh, must you?" Henreitta wailed, but Eliza had already left.

She did not race after Bell, but instead deliberately kept her distance. Once she was satisfied that he'd gone upstairs, she snuck through the parlour and into the ruins of the long gallery. The space must once have been glorious, light streaming in through a multitude of large windows and the central cupola. Now all that remained of the glass were the splinters on the marble floor tiles, while the frames formed a skeletal lattice work overhead. The still room lay ahead and down a flight.

Eliza put her ear to the still room door before letting herself in. All was quiet. Within, the air smelled of lye and the sort of heavy incense she associated with the catholic church. All the ingredients she could wish for were lined up and ordered on broad shelves or housed in apothecary-style drawers, each meticulously labelled. Given Cedarton's long abandonment, she could only assume Bell responsible. He instantly rose in her estimation.

Though the vessel full of leeches rapidly tipped the scales in the opposite direction.

She immediately set out gathering the ingredients she required and adding them to the bowl of the conveniently placed scales. The recipe was a relatively simple one, refined over generations and through her own thorough testing. It was not a difficult remedy to mix, and thank goodness, for she did not wish to be caught should Bell come down. So far, he had proved himself efficient and not the sort to malinger. She supposed she liked him for that. Too many medical men outstayed their welcome, insisting on ruminating over their patients. At least he was decisive, even if his methods—she shot a glance at the disgusting leeches—were spurious. In any case, once this was done, she really did want to look around and see if she could determine what had caused Jane's fright.

"Miss Wakefield, do you have permission to be in here?"

Eliza whirled around in response to the deep

male voice. Jem was poised in the doorway and had clearly been present for several minutes. There had hardly been an opportunity to converse since their earlier reunion, and Henrietta's beady gaze had prevented them from exchanging more than pleasantries at the breakfast table, now, she couldn't help letting her gaze linger. His smart blue coat lent him an air of elegance; his overlong hair was attempting to counteract. The front had fallen over his brow and set one side of his face in shadow, resulting in a mischievous mien that his smile further called attention to.

"It's a break in," she replied, continuing with her preparation. "Are you going to arrest me? Summon the constable? Snitch on me to Bell?"

"He certainly won't thank you for messing about in his drawers." This he said with a chuckle in his voice that made Eliza blush. It was in her mind to say that she didn't think he'd mind at all if it were his drawers she was choosing to mess about in, but they really didn't know one another well enough for her say such a thing aloud, and in any case, it wasn't the sort of thought a young lady of her standing was supposed to even have.

Of course, she did have them—thoughts that were distinctly lewd in nature and hopelessly distracting.

Not that now was the time for such things. "I aim to be done before he's back. Unless you tell him, he won't ever know that I've been here."

Jem pushed away from the door and approached the counter where she was mixing her ingredients into a paste. "What are you about?"

"The remedy for Mrs Honeyfield's toothache. Bell's done nothing for the poor woman, and I don't like to see anyone going around in such a pitiful state. Toothache's the worst."

He winced as if remembering some past episode. "To be fair, he has been busy with—"

"Jane! I know, but he's not a very able doctor if he's only capable of treating one patient a day."

"Two," Jem corrected.

"Why are you down here?" Eliza asked. The paste was thickening nicely.

"Hm, well, let's see. The only interesting person in the entire household abandoned me at the breakfast table with Mrs Prattlebox and a fop set upon eating his own weight in pigeon pie."

"It was rather good."

"So good you left most of yours."

Her stomach gurgled over the memory. She would dearly have liked to have lingered longer at her breakfast but couldn't not seize the opportunity provided by Bell's intention to see Jane.

"'Tis lucky you know an observant gallant." He held out his hand to her, revealing the remains of her pie, wrapped in a napkin.

Eliza gave a longing groan. "Hang on to it for me."

"I've a better idea—bite." Jem held the pie so that she didn't need to stop her mixing. She took a nibble and then another, finally giving in to her hunger. Jem watched her chew, head thoughtfully cocked. "Here," he reached out and dislodged some crumbs from around her mouth with his bare fingertips.

"Oh. Um," she sighed, flustered by how close he was. She was no petite flibbertigibbet, being quite tall for a woman—her whole family bore the affliction except for Caroline—but Jem was easily six feet, perhaps even an inch or two taller, and he was standing exceedingly close. Close enough that she was conscious of the warmth radiating off him, and the scent of the millefleur soap he used to shave. Crushingly aware too of where his fingertip had brushed against her lips. This was not the first time they'd been thus positioned, nor the first she felt the draw in the pit of her, tempting her to further close the gap. At Stags Fell, there'd been too many people about, likewise at Lauwine Hall for all but the swiftest of pleasures, but now, here at Cedarton, there were barely a handful of people rattling about a property meant to house at least thrice their number, surely, they might carve out a moment of privacy without fear of being stumbled upon.

Could they not?

Dare she? What was the purpose of being allowed the freedom of travelling without a chaperone, if she was not to take full advantage of it?

Jem's gaze lingered on her face. His gold-and-green-flecked irises glittered with promise. She wasn't one to have her head turned by a man, but Jem posed a special kind of lure.

Her hands stilled; preparation forgotten. She hardly dared breathe as he traced the shape of her lips.

"Eliza Wakefield. What is it about you that draws me so?" He seemed to be speaking to himself as much as her. "I've not forgotten our last meeting."

Nor had she. She'd kissed him, and Joshua, both, and not felt an iota of guilt over it. Now she leaned into Jem's touch, wanting to experience that thrill all over again.

Why did he not act? Press his suit? Why did he have to choose to be a gentleman in this moment stymied by chivalry and a code of honour, rather than a thoroughly despicable rake?

"Jem," she sighed, straining towards his touch. If he did not act soon, she would take matters into her own hands, and he could thank her for it later. It did always irk her how one came to be forever waiting around for gentlemen to apply themselves.

Eliza wetted her lips. Prickles of desire were chasing over her skin. Her pulse beat loudly in her ears. Dramatically enough he too could probably hear it.

"This is madness," he murmured, warm breath buffeting her cheek.

The only madness was that he wasn't already kissing her senseless when she desired it so very badly. His finger still rested at the corner of her mouth, and he was gazing at her in a way that left nothing to interpretation. This wasn't simply a connection of minds forged over a mutual love of learning, it was physical. It had her heart caught in an iron fist.

She could do it. Kiss him right here and now, and no one would ever be the wiser. Her family were many miles away, no one here at Cedarton was watching over her. She was entirely free to make her own choices.

Jem slid a hand around the back of her head. "Tell me I shouldn't. Tell me to release you."

Eliza clasped the edges of his coat, and instead tugged him closer. "What if that's not what I want?"

"Then we're both cursed."

She kissed him, rising onto her toes to reach, and groaning at his urgent response when their mouths met.

This... this was what had kept her awake and restless through numerous nights since they'd last seen one another. This possibility. This rightness in the way they fit together. It was a ridiculous impossibility, of course. When Freddy talked of finding suitable matches for her and her sisters, she never saw herself as part of that compact. To wed was to agree to a very specific set of expectations, and while she thought she would like children of her own someday, she did not want them to be the totality of her future, not when there was so much to learn, so many other things she might discover or engage with to leave her mark upon the world.

"Oh, God... Eliza. What is it that you do to me?"

Mayhaps the same thing he did to her, drove rational thought aside.

"We can't do this... we shouldn't," he muttered. "We have to stop." Yet how readily he slid his tongue between her lips, clove his body to her. Eliza startled, feeling the ridge of his desire press fast to her front. It made her feel hot and heavy in a very specific place, and eager for something she knew she shouldn't even contemplate while unwed.

Although that rule was not of her making, and she'd grown exceedingly tired of the rules men made.

"We don't have to stop." Daringly she reached down and brushed her hand against the bulge in his breeches. She was rewarded with a sharp intake of breath.

"Eliza. Gads!" He pushed her to arm's length and held her there despite the tremor in his limbs. "I don't know whether to be shocked or delighted." His eyes were fever bright. He took hold of her hands, kissed each curled finger in turn. "You astonish me, always, every time we meet, but it would be wrong and foolhardy to proceed down this route."

"Who's to stop us? If it's what we desire, shouldn't that matter more than anything else?"

"If only all were that simple," his brow furrowed. "Know this, Eliza. There is no part of me that doesn't desire this. You've haunted me every night since we last parted, but it would be wrong of me to allow this to proceed. There are things... things you ought to know about me before we embark on anything others might consider impropriety."

"Things? What things, Jem? Don't say you are bound to someone else."

His gaze snapped back to her face. "Bound? No, I'm not bound. It's not that."

-9-

Jem

One particular person might have had a different opinion about Jem's freedom, but that was because he was an entitled nob who readily mistook desire for affection and lust for love. Jem prided himself on being an honest man, both to himself and others. If he occasionally bent the truth, it was only with exceedingly good cause. He knew he ought to end this right now, tell her exactly what sort of man he was and all the reasons why that made it impossible for them to be together.

"Eliza, I adore you, but I also hanker after other men, and currently Linfield has me in a bind."

The words remained lodged in his throat and couldn't be spat out no matter how hard he prompted himself to do so, not knowing how quickly they would snuff out her regard for him.

Everything had been so much simpler when he thought his opportunity lost. He'd convinced himself that Joshua Rushdale would have wooed and won her by now. That his aunt Mary would eventually write and entirely in passing, remark upon the wedding or some other event where Mr and Mrs Rushdale were in attendance, and then she would recall Eliza to him—the eldest of the Misses Wakefield that came to Stag's Fell last summer with the party from Lauwine Hall. And he would reply, and say "Oh, yes, I recall. Do pass on my congratulations. I'm so happy for them", while he died inside. Yet somehow none of that was real. Instead, she stood facing him, reaching for him now.

He had to tell her. He wasn't interested in a future built on deceits.

"Jem," Eliza prompted.

"I've nothing to offer you," he said with some difficulty. "It'd be wrong to let you assume otherwise." He smoothed a stray strand away from her face. "Eliza, I'm not the man you deserve."

"I don't think that is true, and in any case, we're not negotiating a marriage pact. I'm not seeking to wed."

She wasn't?

"Is this what you told Joshua too? Is this why—"

"You thought I'd marry Joshua Rushdale?" Her mouth hung open in astonishment.

Jem nodded. His mouth was dry, making it difficult to get his words out. It had seemed so logical when he'd thought it over, alone in his Oxford quarters. "It seemed an obvious assumption that you would choose one or other of us after all that happened at Lauwine, and he has the better prospects."

Eliza touched his face, as if with her fingertips

she could read off his skin what he was failing to put into words. "As it happens, much like you, Joshua hasn't been very forthcoming with his attentions or correspondence." She trailed a finger along the ridge of his jaw down to his cravat, then curled her grip around the front of his coat, pulling him back to her so that their warm breaths mingled in the shallow space between them. "Mayhap, I ought to be mad at you both. Instead, I think perhaps I am grateful. Your inaction has allowed me time to think and realise I don't know that I even wish to wed."

"Ever?" he gasped. Surely, she didn't mean it.

"Jem, you must understand that marriage for a woman is to commit to certain duties… duties that would not allow me time for study or the betterment of myself. My life would be dedicated to those and child-rearing, assuming I even survived the horrors of birth. Whereas, if I remain a spinster, then there are no such obligations."

What she said was not unreasonable. He wished there was change on the horizon, a promise he could make that might alter her views, but he couldn't even really offer himself, let alone a means of escaping societal expectations.

"Do you see how I might question the seeking of a husband but might also not wish to live a life devoid of intimacy. You say you have nothing to offer me, but I say that isn't true."

She meant them to be lovers. It seemed unchivalrous to agree and equally discourteous to accept. Yet, he remained tempted. By her lips, which were right there by his chin. By her eyes, so bright with ardour…. He had only to dip his head a fraction and take what was being freely offered. And he need not let the things that had weighed heavy on his conscience worry him any longer. An affair—illicit in its very nature—was a very different matter to a lifetime connection.

She caught his glance. "Do I shock you, Jem?"

"I don't know whether to rejoice that you want me, or feel bitter that you reject the notion of—"

"I've rejected nothing. Merely questioned convention, and now ask that we put aside the notion of plighting troths or tying unravelable knots and the like aside for the time being. Perhaps on deeper acquaintance, we will find that we do not suit as well as we currently think. Or the opposite, entirely. Perhaps I will become so utterly obsessed with you the notion of binding ourselves with golden shackles shall sound like the most perfect of outcomes."

Time—she was giving him time. And whispering to him promises of a future. He could present to her who he truly was, make her understand that… That what, it didn't make him a freak… an embarrassment… a scandal waiting to erupt? He was all those things.

"I have shocked you," she said, bringing him out of his mind and back into the present. They were stood practically chin to shoulder, his hands around her waist, hers resting lightly on his shoulders. "Perhaps you don't believe a woman should allow herself the same pleasures as are readily afforded to men. We should be chaste, goodly… entirely pure."

"No." He pulled her closer. "I'm honoured that you seek to ask those things of me."

"Truly?"

This was foolish, but there was no helping it. In no version of life that he'd ever choose would he walk away from this moment or her and leave her imagining he didn't want what was offered.

He wanted it so badly; he could taste it in the air.

"Goddammit, Eliza!" He crushed his lips to hers, swaddling her in a fast embrace. He kissed her as he'd dreamed of doing on oh so many nights. Those moments at Lauwine Hall had been so fleeting. The three of them tied in knots none of them dared unpick for fear of finding they were the one holding the end of a different rope.

"I've thought so many times about that day."

"Likewise, so many times." Not purely of her, but of Joshua too. Of how it'd made him feel to watch the two of them kiss. The answer was surprisingly complex. Jealous, for certain, but more troubling things too. Desire, coupled with thoughts about what the three of them might do together.

He'd learned just hours before that moment that the lords Pennerley and Marlinscar were engaged in a triadic relationship with Joshua's sister, so naturally such possibilities had loomed large in his thoughts. He knew now, having witnessed Joshua's actions later that day—he'd put that shot in Pennerley's leg—that Joshua would never consent to such an arrangement with Jem or any other man.

Yet another reason kissing her was foolish. Still, he couldn't stop himself.

Her mouth was a revelation. Her touch seared his skin. She was demanding, yielding, soft but fierce. Her hands tucked under his waistcoat seeking skin. He explored the curve of her throat, the shell of her ear, the firm weight of her cherubic behind. She made him stiff with her inexperienced but eager caresses.

The pictures in his mind were all of raising her onto the table, of lifting her skirts and exposing her stocking tops, of then exploring the soft stretch above her garters, of dipping fingers, tongue into the split between her thighs... and maybe, maybe burying himself there.

But she was ahead of him in some regards, eager not just to be led, but to quest ahead. When she set about slipping the buttons of his breeches, his heart grew so big the sound of it echoed in his ears and simultaneously pulsed heat into his cock.

"You've grown stiff," she muttered. "I've only ever seen a man's member limp. Does it hurt?"

"Only in the best way." She pushed her hand inside the cloth and cupped him. The thrill of it stole the last of his shredded restraint.

"Eliza," he breathed. "Have a care."

"I don't know what to do to please you," she confessed into his ear.

"Yet you're managing just fine." He kissed down the side of her throat to the hollow at its base, then all along her collarbone, and the square edging of her dress. The top of her bosom was firm but soft; he flicked his tongue between the fabric and her skin, seeking her nipple. Found it. Claimed it, sucked it into a steepled peak and heard her crow of pleasure in response.

"Show me how I should pleasure you," she demanded, while her kiss followed a similar route to the one he'd just traversed, concentrating on the juncture of his throat and collarbone. She did that simply by being a presence in his world, but he acknowledged the plea in her voice, that part of her that always sought to learn, to discover, to unravel... "Like this."

He guided her hand, showed her how to ring her fingers around his shaft, then guided her motion. Up to the crown, twist, then down. She grazed the tip of his cock with her palm and his breath left his body in an excited hiss. "Yes. Exactly like that. Exactly."

"You feel so solid, yet so smooth. I like holding you, Jem."

He might have said something eloquent about how much he liked being held, but his lips were busy, and he was already weeping pearls for her. She kissed him again, sucking on that same, now rather sensitive spot.

"I want to look." She lifted her hand and tasted the silken fluid he'd spilled there, causing a lightning strike of arousal to hit him. Many's the man and woman who could learn something from her. Jem lifted his shirt tails, expecting her to glance down, drink her fill and be done. Instead, she bent, bringing her nose down level with the wiry bush at his base.

Her eyes gleamed as she peeped up at him, her tongue running along the edge of her teeth. "Might I taste you?"

Taste him!

What was this alternate realm he'd fallen into? His cock bucked hard at the notion. "I think you mean to kill me," he said, his voice reedy.

"Is that a usual response to having one's prick"— she quirked a brow, querying the term—"kissed?"

He would certainly die a little death. "I'm not sure this is a good idea," he croaked.

Eliza dropped onto her knees. She peeped up at him along the length of his body. "I think you'd like nothing more."

Jem gulped. He couldn't deny she was right. This wasn't how things ought to be though, he ought to be pleasuring her, with his lips and tongue, with the slide of his fingertips between the split of her quim.

She pressed her nose against the skin at the juncture between his torso and hip. "I adore how you smell—musky with promise."

He groaned.

"Do you like to be sucked, Jem? I've heard it's a thing that some men—"

"Yes," he gasped. "Yes, I do. Please. Yes."

She grinned, but then stuck out her tongue and stole a pearly bead from the tip of his cock.

Jem's eyelids fluttered closed. Christ, what torment! He wanted to clasp hold of her head, guide her to do more than tease with her tongue tip, to open her mouth and swallow the whole of him right down to the root.

When she tasted him a second time, then a third,

he pressed against her lips, which she willingly parted, granting him entrance to the hot cavern of her mouth.

"Suck me," he sang, his hands finding purchase around her head, while he steadied himself against the cupboard at his rear. He was making noises, nonsensical croons, and rasps, but he didn't think a mouth around his cock had ever felt this good before. She might not be proficient, but she was eager, and he was utterly besotted. She was going to bring him off, and soon, if he wasn't careful. He clasped his hand around the base of his cock, but it wasn't enough.

"I'm close," he warned. "Take care now."

"Do you mean you're going to spend?"

He choked. Eliza drew him deeper. "Going to…" Goddammit, he was already there, and there was no stopping it. The first spurt took her off guard, but she rallied and swallowed; he felt the motion of her throat as his cock released into her mouth.

His mind was a puddle, surely spilling from his ears.

Eliza sat back on her haunches and looked at him. Then she dabbed his spendings from her lips like a duchess wiping away cake crumbs. "That was—"

"Let me do the same for you." He said in a hurry.

She cocked her head. "I don't see how… Wait, you mean, lick between my thighs?"

He groaned at the description, and his cock gave a pulse like an aftershock. In a moment, he'd find her a chair, lift her skirts. Jem slid down the cupboard at his back and landed on the floor on a level with her. "You are astonishing," he said, before kissing her. "How did you even know that such a thing was a thing?"

"I have ears," she said, a tinkle of laughter in her voice.

So, alas, did he. "Someone is coming!"

"Drat!" she mouthed.

Eliza grabbed her bowl, and he his breeches, and they fled deeper into the suite. The backroom housed a large table, and a tray of assorted knives and torturer's implements.

"Anatomist," Jem hissed as much to remind himself as her. They squatted behind the table, and he did his best to right his clothing.

"There's another exit somewhere." Logically, there had to be, as Bell had emerged into the corridor yesterday without disturbing he and Linfield. They both twisted their necks, trying to ascertain the route. There were three choices, and their escape might lie behind any of them. Still crouched, Jem edged towards the nearest.

"Wait," Eliza hissed, still cradling her bowl like precious cargo. "I don't think it's Bell."

"Who else—?"

But no, she was correct. It was interesting how quickly one learned to recognise a person's tread. Bell's gait was more authoritative, and more stride than shuffle. Whoever it was had a more delicate pace and softer soles.

Eliza stood. "Mrs Honeyfield," she said, and returned to the other room.

The housekeeper jumped, fumbling the jar she held, but managing to keep her grip on it. "Heavens, Miss. You reet startled me. Where did you spring from?"

Eliza waved vaguely. Jem ducked back behind the table. Everyone knew what gossip was like in the servant's quarters. The last thing he needed was for Linfield to hear he'd been down here alone with Eliza.

"No, no," that lady was saying. She snatched the jar from the housekeeper's hand and returned it to the shelf. "Those won't aid at all."

The other woman stiffened. "Are ya sure? Doctor Bell said—."

Eliza glanced again at the label. "Kunckel pills won't do a thing for toothache, they're meant for gout and apoplexy, colic even, and I'd question their efficacy even for those. No, they aren't the thing. But see here, I have the preparation I promised all mixed. It's only in need of a container." She turned about to seek a vessel amongst the range of glassware.

"Will this do?" Mrs Honeyfield passed her a small square jar with a cork stopper.

"Oh, yes. Very nicely. Thank you. Here you go. Just rub it on the affected area, and it should alleviate the pain. Although if it's truly bad, you might consider having it pulled. Did Doctor Bell say anything about that?"

"He said his lordship's valet's tha one to ask if ah wants it pullin'."

Eliza gave her an encouraging smile. Was it any

wonder that so few made it to adulthood, considering the many shortcomings of the country's physicians? God forbid they get their hands dirty, or lowered themselves to mix their own medicines. If they did, they might have a better understanding of the worth of each of the ingredients they prescribed, although being fair to Bell, he'd displayed surprising competence.

Enough to possibly forgive him the leeches.

"Use the remedy, Mrs Honeyfield. It's a recipe that's been in my family for generations, and I promise you, Wakefields, to a woman, all die with a full set of teeth still in their mouths. If there's no improvement in a day or so, then you'd best consult with Lord Linfield's valet and have the tooth pulled. I know it's unpleasant to contemplate, but think of the relief."

"Ah'll do that, Miss. Thank you."

~Ж~

Eliza allowed herself a smile once Mrs Honeyfield had gone. She stared at the spot on the floor where she'd knelt but a few minutes ago and sucked Jem's... done that, to Jem. The taste of him was still on her lips, and she didn't regret it one bit. She quickly returned the items she'd used back to their proper places, no sense in inviting Bell's wrath unnecessarily. He never needed to know that she'd even been here.

Only once she was done did she venture back into the anatomy room. Jem was not where she'd left him. She tried the nearest of the doors they'd noted earlier but found only a cupboard. "Jem?" she called, keeping her voice low.

He emerged, not from one of the remaining two doors, but from behind a section of the wainscotting. "You can't tell, can you?" he said, delighting over how seamlessly the door blended with its surroundings. "Those two are cupboards." He waved a hand at the nearest two doors. "The third is Bell's emergency exit. It leads onto the terrace. But this, this I confess I stumbled on entirely accidentally. Rested my hand right on the handle when I was trying to keep tabs on your conversation with Mrs Honeyfield. I'm surprised you didn't hear my call of surprise, for it knocked me right off balance."

She shook her head, not having heard a thing.

"Where does it lead?" she asked. Jem showed her the catch and opened it up again so that she could peer into the space beyond.

"I didn't venture far, there's a spiral stair ahead, but beyond that..."

"I wonder if it's the same—" She shut her mouth abruptly.

"Oh, don't stop, I'm sure you were about to say something devilishly enlightening."

Eliza stepped into the hidden passage. It was rather less dusty than the one she'd explored the previous night. "I'm not altogether sure I should say."

Jem drew his lips into a pout. "Considering the exchange we shared only a short while ago; I can't see what would prompt you to hold your tongue now."

"Very well, this isn't the first concealed passageway I've stumbled on. There's one that runs between my chamber and the library, but there was also a stair that I didn't venture to the bottom of. It's quite possible that it's one and the same with the one you've just found."

Jem's expression grew ponderous. "So, what you're saying is that the place is riddled with secret passages. Passages that one might use to move about unseen—"

"You ought really to wait for an invitation."

He laughed. "Actually, I was thinking of Lady Cedarton's apparition, and how such an array of secret corridors might facilitate in creating such a visitation."

Eliza waded a little further into the gloom. "Ah, yes, that is a possibility. Especially if there is an exit close to where Jane sighted the ghost. We ought to look, don't you think?"

He stepped into the corridor beside her. "Agreed, and if we do it from the inside, then no one will ask why we're patting down walls and bookcases."

"Or volunteer to assist when they might be the person behind it all. Do you think that's what's happening, Jem? Did someone set out to scare Jane half out of her wits deliberately? What in heavens for?"

"I don't know," he said, but after a long enough pause to make her think that he had a range of thoughts on the subject, possibly even suspicions.

"The stair is straight ahead following the corridor. Will you manage, or should we seek out a candle first?"

"I shall manage." Bits of light seeped in through gaps, and after a few moments her eyes began accustomed to the gloom. Progress was nevertheless slow. They frequently bumped against one another, and the stair Jem had discovered proved to be further along than she'd initially supposed. Their direction of travel was difficult to discern, though they must be within the wreckage of the Lady's Tower. When they eventually found the stair and climbed it, Eliza recognised the turn she'd taken towards the library the night before. "There are no more branches. This leads directly to my chamber."

"Perhaps there are other passages, and not all of them link up," Jem suggested.

"Then I don't know how we shall find them without drawing attention."

"Maybe there's a map. Plans of the place in the library. Should we go and look?"

"Wait." Eliza reached for his hand, stilling him as he was about to take the passage to the library. "Do you smell something? What is that?"

"Burning!" they both concluded at once.

Eliza started forward again following the route towards her room. With each step, the scent became stronger. Soon there were distinct wisps of smoke in the air. She broke into a run as best as was possible in the confined space. Jem stayed on her heels. They burst into her chamber through the back of the armoire to find it exactly as she'd left it that morning.

"Look." Jem darted towards the adjoining door. Thick tendrils of smoke were leaking around the edges of the frame.

"Wait!" Eliza demanded, bringing him to a sharp halt. "We cannot both burst in from my dressing room." Perhaps now wasn't the moment to be thinking of propriety, but she had no intention of being sent away in disgrace for having had a man in her room. Said man had the good sense not to argue. He adjusted his route immediately, dashing out into the main corridor, while Eliza entered via the dressing room.

Within, the air was hazy and thick. It burned in her throat, making her cough. A corresponding hack came from the room beyond. Eliza grabbed a muslin kerchief from a basket on the floor and clasped it over her mouth and nose. Her eyes were streaming as she opened the door into Jane's room.

She'd left the sparse room in weary tranquillity; now it was bright as day. Edith was kneeling on the bed, tugging at Jane with all her might, while her mistress remained in an opiate-induced stupor. Around them, the bed curtains burned with a blue-green flame.

"Miss. Oh, miss!" Edith cried on seeing her.

Eliza ran forward, but there was no getting close. The heat repelled her. Jem was knocking on the external door. Clearly having grown impatient, he burst in.

"No!" He caught Eliza as she tried to reach the bed and held her back. "Think."

"Help. Help us, please." Edith bleated. Her plea

was cut short by a choking cough.

There was water in the ewer. An old shawl of Jane's discarded nearby. Jem had her bind it around his arm, then soak the fabric. The canopy caught as Jem gingerly approached. The flames were tearing through it, showering those below in incandescent sparks. "Jump," he told Edith.

She did, giving Jem just enough room to drag Jane, still entangled in the eiderdown, from the burning bed and deposit her unceremoniously on the rug. Her skin was ashen, lips almost blue.

"Out," Jem ordered them, just as Bell burst through the door. George Cluett followed, along with Henrietta. "What the devil?" He sprang back as the canopy fell.

Eliza pushed Edith towards the door. Both Cluetts fell back to allow her passage. Then she grasped one end of the eiderdown, and she and Jem pulled Jane into the safety of the corridor.

"How the devil has she not stirred?" Mrs Cluett asked. She was fanning her face as if that alone would disperse the thick coils of smoke.

Bell dropped to one knee by Jane's side. Someone pushed a coat beneath her head.

"Is she breathing? Is she dead?" Linfield demanded. He'd arrived in his banyan from the far reaches of the house.

Around them, the servants were gathering. Mrs Honeyfield was barking orders. Lord Linfield's valet and a man in rough homespun she supposed to be Gordy the groundsman, began organising a line, while George, in a moment of intelligence, tore a large tapestry from the wall and manhandled it though the doorway. A buxom maid followed, armed with a carpet beater, while Edith curled into a corner, her soot-stained cheeks crossed with tear-tracks.

"Your wife is fine. She lives," Bell replied, having checked both pulse and breathing.

Poor Jane was far from fine. "You gave her too much," Eliza barked at Bell. "And weren't you supposed to be attending her?"

"She was still sleeping, I planned to return later, and nor did I give her too much. I gave her exactly the required dose. If you'll recall, Miss Wakefield, she was distraught."

"And now she is in so deep a stupor as to be insensible to her surroundings, even as they burn down around her."

"As if an inferno could have been predicted. She had a body with her. Where is the maid?" He spotted her. "Careless girl, you've nearly cost your mistress her life."

Eliza barged her way between Bell and the maid. "Oh, don't you point a finger at her. You have no notion of how the fire started."

"It weren't me. It weren't." Edith cried. Eliza pulled her to her, and the maid dissolved into gulping sobs against her breast. "Ah don't know what 'appened, Miss. I swear it. Only, that I came back reet fast like Mrs Honeyfield said I should, an' the mistress was still sleeping so peaceful-like... And then, I dunno. It were fine, and then the curtain were all ablaze, an' I couldn't get her to stir, and she's too heavy fer me t' move on me own."

"Stupid girl, you probably set the curtains alight with your carelessness," Linfield barked. He was peering down his nose at his comatose wife, still laid out on the floor. "Have her moved." He tipped a nod towards Jane.

"I'll deal with the maid, my lord," Mrs Honeyfield stepped in, but Edith clung to Eliza.

"I had no candle, Miss. I swear it, and the coals were burned down to embers. It doesn't make sense."

"Next I suppose you'll expect me to believe it the work of the spectre," Linfield said, already edging away from the source of the mayhem. He tsked as specks of ash landed on his shoulder and flicked them away. "Bell, to where should they remove my wife?"

George and Jem emerged from Jane's chamber at that moment. "It's out," the latter declared, "But the bed's blackened to ruins."

"My room is right here," Eliza gave a nod towards her door. "Unless you think she needs to be further away from the—"

"This will be fine," Bell spoke over her. "Only get those windows open and some air in, and have some cloths set to the bottoms of the adjoining doors."

The servants set to it at once. While they did so, Eliza took a peep into Jane's chamber. The windows had been cast wide, but ashes still swirled in the air, and the scent of burned fibres caused her to quickly cover her mouth and nose. Jem entered behind her. He rested a hand on her shoulder. Eliza longed to turn into him but contented herself with the brush of his fingertip against her neck.

"A candle flame wouldn't cause such an inferno, nor a stray spark. It might burn a hole, but it would not ignite the drapes in so short a time."

"They'll blame the girl."

Eliza scowled. "You don't think her responsible, do you, Jem?"

"I'm not sure what to think. But come from here, let us speak elsewhere. All this ash, it gets in your throat." She nodded her assent and followed him back into the corridor. "I'm sure Bell didn't intend her any harm," he said.

Eliza didn't feel quite so forgiving, and so she pursed her lips. "I should go and sit with her. Ensure no other disasters befall her."

"You fear someone means her ill."

"What other conclusion is there?" She could see it in his eyes that he'd thought the same thing. "Someone set out to scare her last night, and now this. Before, I wondered if it was merely a prank, now, I don't know."

"It does seem rather malicious."

"I'm afraid for her, Jem. I fear someone in this house means her harm."

-10-

Jem

Jem was in entirely too much agreement with Eliza's assessment, though he couldn't fathom for the life of him what anyone could have against Lady Linfield. She was a pleasant, amenable sort, rather too timid for his tastes, but certainly not the sort of woman one imagined having vindictive enough enemies that they'd attempt to burn one alive, or, for that matter, any enemies at all. In fact, the only person who'd displayed any sort of antagonism towards her was her husband.

To reassure himself Linfield hadn't fallen onto the notion of disposing of his wife, Jem sought him out with the intention of asking plainly. He found Linfield in the library reading one of last week's newspapers. He had the broadsheet spread across his desk, examining the print through a magnifying glass.

"Anything of interest afoot in the world?"

"Nothing that's worth wasting my sight over." With a great show of sullenness, he cast down the eyeglass.

Jem picked it up, though he could see the print perfectly well without it.

"There is some article about someone called Hatchett you'll probably wish to drool over. Member of the Royal Society. Says he's discovered 'new earth', not that one imagines it has any practical application."

Jem took a position side by side with Linfield to read the article for himself. There was little reported beyond what Linfield had already told him, besides the discovery having been found during an analysis of a specimen from the collection at the British Museum.

"Where is everyone?" He imagined he would find them all ruminating over the strange fire and Lady Linfield's health.

"Isn't that a jolly good question?" Linfield griped. "Bell, I believe, is at his cadavers. You are here. My wife is no doubt still comatose, though I can't in all honesty say that is a great shame, and as for the Cluetts..." He did not finish that remark, but took to pacing, which seemed an interesting development, as normally George and Linfield were as thick as thieves. Still, there were more pressing matters to address than whatever tiff the two happened to have had.

"It strikes me, that perhaps you ought to display a little more concern for Lady Linfield's well-being," Jem said, instantly earning himself a scowl. "That is, unless you wish everyone to think you're behind the unfortunate bed incident."

Linfield came to an abrupt halt, swirling to face Jem head on. "What the mithering devil are you talking about? An absentminded maid with a stray candle flame was behind that drama. There's no mystery. Ill intent—*pfft*!" He snapped his fingers at the very notion.

"She swears—"

"Of course she does. What servant would ever confess to such ineptitude? Nearly burning her mistress to death, I should think she'd deny it even if we'd caught her holding the damn flame."

While Linfield's argument was surprisingly logical, Jem couldn't quite bring himself to accept it as a true accounting of the matter. That fire had burned too fierce and fast to be anything but deliberate, and the maid had nothing to gain from hurting her mistress, unlike Linfield, who would be only too delighted to mourn the loss of his wife.

"I shall check on my lady's welfare again in a little while," Linfield announced. He forced a smile. "There, will that appease you? I shall take her flowers and candied almonds and play the dutiful husband. I will even listen attentively to whatever raving nonsense she wishes to impart about the phantasms that haunt this old place."

"She saw something yestereve."

"Aye, likely her own shadow. I understand it is quite the fashion, but I confess I have no patience for the timidity and sensitive natures of young ladies. They are so squeamish and ridiculous."

"That is rather a generalisation, my lord."

"Is it? Is it? Name one woman who is not prone

to such fits of blancmange."

"Eliza." Her name burst from his mouth before he had time to think over the wisdom of it.

"Eliza?" Linfield's brows instantly relocated to halfway up his forehead.

"Miss Wakefield." Jem coughed.

"Yes, I'm aware of to whom you refer. What concerns me is how intimate the two of you appear to be." He silenced Jem before he could make any sort of explanation. "Please, I need no further reminders of your previous meeting. What alarms me is that after such a short acquaintance you are on such close terms. Particularly when one suspects that closeness leans to a deeper sort of intimacy than that which you currently afford me. Me." He sidled closer, raising a hand to cradle the side of Jem's face. "The man you loved with considerable fervour until a few weeks ago."

"Loved?" It was unwise, but he couldn't help the expulsion. "It was only ever a physical arrangement. Let us not pretend otherwise."

"You wound me," Linfield theatrically clasped a hand to his chest.

Jem rolled his eyes. "Linfield, please. We have already been over this. You are a married man, and no longer free to—"

"Bugger my fellow man? Jem, dear, has it really escaped your attention that that was never legal?"

"I am fully—"

"Hence a marriage oath hardly seems to matter, particularly as we both know this marriage was forced on me."

"That is wholly irrelevant."

"I need your aid more than ever, Jamie. However, it is plain to see why you're so reluctant to give it. 'Tis more than pretty words you've exchanged with Miss Wakefield, is it not? Or do you expect me to believe the bruise I spy beneath your collar the result of a kiss from one of Bell's leeches?"

He stupidly gave himself away by raising a hand to touch the spot where Eliza had earlier concentrated such attention. Linfield burned him with his gaze.

"Good God, man, look at the state of you. Perhaps it has escaped your notice that there are char marks on your cuffs, not to mention a hole burned through the shoulder of your coat." Such damage had in fact escaped Jem's notice, but he was more flummoxed by Linfield's pointing it out at this juncture when he'd expected an artillery charge over his connection with Eliza.

Linfield stuck his finger through the hole he'd just pointed out. "You're a shambolic disgrace, Mr Whistler. I simply cannot have you in my presence in such a state. You had best shed this ignominious garment immediately."

When Jem didn't leap into action, Linfield added an expectant, "Well?"

Jem gaped at him.

"Off. Off. Take it off." He near wrenched the coat from Jem's back. "In fact, the waistcoat too, and the shirt. The whole lot needs to be removed. Your whole wardrobe reeks of smoke and ashes. I will not have you in my presence stinking like a bonfire." Jem stood bewildered, hands upon his buttons, as Linfield rung for a servant. The more buxom of the two maids appeared, and so quickly that she must have been right outside with her ear to the door.

"Me lord?" She dropped into an idle and very insincere sort of curtsy.

Linfield didn't seem to notice.

"Have a bath drawn for Mr Whistler at once."

"Ah bath! T' be taken t' 'is room!"

Jem swore she was calculating exactly how many trips from the kitchen to his chamber up three flights of stairs that would take, and the vexatious puckering of her features told him she didn't care for the tally.

Linfield tapped his index finger to his lips, oblivious to her lack of obsequiousness. "Heavens, no. There isn't space. Before the fireplace in mine, that's the thing. You'll be more than comfortable there."

"A hip bath in mine would be—"

"Nonsense," Linfield countermanded his attempt to spare the girl's back. "See to it immediately, girl."

"Right away, me lord." She stomped away heavy on her feet and muttering things about her employer that Jem was certain were distinctly rude.

"What the devil are you about?" Jem muttered as soon as the recalcitrant maid was out of earshot. He did not expect or require an answer; Linfield's intent was all too obvious.

He leaned in and pressed a kiss to a spot just below Jem's earlobe.

"Cleanliness is next to godliness." Linfield smiled sweetly. "And you smell dreadful. Not to mention you also seem to have smudges of soot in all sorts of strange places." He made a point of tracing a few of them. "Shall we go up now?"

One hand on Jem's back, Linfield endeavoured to steer him towards the door. "Come now, you're not going to protest taking a bath like some schoolboy scapegrace?"

"You need hardly escort me."

"Oh, I think I must," Linfield insisted. "If you will not satisfy me, Jem Whistler, then you can at least indulge me in this. We will go to my room, you will bathe, and I... I will watch. It will be desperately chaste and altogether civilised. Well, perhaps not entirely chaste... or civilised, but it will be within the bounds of your preposterous terms. Though do not think for a moment that I've forgotten our proposed rendezvous in the third-floor corridor just because it's had to be delayed."

Truly, Jem could not think of a man more self-absorbed.

"Your wife is comatose in bed having almost been consumed by fire. How can you even...? You might at least feign some regard for her welfare."

"Do be a darling, and quit with your admonishments. Truly, Jem, do you wish me to fake affection where there is none? It's a blessed relief not to have to spend my every waking thought wondering how I shall ever get through the ordeal of fulfilling the marriage contract. Of course, I am glad my wife emerged unscathed from this morning's dramatics, but I feel no more affection for her than before. How many times must I state it for you? I find in her nothing that beguiles, charms, or excites my person, nor am I likely to grow into such feelings. Don't mistake me, she is hardly unique amongst her sex in that regard. The feminine form has never been one that captivated my attentions. Some fellows like all that flummery, the softness, the abundance." He made a crude visualisation of breasts to illustrate his point. "Others, however, like you, like myself, are entranced by other qualities. The sort of qualities that only another fellow possesses."

They were not quite so alike as Linfield supposed. "Linfield," he enunciated with deliberate care. "The maid did not start that fire. I am telling you this as a man of science, a man of logic. Someone attacked Lady Linfield deliberately, and the way you are behaving right now rather points at it being you."

Linfield smacked him hard across the face. "How dare you?"

Jem lifted a hand to his stinging cheek. "What other conclusion would you have me reach. You are at pains to point out how little she pleases you, and how crippled you are by her existence. Why wouldn't I think—"

Linfield grabbed Jem's arm and twisted it painfully into the small of his back. "Watch your tongue, tutor, else you might give me even greater cause to loosen mine. I can ruin your Miss Wakefield with a mere suggestion of impropriety with a fellow guest. Cluett may be a merciless tin-kettle, but his mother has a multitude of talents, one of which is as society's premier tell-tale-tit."

-11-

Jem

Jem stood by the linen draped tub, stripped of everything but his breeches and the vaguest smidgen of his dignity. That was about to be snatched away. Linfield was livid, or at least playacting the part. He'd dragged Jem up to his chamber before howling at the servants to get out. The last oversized pitcher of hot water still stood three quarter's full beside him to his right.

"Get in," Linfield barked. Lazy coils of steam rose off the water. It struck Jem that it was six and two threes whether Linfield intended to drown him or coerce him into a coupling. Mayhap he was contemplating both. Either way, he had little choice other than to obey. Threats to himself, he could stomach. Even a long march to the nearest village through the fog might be endured, but he would not have Eliza suffer for his actions.

"I said get in."

There were two ways he could approach this; with a sullen, mechanical stiffness that made plain his indignation, or as if it were simply an ordinary bath, the purpose of which was only to rid himself of the stink of wood smoke and ashes. The former was more likely to spark the spontaneous ignition of the air between them, whereas the latter would require a masterful piece of acting.

"You'll bathe, damn you, James."

James! He was only ever that when he was in trouble, or Linfield meant to compel him in some way.

Capitulating with a sigh, Jem dropped his breeches, then himself into the steel tub. Maybe he was over trusting, but he submerged himself entirely and let the water cocoon him. Sadly, it didn't whisper any insights into his lugholes. When he propelled himself into a seated position again, he found Linfield had taken a perch on the foot of the bed between the curtain swags.

Jem set to with the soap.

Linfield opened his mouth one or two times, without getting as far as speech, but eventually spat out, "I'm not trying to murder my wife. I'm doing my best to fulfil a duty I never asked for and have had thrust upon me. I can't believe you think me that villainous. Nor am I trying to have her declared mad, though considering all her prattling about spectres, one might reasonably assume her to be."

For a wonder, the man managed to sound genuine, if a touch irascible. The earl's plans for his son's future were certainly not being borne with ease, and grace had never got a look in. Linfield was far too used to being the centre of his own world, with those around him all dancing to his tune. It was hardly surprising that being compelled was making him volatile.

"I know she's not what you wanted," he replied, attempting a temperate tone. "And I appreciate how difficult things are."

Linfield considered this with his head tilted almost to his shoulder, and his lips tightly pursed. "There wouldn't be any point in doing away with her, anyway. Papa would only procure another chit. He's positively set on me procreating. 'Can't have the line diverted off to some lesser branch,'" he mimicked. "I mean God forbid that one of my cousins had to inherit."

"Perhaps it won't be so bad on a second attempt," Jem suggested, not believing it for a second. "If you snuff the candles—"

"What? I'll somehow forget it's my wife I'm about to tup? Not likely, not even in the most Stygian of gloom." He made a piteous sound, as though he were facing denizens of the underworld and not the pleasures of a woman's cunt. "There weren't any candles lit the last time." His head hit his hands and bowed forward over his knees. "God in heaven, do you think I'd have subjected myself to Bell's leeches if the matter could be accomplished merely by extinguishing the light? Jem, my prick shrivels at the very thought of exploring her arbour. My cobs retreat so far into my innards they're in danger of becoming lost there. I've thought about this. Turned over every damn possibility. There's only one means of achieving my burden I have any faith in—"

"There are options." Damned if they were going to arc straight back to the matter of him performing. "Davy's gas, and you made mention of a whore who might assist. One capable of getting a rise out of the stubbornest of pricks."

The idea was waved away at once, and Linfield languished between the swags, pouty and indolent. "It was a thought born of desperation, nothing more. It won't work. There's never been a whore yet who could get a rise out of me. Leastways, none of a feminine persuasion. The truth is my prick prefers a different sort of touch. A fellow's touch. I think we can agree, Jamie, can we not, that I spend best when my porthole is plundered and stretched wide by a thick cremorne? And it's likely the only way in which I'll ever manage to impregnate my wife."

"Linfield, for the hundredth time, I'm not fucking you in a corridor." The soap shot free of his grasp and plopped into the water, necessitating him going on a hunt for it. What was surprising was that Linfield didn't immediately dive in with a rebuke, or a counterargument. When Jem finally got a grip on the soap again, and having deposited it over the side, he found Lindfield's dandelion clock of fine hair bobbing in agreement. "Wait, what? I feel I've missed something. You don't want me to do that anymore?"

"Having had time to mull it over, no."

Thank you, Lord!

"You'd need to join us in the marriage bed."

Jem plunged himself deep into the now murky water. Just for a moment there, a fraction of an iota of a second, he'd thought Linfield had seen sense. Fool him for thinking that Lord Nickninny would ever propose something that wasn't wild, stupid, or deranged.

He came up again once his air ran out, and still exasperated, scrubbed the water off his face. "You're suggesting I prick you while you prick your wife?"

"Yes. I thought it was rather—"

"Have you taken complete leave of your senses?"

"—elegant."

"I'm never agreeing to that. It's a nonsensical idea. More stupid than doing it in the corridor, and letting Bell's pets feast on your cock, and everything else that's been suggested or tried all put together." Although really, he oughtn't be surprised. When had Linfield ever said anything rational or sensible? Jem struggled to think of an occasion in the entirety of their acquaintance.

"You maintain all my ideas are nonsense, but nearly all of them you've gone along with, anyway. Why should this time be any different? Especially when this time, it matters. Really matters. It's the only hope I have of siring the necessary tailfruit to soothe my sire's grumbling."

Jem opened his mouth but found he was profoundly lacking in coherent arguments. "You don't think she might—"

"Object?" With the turn of a narrow wrist, his employer swept aside the notion as if it were a trifling thing, not a matter of considerable importance. "James, she's a lady. She's uninformed. I shall simply explain that a fellow's goujat is sometimes involved in such matters. It's not as if you're going to be touching her, and there's no deception about the matter, so you can't object on those grounds. It won't be like the corridor thing at all. This will be all entirely in the open."

Evidently his objections were irrelevant, too. "I'm not doing it. You're insane."

"I'm perfectly reasoning, and you're only being objectionable about it because your head's been turned in another direction, and I might add, Jamie, that I find that extremely irritating. You're here for me, not to consort with—"

"Don't," Jem barked, cutting him off before he said something unforgivable. The outburst earned him a ridiculous pout, the sort that would put a lady of the ton to shame.

"Well, if you weren't being so tiresome about the matter, we wouldn't need to have these little ripostes."

"Better tiresome than a fool. While I agree that Lady Linfield is likely ill-informed of the marriage acts, I question her total ignorance of the matter." She was Eliza's dear friend, after all. "I'm not climbing into the bed of a woman who hasn't explicitly invited me there."

"Oh, is that the issue?"

"Linfield, no!"

"She's my wife, Jem. I married her. She'll do as bid, like the meek and obliging creature she's been brought up to be. If it's my decree that another fellow is a necessity in our bed, then that's the beginning and end of the matter. Be thankful I'm not asking you to do the job for me." The grin that stretched wide his lips said he'd certainly entertained the notion. "You're far too swarthy." The Bellingbrook stock were all wan to the point of anaemia, with heads full of silky near-white hair, and spindly limbs; any deviation from that norm would rouse suspicions and set tongues wagging.

"You're damned right I'm not. Just what sort of gentleman do you think me?"

A great spurt of water hit him in the face, courtesy of Linfield clapping a hand across the surface. His eyebrows were raised. "James Whistler, I know exactly what manner of man you are. One with similar tastes and weaknesses to myself. That is why we're friends." Linfield leaned forward, propping his elbows on the rim of the bath and soaking his coat cuffs. "You'll help me bed my wife, Jem. You'll plunge your ramrod so deep in my arse there'll be no question of me spilling and the act bearing fruit. You'll do it because if you do not, there will be consequences."

He refused to play into Linfield's hand by asking what form those consequences might take; he could imagine well enough. Linfield could break him.

"The answer's still no."

Linfield's nasal huff, followed by a smile full of teeth, made the hairs all over Jem's body rise. He watched in alarm as Linfield sauntered across the room and gave the bell pull a sharp tug.

"What are you about?"

"Ringing for my valet."

"Why? Do you mean to eject me from the house

naked?" In anticipation, Jem began propelling himself upright.

"Sit down!"

The snap of Linfield's voice, so unlike his usual nasal whine, had the desired effect. Jem fell back onto his arse with a splash that sent water sloshing over the sides.

"Much as that might amuse me, no, I'm not about to eject you. That would hardly achieve my objective, would it? I need you. However, it has come to my attention that one of my guests is not quite the person they appear, but is in fact a harlot given to unbridled salaciousness. She is thus quite unsuitable as a companion for my wife, and I will be sure to make that known."

"Goddamn you. Eliza has nothing to do with this. Will you leave her out of this matter!"

"Oh, Jamie. Numbers may evade me, likewise Latin verbs, but I assure you that both of my oars are in the water. She has *everything* to do with this. Your entire demeanour has changed since her arrival. You're wholly diverted, you deny me, and that is most unacceptable. Moreover, am I wrong in thinking that it's her opinion you're afeared of, and which is preventing you from being your usual agreeable self?"

"What you're asking of me—I think it's monstrous. I expect Eliza would too, but that is hardly the point. I expect every person in this house would think the same if the matter were put to them."

Linfield sashayed back towards him, waving a

hand from side to side as if he were felling beasts to clear a path. "No, no, you must explain this to me. What exactly is so monstrous? The act of fucking me? Could it be that to which you refer? But surely not, for you have done that more than three dozen times over with no objections. Maybe it is the notion of me siring a child you find objectionable."

The notion of a junior Linfield was certainly no great delight.

"But I do not think it is that. One must therefore conclude that it is my lady wife you object to. Yet, how can that be so, when you and Bell have regaled me at length with her virtues."

"Linfield, you can't truly expect me to fuck you while she watches...while in her presence." He amended, pre-empting an offer to bind the lady's eyes.

"Why the hell not? Why should it matter where my prick is bedded at the time? If I had proposed such a passion not so long ago—not now, because since the arrive of Miss Wakefield you have become entirely irascible, but a short time ago—you would have had no objection to fucking me while I fucked another. None whatsoever."

"That's not—" He intended to say true, but it was. He would have done it, and he'd have enjoyed it. His damned traitorous prick was excited by the notion even now. And that was a problem, given that Linfield had a bird's eye view of it in all its naked glory.

Indeed, Linfield gave a mirthful snort. "See, you're not so terribly appalled by the notion."

Apparently, he could be appalled and aroused simultaneously.

Gentle fingers brushed through the hair on the back of his head, then seized his chin, turning him so that he was peering up at Linfield standing next to the tub. "Jamie... Jamie," he sing-songed, while his thumb swept back and forth across Jem's lips. "Do it, and I'll have cause to be extremely grateful. You won't only have my backing; words can be dropped in other ears. One does know a number of very flush and powerful men."

A lump clogged his throat that he tried to swallow out of existence. Linfield certainly knew how to bait a trap. If he ever managed to apply himself to something other than racing and roistering, his mind might sharpen into a tool worthy of the position he'd someday inherit. It was only a shame that he was applying himself in Jem's direction. Shit! He could see no way out of this bind that wouldn't compromise Eliza's reputation, which left him with no alternative but to forfeit her affections.

It was bad enough that she'd learn of his fascination for his fellowman, but to do so with her dearest's friend's husband while he attempted to plant his seed, she'd be appalled at him, would lose every ounce of respect for him. Nor could he blame her for it. Damn and blast, but he may as well write to Joshua Rushdale this very minute and congratulate him on his victory, for he would surely win Eliza's heart with only a fraction of effort. Joshua...glorious, dependable, solid, Joshua, with his clever hands and silver wings in his hair, was everything he wasn't and would never be. A magistrate, the brother-in-law of a marquis, flush with funds, and most importantly, not a sodomite or a prospective third wheel in a marriage bed.

"Linfield, please!" He stretched out an arm to the viscount, whose gaze slid over him hot and eager. "If you eject her, I'll leave, too."

"If you leave these walls against my wishes, I will take great relish in telling Henrietta both yours and Miss Wakefield's histories and I will be especially distraught about it."

"So, you're going to blackmail me into this?"

"If it's good enough for my father, then it's good enough for his son. Mayhap you should think more carefully about who you fornicate with while under my roof going forth."

Lord have mercy on him. "Linfield, it's not like that. I've never... We haven't—"

"You may claim it, but the evidence rather says otherwise."

Jem flinched as Linfield brushed a thumb over the mark on his neck. "Although, I suppose I could be persuaded that you were in fact assaulted by one of Bell's pets. The bruise is rather like those currently mottling my cock. Let me show you, that we might compare."

"Linfield, I don't want to—"

Too late. His falls were already undone, his semi-erect cock flapping about in Jem's face. Mottled was an accurate description. The normally pale skin was broken up by circles of blue-black bruising.

"Similar, don't you agree?"

Jem lowered his gaze, his capitulation already a given. "Similar, yes."

"Let me kiss it better for you. How awful for you to have been so assaulted. Bell must be made to keep a close guard on his pets." Dry lips pressed to the mark Eliza had left on Jem's neck. Then Linfield's prick was brought back onto a level with Jem's head. "Do the same for me, eh, my love?"

"Your valet's about to arrive."

"Aye, and if my knob's not being well petted by that point, Miss Wakefield will be the biggest social pariah of the decade."

There was nothing Jem could do but open his mouth.

~Ж~

Being forced to fellate a man with more funds than sense ought to have made Jem bloody irate, and it did, but it also turned out that his cock rather liked him being coerced. He could tell himself all he liked that it was the fact he was sparing Eliza future ignominy that made the act palatable, but a maggot in his core said otherwise.

"Jamie, Jamie, the man with a saint's name and the same willingness to serve his lord." Linfield pulled him in close so that Jem's nose butted up against his silken mat. It sent a shot of arousal right down through his pleasure centres. "Take up your cudgel, Jem. Let me see you soap it while you swallow."

They were past the point of resistance. He did as instructed, minus the soap, so that he was soon groaning around the wedge in his throat and drooling saliva over his chin.

"You're so good at that, Jamie. So, good." Linfield stroked one hand along the line of his jaw, the other remained fast upon the back of Jem's head. "Take it like a good boy, that's it. That's the man I know. The one who lives for something other than maths and verb forms. You realise you'll never be able to do this for her."

He didn't want to think of Eliza right now.

It was too late, of course. There was no way of untangling his passion for her from his relationship with Linfield. His lordship's ramblings were making sure of it. He did not seem to grasp that there were great gaping holes in his logic.

"What will you do when you're desperate for a prick in your arse, eh? Tell me that, Jem. You're never going to stop wanting it."

What would he do?

His mind provided a bright clear vision of Eliza naked on her hands and knees behind him, her tongue tip tickling his arse without an ounce of shame.

He did not share his vision with Linfield, but greedily kept it all for himself just as he'd stowed several other precious memories. Eliza as she had been last summer, in her sprigged summer muslin, brimming with life and knowledge, the most enchanting being he'd ever encountered. So, alive.

So, engaged. Her thoughts outpacing his. The day was bright and fragrant. They were in Lord Marlinscar's garden. And his guests' voices formed a constant murmur on the breeze. They hadn't deliberately meandered away from the party. There was nothing salacious about it. They'd simply been so deep in conversation that their environs had lost all meaning.

She'd been telling him of her home, of the people who depended on her, the babies due to arrive, and all the things she would do if she owned an estate as large as Lauwine. He'd spoken of Stags Fell and growing up there, which had inevitably lead them to the topic of high-pressure engines, the possibilities that would open from the development of steam locomotion, and all the other riddles of the world that mathematics could be used to solve.

It was entirely accidental that they'd ended up in the middle of the hedge maze. Having reached that dead end, she'd turned and faced him. The breeze had tugged a few curls of her hair loose, so that they framed her face, and her eyes were full of delight over his scientific explanations. Every other woman he'd ever conversed with on such topics, except for his cousin Bertie, had only had yawns for him. He hadn't planned to do it, it just happened. He'd reached out a hand, cupped the side of her face, and she'd leaned into him, lips parted. The warmth of her breath touched him first, sent a rush of heat through his body, that only increased when true contact was made.

She was perfect and giving, and her presence

filled the whole of his mind. He wanted to crush her closer, peel away the layers of their clothing and throw off the civility along with each item until all that was left was the raw, unfiltered versions of themselves.

Her mouth was a revelation. Her scent enthralled him. His heart was racing.

"Jem." Her hand pressed against his sternum, creating a degree of space between them. There was a small V of concern between her brows.

"I'm so sorry, I didn't—"

"It's not that."

She flicked a glance over his shoulder, which he followed, to find Joshua Rushdale standing in the entrance of the maze's central folly.

Joshua had spoken to him of Eliza. He was every bit as enamoured of her as Jem. They hadn't sworn a truce, but he still winced at the hurt he saw reflected in his friend's eyes.

"My apologies, I didn't realise." Joshua bowed his head then the interior darkness of the building swallowed him up.

"Shit!" Jem had hissed and followed it with an apology. "I should speak to him."

Eliza again stayed him with the press of her hand. "Actually, I think I should speak to him."

The world felt cold without the warmth of her body fitted against him. He'd worn a groove into the flagstones, then followed her within. Whatever speech had happened between them had obviously been uneasy. He arrived at the tail end of a sentence.

"—assumed, when I should not have done so.

You'd given me no reason to think—."

"I don't wish you to think things are other than they are. Jem is—"

"Magnificent. It's not difficult to see why you'd lean towards him. I haven't his intellect."

"That's not true. You're learned in different ways. Joshua, I don't want you to think that I've made any sort of choice. I didn't even comprehend until this moment that there was a choice before me."

Jem came closer. If this conversation was to be had, then it was one that ought to include all three of them. Heartfelt words followed. Words and pleas, and heartache visible in all their faces. It was inevitable that one, if not all of them, were going to be hurt by the threads of desire that now linked them all.

He knew a solution but couldn't bring himself to propose it.

"Gentlemen, I'm away home tomorrow. I do not wish to make this parting sad. You have both brightened my world these last weeks. Neither of you can ask me to hurt the other. I won't. I don't want that. Shall we agree to remain all friends together?"

What else could they do but agree?

Even now, he couldn't find it in him to hate Joshua. He liked him too much. He'd spent days in the Stags Fell workshop with him, inhaling his scent, watching him rub the tension from his brow whenever his sister caused him a headache. People misunderstood him. They mistook kindness for weakness, and enduring love for his sibling as an endorsement of her behaviour. But all you had to do was look a little deeper, and the truth was obvious. Joshua craved novelty and companionship every bit as much as his sister did, only in Joshua's case, he was afraid to let go of his security to secure it.

So, Jem kept his thoughts to himself, and didn't say anything about triangles. Only in his imaginings did the afternoon end with the three of them entwined, loving one another as if three people doing so was the most natural arrangement on God's earth. Both of them kissing her, together and apart, exploring her body in a similar way. Tupping her together. Fucking her in a wide assortment of arrangements. And fucking each other too, while she watched and encouraged them.

He was a fool even to dream it.

Still, the fantasy of it was enough to bring him off. He spent, sending opalescent streamers across the surface of the water.

Linfield pulled free of his mouth, and for a moment, Jem thought he meant to splatter his face, but he barked a command instead.

"Get out and lean over the bottom of the bed."

Jem blinked. It'd been some time since Jem had last had his furrow ploughed. Usually, Linfield liked nothing better than to lie prostrate and utterly indolent and let someone else do all the work. Perhaps that was another contributing factor in his inability to tup his wife. It required actual physical exertion.

"What?" Linfield demanded. "I'm ramrod hard, and I need the practice."

Rivulets chased down his body as Jem complied. There was no towel with which to dry off, and indeed, Linfield hadn't the patience to wait for such a thing had one been available. He was behind Jem the moment his knees hit the edge of the bed and had a couple of fingers pushed inside him in a trice. It was uncomfortable, even with a slather of oil, but titillating in the same way having Linfield's cock pushed into his mouth earlier had been.

Jem took refuge in his memories again. Stags Fell remained his favourite place in all the world. The scent of oil and grease combined with an underlying metallic tang, and instead of jacquard beneath his body he imagined the pits and grooves of the workbench. His various cousins were around him. Pip at his chemistry set, Sheridan composing by the fireside, Bertie tailored to within an inch of her life in attire a dandy would aspire to look half so handsome in. In another blink, they were gone, and his sole companion was Joshua.

The stub of a pencil sat tucked behind his ear, while delight crinkled the corners of his eyes. He'd just solved a page of rambling equations and arrived at the same answer as Jem. They were positioned either side of the bench, their brows almost touching. His nostrils were full of the other man's scent, and he couldn't stop himself from peeping inside the open collar of Joshua's shirt. They'd both stripped off coats and cravats earlier when they'd been meddling with piston parts. There was still grease on the tip of Joshua's index finger and all Jem could think of was how desperately he wanted the other man to put that greased digit inside his bum.

Well, he wanted more than a finger, but he also knew that Joshua would never speak to him again if he suggested it.

"Damn, you're tight. You're squeezing me." Linfield licked the beads of water from the space between his shoulder blades. "Do some of the work, damn you. Push back. I've barely half my cock in you."

"If you want to get balls deep, you might consider foreplay."

"Dammit, I've already made you go off."

Linfield had had next to nothing to do with it.

He shoved instead. Jem felt the sting through to his nose. But he took it. He breathed through it, knowing it would be over soon, and that Eliza would be safe, while also accepting that while his mind rebelled at his current situation, his body sure as hell liked it.

"You love it. Admit it, Jamie, you live for these moments. There's no way you could live without them. You like taking it, and you like giving it." Linfield groaned indulgently and started massaging circles into Jem's flanks. "Oh, fuck, you're a nice ride. This can't end, Jamie. It can't end. It's too good between us. This is too good."

Jem tactfully kept the fact that he was thinking of another man to himself.

"She can't have you. I won't allow it. You're mine. Fuck, it's coming..."

Those last words squeezed free of Linfield's mouth as his load released. Jem rolled over once

Linfield was done.

"Bring yourself off again."

He might be erect, but he had no desire to perform. "I'll be more eager for what you want me for later if you deny me the chance to finish now."

The notion seemed to confound Linfield, causing him to scratch his head and then his balls. "You've changed your tune. Figured you'd be doing anything at all to delay proceedings. Shall we say after dinner tonight, then?"

He was an idiot. "You said you would exhaust other options first."

"What other options? We both know my cock's not going to stand for her without assistance. Your assistance. I'm not interested in potions and leeches and whores—"

"There's Davy's gas."

"And do you have this gas?"

"I can make it."

Linfield chewed over the prospect while he righted his clothes. "Fine, I'll partake of your gas, but I don't anticipate—how was it you described it? That it'll put me in a theatrical mood."

Honestly, Jem didn't know that it would work either, but he had to try. He would try near anything at this point. The chamber door opened, and Linfield's harried valet scurried in.

"Good, you're here. This bathtub needs emptying."

"Of course, my lord. Right away. Mrs Cluett asks if she might have a moment of your time? She's in your study, my lord."

"What the devil's she in there for?" He eyed Jem suspiciously, like he might have something to do with it. "Stop loafing around the place, James, and put some clothes on. Don't you have an element to extract?"

"I'll fetch you some clean things," Linfield's man remarked.

The door banged behind both servant and master as they exited.

Jem slumped against the bedspread and pulled a pillow over his face. "It's not an element, you dolt. It's a compound."

-12-

Eliza

Jane continued her drugged sleep, stirring occasionally to murmur softly and turn over, or to cough ash from her lungs. Eliza had washed the soot from her face and clothed her in a clean shift and neither had woken her. Given Jane's vulnerability, Eliza was determined to stay by her side.

Eliza perched on the bed to begin with watching Jane sleep in frustration. Then, as the afternoon drew on, and a fine misty drizzle steamed up the windowpanes, she took to pacing the uneven floorboards while her mind conjured endless cycles of knotty thoughts. There did not seem to be one single thread that she could pull on to begin unravelling the mysteries here at Cedarton. Questions merely led to other questions, rather than answers. What was certain to her was that foul play was at work. Eliza no more believed Edith responsible for the blaze that had almost consumed her mistress than she believed Jane had seen an actual apparition the night before, or that Linfield had any regard at all for his wife.

A loving man, even an undemonstrative one, would have shown some regard for the fate of his wife. Linfield had been dismissive, almost irritated by her misfortune. Heavens, could he not see that someone among them meant Jane harm?

Or perhaps the issue was that that someone was him, the man that Jane had, in good faith, wed. She could only pray that time proved otherwise. For dear Jane, this was the sorriest of sorry situations to be trapped in.

There was no joy to be found in this accursed place, other than the sort to be found at another's expense. At least, not for Jane. She could not deny there were bright sparks for herself. Jem was here, and Jane's misfortune could not eradicate the pleasure that awoke deep in her chest every time her thoughts strayed in Jem's direction. She fluttered her fingers against her throat, recalling the sensation of his lips there, and then her brazenness at taking him in her mouth. It made her giddy in a senseless way... an undignified way, yet she wouldn't exchange that singing sensation under her skin for... Well, a lot of things.

It was not pleasant to think her joy had come at Jane's expense. If she had stayed by her side, then Jane might not have brushed against death in such a horrifying way.

Her gaze strayed again to the pale form occupying the bed. *Why in heaven's name did you marry him?* He was exactly the sort of aristocratic bully they had decried at their meetings of the Women's Natural Philosophical Fellowship. Cruel. Selfish. It wasn't even as if love had blinded Jane to his qualities; she was no love-struck goose. Something had to have persuaded her, some so far undemonstrated quality, or an outside pressure. Why else would she marry a man she had no regard for and who seemed unlikely to ever grant her a smile let alone a boon or affection?

As dusk arrived, and the drizzle continued, Eliza pulled a chair over to the hearth. Mrs Honeyfield had been and gone twice, providing her first with a pot of tea and seed cake to nibble on, then later with a fine chicken broth for Jane. As Jane slept on, Eliza had partaken of the broth as it seemed certain it would grow cold long before her friend ever stirred. The next caller was Betsy. Would she like her dinner on a tray, or did she mean t' join the gentlemen? Mrs Cluett wasn't going down, having being terribly taken by the shocking events of earlier.

It didn't surprise Eliza in the slightest to hear that Mrs Cluett had taken the opportunity to make Jane's misfortune all about her. Suffering a nervous disposition—pah! That woman was no wispy dumpling, she was forged of steel beneath her pillowy outer, of that Eliza was sure. She'd met her type before. Women who circumstances had honed into survivors. But then, was that not most of them?

She declined the offer of Mrs Honeyfield coming to sit with Jane while she dined. She was not keen to eat with Linfield and his cronies even for the chance to see Jem. Nor had she yet forgiven herself for her earlier absence. No, she would take her meal on a tray, and stoically endure until Jane was whole and hearty once more.

Betsy nodded her head like a sagely old crone at this announcement. "I thinks that's probably for the best, Miss Wakefield. I know it's not for me to say, but I don't rightly know that it's safe or altogether proper for ya to be alone wi' so many rogues. I know he's me master, but the rumours, Miss… They say he's all manner of vices. Mrs Honeyfield won't even let us maids wait on t' gentlemen t'night. We 'ave t' stay in servant's quarters, and let footman and Lord Linfield's man, Clement, attend 'em. If that's not signs of rakery and him being a bad 'un…" She nodded her head. "It's not reet, you and hers haven' t' stay up on this corridor next t' tha great ghastly hole at end. It's like a gapin' sore 'tis. I tell ya, Miss. I was talkin' to me cousin just last week. Wednesday, it were… Yes, Wednesday—that's me afternoon off— an' she said—"

"Betsy," Eliza interrupted, seeing the girl was in no hurry to leave. Her amble around the room, ostensibly to gather bits of crockery had so far taken her to every surface bar the one in need of clearing, and she didn't care for how her fingers had a habit of wandering over things they had no business touching. The maid was a fair few years older and a deal less delicate than Edith, and far too gossipy and proud of herself to win Eliza's admiration. She piled the used crockery onto the tray they'd been delivered on and held it out to her.

"Oh, ta, Miss." Betsy accepted the burden with a

sigh. "As I was sayin', best ya stay up here outta sight, like. Though, I'm sure I can't picture what four upstandin' gentlemen could get up t' that make it necessary to keep us women outta sight."

She cocked her head as if expecting Eliza to enlighten her. Eliza forwent that pleasure. She was sure the girl was fully versed in the dangers inherent in such a situation to both one's person and reputation. Civility, after all, was only ever a veneer pasted over a base form of sin. Every preacher in the land sang that song from the pulpit on a Sunday morn, and a Yorkshire-born village lass like Betsy was no hothouse flower from whom the hard realities of the world had been hidden. She'd likely witnessed all manner of bawdy behaviour afore she'd even walked on her own two feet.

"Is Edith recovered?" Eliza asked as she guided the girl to the door.

"Aye, Miss, tha Mrs Honeyfield gave her a proper scolding. Bet her lugs are still ringin'. I know mine are jus' from hearin' it. Surprised she didn't belt her too. It's only cause we're so short a hands she weren't got rid of reet away."

"Well, I'm glad she still has her employ. She didn't deserve to be dismissed, nor a hiding either." She hadn't deserved any punishment. Poor Edith had suffered aplenty already. "It wasn't her fault."

"Weren't it?" Betsy's attention perked up. "T'was someone's, Miss, an' Edith was the one watching over t' mistress at the time. Ah reckon she dozed off, meself, an' so does Lord Linfield's man. He reckons she probably knock't candle over. I dunno mind. I think it were Old Lady Cedarton's doing meself. I bet the old hag's out for vengeance. Doesn't want Cedarton t' 'ave a pretty new mistress. Dun't want any of us here. You be watchin' yerself for 'er now, Miss. Ya wouldn't want t' be tumbled up in 'er malice."

"Thank you. You may go now, Betsy." She had no time for ghosts, vengeful or otherwise. Whatever haunted Cedarton's corridors was no spirit, rather a would-be murderer of an altogether earthy guise.

The girl bobbed her another curtsy, then balanced the tray on her hip so that she could reach for the doorknob. Eliza held it open for her. She breathed a sigh of relief when the maid was finally gone, only for her to poke her cheeky face around the jamb again not two ticks later.

"Beggin' ya pardon, Miss, but Mr Whistler wonders if—"

Jem.

Jem... she could see him now. Standing behind Betsy in the only slash of light in the gloomy corridor. Candlelight from a wall sconce caught in the fine strands of his hair making the soft browns and golds shimmer. His eyes were soft as she stepped into the beam to greet him.

"Miss Wakefield, I—"

"You may leave, Betsy." She ushered her off.

The girl went, but she gawked at them over her shoulder for the length of the corridor and even had the audacity to linger at the turn, while she rearranged the items on the tray.

Eliza and Jem exchanged huffs of disbelief when

she finally turned the corner.

"I pray my presence at your door hasn't metamorphosed into a tale of an illicit liaison by the time she reaches the kitchens."

"Oh, I imagine we've kissed and agreed the time of our elopement afore she's even reached the back stairs. We'll be halfway to Gretna Green before she enters the kitchen, and one of them will be up to see I haven't abandoned my post and that I still require dinner within a half an hour. Betsy will naturally volunteer."

The pinching of his brows rather suggested Jem didn't relish so much embellished gossip circulating.

"Don't fret so," Eliza soothed. "No one will take her seriously. I'm sure they all know precisely what manner of person she is and tolerate it because nothing speeds away the tediousness of endless chores than a good gossip about one's supposed betters."

"Supposed?"

"Well, I don't consider myself better than anyone else, just fortunate enough to have been graced with some education and not to have been born into a hovel."

"Ah." He found his smile, and Eliza tilted her face up to better appreciate his handsomeness, feeling strangely shy after the circumstances of their last parting. They'd changed things between them, but then they'd been torn asunder in a fashion that hadn't lent itself to reassurances. Eliza reached up to touch his face, but he caught her fingers before they came close to making contact and pulled their hands down into the shadows between them.

"Take care, Miss Wakefield. There are eyes aplenty in these old corridors, not just those of a tattle-tale maid, and few of them kindly." Still, he held her fingers and gave them a reassuring squeeze. "How is Lady Linfield? That's what I came to enquire."

"Settled." She squeezed his fingers back, noting the calluses at their tips, and smoother patches of skin, perhaps wrought from chemical burns. "Still in a very deep sleep, thanks to Doctor Bell's heavy-handedness with his dosing." He could surely have knocked a cart horse out with the amount of opiates he'd administered to Jane.

"I imagine he would tell you that sleep is the ultimate restorative."

"Yes, I imagine he would, and he'd probably have a few other scathing things to say." Wretched man. And the worst of it was that she couldn't even in good faith argue with him. "It'll be a relief to see her wake again." Only then would she know if Jane was truly well and not injured in some unforeseen way, or still suffering the delusion that a ghost walked Cedarton's hallways.

"I think we all will."

"Not her husband," she muttered, bowing her head.

Jem twitched as if struck by her words. When she looked at him, his jaw was clenched. "He's resentful," he admitted. "It's not a match of his choosing, rather one that familial obligations obliged him to make. I'm sure in time..."

Would time make a difference? She wasn't so sure, and remained unconvinced that Jem believed any differently. A shadow lurked in his eyes when he spoke of the pair that made her suddenly mistrustful. She knew him as a soulful and clever man, but she would do well to remember that he was also one of Linfield's barnacles and a man who hadn't hesitated over agreeing to a passionate affair with her.

"Is that the only reason you are here? To enquire about Lady Linfield?" She took a step back towards the doorway, making him blink at her obvious retreat.

"No... No, that wasn't entirely it. I thought... rather, it occurred to me that you might... That you might appreciate something with which to help you pass the time. I know how slowly the minutes can crawl when one is confined. I brought you these." He scooped a pile of books off the window ledge and thrust them into her arms. "I wasn't at all sure of your preferences... but, well... they are what they are. You may put them aside if they don't suit, and I won't be at all offended."

Well, he might be one of Linfield's cronies, but he was not at all like that man.

"Thank you." She accepted the gift with a smile. "It was a kindly thought."

"Perhaps. You may not think so when you give them a look."

Given the weightiness of the pile, Eliza took them to the table she and Jane had sat at yesterday afternoon exchanging gossip. Jem didn't enter the bedchamber, but lingered on the threshold instead as if he expected a raucous alarm to sound if he did anything so transgressive as entering.

Eliza opened the cover of the topmost volume. It was a novel. Something her younger sisters would have delighted in and had likely read a dozen times apiece. It would, she supposed, pass some hours, though Cedarton had mysteries aplenty of its own, without the need to dive into those of an imaginary abode.

"Mrs Cluett was keen to lend her expertise," Jem explained. "That top volume is one of her recommendations. She was rather dismissive of my choices, said they were not at all the sort of thing a young lady would appreciate, but then I said to myself, she doesn't know Eliza as I do, and I made the rest of the selections accordingly."

Intrigued by his words, Eliza opened the second volume, the title of which startled a gasp of delight from her lips. A treatise on algebra, and below it, *Zoonomia part one* by Erasmus Darwin.

"That latter one I managed to persuade Bell to temporarily part with. He was not entirely complimentary about its author, but agreed there was merit to the discourse. There are chapters about motion and various organs." He took a tentative step into the room, leaving the door wide open, then another few bolder steps when he wasn't immediately struck down for the transgression. "I thought you might especially appreciate the chapters on diseases and the oxygenation of the lungs and placenta." He pointed them out in the index with one long finger.

"Fascinating," she agreed, provoking a broad grin from him that was at once both boyishly charming and intellectually gleeful.

"I'm sorry I'm making such assumptions, and I shouldn't. Maybe you'd have preferred a stack of novels—"

"I definitely wouldn't."

"It's just, I've never met a woman with such a similar passion for science as myself."

"These are all marvellous, and I will thoroughly enjoy them all." Though she would also not be surprised if Jane woke the moment she turned the first page. That would be a very Jane-like thing to do. She'd never decried Eliza's thirst for knowledge in the way others did, but nor did she entirely understand it, and she did possess a remarkable knack for derailing Eliza mid-thought.

"I believe I'll start with Mr Darwin, and then move onto the mathematics. Shall I follow it well enough, do you think?"

"Oh, I should say so. I'm afraid there are rather a lot of my notes in the margins. I hope you won't mind them. I do like to make sure I'm following as I go along."

"I shan't mind them at all." She would read them all and perhaps add a few of her own that he might read once she'd returned it to him.

"I ought to go," he said throwing a disheartening glance towards the open doorway. "If Linfield catches wind..." A dark thought, judging by the storm clouds that gathered in his eyes, hit him causing him to pause. "No matter. I shouldn't linger. I'll let you get back to nursing Lady Linfield."

"An overgenerous description," Bell said from the doorway. He entered, leading with his completely unnecessary cane, the ends of his wig trembling. "How is my patient?"

"Sleeping." Eliza could not find it in herself to be entirely welcoming.

"Best restorative for a woman in her position."

He lingered only long enough to take Jane's pulse and lift her eyelids to shine a light into her pupils. They were, Eliza observed, still narrowed to pinpricks.

"You drugged her far too severely," she admonished.

"Are you a qualified apothecary, Miss Wakefield?"

He knew she was not, as only men were permitted to qualify.

"Then I will take your advisement with a pinch of salt. Lady Linfield will awaken when her mind is fully rested and her wits and senses restored. That is the outcome we all desire, is it not?"

Grudgingly, she admitted so, but that didn't stop him being a pompous twit.

-13-

Jem

"...unbuttoned my breeches,
My prick in full vigour does stand;
Don't be like affected coy bitches,
But lake it while stiff, in your hand."

Bravo," Cluett called, drumming his hands on the tabletop, as Linfield raised a glass in a salute to himself and his successful rendition of Bumper Allnight's verse. The recital had been in full swing for around twenty minutes, following an irritating game that involved making lewd noises with one's armpits. It was the sort of schoolboy nonsense Jem had indulged in with his cousins when they were barely out of their skeleton suits.

Bell gave dry applause, while Jem found his fingertips curled into his thighs. The evening was progressing about as well as he'd imagined it would when he'd arrived at dinner and noted the absence of the ladies.

Some three bottles of port apiece farther into the evening, Linfield was at his treacherous worst, and Cluett was barely able to put three words together in a comprehensible order.

"Drink up, drink up laddies." Linfield encouraged. Jem rose his glass and took first a sip and then a draft under his host's beady observation. He was already a bottle and a half behind. Even Bell was ahead of him. His lips were stained crimson and the blush in his cadaverous, sunken cheeks was more vibrant than that of a maiden's in a brothel.

"Do you not like my rhyme?" Linfield stalked around the table and put his lips irritatingly close to Jem's ear. The man reeked of sour grapes and desperation. "Must I learn it in Latin to meet your approval, Sir Tutor?

"*Meus phallus in vigore stat; vena osculum me et accipe me in manu tua.*"

Cluett applied his knuckles to the table again. Bell rolled his eyes, while Jem made a show of befuddlement. The man's Latin was atrocious.

He'd felt the man's gaze too viscerally throughout the recital as it was. He didn't require a further agonising rendition, having perfectly understood both the writer and Linfield's intent. The former imagined women as things for men's entertainment, while Linfield attributed Jem the role. Clearly having got his way earlier, his lordship was now convinced of his victory and envisaged them fucking like bunnies in the not-too-distant future. Except Jem was not won over to the cause. His prick shrivelled at the very thought. He had capitulated in one instance to give himself time to navigate himself out of the current dilemma. God dammit, if it weren't for Eliza and what he feared might happen if he left her in this place unprotected, then he'd have taken his chances in the mists already and left both Cedarton and Linfield behind without a backwards glance.

He could scrape by without Linfield's coins in his purse. He was never going to starve. There was always a place for him under his uncle's roof. It just came with expectations of a different variety...namely, his auntie Mary's desire to saddle him with a bride.

Right now, that seemed preferable to staying here. Not to mention that his arse still smarted a little from earlier.

"Should we away to bed?" Linfield purred, like he was already having his prick sucked.

Lord, no. He'd rather stay awake until dawn listening to his compatriots performing one of Beethoven's piano sonatas on their armpit trombones. "Growing old, my lord? We're still some minutes shy of witching hour. Surely we don't need to toddle off yet, or do we need to secure you a bath chair and ear trumpet?"

"Ah, showing your teeth, dog." Linfield slapped Jem on the back, good naturedly, before leaning in uncomfortably close, and snarling. "Watch your tongue, tutor. Recall, I'm acquainted with your weaknesses, and you will spend the night precisely where I bid you to spend it." He straightened and seized up the bottle standing by Jem's glass. "Drink up, you filthy laggards." The rim of the bottle was rudely thrust against Jem's lips. "Down it. Down it. Down the whole damn lot." With Linfield's clawed fingers digging into his shoulder, Jem had little choice but to do as instructed and swallow the syrupy liquid.

The swill sat heavily in his belly and left a musty taste on his tongue, which he tried to remove with the back of his hand, while Linfield set the empty bottle spinning on its side.

"I think it's time for a game, gentlemen."

"If it's cards, you may count me out," Bell remarked.

George deflated at the dismissal, but roused immediately to cry out, "A game of chance."

"No, one of stealth. Do you think you can outwit us, Georgie dear?"

"Easily." The keen fool was already half out of his chair. Stealth! If he could still walk ten paces in a straight line it would be a miracle, but George didn't let that curtail his faith in himself. He straightened himself up, holding onto the table. "What do I have to do?"

"Evade us, of course. We'll have a ghost hunt. You'll play the part, and we'll stalk you. You must look the part, of course."

"A ghost hunt?" George's beady eyes crossed. "I hardly need to play the part, this place is already crawling with them according to your wife."

"Women are such fanciful creatures. Here..."

Linfield had clearly planned in advance, for he gave his man a nod, and the valet produced a woman's nightrail.

"Put your costume on, George."

George pulled the white cloth over his head.

"Not like that, you dolt. Whoever saw a woman with a coat and cravat under her shift?"

"Mercy, my lord," George protested, all fingers and thumbs. He'd managed to poke his head through one of the voluminous sleeves. "The ones I've been acquainted with have worn nowt but stockings and skin beneath. I'll freeze my nads off if I run about this place like that. Your halls are colder than a witch's tit outside of this snug."

"Then you'll have to run swift enough to keep the chill off. You may keep your stockings and shoes."

As if that were any concession.

George grumbled and groaned, but nevertheless stripped off his clothing and donned the nightrail over his birthday suit, while Jem and Bell averted their gazes. Linfield produced a mob-cap for George to pull down over his hair.

"Perfect," he announced.

"And now I suppose you expect us to tear around after him?" Bell gave his eyes a laconic roll. The man could move swiftly enough, when pressed or caught up in a matter that excited him, but he was not the sort for childishness or unnecessary exertion, and he'd endured a deal of the former this evening already.

"That is generally what a hunt entails, Ludlow, my dear fellow. Oblige me, this once, won't you, and I shan't bat an eyelid when you next bring a corpse through my door. Up now. Up, varmints!" Linfield propelled them onto their feet, with a series of gesticulations worthy of an orchestral conductor. "Georgie, get ready. Gentlemen, all is fair game within the bounds of Cedarton's walls. The first to capture the ghost, may claim the victory. George, if you've managed to evade and outwit us by the time the clock strikes one, then..."

"Then?" All three of them prompted in unison. Open-ended agreements weren't something one wanted to agree to, especially with the likes of Linfield, who was a known snake, and couldn't be trusted to play fairly.

"Then the victory is his?"

"That's it?" George grumbled. "No prize other than a pat on the back? I'm foxed, but not foxed enough to risk a chill for less than a guinea apiece."

"I can think of better things to do with my guineas," Jem muttered. In hindsight, he ought to have kept his mouth shut. Protesting only served to make Linfield more determined they would all run around like blind mice to suit his whim. "Ten guineas to the victor."

Dammit, that would mean coughing up over three guineas apiece, money he could do without throwing into George Cluett's pockets. Naturally, George brightened. An avaricious smile snaked across his face, and he started skipping from one foot to the other in readiness. Bell continued to hesitate, which at least served to make Jem's own reluctance less remarkable.

"What's the issue, gentlemen? Afraid you might meet our resident white lady and piddle yourselves with fright?" Linfield gave a raucous, nerve fraying laugh. "She's not real, muttonheads. She's merely a delusion of my wife's. Start running, George. I'm going to start counting now." He did just that, beginning a droning amble towards a hundred that sped as the digits increased. George vanished from sight as the count climbed towards thirty, whereupon both Jem and Bell were obliged to find their feet. The physician positioned himself at the exit that led towards the stairs. Jem hesitated, wondering if it was safer to follow his lead, or flee in the opposite direction. Linfield was already shooting him lascivious looks that spelled his intent out all too plainly.

It was the perfect reason not to linger. If he managed to outpace Linfield far enough at the start of the chase, then he ought to be able to stay out of his grasp for the duration, particularly if he ventured into the parts of the castle that were dank with ruin and best left to fester in peace.

"Ninety-nine, one hundred," Linfield finished.

Jem sprinted for the glass-scattered remains of the former solarium via a circuitous route through the first floor rooms. From that chamber he would be able to circle around the outside of the building, then enter again through the window into the dining room with the dodgy latch. Then... then with luck he'd make it down to Bell's surgery, and from there into the tunnel between the walls where he could hopefully wait out the hour unmolested.

That was assuming Linfield didn't know about the hidden passageway, but even if he did, he had no idea that Jem knew. Hopefully, he'd be busy stalking corridors and looking under beds and inside closets.

The first part of the chase was the most precarious. Unfortunately, George seemed to have had a similar path mapped out, for Jem caught sight of him as he nipped across the entrance hall. The last thing he wanted was to actually catch the man and then endure a second bout of this nonsense, or worse, whatever Linfield's mind conjured next.

He took a right into the Lady's Parlour and hefted open one of the sash windows, then slipped out and lowered himself onto the window ledge below, and thence into the channel that bordered nearly the whole of the property. With the window pulled down once more, hopefully Linfield wouldn't notice it was unlatched. Jem then snuck around to the west facing side of the castle. The mist that had swaddled the property for days still sat heavy on the surrounding moorlands. Coupled with the dark, it made it difficult to scry more than a few feet ahead. Once or twice, he thought he saw lights amid the gloom, or heard the whisper of voices, but he dismissed them as phantoms of the fog. The walls were a certainty, so he stuck to them, making sure to take care when passing any windows.

He slid in through the back entrance onto the boot room, then skirted the servants' quarters to reach the tunnel that lead to Bell's domain.

Would Bell himself be there? Would he find him at his studies, rather than humouring Linfield by chasing around the castle? Would Linfield have struck out in this direction thinking it a likely place to find Jem?

The rooms were blissfully silent as he passed through and slid into the concealed passageway.

Of course, he had not accounted for the lack of a light source, leaving him to navigate the inky darkness by touch alone. He got turned about at the first junction and found himself in a suite of rooms he'd never seen before. Cobwebs hung like sails from the ceiling and black mildew had created a canvas of lurid figures across the whole of one wall. The chamber was sparsely furnished. Jem pulled aside one dust-drape and uncovered a child's rocking horse. Deeper into the chamber sat a replica of the castle, inhabited by a miniature lord and lady, though most of the maids and footmen had been knocked to the floor and trampled. Both a cleaver and flame had been taken to the Lady's Tower so that it stood as soot blackened and damaged as the real tower. He noticed himself then, positioned in his chamber, and Bell in his surgery downstairs, Jane, Eliza and both the Cluetts all positioned just so. Lady Linfield's bed had been burned in the middle, and her dolly's face damaged so the face was melted on one side and her golden hair singed back to her waxen scalp.

He stepped back from the horrid display with a yelp.

What devilry was this? Someone's recreation of the events after the fact, or the place where they had plotted their actions?

Who even knew of this chamber besides him? Linfield claimed to never have set foot inside

Cedarton prior to the party's arrival here, but they had only his word for that, and his word was hardly reliable.

What if he truly had come here to enact some dastardly plan to rid himself of his unwanted wife, and not just to avoid the aftermath of that disastrous carriage chase.

If he murdered her, he'd likely get away with it. He'd claim the privilege of the peerage and the House of Lords would acquit him without punishment. They mercilessly honoured their own.

Was Linfield really capable of such villainy? He was a tyrant to be sure, but more mischief than miscreant in Jem's experience. And would he really subject himself to Bell's leeches if he meant to do away with his wife? Her death would rather render the need for a cockstand unnecessary.

But if it was not Linfield behind this ghastliness, then who? And why? Who could possibly wish Lady Linfield such ill? And why create such a rendition of the castle? The rooms were arranged to the last detail, including the deserted area he and Bell had explored hunting for clues as to what Lady Linfield had seen, right down to the mice and the candle left in the middle of that dark painted otherwise empty room. Even this suite tucked away at the rear of the west tower was reconstructed with its cobwebs and replica house.

Perhaps he needed to further question Eliza on her friend's past.

Jem found a candle stub among the detritus, and with a trick for making sparks he'd learned as a child, kindled a flame to light his way through the concealed passageway. He did not attempt to exit the suite via its actual door, being too afraid of finding Linfield on the other side irate over having his secret lair uncovered. Although, in truth it was not a very Linfield sort of room. Cedarton's master was a creature of comfort and privilege. He disliked filth, sneezed over the tiniest bit of dust, and was not overly fond of eight-legged beasties.

Truthfully, Jem was more worried about being found and pressed into some manner of fornication. Much better not to risk it, and to remain out of sight.

-14-
Eliza

Eliza's head had nodded towards her chest somewhere between the paragraphs detailing the instincts of newborns to suckle at their mother's teats and certain ladies being too refined to nurse their own children. Mr Darwin's book was not providing her with the wealth of new information she'd hoped for, rather, she found herself inclined to agree with Doctor Bell as to the worthiness of the tome. It contained a few points of discourse but was mostly a catalogue of things anyone with half a brain already knew.

She was abruptly startled out of her doze by the chamber door slamming against the wainscotting. The book slid from her knee, landing open face down. Lord Linfield's spry form appeared out of the gloom and lurched towards her. His hair was standing practically on end, and his cheeks and nose were both ruddy, making her wonder if he'd just encountered Cedarton's white lady.

It was apparent from the whiff of alcohol about

him once he got close enough that this wasn't the case. He stopped, and peered down his rather sharp nose at her, and barked, "Where is he?" before scowling in a fashion that caused his chin to disappear inside the folds of his cravat.

"Excuse me?" Eliza retrieved the borrowed book from the carpet, then rose, clutching it as if the leather and parchment might lend her strength. When a man barged into one's chamber unannounced, it was rarely for savoury reasons. "Wh-where is who?"

Linfield's drink-addled brain must have comprehended her misapprehension for he took a deliberate step back from her person, chewing on his ruby-stained lips.

"Jamie."

"Who?"

"Jamie... James... Jem. Mr Whistler." He spat the latter at her like an insult. "Where else would he hide but here?"

Hide? What the devil was he hiding for? "Well, I'm sorry to tell you that he's not here. There's only your wife and I, as you can plainly see."

Linfield blinked. His scowl grew as his gaze darted about the room. Clearly, he expected to find Jem secreted behind a curtain, or perhaps slotted under the bed alongside the chamber pot.

"But!" he blurted when it became apparent neither were the case. Why he'd ever imagined it so, she couldn't imagine, but then, drink-addled men often assumed things erroneously. Her father had always seemed to imagine he had a surplus of coins when in his cups, rather than a mortgaged house and five children. He'd always believed he was the best tenor in the county too, when in fact he could barely hold a note and was a baritone, anyway.

"There's just the two of you here?" His eyes narrowed again.

"Aye," she confirmed. "Just me and Jane."

"Hm." His nostrils thinned to snake-like slits. "She's fine?"

"Huh?" Startled, she found him throwing a look towards the bed, and a rather softer one than she'd previously seen him give Jane.

"Sleeping," Eliza ventured. Jane was still yet to wake. Fine wasn't something she felt she could commit to. "When she wakes, I'll tell her you looked in on her."

"You will?"

"Of course."

He rubbed his eyes while Eliza failed to stave off a yawn.

"Whistler's not been here at all?"

"No." He hadn't. Leastways, not since before dinner, and she was bright enough to know when to spare unnecessary details.

He hmm-ed a bit more. "Felt sure he'd be here."

"I'm afraid not."

"I'll leave, then, and seek him elsewhere. We're having a game."

"Ah. Well, he's really not here. I've not heard anyone pass by either." Actually, that wasn't wholly true, she'd heard Betsy a while back, idling about and taking her time over whatever task Mrs

Honeyfield had presumably given her to do.

Linfield, it seemed, had already exited the conversation. He turned on his heels and marched back towards the open door.

"Goodnight," Eliza called after him. He did not return her adieu.

What a strange, strange man her friend had married. It was hard to know what to think of him. At least on this occasion he had found some measure of interest in Jane's welfare. Perhaps he wasn't such a villain after all, simply peevish over having a bride thrust upon him. She knew she wouldn't care for such a thing. It was bad enough when Freddy got it into his head to include her in his matchmaking schemes. Thankfully, he was truly atrocious at it, so she'd been spared the irritation of finding herself beset by suitors. Although her brother's incompetence was a shame for Caroline and Maria, who were both very much in love with the idea of being in love.

Maria fancied having a host of suitors, while Caro was all for having her heart broken and then mended by the arrival of a handsome prince.

Eliza closed the door and secured the latch. Whatever that had been about, she had no desire to experience a repeat. Thus, she was prompted to secure the entrance via the dressing room too. Really, it always made sense to lock one's door when staying in a strange place, but she hadn't thought it a necessity when she was nursing the lady of the house.

She was about to fall back into the chair by the

hearth when a knock turned her attention to the armoire. Heavens, there was another entrance she hadn't accounted for.

Eliza cautiously grasped the handle and pulled. For a moment, all she revealed was inky darkness, then a hand reached out and tugged her into the passageway beyond. Here, in a pocket of light formed by a stubby candle, she was finally able to see the figure holding her.

"Jem!"

"Who else?"

"In this place, I'm sure it could be anyone or anything."

"Did you think me a ghost?"

His hold on her was far too warm for that. She imagined a spectre's touch to be chill, that there would be no vitality about it. And while she was sure such an encounter would make her heart race, it wouldn't be akin to having Jem's breath on her skin.

"Lord Linfield was here looking for you."

"Yes. I overheard you. Thank heavens he didn't think to open the wardrobe."

"Were you spying on me?"

"Eliza, of course not. The passageway seemed a good place to make myself scarce. I'd rather avoid his lordship's company for the moment."

"Don't you care for his games?"

"No. Not presently. Not so much. Eliza... I didn't know if you'd be awake. I wouldn't have lingered if you had been asleep, so I pray you won't think me horribly creepy."

"I don't think that. Though standing watching

me sleep would definitely have been odd."

"I'm glad you are awake. I found something. Something peculiar." He described the details of the cobwebbed room to her and the dolls' house he'd found there. "What do you think it all means?"

Eliza shook her head. "That someone means Jane ill, but that's hardly a revelation. I'm certain that maid wasn't responsible for the fire."

"Linfield?"

She'd felt almost as certain of his guilt earlier as she'd been of Edith's innocence, but now... "There's plenty of reason to suspect it, but I don't know, Jem. Something doesn't feel right, especially after what you've just said of that strange room. Maybe I just want to think better of him. To believe that Jane hasn't landed in such grim circumstances. He asked after her, almost seemed concerned, but I'm still not sure he cares much for her."

"That could change. They hardly know one another."

She nodded, but swiftly turned it into a shake. "You're saying that, but you don't really believe it."

"I don't know, Eliza. I think there are some things they need to figure out between them, and maybe then they'll learn to rub along together well enough. Lady Linfield seems very amenable."

"She is. Very. She's a delight. I cannot understand why he can't see that."

"We're often blind to what's in front of us. Plus, it's taking him a little while to adjust to his new circumstances. Eliza, his sire did compel him to make the match, and who among us likes doing what our guardians tell us to do? Is it then really any wonder he's somewhat resentful?"

"Jem, you're agreeing with me. Do you see what I mean about the notion of him being the guilty party feeling wrong? You started out arguing it was him and wound up defending him. Then again, you are his friend."

"That's a stretch. I'm his tutor."

"A little more than that, I think."

Curiously, his whole posture, from shoulders to shins stiffened as if he were bracing for horrible news.

"Jem, you're practically his social equal."

That startled a laugh out of him. "Sorry! Hardly. Eliza, he's the son of a peer. I'm the orphaned nephew of a minor baron. I told you earlier, I'm a dreadful prospect."

"You did." She fingered the silk of his cravat. "And I told you I'm not looking for a husband." She lifted onto her toes then, while also pulling him down to her and brushed a kiss to his lips.

"That you did."

"Why would I want to be pinned down?"

"Hm," he mused, and fastened his hands around her wrists. "Why indeed?" With no effort at all he edged her backward into the wall, where he held her trapped, with her wrists raised to either side of her head. "I mean, there's nothing fun about that at all. Nothing distracting, or inspirational." His breath buffeted her cheek as he bent his head while holding her gaze. His lips skimmed shy of her mouth then down the side of her neck to the hollow at its base.

"No, you definitely wouldn't want to be pinned in place by a man. Teased... Tormented... Think how appalling it would be if he kissed you." His lips grazed her skin, sending prickles of excitement flowing out from that point of contact. "Stole not one kiss, but two... Took certain liberties with one's clothing." He drew the pin holding her dress front at the shoulder from the fabric with his teeth and dropped it to the floor. Then did the same to the other shoulder. Beneath, the two sides of the dress fastened with a simple drawstring. Below it, she wore only a chemise and simple waist petticoat.

"Jem!"

He kissed the top of her right breast.

"What are you doing?"

"Pinning you down. Playing the rake. Don't tell me you've never attended a ball and wondered what it would be like to feel lips on your skin... a hand beneath your skirt. Your sisters, your brother, the other guests... they're only a few steps away. We could be caught at any time. There's just a simple door between us and scandal."

That was more or less true of their current situation. If Jane woke... If Linfield returned and demanded entry.

"Tell me to behave and I will. Or don't..." His grin grew as salacious as it was broad. "Please don't."

"Jem," she returned, nervousness making her own smile extra wide. "I don't... I don't want you to stop. Please, don't stop!"

The touch of one person's lips to another's oughtn't to be so distracting. It chased intelligent thoughts from her head, trapping her in a world of sensations, where all that mattered was the next touch, and the next. She strained against his grasp, but he wouldn't release her. His fingers curled against the pulse points in her wrists. She could hear the thunder of her own blood in her ears.

"Are you going to be a good girl if I release you?"

"What are you going to do?"

He tugged open the bow resting between her breasts. Her chemise was of the drawstring variety too and opened just as easily. The tip of his tongue touched her skin, making her gasp. Then his mouth closed over her nipple.

Mr Darwin's book hadn't included any mention of the pleasure of having a man's mouth wrapped around one's nipple. It stole her voice. Made her blood sing. Heaviness pooled between her thighs. It was the sort of ache that made her lean into his heat and made her disobedient. Instead of keeping her hands where he'd set them, she tangled her fingers in his hair and held him in place against her breast.

Damn, that felt like nothing she'd ever felt before. Better than syllabub, or the feel of the sun on her face. Better than sagging into a chair after a long hard day, tired but relieved to have survived all that had been thrown at her. Even better than having him fill her mouth earlier.

"Jem," she cried, not wanting him to stop, but simultaneously seeking to lift him to her.

"Eliza… I… still… think I… owe you a favour… or two." He punctuated his words with movement, each subsequent kiss alighting on a different part of her body. It shocked her when he planted the last of them on her bare thigh above the garter holding her stockings up. He'd bunched her petticoat and dress. "You gave me something precious earlier. I've been thinking all afternoon about returning the favour."

His attention slid further up her thigh.

"I wonder, Eliza, are you as familiar with this concept as you were with fellatio? It has a Latin name too."

"I've heard the term," she squeaked, sounding far more girlish and innocent than she normally did.

"Ah, so it's a thrill you've yet to enjoy."

"I don't raise my skirts for any old fool."

"Just for this one," he muttered, but he looked up at her, and his eyes were shiny even in the gloom. "I can smell you, and it's damn near driving me insane. I'm going to lick you. I'm going to taste the split of your pussy. Fuck you with my tongue."

"Is that—"

"It's safer than the alternative."

"But what if I want the alternative? If it's your prick I want, not your mouth, or your fingers. What if that's what I want to feel?"

"Shh, shh!" He reached up as if to cover her mouth and stop her making such a demand, but he was on his knees, and she was a tall woman. His hand found her bared breast instead and took possession of its fullness.

"Jem, come to me," she pleaded, wanting his arms around her, and his mouth on her lips not lower down.

"One taste. You'll let me have that, won't you,

Eliza?"

She couldn't help holding her breath. She didn't precisely say yes, but she did nothing to stop him either.

He licked her right along her split as he'd promised. It made her tingle all over.

"Now come here."

"You're sure you wouldn't rather I stayed here?" he asked, cocking a brow.

The honest truth was that she wasn't sure of anything anymore. This man on his knees before her turned her ordered and methodical world into one of madness and emotional intoxication. "I want you to kiss me."

"That I can do." He kissed her pussy, exactly as he'd earlier kissed her mouth, teasing her lips open and pressing his tongue inside. Being touched there, it made her insides sing too hot. He was aware of that; she could feel the smile on his lips as he fed the flower of need blooming within her. Ruthlessly, he further awakened that ache. Now she understood it, why she saw women who'd sworn off ever lying with a man again birthing their fifth, or sixth, or thirteenth child. There was something so agitating, so distracting about what he was about. She couldn't help but groan. Those noises even escaped when she rammed the heel of her hand into her mouth.

"Ah, don't do that. Let me hear you." He rose and peeled her hand away from her mouth. His eyes were fiercely bright, ringed with a halo of desire. "I like hearing how I'm affecting you. Those noises are like precious gifts and a set of instructions rolled into one. How can I know if I'm pleasing you if I can't hear your purr?"

"My heart's thumping," she confessed.

"Eliza." He kissed her long and fierce, until she was almost insensible from the taste of him and clung fast to his head and back when he sought to speak. "If you won't let me kiss your cunny, then will you let me finger it?"

"I don't know what that means."

"I think you do."

He pushed his hand between her thighs. Eliza's breath caught as his fingers moved slowly upwards, sliding easily in the wet-heat of her arousal. He found the bud at the top of that avenue, causing her to damn near swallow her tongue.

"I think you've probably explored this devil's doorknob before, but it's always different when it's not your own fingers doing the tracing."

She couldn't hold it back and cried into his shoulder. Writhed and gasped at his perfect touch. No longer did she attempt to hide the sounds of her pleasure, but mewled over each gentle brush, and crooned when his strokes grew bolder, heavier. His touch wasn't quite so soft then. His thumb took over where his fingers had been, while his first two digits delved inside of her, then pumped back and forth.

"It's just a taste, just a taste for now, of how it'll feel when I'm finally inside you."

"Why not now?" She was too far gone in her pleasure to think of the ills that might result. Besides, there were potions she could brew.

"Reasons," he replied cryptically. "I don't want

the first time I lie with you to be in a rat-run of a corridor with cold stone against your back. Eliza, you deserve better than that.

 "What if I want that?"

"Eliza, I don't need to fuck you to bring you off. We don't need to cross that boundary tonight. Trust me. I want you, but fucking... Well, it's always a little cock-centric. I'd rather tonight was about your bliss."

His fingers stretched her again, but this time he curled them, so they brushed against the wall of her sheath. Here she discovered was a previously unknown pleasure-spot. Being touched there caused her to greedily rock against his thrusting hand.

Jem kissed her neck. She could feel the tickle of his cravat and collar against her breast and lower, her arousal dampening his shirt cuff. Something was building. She was teetering on the edge of it. The muscles in her cunny tightened around his fingers like they could squeeze further joy from him or perhaps trap him there so that he might always pleasure her.

"Let go, Eliza. Let me give you this, as you gave it to me."

She reached that precipice then and crashed headlong into the maelstrom beyond. She floated in that state of bliss but moments, but what momentous moments. Every cell seemed alive and united and every nerve sang. It was a taste of heaven, and she wanted more. "Jem," she rasped.

"I know," he gasped hot into her ear. "You're a goddess, and I know." He kissed her again as she rode out the last of her peak.

Then, he sucked his fingers clean.

-15-

Eliza

"Jane. Thank the Lord, you're awake. I was starting to think you'd never open your eyes again."

Dawn had arrived and passed. The morning was swaddled in mist again, the mullioned windows blanketed in yet more drizzle. Eliza had slept fitfully in the chair, though she'd turned to the wardrobe smiling each time she'd woke and clenched her inner muscles. The sensation of being stretched by Jem's fingers lingered long after he'd departed.

"It'll raise suspicions if I'm missing too long," he said, recalling to her the fact he was midway through a game of hide and seek with Linfield and his fellow guests when she'd tried to coax him to stay and let her have her wicked way with him. His cock had been standing ramrod stiff behind the placket of his breeches, and she'd found it near impossible not to reach for it, to run her fingers over it, and rub it.

Jane blinked rheumily at her but struggled into a sitting position. "How long have I slept?" she asked, as Eliza fussed and plumped the pillows behind her. She gave a rather extravagant yawn.

"A whole day and then some." Eliza smoothed the covers over her friend's lap, then perched on the side of the bed. "Doctor Bell gave you some drops. Do you recall any of what happened before that?"

Jane frowned at her so that furrows appeared in her usually unlined brow. "My head is so thick I can almost taste the wool in my thoughts. I'm not sure."

"You don't recall what you saw on the second-floor corridor?"

Her friend's expression further clouded. "I don't," she said after a moment's consideration. "At least I don't think I do. What did I see? Not Lady Cedarton's gho—Wait!" She gave a sudden sniff. "Whatever is burning? Can you smell smoke? Eliza, is that fire? Is something... the castle alight?"

"Rest easy, friend. That drama is over. There was—there was an incident while you were resting, but no one was hurt. Only furnishings were damaged, specifically, your bed. That is why you are in mine."

She watched Jane turn her head to look around her, taking in her surroundings. Her frown deepened, and her jaw worked as though she was chewing over the problem. "I think you had better tell me all that I have missed, for it seems to be rather a lot."

"I'm not sure it's wise to overtax your mind at present. You've only just woken."

"Eliza Wakefield, if you will not tell me, then I shall summon Mrs Honeyfield and compel her to talk. What in heaven's name has gone on?"

Eliza clasped her hand and explained both about the ghostly figure and the burning bed with as little drama as possible so as not to excite Jane's nerves. Her friend listened intently, with hardly an interruption. When the tale was told, she put her head in her hands. Her shoulders shook. "Jane?" Eliza reached for her in alarm, intending to swaddle her in an embrace, but Jane lifted her head, and Eliza realised that she was laughing.

Admittedly, it was a dry, hysterical sort of laugh. "What a hideous mountain of nonsense I've got myself ravelled in," she declared, "And all because of one foolish, foolish mistake." She pulled one of the pillows out from behind her back and beat her fist into it. "I never wanted to marry Linfield, Eliza. In any other circumstances I would not have, but my situation left me with little choice."

"What situation? Whatever do you mean, Jane?"

Jane opened her mouth, failed to speak, choked, and set her fist to her lips.

"Now, now," Eliza soothed, muttering comforting inanities, while attempting to brush Jane's hair back from her damp brow.

"You don't understand, and I should not tell you this, because you will think very ill of me indeed, but—" She clasped tight Eliza's hand and only mouthed her next words. "I'm increasing."

Eliza frowned. She pried her hand loose from Jane's overtight grip. "I don't understand. How is that possible? I don't mean… What I mean is, how? You said you and Lord Linfield hadn't consummated the marriage yet." Realisation struck the moment she'd spoken the words aloud. "Ah! That is why you are in such a pickle over his failure to bed you. You need him to believe it is his."

"You see. Now you think me monstrous," Jane wailed. She scrubbed at her face, as tears began to trickle down her cheeks. "I know... I know it is dishonest of me. You mustn't think I don't know my own deceitfulness, but.... Oh, Eliza. I didn't know what else to do. My parents are unaware. They negotiated the marriage with the earl and presented it to me as the greatest of triumphs. I don't suppose they gave any thought at all to Linfield's reputation, only to how it would elevate us in the eyes of society. There was no possibly way I could refuse, especially when it seemed such an obvious way out of a terrible pickle."

In Eliza's mind a pickle was something of a trivial nature, which could hardly describe the current situation.

"Jane, you need to tell me what happened. Were you attacked? Forced? Is this why you left Scarborough in such haste? I thought there must have been something, after all you had said about loving it there. And who knows? Someone one must know."

Jane hid her face again. "The situation is entirely born of my own folly. I was blind, duped... Understand, that I loved him, Eliza. Utterly. Devotedly. Even now, I cannot look back on that time and regret a single moment of it."

"Did he make you promises?"

Jane swiftly shook her head. "He did not, but I was certain he would ask for me. How naïve I was. He never intended such a thing. Nor was it in his provenance to do such a thing."

Little by little a picture was building in Eliza's head. "He has a wife already?"

Jane, sniffling into her sleeve, looked up and nodded. "I'm so ashamed. He thought from the outset that I was a wanton. And it is true. I was all too willing to give myself to him."

Eliza found herself blushing, thinking back to all the things she'd said to Jem just a short time ago. If there was a wanton among them, then she deserved the title as much as Jane, perhaps doubly so, for she had been forthright about the fulfilment of her desire, while being equally dismissive of the notion of matrimony.

"You are quiet," Jane said. "You believe it too, as does Linfield. It is why he will not lie with me. Is it something about my aspect that announces it? I confess, I was horribly enamoured of tupping. It's so... so utterly distracting. I suppose the sin must show on my face."

All Eliza could do was shake her head. "Yours is a lovely face, Jane. I have never once looked at you and seen a single trace of sin about you."

"You are a dear," Jane replied mutinously, clearly unwilling to believe herself anything other than monstrously disfigured. "But perhaps it is only that you are so good yourself that you cannot discern such things in others. Linfield sees it. I cannot rid myself of his disgust. It clings to me. He was appalled by every aspect of my person. He would not look at my breasts, was utterly horrified that I was in anyway eager for the coupling."

"Yet, he is no saint to judge you."

"Things are different for men."

"Only because we allow them to be. I am quite certain nothing you have done prompted his revulsion, rather some flaw of his."

Jane remained unpersuaded, shaking her head so vigorously she was sure to give herself a headache. "I cannot erase his disgust from my mind. Truly, I think he detests me."

Eliza resorted to biting her lip. Based on what she had witnessed, it was difficult to refute that notion. He'd shown the least concern of any of them over Jane's safety and had been all too eager to have Bell dose her with laudanum.

"To think, I intended to wait naked for him in his bed. What madness persuaded me that was the best course of action? I can see now it would have been utter folly. It is no wonder that Lady Cedarton appeared to thwart me. I'm not a worthy mistress of this house."

"Jane, you are being overdramatic. I'm certain that there's a plain explanation for what you saw, which I'm quite certain was no phantasm. It seems rather there is someone here who means you ill."

This surprisingly stilled Jane's tears. "Whatever do you mean?"

"That you are being targeted. The sightings, the fire... Someone means to scare you out of your wits, or worse."

"But why? Unless they know." She pressed her hand to her stomach. "How could they? I've told no one besides you, and I've taken every care to disguise it. Besides, 'tis not as if anyone else knows that he hasn't performed his duty. Whoever heard of a man reluctant to bed his bride?"

"Someone must know. A maid. Your lover."

Jane shook her head even more vigorously. "I've bled. I've made sure of it. Mrs Honeyfield has even commented on it, since it's been her job to see to sending out the laundry until we can take on more servants. I think she meant to be kind. 'Tis everyone's assumption that a newlywed woman is consumed with the task of producing a brood. As for him... He would not tell anyone. It would lessen his standing to admit he'd sired a by-blow. Besides, I doubt he even knows that I am wed."

"Well, someone means you harm, and if it isn't to do with your—" Eliza inclined her head towards Jane's midriff. "Then what is behind it?"

"Have you a theory?" Jane asked, clasping her hands into her lap, precisely as she'd done when they'd been schoolgirls together at the start of whatever philosophising Eliza had been about to embark on.

"I don't know that you're taking this entirely seriously. Jane, you were almost burned alive, and you are the only one besides the maid who left who has seen the ghost."

"It's not that I mean to be flippant, it's just all so preposterous, it's difficult to be serious. And Eliza, we are so pitifully few here, do you really mean to imply that one of my guests wishes for my death? Whatever motive do you prescribe them?"

That was the part that truly had her stumped. The Cluetts were gossips, but not malicious as such. Although she had witnessed that exchange between George and Lord Linfield in the library. Perhaps if she could get a glimpse of that paper they'd fought over, it might shed some light, though she hardly saw how. Jane's death wouldn't benefit them in any case. As for the rest of their party, Doctor Bell and Jem were both employed by Lord Linfield. She trusted Jem implicitly, and Bell had no obvious motive. As for Linfield himself...did he truly despise his wife that much? What would her death possibly gain him? Jane's possessions, her very body were already his to do with as he pleased.

"Perhaps he has a mistress," Jane mused.

"Here? Right now, at Cedarton? Wherever do you imagine he's hiding her?"

"Oh, you! I was only speculating aloud. However, would it not explain so much? What's not to say the ghost I saw was in fact his mistress?"

"I would say that this is not a novel by Mrs Radcliffe." Although to be fair, it was becoming almost as far-fetched as one.

"And yet you cannot entirely dismiss the notion. I was almost burned to death in my own bed while drugged into an opium stupor, we are entirely isolated by the fog, and you at least believe my husband a villain."

"I think your mind's addled by the ludicrous dose of opiates Bell gave you," Eliza huffed. "I never once said he was a villain."

"But he is your primary suspect, or is it Bell? I'm confused. Perhaps they're in coalition?"

"Jane, I neither said nor implied—"

Her friend's impish smile lit up her whole face. "You didn't not say it, either. Nor do you entirely deny the possibility."

"It is true that Bell left breakfast with the express intention of going straight up to see you, but he was not here whence I arrived." She would have to check with Edith and Mrs Honeyfield to see if he had been and gone. "I suppose that might be construed as suspicious."

"Perhaps he required something from his rooms first?"

"No—I would have seen him. I went down there right after he left to come up to you to make Mrs Honeyfield the remedy I'd promised her."

"How is she today, do you know? Toothache is quite the worst."

"Not entirely the worst," Eliza muttered. She'd had it from enough to believe it that there was at least one thing worse, and probably a good many if she were to really compile a list.

"I'm going to rise now," Jane insisted, casting back the covers. "If there's a rotter about, then I'll at least face them with my stockings on." She was most of the way through dressing, Eliza serving as her maid, to assist her with the pinning of her bib-fronted bodice when she suddenly went rigidly stiff.

"You don't think he's bedding the maid, do you? And that she's some notion that if she removes me then he'll be entirely free to dote on her?"

"Jane." Eliza dismissed the notion immediately. It wasn't even worthy of speculation. "Linfield's a snob. Do you really think he'd lower himself to—?"

"I think he might take what he figured he was entitled to. He's a reputation as a wretch, after all."

"He's a reputation for wild escapades involving wheeled vehicles, and drunken behaviour, not as a whoremonger. Besides, he has a willing bride all too ready to tup him any time or in way he might choose, but he's not showing any appetite for it. So, no, I don't think he has a mistress. In fact, I think he lacks the sort of urges—"

"Oh...oh," Jane frantically tapped Eliza's forearm interrupting her. Then squeezed it so tight it left a mark. "What if it's Henrietta?"

Eliza laughed, but found her mirth faded quickly. "You think Henrietta is his mistress?"

Jane replied in hushed tones. "Well don't you find it odd that a gentleman brought his mother along to a house party? It's not that sort of house party. There are no young women here seeking husbands. There's no one for her to talk to, or chaperone. It's entirely odd."

"Yes, but his bosom friend's mother!"

"Perhaps he prefers older women? Perhaps she has it in for me? Maybe she expected to be his viscountess, and our marriage has robbed her of that. It was all arranged quite without our input, negotiated between my father and the earl. It would explain Linfield's behaviour too. Why he's so loath to bed me and being so mutinous in general."

As explanations went, it was far-fetched, but no more implausible than any other. Agitated by the course of her thoughts, Jane proceeded to march back and forth worrying the sides of her frock.

"We should take tea with her, don't you think?"

"That depends. You don't mean to ask her outright if she's your husband's mistress, do you, Jane?" Like many of the meek creatures Eliza had encountered, when cornered and roused, Jane could be decidedly plainspoken and vicious. But this was not the moment for candour.

"Gracious heavens, no. I think I can manage more subtlety than that. But I shall talk to her of Linfield, and we will see where that leads. One thing I have observed is that once Henrietta sets off, she goes on and on for as long as you've a mind to listen to her."

"Perhaps she might know what happened in town that prompted Linfield's exodus to the countryside too?"

"Exactly. I would like to know that too."

And what her son and their host had fought so violently over the night afore last.

Jane rang the bell, and by and by a maid arrived. It was not Edith but Betsy. "Please ask Mrs Cluett to join us for tea in the drawing room. We'll go down there now."

Curiously, the maid's face brightened at this announcement. "Reet away, me lady," she agreed and took herself off swifter than Eliza had previously imagined her capable.

-16-

Eliza

When Jane and Eliza reached the drawing room, they found it already occupied. George sprawled in the armchair closest to the fire, one leg hooked over the arm and the other stretched towards the grate. He righted himself with an irritating degree of indolence.

"Ladies, am I in your way?"

That much was apparent, as Jane took the other chair, while Eliza moved one from across the room, so that when Henrietta arrived, they might all sit together. The servants arrived but a moment later with a selection of cold cuts and buttered bread, along with Jane's favourite potently brewed tea, and the seemingly ubiquitous bergamot marmalade. Only when there was a cup cradled in her hand did Eliza observe Jane to be truly at ease.

"We had hoped your mother would join us," Jane remarked, finally startling George out of his seat and onto his feet, allowing Eliza to slip, at least temporarily, into the space he'd vacated.

George offered them a rather sickly smile. "Oh, I doubt she'll come down. She's feeling wholly out of sorts."

"No, George, I'm simply out of sorts with you."

Henrietta stormed across the room like she was shipboard and bracing against a gale. She was swaddled in a cashmere shawl of particularly fine quality and a woollen day dress of apple green that flattered her complexion and made her look much younger than her years.

Eliza swapped seats, allowing her the comfort of the chair closest to the blaze, recalling her complaints about the cold on her first evening here. It hardly seemed possible that was only the day before yesterday. So much had happened, it seemed as if she'd been at Cedarton for days upon days between ghosts and fires and intrigue, and of course, her delight at finding Jem here. Thinking of what they'd done in Bell's laboratory and the secret corridor brought a smile to her face that she tried to hide with her hand. George, nevertheless, caught it, and clearly thought her to be smiling at his telling off, judging by his scowl.

There was no opportunity to correct him, for Henrietta made a frantic shooing motion with her hand and set her son on his way with a command of, "Go, George. I'm entirely too horrified by what you have done to look at you."

Jane waited until the tea was poured and George had vanished into the depths of the library before mouthing, "Heavens, whatever has he done?"

Eliza leaned in, equally eager to hear the answer

but dubious whether they would hear the truth. After what she'd witnessed between Linfield and George, it seemed to her there were matters afoot that Henrietta might not wish to impart. That was assuming her son's sly behaviour and her current vexation were related.

"It's really nothing to be concerned over." Henrietta smoothed her brow with her fingertips. "Sons are always so taxing. You might recall I warned you of that when you have your own." She forced a smile. "But let's forget George for the time being. How are you, Jane, dear? After so many shocks, I'm astonished to see you risen. And shall we pour this tea?"

Jane at once set about pouring. "No good ever came from idling. I did not wish to remain bed-bound unnecessarily."

"Hardly unnecessarily. Jane, dear, we've all been terribly worried about you. Such shocking turns of events, and you're so dreadfully pale. Are you sure you wouldn't be better from further rest?"

How swiftly she diverted the subject away from George. It made Eliza even more curious to learn what he'd done, and whether it was related to any of the current mysteries at Cedarton.

"Her pallor is likely down to the lack of daylight. This whole house is steeped in gloom. It will be a relief when this fog clears, and we can all venture outdoors and enjoy the gardens. I for one am looking forward to a trekking up onto the surrounding moors."

Eliza's statement was met with a look of absolute

horror. Henrietta, she concluded, was the sort who took a conveyance even to cross a square in order to visit a neighbour and would be horrified to learn that Eliza regularly wore out her soles by hiking miles across the open countryside.

"I did so desire your company too," Jane added, handing Henrietta a cup. "There are things I wanted to ask you, woman to woman, for I find myself sadly uninformed about certain matters, and that doesn't seem at all proper. I thought you might be able to shed some light on them."

"Oh, my girl! You poor, uneducated blossom." She clasped a soft hand to her ample bosom. "Of course, I will aid you in whatever manner you desire." She shot a glance at Eliza. "But perhaps such talk is best conducted purely between ourselves." She continued to turn her head to look between Eliza and Jane and muttered something about married women.

Eliza choked back a laugh, that she turned into a cough. "Crumbs," she explained. "Caught in my throat." She lifted her tea, and took a gulp, before taking the cup and saucer with her over to the window bay. Outside, the fog remained thick and isolating. Never mind trekking the moors, as soon as it cleared, she intended to head into the village and seek out the maid who'd been scared off.

"I didn't mean..." Jane began.

"Oh, it's quite all right." Henrietta patted the back of her hand. "You are still newlywed. What is it that..."

"Actually, you and George were the first to reach

me after my shock the other night. I wondered what you saw."

"Saw? Why not a thing, I assure you. You fell into a faint in George's arms, or rather I should say he caught you. Likely he saved you a nasty bump. I guess the great lummox has his qualities. I'll not let it be said that I didn't bring him up to be a proper gentleman. We heard you cry, dear. We'd been in my room talking, and he rose in a trice, ran straight out to you, and a good thing too. I followed; I'll admit rather more timidly. Then, everyone else arrived hardly a moment later. I didn't see a thing, I'm afraid."

"Not a shadow? Something out of place?"

Henrietta decisively shook her head, then sipped her tea.

"I'm sorry that you rose from your bed simply to ask me that."

"No, no, It's fine. There are some other things too."

"I'm afraid I can tell you nothing of the fire. I was near last to arrive. I suppose the girl's been dismissed. Silly creature. Awfully clumsy. The result could have been dire."

"I didn't mean that, and if it was just a clumsy accident, then I think we might extend her a second chance and be glad if she stayed on." Jane raised her head to seek Eliza's backup. "We're too many for the few servants here as is without dismissing them and causing discord. No, what I want to ask you about is why we're here at Cedarton?"

"Why we're..." Henrietta's mouth closed tight,

while her hand jiggled, causing tea to fill the saucer. For a moment, Eliza thought she would bring the saucer to her lips as she herself would have done if she were home before the kitchen fire, but instead Henrietta set the porcelain aside. "Whatever do you imagine... I'm sure I don't know anything. Not more than you, Jane, or even Eliza, who has only been with us since yestereve."

Unrelenting, Jane pressed again. "But something happened in London, did it not, that caused Linfield to insist on us coming here? I feel certain you must know what it is. Won't you share that knowledge with us?"

"Oh! Oh, you mean that. Why I thought... you mean, you don't know? But talk in town has been of little else."

"I have not been in London. Our marriage took place in York."

"I see. Well."

Jane levelled her guest with doleful eyes. "You see, I'm quite oblivious. I beg you to take pity. Won't you enlighten us?"

"My dear, of course. Yes." She nodded her head as she took a tight hold of Jane's hand. "You should of course know all. I cannot believe... Why that man! To think that he has not told you, his wife." She settled herself like a nesting hen. "You must know I'm not one for gossip, but there has been a deal of speculation about the incident. It was an accident of course. You must not imagine that you're wed to a murderer."

"Beg your pardon!" Eliza gasped, returning in a

hurry from the window bay. She pressed a reassuring touch to Jane's shoulders, and found her friend seated with a rigid spine.

Henrietta seemed to be enjoying the discomposure she'd prompted. She was fluffed up and literally bursting to get her words out. "It's all quite frightful. Are you sure I can't spare you the details? Perhaps we could talk of something else. I heard the groundsman talking to one of the maids earlier, about a gang of smugglers operating hereabouts."

Smugglers! They were at least thirty miles from the sea.

"Henrietta, won't you please tell us about London and whatever has transpired?" Eliza settled on the arm of Jane's chair. She had not minded Henrietta much before this point, but her tolerance for the woman was rapidly decaying. She was the most intolerable tease, drawing this out, and making them work to hear whatever disturbing wisdom she had to depart for the sake of dramatics. It was surely for dramatics.

"Dear Jane," Henrietta clasped both her hands tightly. "Let me put this to you in the most straightforward manner as possible. A woman died, and while Linfield cannot possibly be seen as culpable, it was his phaeton that struck her."

It was clear from the anguish on Jane's face that the words 'culpable' and 'murder' were still ringing in her ears exactly as Henrietta intended them to. "Perhaps you might start at the beginning of this tale rather than it's centre."

"Of course, Miss Wakefield. Jane, you may not be aware, but your husband is a sportsman with a passion for carriage racing."

"Wait!" Eliza hopped onto her feet again. "I read about this in the newspaper. A woman ran into the path of the racing carriages and was struck. I believe she died at the scene."

"Yes. Yes, exactly that," Henrietta huffed, evidently put out to have the story stolen from her, but equally determined to steal it back. Eliza only too happily let her, choosing only to add helpful additions to better steer the narrative, and ensure Henrietta left nothing out.

"Oh, but this is frightful," Jane said, tears brewing in her pretty eyes.

"Very." Henrietta agreed, still clutching Jane's hand. "George witnessed the whole thing, being part of the race. He managed to swerve to avoid her, but Linfield hadn't the time. His horses ploughed straight into her, and the carriage did the rest of her work. Cut her down and broke her neck." She made the sign of the cross. "God rest her soul. Doctor Bell attended to her, along with the other fellow, Whistler."

Jem had witnessed this.

"It's frightful. Truly frightful, but you mustn't fret over it, Jane. It will all blow over soon enough, as these things inevitably do, and you can go back to London. There really isn't any question of it being his fault."

"His fault. Why would anyone even suggest it was his fault that a stranger ran out in front of him?"

"I'm sure I didn't mean to suggest—"

"Then why would you say it?"

Henrietta threw up her hands. "I was simply repeating what others have said. I didn't mean to suggest I thought him responsible. Though I do question the need for gentlemen to turn every blessed thing into a sporting event. All they care for are wagers and..." Her words petered out. "My apologies. We all have our little flash points, and gambling does tend to spur me into a froth. So wasteful, and entirely unnecessary."

"Is that why you are vexed with George?"

"I beg your pardon, Miss Wakefield. Whatever are you implying?"

"Nothing. I'm sorry. I think I misheard what you were saying. Forgive me." She gave the older woman a curtsy.

"Yes, well."

"Linfield's not in debt, is he?" Jane half rose from her seat in alarm. Eliza nudged her back down again, by thrusting a plate of cake at her. Her friend's sweet tooth instantly won.

"Linfield? Heavens no," Henrietta gave an awkward little chortle. "Of course not." She stood. "Do you mind awfully if I go, Jane, dear? I fear I have a frightful headache coming on. I should probably seek out Doctor Bell and see if he can't provide something."

"Of course. Eliza, maybe you could—"

"I'll see Doctor Bell at once."

"Mrs Cluett," Eliza called, bringing her exit to a momentary halt. "What was the name of the girl? I can't seem to recall it."

"The girl?" She blinked at Eliza as if she were a boggart straight off the moors. "I'm sure I don't know. Fairfield, Furlough, Finlay, was it? It hasn't stuck in my head. I don't know why you imagine it would."

"How awful to be cut down so cruelly and not to be remembered," Jane remarked once Henrietta was gone. "Why do you think she did it? And why did you ask Henrietta her name?"

Eliza cast herself into the seat the older woman had vacated. It was lumpen and not terribly comfortable and had the sort of back that induced one to slouch. "I don't suppose we'll ever know her reasoning."

"Addled in the head, do you think?"

"Oh, yes, delicate and hysterical, I imagine. Isn't that always reportedly the case?" She sighed, vexed by the injustices of the world. As if anyone ever ran into the path of a carriage without a sane and sound reason. "I just wondered if she knew it. I don't know, Jane, none of it seems at all connected to what's going on here at Cedarton, but somehow, I'm sure it must be. Did you see how prickly Henrietta was at the suggestion that Georgie was in debt? I think him swerving to avoid that girl cost him far more than the race."

"Maybe, though you did rather insult her."

She'd merely been plainspoken. "I saw George rifling through the desk drawers in Linfield's study the night afore last and watched them knock one another about over it. George was looking for something. He didn't find it, but he found something, and whatever it was made Linfield fiercely cross. I'm not sure that it was just money that George lost."

"Do you think Henrietta knows?"

"Of course she knows. That's why she was so out of sorts with him."

"Well, what do you think he lost?"

"I don't know. I'm not sure it even matters, outside of it being a motive for mischief." In truth, she was more interested in whatever it was that George had found and that he'd refused to hand over to Linfield.

Meanwhile, Jane had left her chair to rummage in the sideboard. She straightened after a moment, triumphant, an old newspaper clutched in her hand. "Here, there's a piece about the race. It seems some other fellow won. Just nipped ahead of Linfield due to the collision, but doesn't that mean...? Wait, it says the result was declared void, and no winner was named. So maybe your theory of debt isn't right."

"They might have made a wager between themselves, separate to the overall outcome of the race." Eliza perused the article over Jane's shoulder. It was the same one she'd read before. The details were scant, and largely concentrated on the race, rather than the poor woman's untimely death. However, Henrietta had mentioned Jem's presence at the event, so she meant to find him and ask him about it. She wouldn't leave Jane here alone though.

"You know, I'm inclined to agree with Henrietta," her friend declared. "What the devil is the point in it all? Why wager something you can ill afford to lose?"

"External pressure. Isn't that the reason why most of us cave in to doing things we really oughtn't? You wouldn't be tied to Linfield otherwise, nor he to you, and then you wouldn't be here in harm's way."

"It could simply be coincidence that I'm the one who's seen the ghost, and my bed curtain's catching fire."

Eliza huffed, grateful at least that her friend hadn't suggested a supernatural cause.

"Also, I don't rightly see what George owing Linfield money has to do with me."

Nor did she, but she was certain there was a connection. Something connected all the things going on.

"You're cogitating," Jane said. "Have some cake, it might help. Cake always helps me to think things over." She mopped the crumbs from the plate she was holding, then helped herself to another slice.

Eliza didn't require cake. She needed to talk to Jem. There was no way to unravel this puzzle without all the pieces, and presently she was missing far too many of them.

-17-

Eliza

Although she'd been reluctant to leave Jane unattended, Eliza realised it would be impossible for them to spend every moment together, and indeed, neither of them would want such an attachment. They were both independent women in their own ways, and so after they'd drained the teapot, Jane had taken the remainder of the cake through to the Lady's parlour where the light was better, and she had her lace-making things laid out on a cushion. Eliza had watched her manipulation of the bobbins for several minutes. It was a skill she'd never mastered herself and could find little patience to learn, but one she admired. The constant motion though was lulling and soon her eyelids began to sag. Startled to her feet by the act of dozing off, she declared the need for a walk and Jane waved her on her way.

As it remained decidedly inclement outdoors, Eliza proposed to take herself on a tramp about the castle's rambling architecture with the dual purpose of poking into its many corners and secrets while simultaneously tracking down Jem without being seen to be seeking him out. Alas, she did not find him on her walkabout in any of Cedarton's many reception rooms, which was how she eventually found herself outside of Bell's surgery in the basement.

"Miss Wakefield?" Bell opened the door to his lair, a book open in his hand, which he snapped shut on seeing her and peered at her down the length of his hooked nose. His wig was slightly askew, making her suspect it had been hastily plopped back on his head in response to her knock. "Is there something you require my assistance with? Having been regaled with your skills, I find that somewhat unlikely. Is this perhaps a courtesy call? Have you come to tell me you've cured all the local ails, and my services are no longer required by his lordship?"

He still sounded haughty, but somewhat less hostile than on their initial introduction. He was, she thought, poking fun at himself as much as her. Nevertheless, she could not entirely warm to him.

"I wondered if you knew where I could locate Mr Whistler?"

"Of course you did. He is a very sought-after fellow." He seemed about to send her on her way, when he instead took a step back and pushed the door open wide so that she was able to see inside the surgery. "*Et voilà!*"

The chaise had been displaced to beneath the high, narrow window which currently bled a meagre drizzle of light on Jem tinkering with a set of chemical apparatus. His outfit was of deep, dark, green, and he was without coat or neckcloth, stripped to his shirtsleeves, which in turn were rolled up to his elbows, revealing them to be covered in a fine dappling of golden-brown hairs.

There was something supremely enchanting about catching him so dishabille.

Too often, she'd despaired over those whose heads were turned so readily, but Jem... Jem seemed to generate his own gravitational field that drew her in, and as much as she wanted to declare that it was wholly his genius that generated that attraction, truthfully, simply gazing at him filled her with all manner of soft indefinable feelings, and a longing to brush up against him as a cat might do.

It was that desperate pull that also stalled her from striding straight past Bell. She could not let her attraction to Jem get in the way of her plans. They had agreed to mutual exploration, but she would have to keep a fast check on herself to avoid growing unhelpful emotions. Therefore, she forced herself to stall their meeting, and used that moment to study him at work instead.

"Maybe I shouldn't interrupt."

Bell coughed into his fist. "Chemistry is not his natural occupation. It's taken some considerable effort to get to this point. I daresay he might be pleased of someone to show it off to."

She was intrigued. "Is it something to do with his puffing devils?"

"Lord, if only," Bell gave a dry chuckle, and ushered her in so that he could finally close the door behind her.

Jem must have heard them, for he turned toward them, his eyes flashing green and gold. A grin then stretched across his face, broad and welcoming. "Eliza." He made come hither motions until she joined him by the table. "You'll excuse my state of dress, I trust. I thought you busy with Lady Linfield, or I'd have hunted you down to assist with all this. Brewing potions is more your field, I think, than mine. Really, I could use the expertise of my cousin Pip, but I think I have this all working nicely now. The heat source has been the worst of it."

Indeed, it was her forte, at least in terms of brewing herbal remedies. "Should I be donning an apron?" Doctor Bell passed her exactly such an item. It was of the sort more usually found on a butcher but served the desired purpose of keeping her clothing clean. "What is this? Not your usual sort of experiment." A flame sat heating a bubbling vessel, from which a glass pipe led to another larger vessel situated upside down in a vat of hot water. She had seen depictions of such arrangements attributed to Lavoisier for the collection of gases.

"No, the mysteries of steam and pressure have been sidelined in favour of chemistry today. I have one of Davy's pamphlets." Jem rustled through a sheaf of papers covered in scrawled calculations but didn't seem to find what he was looking for, until he looked up and spied Bell and the book. The doctor had reopened it and was studying its pages again.

"Ah, you have it. Do you know of him, Eliza? Not Bell, I mean, Davy. In his role as a superintendent of the medical pneumatic society he's been studying the effects of an array of newly separated gases. This is what I'm trying to replicate."

Of course, she had heard of Davy. He was busy shaking up many of the fundamentals of chemistry, and while she wasn't as well versed in the subject as she'd like to be, she did follow along as best she could.

"Will it help drive your engine?"

"Oh, heavens no. No, I don't think so. These are his instructions for the preparation of nitrous oxide. And the study of its effects on the body. The earlier preparations involved zinc, which would have been a problem as I don't have any, but the later ones involve bubbling nitrate of ammoniac though water and then collecting the gas." He pointed out the inverted jar.

"I see, but to what purpose?"

Jem frowned, but quickly shrugged off the question and gave her a smile. "Well, you may have heard tell of laughing gas. It's been quite the thing in certain circles of late."

She had. Her friend Bella Rushdale, now the Marchioness of Pennerley had written to them of an evening soiree she'd attended with Lord Pennerley and all manner of artists and bohemians, where silken balloons containing the substance were passed around, and had succeeded in making everyone quite giddy and dreadfully merry. "And this is that?"

He nodded with great enthusiasm. "So then, are you saying Lord Linfield demands you produce it to use as a form of entertainment?"

Doctor Bell gave a curious guffaw. Whereupon he and Jem exchanged equally curious glances that ended with Jem shaking his head, and Bell relinquishing the book into his hands. This Jem immediately passed to Eliza and turned out to be Davy's treatise on the subject, published only the year before.

"In a sense. However, you needn't worry. His intention isn't to pass it around his guests. It's purely for his personal consumption. And he didn't so much deliver me the task as I suggested the experiment."

"Because he cannot wait until he returns to town to sample its effects?"

Lips pursed and cheeks sucked in, Jem seemed to be determinedly fighting off a smirk. "I guess you might say that's about the gist of it. Linfield's not what you'd call a patient man. What he wants, he generally wants right now."

That was usually the case with the aristocracy; impatience was baked into their marrow. At least it was a relief to find Linfield wasn't intending to cajole his guests and his poor wife into partaking of this newly discovered laughing gas. Fortunately, but slightly bilking too, since it would mean she'd be deprived of the opportunity to experience the effects for herself, out of a purely academic interest, of course.

"Will you not sample it too?"

Jem nodded at once. "Oh, definitely. Any true scientist knows that you ought to verify outcomes and potencies for oneself." He tapped a finger against the pages of the open book in her hands. "There are a range of reported effects according to this study. The only way I can be certain I've collected the correct gas is to test it by inhaling and verifying the results."

How quick he was to smile. How full of vitality he seemed in that moment. The very air around him seemed to thrum with excitement. This was how she'd observed him in the engine sheds at Stags Fell as she showed off his workspace, his engines, and the rudimentary plans to create his own puffing devil locomotive.

"Options besides dosing yourself are available," Bell remarked. "It is not always necessary to experiment on oneself, or even advisable."

"In your line, perhaps," Jem replied.

"Practicalities abound."

"Yes, I don't suppose one can really extract one's own heart in order to poke about in the vessels to determine how it malfunctions." Eliza's remark succeeded in making both men gawp at her. Jem's surprised gurn cracked first. "Oh, I think she has the right of you there, Bell. You do like to poke around in viscera."

Bell rolled his eyes. The tilt of his head set his wig at an even more alarming angle. Irritably, he straightened it. "You might be more thankful for my studies. If it were not for myself and other anatomists, medicine would not be progressing, and the various quacks and charlatans would still hold reign with their archaic notions of humours and bloodletting."

"I'm delighted to find you don't hold to those practices," Eliza said. "For it is a novelty to be sure to find a physician who doesn't rely entirely upon cupping and drawing as if it were some magical panacea. I only pity the poor souls whose cadavers you torture to obtain such knowledge."

"I see you question my ethics, Miss Wakefield."

Indeed, she did. Ludlow Bell was precisely the sort of carrion crow that paid to have decent folks' endless peace disturbed by having them dug out of their graves and dissected on his table like giant joints of meat.

"A body is but worm food, Miss Wakefield. It is of no practical use to its previous owner, and I should think as a self-proclaimed scientist, you should appreciate that in order to mend a thing, one must first understand how it is that God intended it to function. Only then can one determine how disease, poverty, and malnutrition can alter that vessel."

She did understand that, but bodysnatching had become a worrisome hazard of death.

"I suppose you're a pickler, Doctor Bell. Are you a pickler?"

"Only if there's a purpose to the pickling. Preservation for the purposes of study, or comparison is wise, as is it beneficial to catalogue the mutations and deviations from the norm. Pickling things purely for non-scientific or monetary purposes, I cannot condone. But the trade of organs, teeth and the like is hardly a new fad. The church has always encouraged such things in the form of relics."

"That is hardly the same."

"It is exactly the same."

"My friends," Jem stepped between them. "Must we be so hostile to one another? Might we not put aside our differences of opinion and focus on the experiment happening before us? Eliza, perhaps you'd be so good as to take some notes for me? Bell—"

"It rather seems that my assistance is unnecessary. You have yourself a scribe, what more could you need? I have matters of my own I can attend to." He stalked off in a long-legged stride, a deep frown etching his face that made his skeletal slenderness all the more pronounced.

"He's awfully pompous," Eliza remarked of his disappearing silhouette.

Jem looked up from his task of adjusting various portions of his apparatus. "I think you scare him."

"What could he possibly find terrifying about me?"

"Fears for his livelihood, I should imagine. Eliza, one only has to know you for a short while to realise how terrifyingly bright and adept you are. If a marquis chose you over a physician, and Bell is by no means the only one trained in progressive methods, then surely that's a sign that their days as an exclusive club are numbered."

"Not while women remain barred from the universities and lecture halls."

He nodded. "I concede that is an issue, but it is not the case everywhere. They may be few in number, but there are women now with university degrees in both philosophy and medicine."

"Barely a handful compared to the many, many men, and none here in Britain, only in Sweden, and Bologna, and other such far places. They may as well be on the moon, for they are just as inaccessible to me as an orb in the sky."

"You could learn Italian," he said. She was tempted to kick him, but he was fiddling with the equipment, and she didn't wish to disrupt his experiment. The acquisition of another language would not swallow up the distance between a foreign university and her beloved Yorkshire.

"My French is barely passable. It would likely be a waste of my efforts to attempt another language as well. No, I shall keep up with my studies as I've always done and learn from books and the other resources around me."

He nodded. "I didn't mean to insinuate otherwise or tell you what to do. You may borrow that book, if you like, once I am done here. Though I warn you, you may be horrified by the number of lives sacrificed to the cause."

"Lives?"

"Small mammals, primarily. Though there are sections of study dedicated to the effects of various gases on fish and reptiles too."

"I see," she said. "Poor beasts. It's such a shame that progress must come at such a gristly cost." Normally she'd have her nose thrust inside such a tome immediately, but the live experiment being conducted before her currently held her attention. "Is your gas ready?"

He nodded. "I think it may be." From under a sheaf of papers, he produced a waxed silk bag. This he attached to the glass apparatus by means of a tube attached to a small tap in the vessel where the gas was collected. "Are you sure I can't tempt you to partake in this experiment along with me? One of Davy's observations is that it opens the mind to endless possibilities. He found his thoughts awash with unique ideas and all manner of possibilities."

She was tempted, for knowledge of all kinds was indispensable, but nervous too of filling her head with vapours and having her thoughts slide away from her. Cedarton was a dangerous place to not be in full possession of one's faculties. She'd taken tincture of poppies once, to ascertain its effectiveness in numbing pain, and experienced its benefits, but saw also how it melted the mind, as did so many other remedies recommended and described by both Culpepper and Elizabeth Blackwell.

"Don't feel I am pressuring you. You may make your decision after I've taken a good dose of it, and you've witnessed the effects."

He bled off some of the collected gas, until the small bag inflated. Then, once the tap was shut off, Jem nipped closed the neck of the sack. "If you could turn to a new page for me, then I'd appreciate you transcribing any observations and findings. Davy reports taking up to twenty quarts, and regularly imbibing six, but I think what we have here will be more than sufficient for this trial and to satisfy Linfield's requirements. At least, hopefully."

He brought the bag to his lips and covered both his mouth and nose. Eliza watched his cheeks grow flushed, and a smile crept over his face. His eyes shone bright making the hazel tones stand out against the deeper, forest green.

"How does it feel? Is it acting in the way you expected?"

Jem seemed to struggle with the formation of words for a moment. He moved his tongue around his mouth and over his teeth, before finally bringing his fingers to his lips. "Presently, it's all in my head, making it feel strangely thick. I would not describe it as a particularly pleasurable—Oh! Oh, wait. It's spreading." He stretched out his arms and proceeded to weave patterns in the air with his digits. "That is curious, and—" He brought the bag back to his mouth and took another few deep inhalations. "It is most curiously pleasant, especially in the extremities. I don't quite know how to best describe it."

"All of your extremities or just some of them?" Eliza enquired, while doing her best to both keep an eye on him and transcribe his thoughts precisely and concisely. The nib of his pencil was worn and made her writing smudgy, but there was no pen or ink to hand.

"Most all." Jem continued to weave his patterns for several moments. "It subsides disappointingly quickly. I suppose this is why Davy reports inhaling for up to twenty minutes. It is curiously freeing though." He seemed to be fighting to spit out his words now. "My mind is quite open. There are so many thoughts. Such clarity." He took yet another draft.

"But what is the purpose of it? What is its practical application? Please tell me this is not simply a study in depriving yourself of reasoned thought."

"My paymaster's purposes I'm not at liberty to depart."

"Is it for a medicinal purpose, or a recreational one? Tell me that at least."

Jem dragged a nearby stool to him and balanced on its surface. The dreamy expression on his face lingered, and as he raised the bag to his lips to inhale again, Eliza found herself reaching out and staying his hand.

"Is he ill? Is Linfield unwell? Is that why he's here at Cedarton?"

"Eliza cease. You're asking for knowledge that I'm truly not at liberty to reveal."

"So, he is sick?"

"No."

"Then tell me why he has not bedded Jane."

He coughed, and his cough turned into a laugh.

"Nothing, but nothing escapes you, does it? I suppose she has told you that. I told him that she wasn't so ill-informed as he liked to think. Even the most modest of maids have some notion of what occurs in the marriage bed, unless they are city bred and entirely without ears or eyes."

"Jem, she is my friend. I will not have you disparage her."

"Lord, no, I mean her no disrespect. A woman

ought to know these things. I think it's scandalous that so many are so desperately uneducated. I only mean to say that Linfield imagines her so thoroughly green that she'll believe any old nonsense he feeds her. I think she is probably rather wiser than he."

"You are talking in riddles."

"That is probably for the best."

She observed him for some minutes more, jotting down her observations of his appearance. He took to waddling around the laboratory as if he couldn't quite decide where to put his feet but following a more or less clockwise direction around the worktable. Occasionally, he would mutter a few words, or release a chuckle. When he reattached the waxen sack to fill it a second time, Eliza slid her hand over his, which caused him to stare most intently at the point of contact.

"I think I might like to try it."

His head twitched to one side.

"Unless there is some inherent danger of which I'm unaware?"

He gave his head a miniscule shake, then swallowed so that she could see his Adam's apple bob. "Davy records the results of several women partaking, and none describe ill effects, only amplification of their general disposition. Those who are of a flighty and delicate nature, react as flighty, delicate creatures are wont to. But Eliza, you have never been those things."

"Indeed, I should think not. Shall it make me giddy?"

"It's heady," he replied. "But come rest against

me as you breathe, in case you should feel the need to fall into repose." It seemed to her that of the two of them, he was more likely to fall into indolence. Jem moved them over to the chaise and sank against its backrest. Rather shockingly, he positioned her so that she rested her back to his body. "I'll cover both your mouth and nose. Deep even breaths," he murmured soft against her ear. "Get it right to the bottom of your lungs."

The effects stole through her body from her chest to her toes, creating a sense of muscular power. However, it was not a thrill in her extremities she experienced, but rather an abrupt and involuntary urge to laugh. This she did the moment the bag was removed from her lips, while the tip of her nose tingled, and her cheeks warmed as they might when coming into a warm kitchen after a walk on a frosty morn.

"What is so funny?"

Jem's words whispered against her ear made it tingle in turn, as if his breath were possessed of feathered fingers, and each was caressing the skin in a way that filled it with delight.

"You did say it was called laughing gas."

"I did."

"I can't stop myself," she giggled, and touched her lips with her fingertips, as if by doing so she might control herself.

It did not work.

"What do you feel, Eliza? I'm finding my thoughts are much diverted, and it's difficult to remain focused on what remains external, the internal calls so loudly. But then, you are here, and you are in here." He tapped his skull. "My thoughts are all of earlier. What we did. Eliza, there's so much more I want to do with you. So very much more." His lips grazed the back of her neck. "You don't regret it, do you?"

"Of course not. Why would you think—?"

"Only, that I feel such a cad. Eliza, you must know that I want you to be mine. I want to know you in all ways, and for us to be together. I can't stop thinking about you. My head is bursting with you, and every detail of earlier. How your mouth felt wrapped around my cock. The heat of it. The taste of myself on your tongue. Friggin' your pearl yestereve. I want to do it again. To lick you. Kiss you. Touch you. To bring you the same measure of pleasure. Nay, even more, for you deserve to be worshipped."

"Jem," she chuckled. "Perhaps you have imbibed a little too much."

"Not at all. The effects subside rather quickly. I'm speaking only the truth. I adore you. You're the most intoxicating of creatures that ever lived. There's never been a woman in my life to whom I've felt such a desperate affinity. I was so, so sure that Joshua would have won you. Christ, I wish that I could give you the life you wish. I would do so in a heartbeat. All the learning you might desire, and all the acknowledgement too."

What else could she possibly do but smile at such at notion? "You enthral me too, Jem. You are not like other men of my acquaintance, you are not pompous and over-inflated in your opinions, you delight in the workings of the world as I do, and you see me. You never belittle my accomplishments."

"Belittle them? I should like to sing them to the heavens."

"Yes, but don't," she said, turning and catching hold of his hand as he made to raise them and exalt her to the ceiling. In so doing, she knocked the bag from his hand, which escaped across the floor, emptying its contents into the air of the room. "Drat," he muttered.

"I'm sorry, I didn't mean—"

Jem put his hands over hers. "It doesn't matter. There's more brewing, and I think I have the measure of its effects."

They both stared at their entwined digits. To Eliza it felt hopelessly right. "If you wish him mirth it will surely bring it, or do you mean to open his mind?"

"Ah." Jem's teeth rasped against his lower lip. "It's a rather delicate topic. Might we avoid it? I don't wish to think of Linfield when I am with you, anyway. I'd rather think of us, and all the things we might do together." His expression sobered a fraction. "But what of Joshua?"

"What of him, Jem? I have not heard a whisper from him since that day. It seems so long ago, and so impossible as to have been anything more than a daydream."

"It was not. I was there." His look said he could still feel the collision of their lips as vividly as she did. "Then, may I kiss you?"

"May you? Lud, I thought you'd never ask. I

should like that very much. But wait." She stayed him with her hand against his chest. "What of Doctor Bell?"

"Bell? Ah, yes, Bell." Jem shot a glance over her shoulder, but he didn't turn his head. "He won't disturb us."

"Jem, he's right next door."

"You're right." He hollered. "Ludlow, don't you dare come in."

Eliza covered her mouth with her hands, then laughed, her incredulity infectious, so that they were both beset by giggles.

"I can't believe you did that? Whatever will he think?"

Jem caught her hand. Raised it and kissed her knuckles. "Do you know, I don't actually care. He may imagine whatever he wishes. We will know the truth, and that's all that really matters."

"And what is the truth?"

His arms slid around her. "That I want you all to myself for now and always."

"Is that so?" She challenged him with the arch of a brow.

"Aye, it is so. Will you come up here?" He patted his lap, only when she rose to oblige, he lifted his legs onto the chaise. "Straddle me, as a man would a horse."

"Next, you'll propose that I ride you like one. I thought you wished to kiss me."

A flush rose through his neck into his cheeks. "You see into my head. God, Eliza. I swear my prick's crying out for you. And yes to kissing. Don't you recognise a man when he's desperate?" He tugged her down on top of him and stole the air from her lungs as his kisses teased the seam of her lips, and his tongue led hers in a merry dance. They were both breathless and still lively as spring lambs when they pulled apart.

"Should I kiss you elsewhere too?" She reached for his falls, eager to reacquaint herself with that part of him too. Feeling the velvet heat of his prick before had only cemented her desire to further explore the relations that happened between a man and a woman, and how such connections came about in practice.

"What he'd most like is to slide deep into your cunny."

"How scandalously you speak." Their mouths were mere inches apart now, her straddled over him, his hands, one on her waist and one beneath her skirts, on the bare flesh of her thigh above her stocking top. He ticked a finger from side to side across her skin. "Are you in fact, a roué, sir? Set on deflowering me?"

"I confess, such a temptation has crossed my thoughts."

"But surely not, you being such an upstanding and studious gent."

"I fear I'm not the man you believe me to be, although I am both upstanding and studious."

"And what man is that, besides the one I want?"

"Eliza."

She pressed a finger to his lips. "Just kiss me again."

Her hands clamped around the back of his head, pulling him closer. For a second a fear stole through her of what he must think of her brazenness, but all that dissipated as she heard his groan, and his lips caressed hers.

-18-

Jem

The effects of the nitrous oxide were curious. To begin with, Jem found them irritating and somewhat dulling. His thoughts became woolly and thick. That sensation had quickly passed to be replaced with one of muscular power and invincibility that stole through his body, starting in his chest and spreading out through muscles and tendons to his extremities.

Clarity of vision, a sharpening of his senses followed, or rather his mind became unburdened. When he stubbed his toe as he moved, he found it did not hurt. No wonder Davy had collected a coterie of poetical barnacles to his person.

And then... Then there was Eliza. Eliza who was all and everything. His greatest desire and a folly he ought not to commit. It would get back to Linfield. The man had no real talents to speak of but a nose for sniffing out subversion, and Jem couldn't let that happen. He had to protect Eliza, ensure her reputation.

Simultaneously, he would not pull away from this. Here she was in his arms, a dream come true, groaning from their kisses, her agile fingers tugging on the front of his shirt as if she meant to tear it from him. This could be his one and only chance to be with her. The events Linfield might demand of him this very night were rapidly spinning his future out of control.

Lord help him. Knowing she wanted him as ardently as he wanted her only made holding back so much harder.

Would she hate him come tomorrow?

Why was everything so monstrously muddled?

He'd put such hope into the gas, imagining it was his route to freedom, but realistically, while it certainly brought a pleasant tingling to his extremities, he couldn't swear that it was responsible for his current rise. No, in all truthfulness, his current priapism was down to her. To Eliza. Her taste. Her presence. The sweet promise of her honeyed cunt enveloping his prick. She did not need to touch him. She simply needed to be. Of course, when she did touch him... Well, then there was no escaping the thrall she held him under, and nor did he desire to. Every little thing about her called to him. Her voice, the sweet-luscious curves of her body, her mind. Predominantly her mind. He loved that she was not meek, nor a mild-mannered infant dressed up and paraded as breeding stock. She had her own thoughts and her own plans, and if there were a way to give her all that she desired, he would do it in a heartbeat.

Pity then, that in truth he could offer her little more than this moment. To promise more was impossible. He had not the funds to keep her, and besides, if he was forced to comply with Linfield's diabolical plan, then she'd likely hate him forevermore.

Dammit! The only reason he'd ever fallen into Linfield's trap was because he'd been so desperately trying to relinquish his desire for Eliza... and forget Joshua, and all that had happened between the three of them that day.

Lord, did he ever want to tup her, but he was not such a cad as to go ahead and do it, not knowing that she would regret it come the morrow.

Jem broke off their kiss. Her eyes were glittering brightly. Her skirts spread all around them while she rose her puss against his eager cock. "I'm going to shuffle down the chaise. I want you to stay right where you are."

"And do what? I'll be perched practically on your shoulders if you lie flat."

"Yes," he agreed. "You could perhaps grasp the back rest here." She cocked her head perplexed, but obeyed. Jem shimmied his body down between her thighs, until his head was lost beneath her skirts. A smooth expanse of bare skin stretched from where her garters held her stockings in place to the thatch over her muff. Jem tickled the split of her cunny with his tongue then dived in deep, covering himself with her honey. It'd been a long while since he'd lain with a woman, and there'd never been any he'd cared strongly about. Such occasions had been fleeting transactions, indulged in to service an itch. This was different. Each inch of him wanted every inch of her. His cock was like rock and the rasp of his shirt over it almost painful. He didn't let it dissuade him from his goal. He meant to bring her to bliss with his mouth in the way she'd dissuaded him from doing the previous night.

"Oh! Oh!" Her gasps which started out as mere murmurs were like a siren's call to him. They spurred him to greater effort. He sucked on her nub and licked it until it stood out taut and eager for his touch, until she trembled with each passing of his tongue and then wrenched all her skirts aloft so that she could tangle her fingers in the strands of his hair and watch what he was about. "I hardly know what you are doing to me, but don't stop. I beg you, don't stop. It feels…"

"What does it feel like?"

"Like everything is becoming tight. Like it's building towards some sort of crescendo."

He purred against her skin. "Well, that is the idea. I like watching you come, Eliza." He'd left her the previous night with fire in his veins after watching her spend on his fingers, and since facing Linfield with such a stick in his breeches would have led to much hellish awkwardness, he'd tossed himself off ahead of rendezvousing in the drawing room again. Bell had won the game and compelled them all to their beds as his prize alongside taking their guineas.

"Come…" Eliza echoed, tipping back her head and giving in to the sensations. "What a curious way of putting it."

"Does it not make you feel as if you'll come apart into a myriad of pieces?"

"I think... I don't know. I may need to experience it again to properly quantify the experience."

"Then it's a good thing I'm here to serve."

Jem felt the *tick tick* of her pulse beating against his tongue, the firmness of her nub as it swelled, growing tight and hot as his prick grew tighter and hotter too. He wanted this moment more than anything else right now. This explosion would see him through the dark days that were surely ahead. He gave her pearl another long suck, then licked the flat of his tongue against her opening before jabbing the tip between her swollen lips. The taste of her exploded more fully on his tongue.

Lord, he wanted so much more.

So very much more, but he'd content himself with this. His tongue inside her opening, the gasps, and rough noises of her pleasure playing like music for his ears alone. He'd take this offering and stow the moment away in his heart.

Delving deeper with his tongue he met resistance. She was *virgo intacta*. Hardly a shock, yet it brought home exactly the manner of fire he was playing with. God help him for the fool he was, but he wanted her.

"Don't you want to put your prick in me?" Her cry was practically a siren's call for him to do just that.

"Yes," he gasped. "So much, but not here, not now, not like this." When it happened—if it happened—he wanted it to be on terms they both fully understood and were happy with. He would not have her regret it afterwards. He would not have the memory of their first time together tarnished by the secrets he held. Truthfully, he wasn't worthy. But still, he was taking what little he dared. Fucking her with his tongue, his arms curled around her thighs pulling her fast to his mouth, sealing them together so that when he felt the rush against his tongue and her cries sang out, he was right there with her until the very last pulse of it died.

She sagged with a cry, her fist pulled tight against her lips, as she slithered down his body to kiss him while his lips and chin were still covered in her dew. "I feel almost completely boneless, like I should just like to lie here for an age and hold you fast." She lay against him as if to do precisely that. "Yet, part of me is still eager and desirous of more. I know how to make sure there are no unwanted surprises from us lying together, so you needn't fear, if that's what holds you back."

He brushed the escaped wisps of her hair back from her face. Her eyes were shiny, alight with desire and love he didn't deserve. "Bell is still next door."

It was an unnecessary reminder. Ludlow would not disturb them. Likely enough the fellow had his eye to the keyhole, which was reason enough not to strip every inch of fabric from her and tumble her until they were both so exhausted that they could do nothing but fall asleep. However, it was also an acknowledgement that the world existed outside of these humble laboratory walls.

"But we surely cannot leave you so" —she traced a line along the length of his shaft— "risen."

"I will not prick you now, Eliza."

The fine row of her teeth dug into her lower lip. "Then, will you at least allow me to lie here beside you and watch you toss yourself off."

He coughed out an 'O' of surprise, then lifted his head to better look at her tucked against his shoulder. "You want to watch me toss myself."

She was all impish delight. "Aye. I do. Rather fiercely to be truthful. It's something I've wondered over. I know it's a thing that men do. Why even the smallest of boys seem to have a rapacious fondness for playing with their bits."

"I prefer not to think of small boys, but you are not wrong. Big boys like playing with their cocks too."

Impudent miss that she was, she reached down and tugged his shirt tails out of the way so that his erect prick was displayed in all its glory. "Show me."

He laughed, though nevertheless cupped himself. "You want me to show you how I coax myself into spending, is that right, Miss Wakefield?" he asked, stroking up from the base to the tip. "Is this a serious study? Shall you take notes?"

She bopped him on the nose. "It most definitely is, Mr Whistler. I will restrict myself to observations and record my findings later. Will you shoot yourself in the eye, do you think?"

"With you here watching? Aye, I just might."

Her gaze remained rapt upon him as he stroked, though it flitted between his hand and his face. Jem knew he'd pinkened around the cheeks over the scrutiny, but her presence coupled with her studious, yet excited expression kept him focused on the task. Did he draw it out a little, make a show of it for her? Well, of course he did. Who the hell wouldn't? Linfield sometimes got it into his head to make Jem stand about in the altogether tossing himself, but that was about power not fascination. There was no love in that act, whereas now it was all about the connection.

"It's coming," he warned her, his breathing getting away from him so that his words became drawn out, the syllables stretched by the pleasure congregating at the base of his cock. She watched him come apart. And while he didn't shoot himself in the eye, he did make a proper mess of his waistcoat.

Eliza provided him with her handkerchief, a large practical cotton square embroidered at the corner with her initial. As he made to mop himself off, she leaned over and kissed him. "Your eyes are so shiny right now, and so green at the centres. Thank you for showing me."

"Did you like the display?"

She rolled over and hopped off the chaise, shaking out her skirts. Much of her hair had come loose from its pins. "I did. Rather a lot. I think I should like to see it again. Perhaps with you naked as a newborn."

"Being naked as a newborn with you certainly appeals." He straightened his clothing out as best he could, though he had to abandon the waistcoat. Then he went to check on the chemical equipment. It was still bubbling away merrily, though he suspected he had more than enough nitrous oxide now to send Linfield into a state of extreme theatricality. Perhaps that would even be a good thing. Not because it would enable him to fuck his wife, but because he might be rendered so indolent in his rapture as to forget to summon Jem to assist with the task.

-19-

Eliza

The scream curdled Eliza's thoughts. She knew at once from whose throat it had been torn. "Jane!"

She had barely righted her clothes before Bell streaked across the room without so much as an *excuse me*. Both she and Jem sprinted after him into the corridor. They caught up to him in the subterranean passage Eliza had heard the servants describe as the rat-run.

"Why have you slowed? Let me through." Eliza made to elbow her way ahead, but Bell stayed her with a hand clasped about her upper arm.

"Straighten your hair, Miss Wakefield. Whatever mischief is afoot won't be helped by you appearing disorderly, that much is assured." She reached a hand to it and found the coil of it that had previously been fastened at the nape of her neck partially unwound. This she restored with the adjustment of several pins.

"I can hear Linfield. Discord amidst the

newlyweds?" Jem said, arriving at their heels. He'd taken the time to pull on his topcoat, but he was still missing his cravat, nor had his shirt been fastened at the neck. "Eliza, your earbob." He passed her the jewel that she hadn't noticed was even missing.

"I fear it likely something of that nature," Bell's bewigged head was tilted to better hear the rumpus. "There is never a moment of peace in this place. Not a blasted one. If it's not arguments, it's phantoms, and if it's not phantoms it's melodramatic maids or our fair hostess taking another turn." He advanced a couple of steps, before straightening up and proceeding with his usual long-legged stride. "Miss Wakefield. Jem, I think we might advance to the stairs. The wailer I believe is Mrs Cluett, not Lady Linfield, and if I'm not mistaken, young George has embroiled himself too. No doubt rallied to his mother's cause."

"So not a marital tiff." A deal of tension seemed to fall from Jem's shoulders.

"I definitely heard Jane."

"Then I fear whatever has occurred must have embroiled them all."

"I pray that we're not about to walk into the aftermath of another spectral visitation," Jem said. "They are most perplexing, and I do not care for the puzzle of it. In fact, I do not care for any more supernatural nonsense at all. Whoever is playing these games must desist in them."

"Then you truly believe this all a person's work?"

"Of course," he shot back, prompting Eliza to exchange a look with Bell. She did not truly doubt that fact for herself, only a part of her wondered. There were no explanations to be had for Jane's visions, nor her bed curtains' spontaneous ignition. She believed the maid. Matter of fact, she readily believed her testament over any other given her by the inhabitants of this place.

"Is that your opinion too, sir?"

Bell tugged on the end of his ringleted wig. "Most malice does have a human hand in it, and I confess, I spend enough time alone with the deceased to question the notion of vengeful spirits. One would think that if they were a reality then some of the souls that have crossed my dissection table would have objected more strongly to their treatment, both in their last moments of life, and in their eternal slumber. Yet not one has ever risen to haunt me."

That was certainly something to ponder. "Perhaps it was the nature of Old Lady Cedarton's death that's caused her to..."

Jem shot her a questioning look over his shoulder before he turned the bend.

Doctor Bell huffed. "Miss Wakefield, believe me the folks whose bodies have reached me have plenty that might prompt them to stir from their eternal rest, but perhaps we might ponder this matter later? It rather relies on the notion of a soul, and I can tell you that I have never found evidence of such a thing's existence."

"Nor would you, for in death it's departed."

"Or wasn't there to begin with."

"You're an atheist, sir?"

"Agnostic. There are no rational grounds for the justification of a divine beneficent force, nor a maleficent one."

Indeed, it was a discussion for another time. Eliza lifted her skirts and hurried up the first flight of stairs. For some reason his words disturbed her in a way she couldn't rightly fathom. She was not an overly religious woman. Of course, she attended church as any good woman did, and said her prayers, but to go as far as claiming that the existence of a soul—and the Almighty—was no more than a myth.... Well, coming from an anatomist, it gave her the shivers.

Midway up the second flight of stairs, Eliza caught sight of Jane in the shadowy entrance hall. Despite it being only mid-afternoon, the large fireplace was lit, along with a number of cheap tallow candles, the stench of which permeated the air, adding to the sense of neglect and ruin that lingered over the whole castle. Several long shadows cast by the various stuffed stag heads loomed large across the chamber floor, so that it appeared as if two great grasping hands stretched out to seize the occupants scurrying about the cavernous interior. George and Linfield were lobbing items at one another.

Jane collided with her as she reached the top, drowning her in a cloud of rose pomade. "Eliza." She threw her arms fast about her and proceeded to snuffle against Eliza's shoulder.

"Dear, what has happened? What ill befalls you now? Not another scare... another sighting?" The room's other occupants were in such a state of chaos it was impossible to tell what was going on.

"What I have seen is nothing worse than hell itself. Oh, I wish I could cut it from my mind."

Eliza coaxed her upright, and hands clasped fast to her friend's cheeks looked her square in the face. "Jane, what in heavens have you seen? Old Lady Cedarton? Has she appeared to you again?"

Her friend released a hysterical cackle. "Old Lady Cedarton. Oh, dear no, 'tis much worse than that. I am made wretched... wretched. 'Tis all a farce, a marriage in name and naught else. His affections lie with another. Eliza, it is as we suspected, he has a mistress, and that mistress is Henrietta."

"Henrietta?" She could not keep the astonishment from her voice. "Come, you must tell me all. Surely, there is some misunderstanding."

"'Tis a gift-horse of a marriage." Jane clasped Eliza's hand in a fearsome grip and dragged her through into the dining room away from the others. Here there was no fire lit, and the air held enough chill that their breath steamed before them. Outside, the daylight was already fading into night, making the rain streaming down the glass seem like a blackened waterfall. Jane cast herself into a chair and slumped against the table, only to bob back onto her feet a second or two later and begin a military-like march before the empty hearth.

"Jane, that seems... surely you're mistaken."

Her friend planted her hands assuredly on her hips. Her delicate feature screwed into a frown. "Mistaken, I am most certainly not. I saw them together, as plain as I see you. Heard her giggling and playing the coquette and caught him with his...with his falls unbuttoned and his... his... It was in her mouth. In her hand... No, both, I believe."

"In the hallway?"

Jane laughed. It was a laugh bordering on mania. "Is that the only part of this you find far-fetched? That he should make merry with his mistress in our hallway rather than a bedchamber or another room with more comforts?"

"Jane, that is not at all what was in my thoughts. I merely question what you think you saw."

"Yes, as everybody does. I see spirits after all. I am most unreliable. He... Linfield has already tried that line with me, but it is no fallacy. I know very well what I saw. I am not mistaken, and if you try to convince me otherwise, I will know you are no longer my true friend."

That was just enough of a retort that a rush of heat bloomed across Eliza's cheeks. "I don't mean to call your judgement into question." She simply wished to calm her down. Jane's limbs were aquiver, her heels drumming against the floor, and her poor lower lip was now bitten into ruddiness. "It's only that I have such a scant understanding of what has occurred, that it all seems outlandish. Perhaps if you give me a fuller picture."

"I do not see how much fuller a picture I can give. Eliza, she was kneeling before him, and had her hands on his..."

"Prick," Eliza suggested.

"His...prick...yes." Jane dragged her tongue over her teeth as if to remove the stain of the word from their surface. "And she was bent as to kiss it. He was encouraging her, while she whispered all manner of sweet talk to him." Emotions getting the better of her, Jane slapped her hand against the back of a chair, only to wince at the impact and curl her fingers before bringing them to her lips and spilling a fresh round of tears over them.

"How horrid for you. I wish it were otherwise and that your husband has not proved himself the rogue his reputation foretold. However, it does not follow that one incident equates to an ongoing arrangement."

"What else would it be? He spurns my affections, and now it is clear why. What use has he for them when he has his whore staying alongside us under this very roof? Did we not... did we not both observe that it was an oddity for a man to bring along his mother to such a gathering? Well, now I should say the purpose of it is entirely clear. Oh, I hate this place. Hate it, and despair of it. Nothing but calamity has befallen me since entering this accursed castle."

Then clutching her belly, she burst into another round of angry sobs. "'Tis all bad. I am ruined. How shall I ever convince him the child is his, when he is untempted by my person, and our marriage remains unconsummated? He has her. Does not need me. Is only disgusted by me. I should scratch her eyes out if I could. Why must she be here? Why must she have his love?"

"Jane, you do not know that is the case. You are shocked and overwrought, and with sound reason, but you jump to conclusions that may not be facts.

Come sit." Eliza drew out two chairs from the dining table and having positioned them facing one another propelled Jane into the first, before settling in the second. Thence, she clasped Jane's icy fingers and held them in a comforting grasp. It was deuced cold in this chamber, and she longed for a warmer locale to have this conversation but having only just managed to get Jane to settle, she did not want to divert her attention even to secure them both some warmth.

"Tell me from the point that I left you at your lacemaking all that occurred. Do not leave anything out. Do not speculate. Tell me simply all as it occurred."

Jane mopped her face with her kerchief. "Linfield claims my mind is addled, that he was merely taking a piss in a chamber pot. As if I am so foolish to believe that. Does he imagine me blind? Am I to suppose Henrietta was holding it for him? It is so preposterous."

"Jane," Eliza coaxed softly. "From the beginning."

Jane's thoughts were soon wrangled into a narrative, one in which she'd been engrossed with her bobbins and making steady progress. Mrs Honeyfield had brought her more tea, along with marmalade and bread, but she had not eaten because she'd been disturbed by the sound of footsteps hurrying about, and the banging and creaking of many doors. "Trust me, I was most wary of investigating, for Cedarton has proved itself an unfriendly place, particularly to me, but I will not be enfeebled, or made to tiptoe about the place in fear of being alone. I cannot ask you always to be here with me." She squeezed Eliza's fingers tightly. "I may not like it here, but it is my home, and my right as Lady Cedarton to live here. Anyway, I lingered a while, wary of investigating. I was sure that you would return afore long, and then we might look together. Cedarton is not so extensive that you would not be able to traverse the whole of it inside an hour, not even if you had ventured into the ruins of the Lady Tower. You did not, did you, Eliza? It is quite unsafe, and the rain has been so utterly relentless this afternoon."

"I did not. You need not fear."

"That is good." She tried to pat Eliza's knee while still clinging tight to her fingers. "But the hour passed, and you did not come, but the noises continued. I felt quite sure that someone was meaning to frighten me with a trick, so I did some tiptoeing of my own. You'll recall that I can be quite light on my feet. Was I not often applauded at school for the lightness of my gait when the dance tutor came?"

"You were, Jane. Often and heartily. You always had the lightest step amongst us."

"Precisely, and so they did not hear me." She shot a gaze at the door onto the hallway. "Eliza, they were in the Billiards Room together. Linfield had his back to the table and Henrietta was knelt on a footstool alongside him. She must have fetched it from the Hunting Room next door, for I swear I've never noticed it in there before. Anyway, she was kneeling, right before him. Should I show you?" She made as if to fall to her knees.

"No need."

"Well, she kept talking to him in a coaxing fashion, saying all manner of sweet and encouraging things."

"What sort of things?"

A blush scalded Jane's ashen cheeks. "I'm certain I shouldn't wish to repeat them in full. It was all about Captain Standish and how she'd soon persuade him to stand for the ladies, and Linfield saying that man Thomas was not at all eager, but if she had it in her, then...then he could see to giving her what she wanted, as a show of his gratitude and the like."

That did sound rather damning.

"Well, I'm sure I didn't mean to burst in as I did, but I couldn't rightly stand there and let them carry on canoodling unchallenged, not when it became obvious from the bobbing of her head that she was not just fondling his...thing... gentleman's thing... but kissing, nay even suckling him down there—"

"No, I suppose not."

"Suckling like a babe would at a teat." Her voice was rising again, growing increasingly shrill. "Of all the things! I'm quite sure I didn't comprehend that one might even do such a thing before witnessing it. It doesn't seem at all right or proper that a dame should do that for a man. Not that any sort of congress is entirely right or proper, but..." She fell into momentary silence.

No indeed, fucking was not proper, nor sucking,

but wickedly delightful all the same. 'Twas hard not to recall the joy of taking Jem thus only yesterday morning, and how glorious it had felt to have him return the favour in the surgery just now.

"Of course, if that is what he requires in order that he bed me, then... then of course I will obey him in this whim." Jane's wild eyes briefly closed, and her face screwed up into a knot. "Oh, I do not understand why he would do this. I swear I have made myself as amenable to him as any woman possibly could. Why does he choose to fornicate with her and not with me?"

If there was an answer, then alas Eliza didn't possess it.

"Why, Eliza? Do I revolt him so very much?"

"I am sure that is not the case."

Linfield was a queer kettle to be sure, if he desired Mrs Cluett's favours over those of his new wife. Not that Henrietta didn't have her charms, but Jane was his to use how he wished, so unless he had somehow discerned the Jack in her cellar... Could that be it? It seemed most unlikely, there was as yet no obvious thickening of her waist, and he had hardly been so intimately acquainted with her person to note such a thing.

"Jane, I know you will not like what I have to say, but I think... I think you're going to have to address him on this matter."

"Speak to him about it!"

Eliza gave a decisive nod.

"You did not hear him, nor all the foulness he threw at me. At me, who had done nothing wrong, only expressed my horror over finding him so compromised as any wife would surely do. It is deplorable of him, it truly is, for him to have brought that woman here."

"Jane, I'm still not entirely certain she's his mistress, and this wasn't anything more than an opportunity seized in a moment."

"He promised her recompense."

"I did not say there wasn't a bargain struck, but it does not necessarily follow that it's an ongoing arrangement."

"If it's a first, then that is almost worse, for doesn't it only emphasise his repulsion for me?"

Refusing to support the way Jane seemed determined to demean herself, she sucked her lips into a pucker. "The only way you'll know the truth is if you talk to him. I know you do not wish to and with every reason. He owes you an apology, plain and simple. But Jane, you have both sworn oaths and agreed to this union. If you cannot make good of it, then I fear you will both make one another very unhappy."

"But to address him so directly on such a topic, and after how violently he swore at me? I don't think that I can. And even supposing I do, what if he tells me that he won't be rid of her? Or that he means her to continue to share our home, and intends to go on making use of her favours? What shall I do then?"

"Persevere." Eliza offered her another hand squeeze. "I am so sorry that this is your lot, Jane. It is undeserved, and alas convinces me that I will preserve my spinsterhood."

"Truly?" Jane queried, letting go of Eliza's hand to rub and dry her eyes. "But I thought I detected a fondness between you and Mr Whistler. Surely you would take him if he offered. Wouldn't you, Eliza?"

She could not be certain that she would. Though she didn't say that, it must have been clear in her expression for Jane worried her poor lip again and tutted, then took to patting her hand as if she were the one in dire need of comfort. "I pray only that you don't make my mistake, Eliza. Do not think you can love and be free, for you cannot. Not without consequences, and such folly is precisely what has led me here to this doomed marriage, in this wretched place. Had I not been so naïve, so foolish, then I would have had the option to object to my father's negotiations with Lord Bellingbrook."

"What is done is done and can't be altered," Eliza advised.

Jane's sighs seemed to wriggle up from her bowels. "You are a goddess among friends, Eliza. I cannot thank you enough for being mine. Almost everyone would have severed our friendship the moment they knew of my predicament, but not you. You are more steadfast. You are a true friend. A saint amongst them." She fell into wretched silence, whilst chewing on her lower lip.

Eliza heartily wished she had more wisdom to offer and could do more than offer her friendship and support for she could see that Jane was trapped. Both here in this mouldering ruin of a castle and in the bed she'd made for herself by tying the knot with Lord Linfield. And indeed, the one she'd made for herself by trusting a previous man's word.

She would gladly wring his neck if she ever discerned his name.

Jane took to her feet again. Indeed, Eliza followed her up, for it was overly cold to linger too long in one position. The damp had a way of inveigling its way into your joints if you did, and she was young still to be complaining of aches and cramps and stiff limbs.

"I must compose myself before I even think of confronting him. I am so torn." Jane was marching again. She seemed to think best on her feet and in motion. "In truth, I confess, I do not desire him, and if the circumstances were other than they are,"—she cradled her arms around her middle— "I think I should be wholly relieved that he does not care to bother me. But they are as they are, and he must bed me. Eliza, he must believe this child is his. All must think it. For I fear for both our fortunes if it is found out."

'Twas the only thing persuading Eliza to hold the information close. It was not a deception she cared to be privy to, though she completely understood the necessity of it. Jane ought not to have wed him, but that was done and past. The best had to be made of the circumstances. Also, she rightly feared Linfield's reaction were he to find out. She already held a deep suspicion of him. Too much circumstantial evidence pointed to his involvement in all the ghastly goings on. Perhaps Jane was correct, and Henrietta was his long-term mistress. Perhaps they were co-conspirators in trying to relieve Jane of her wits.

"Will you come with me to the Lady's Parlour?" Jane asked. "Only it is too chilly here to think properly. My toes are like ice, and I mean to return to my bobbins. I know the activity will help me straighten out my thoughts. They are in a frightful whirl."

"Of course, I will come."

They did not return the way they had come but wove a path through the drawing room and its antechamber and several small rooms to reach their destination. Whatever squabble had abounded between Linfield and George seemed to have ceased. Nor could they hear Henrietta's screeching any more.

"How did George come to be involved?" Eliza asked as they walked with their arms linked, and Jane's wrap about both their shoulders.

"I think he must have heard my cry. He arrived from the Hunting Room and quickly discerned the cause of the discord. Then he grew enraged, though I'm not sure who he was most angered by. He took up a billiards cue and tried to jab Linfield." She made a forward thrust as to demonstrate, dislodging the shawl, which Eliza caught. "But he had no kind words for his mother either. She got out of his way when he raised his hand, else I think he would have struck her too."

"He landed the blow to Linfield, then?"

"Yes. Perhaps. I'm not rightly sure. But Linfield started throwing the billiard balls at his head, and that's when he chased George out into the hallway. I do hope the Cluetts will leave. I pray that when we go to dinner tonight it will be two less around the table, and a swift end to all the discord. Then, I shan't have to say anything to Linfield, nor smile at that snake of a woman. To think she has been nothing but sugar and kindness to me, but it has all been a lie. In all my days, I don't believe I've ever encountered such a duplicitous," —she swallowed what was surely an awful name, before substituting— "woman."

That she was duplicitous herself did not seem to cross her mind. It made Eliza wonder if anyone in this castle was entirely honest. And what of the argument she had witnessed between George and Linfield? How was that connected? She felt certain it had to be.

They reached their destination, and Eliza went to stoke the fire, while Jane settled at her table, the cushion with her lace pinned to it before her. A horrific thought struck Eliza as she stabbed the coals. What if Linfield had in fact already been wed before he recited vows to Jane? What if he was in fact wed to Henrietta, and it was Jane who was the interloper? That might explain a good deal about why the "spirits" were haunting her and proving shy of anyone else. No one besides that one maid who'd left her employment had witnessed the visitations.

But no, it could not be. She'd overheard George as he'd begun to recite the names on that certificate. He'd said Jane, hadn't he? But then why had Linfield flown into such a terrible rage?

Ought she to voice her concerns to Jane? Oh, but she couldn't, not without certainty. It would destroy her friend utterly. No, she would have to find the certificate George had claimed and view it for herself.

-20-

Jem

As Jem digested the scene before him, he heartily wished that he'd remained below stairs in Bell's surgery, Eliza in his arms and his experiment bubbling away in the background, for it took only moments of listening to Linfield and George shouting into one another's faces to establish the facts of what had occurred.

He had wondered over Mrs Cluett's inclusion in their numbers. The answer now was delivered without preamble. The lady was present as she had no other place to go, George having thrown the deeds of her abode into the pot as his stakes for that disastrous carriage race. George, naturally, had a scheme in play to rectify his loss. Meanwhile, his mother had plans of her own to restore their property, and Jem couldn't even be sorry about her attempt. If it had worked, then it would have absolved him of the martyrdom currently in his future. As it was, the billiards room and much of the entry hall stood wrecked, pictures and vases smashed, and billiard balls scattered about the place as though lawn bowls were being played.

"You had no right, George. Nor have you any to interfere now. I earned that property on my back, and if it pleases me to restore it to my ownership in the same manner, then it is no business of yours."

Henrietta in her fury was certainly a sight to behold, puffed up and red in the face. If he was not mistaken, her accent had taken on different inflections too, betraying perhaps the area of her birth. It was neither local nor London born.

George was not heeding his mother's calls; despite the fact she was simultaneously hanging onto his arm while batting him with her reticule. No, his focus was all on his former bosom companion, who had yet to exhaust the supply of billiard balls and was still pitching them at George's head, displaying considerable skill in the process. Evidently, he'd have made a fine cricketer if his passion had not been subsumed by carriage racing.

"What manner of scoundrel preys on a fellow's mother?"

Linfield, his floss-like hair springing out from his head in hereto unprecedented fluffiness, was reared in spiteful glory, his shoulders back, chest out, and a hopelessly malevolent sneer on his aristocrat lips. "What manner of fool gambles his mater's bed out from under her? I, in my benevolence as your friend, was assisting in righting your wrongs, providing the lady with an opportunity to rectify your mistakes."

"You are the one responsible for her situation.

You need not have called in the debt."

"George, if I choose to work—"

"Mother!" He shook her off and made a futile attempt to waft her from the room, succeeding only in propelling her as far as a chair. This she perched on like a turtle dove, all plump elegance and not an ounce of remorse about her. George turned from her and made a spring for Linfield's throat. Clearly, not having expected things to progress quite so rapidly, he succeeded in knocking Linfield off his lordly feet with a blow to the chin that sent him careening backwards into an ancient and rather rusted suit of armour. Both mail and master crashed noisily to the floor, while George swung his foot back to deliver a boot to Linfield's arse, only to be stopped by his mother's shriek.

Henrietta had lost all her studied congeniality and harkened at him like a fish wife—or at least fisherman's daughter. "For goodness sakes, George, pull yourself together. Are you trying to have us banished from polite society forever, not to mention turned out into this godforsaken wilderness that surrounds us? We have no place to go, and no money, thanks to your efforts. You should be licking his arse, not trying to ram your foot up it. I kept you out of my business when you were small, but I do sometimes wonder if that was the right course. You'd have a better head on your shoulders if you'd been an apprentice of ill fortune as I was, rather than that of the pampered toff you aspire to be. I should never had sent you to that ridiculous establishment. What did they teach you save ciphering and sums you could have picked up at Sunday school? And all for an exorbitant fee. It has left you with neither brains nor brawn to speak of, nor the wherewithal to even woo yourself one of the scores of widows with more money than teeth to keep us flush. You are truly hopeless. A failure. At least if I'd kept you with me, you'd know when being prepared to get on your knees and open your mouth was to your net advantage, instead of being the overstuffed buffoon that you are. All this mither and mayhem you've created, and for what? For one measly suck that would have saved our fortunes."

At this point, she sniffed, and turned imperiously to Lord Linfield, whom Bell had had the presence to assist to his feet. He was sporting a rather long gash to his cheek, at which he was dabbing gently with a fresh handkerchief, also supplied by Bell.

"My lord, I hope you will excuse my dimwit of a son. The offer remains, perhaps we could retire elsewhere and—"

"Mother, I am not about to let you—"

"Let me, George?" Oh, she was terrifying in her ire. Terrifying and magnificent. On her feet again and spitting like a swan. "There is no letting me about it, George Hector Cluett. You are not my master. If it pleases me to suck the knob of every goldfinch you know to better our lot, then I will do it. I'll spread my legs too, if it pleases, but as it happens, a suck would have done. The deeds, George, the ones you lost. They'd have been mine if not for your interfering and Jane and her ghastly howling. And all for the price of one paltry spending. I gave you one simple task. One. To ensure the maid stayed at her making, but you could not even handle that. I did not realise it was so damnably difficult to turn a key in a lock."

She sank again, into a disconsolate rage and scowled into her handkerchief. Jem could not precisely ascertain if she was truly overwrought or simply making a good display of it. Linfield remained unmoved by the display. His lips pinched into a sour glout, which served to make his thin nose more pointed and his voice emerge reedy. "I will not retire elsewhere with you, madam. In fact, I think it best if you and your son leave this house."

Henrietta wailed. "Fool. See what you've done."

George pulled his shoulders back. "What *you* have done, mother. It was not necessary to debase yourself. I have things in hand. We will not be leaving." He turned his attention back to Linfield. "My lord forgets something."

"You will leave," Linfield insisted.

"Truly? That is your final edict on the matter?" George speculatively cocked a brow.

Interestingly, Linfield quailed. "You wouldn't."

George responded with a sly "*Hm*", whereupon he licked his lips.

Linfield pitched another ball at his head. It arched wide, struck the wainscotting and dropped to the ground with a thud.

"Should we retire to your study to negotiate, Eustace, or would you prefer all these souls be privy to the matter?"

After a moment of mincing vacillation, Linfield mutinously charged past George with his head held high and a bitter sneer on his narrow lips. Cluett swung at once to follow him, and the two disappeared into the west wing, presumably to negotiate matters in a manner satisfactory to them both. Henrietta watched them leave with a calculating expression, if ever Jem had seen one.

"Well, I suppose it saves me the bother," she muttered. "It wasn't as if he was readily upstanding."

She was speaking to herself rather than them, but her utterance still sent Jem into gloom. If one experienced in the arts of pleasure could not get Linfield to rise, then it was unlikely Linfield would be upstanding even after partaking of the laughing gas. The frightening possibility of his lordship hauling Jem directly into his wife's boudoir loomed larger.

That was assuming this afternoon's activities hadn't put a blight on the whole notion of fornicating. Jane would hardly be receptive to Linfield's advances after catching him with his breeches down and one of their guests sucking on his knob.

Henrietta left a moment later. Jem turned to Bell and found the cadaver carver arranging the suit of mail on the floor. "What just happened?" he asked.

Ludlow gave him a bony shrug. "Damned if I know, but it may have bought you a reprieve for a night or two. Be thankful for that and don't question it. I'm sure your mind is better applied to other matters."

On both points, that remained to be seen. It was equally likely that Linfield would use the discord as an excuse to hasten matters. He liked nothing better than to fuck after a bout of drama. As to the application of his brain, he wasn't of a mood to fathom equations, and there was hardly a rush to do so since he would have no time to apply himself to building his puffing devil until Linfield had passed the Oxford exam.

"Pass me that cuisse," Bell waved him at a piece of the fallen knight, which Jem dutifully retrieved. They spent the next half hour or so reassembling the metal skeleton on its stand. At the end of which, Bell remarked, "You're playing with fire, dallying with that lass, and before you mutter anything nonsensical about love and future commitments, I'll remind you of your current circumstances."

Of those Jem remained painfully aware.

"I'll also thank you not to use my surgery as your trysting place. If he discovers you, there'll be hell to pay, and I don't intend to be tangled up in your folly. He might be as thick as clarts, but his patronage is well worth the bother of tolerating his whims. Perhaps you ought to remind yourself of that."

He reminded himself upwards of a dozen times a day. "Being coerced into acts I find distasteful rather puts a blight on things."

"You did not always find them so distasteful," Bell correctly observed.

The knight properly restored to the stand, they both ambled towards the basement surgery again.

"There was something in it for both of us at the start." Escapism, primarily, but it'd been something. "That is no longer the case. He has me cornered, Ludlow. I can wish it otherwise, but it is not. These events of this afternoon will not have changed a thing. Henrietta's testament reached my ears even if it didn't reach yours. She couldn't get a rise out of him. Thus, he will destroy whatever future I imagine, whether it was ever anything more than idle fancy or otherwise." Only when Bell's brows almost vanished under his wig did he add, "She'll not want me after she hears of me buggering him in her devoted friend's marriage bed."

His friend's naturally stern face softened around the eyes. "True enough. He has you by the bollocks. I suppose he has threatened to ruin her if you don't comply."

"Ha, it is almost as if you know the man."

They both of them shook their heads.

"What he lacks in genuine intelligence he makes up for in raw cunning and cruelty," Bell expanded. "'Tis a pity there is no examination for that, for he would excel, and the earl would be delighted to learn his son is in fact a wit and not a twit."

Jem laughed despite the churning in his guts. He supposed black humour was what he ought to expect from a fellow who cut up bodies for fun.

"I could share my collection of pickled scrotums with you to lift your spirits if you like."

Jem pinched the base of his nose. Bell was an odd fellow, but he was learning to appreciate him. "I pray you jest."

Bell treated him to a rictus grin in return, leaving him still in doubt.

"I think I will spare myself the joy, though I will come and attend to the gases I have bubbling. I think there is probably more than enough now to send every person in the place into raptures."

"Then I will attend my leeches. I've a batch newly hatched this morning, and eager for a meal."

"Well don't look at me."

"No?" Bell flashed him another of those death grins. "Very well, I will ask Cook for some liver. Anon." He turned to the kitchen, leaving Jem to trudge back along the rat-run alone.

-21-

Eliza

If there was one thing Eliza truly despised it was to sit idle, particularly when there were tasks to be done that she was itching to apply herself to. She had tried to entertain her mind with a book as Jane sat at her lacemaking—it was clear that her friend wasn't so much unknotting her thoughts as avoiding them—but she could not focus on the pages. Afore long she began strolling, taking turn after turn about the lady's parlour, and thence a little further into the neighbouring room where she came upon a game of peg solitaire to occupy herself with.

She was in this adjoining room, perusing the artworks there, some of Cedarton in its former grandeur, having tired of the game when Linfield presented himself to his wife.

"May we speak, madam?" he said. "I am relieved to find you alone."

Through the open doorway, she saw Jane lift her attention from her bobbins. "Linfield." She cast a tremulous look in Eliza's direction, but Eliza made sure to step back into the shadows so that she wouldn't be observed. She did not intend to leave her friend alone with this man, even if the devil was her husband, nor did she wish him to be aware of her presence. Better she remained a silent witness to whatever manner of tête-à-tête he intended to have.

Jane turned in her chair so that she faced him and settled her hands in her lap, presenting herself as the very model of an obedient wife. She had always possessed a mildness that Eliza could not wear even as a mask.

"Have you come to tell me the Cluetts have departed?" Jane asked.

There had been no evidence of such a thing, and they surely would have heard the commotion in the hall, and indeed the courtyard beyond the windows.

"I have not," he replied stiffly.

Linfield did not sit, but took up a position before the fireplace, with his back to the blaze, selfishly seizing most of its comfort for himself. He was a peacock of a man, spoiled and so certain of his own value, that he could not comprehend his various obvious faults. Eliza could already envisage him somehow making this whole episode Jane's fault.

"They will be remaining."

"No!"

Though Eliza could no longer see her, Jane's pain was evident enough from her cry, and thus, thank heaven, meekness was dispensed with.

"You cannot mean it. Linfield, please. You surely do not mean me to accept your mistress in our home? Only the cruellest... Why must you punish me thus? What have I done? I wish you would tell me so that I might make it right. Have I not been a good wife to you? I am more than ready than to fulfil my duties, have been since we spoke our vows. If I displease you, then you have only to say, and I will alter my ways."

"Madam, your actions have no bearing on the matter. Our guests will stay. It is my decision, and I have made it."

Pompous whelp!

Jane began to pace. Eliza caught glimpses of her as she passed back and forth before him, her head bowed, and her pretty face so riddled with anxiety as to make her seem twice her age. "Is it my talk of spirits that has offended you so, turned your heart so thoroughly against me?"

"Madam, you did not possess that to begin with. Let us not pretend that this arrangement between us was made as a declaration of love. I was bullied into it, as I suspect were you. And as to your theatrics, they are irritating, but given there is precious little in the way of amusement to be had in this place, I suppose I should at least thank you for the entertainment of them."

Certainly then, he did not afford them any belief, but nor did he speak as though he'd had a hand in creating the disturbances. It was possible that he was a fearfully good actor, but from what Eliza had observed of Lord Linfield so far, he was a shallow creature, not likely capable of anything so complex as the level of deception such a ruse would surely require.

"As to the matter of Mrs Cluett, you are erroneous in your assumption. She is not my mistress, nor ever has or will be."

"But I saw—"

"Whatever you imagine you saw, madam, I assure you, you are quite mistaken. You do after all frequently see things that are not there."

Jane stomped to a halt and whipped about to face him. "Linfield, your falls were down. Despite what you may think, I am not such a nit that I cannot discern what is plainly happening before my face. Whether you call her your mistress or not, you were trysting with her."

"It was no tryst," he snarled. "As if I would choose..." He threw up his arms in frustration, thence cast himself onto the settee before the fireside, a position from which Eliza could see his reflection. "She is not the sort of person one would tryst with. She cornered me." He lifted his feet up, so his heels were pointed toward the sash windows, then grasped a teaspoon from off the plate of offerings Mrs Honeyfield had earlier supplied and drummed it against his thigh. "Is this tea still warm?"

"What?" Jane crossed to the table and tested her hand against the side of the pot. "'Tis warmish. Should I ring to have some fresh brought?"

"No, no. Pour it. I need something to wet my throat, and I don't suppose you've anything stronger to hand."

"I should think you'd be appalled if I did."

"Aye," He took the offered cup and spoke into it.

"I should think I might. One wouldn't want a lush as a wife."

"Well, I don't much care to have one as a husband."

Much to Eliza's surprise, Linfield snorted in mirth. He set his heels back on the floor again. "Why madam, I see you are not quite the timorous mouse you've been pretending to be. Perhaps we shall manage to get along together after all."

"You are not forgiven," Jane snapped. "Do you truly expect me to believe that Henrietta waylaid you in such a way that you could not be free of her? If you wanted to get away, you surely could have done so. Therefore, it is reasonable for me to suppose that you did not wish it, that you were in fact a willing participant, that you even encouraged her to act—"

"Is that my mother's bergamot marmalade?" he asked, squinting at the table, and cutting Jane's building tirade to an abrupt cessation.

"It is," Jane snapped, halting her march. She glared at him; fists tightened in frustration.

"Oh, sit yourself down." He reached for a plate and knife and began ladling marmalade onto a thick cut slice of bread. "All this frenzy over nothing. Calm yourself, Lady Linfield, afore you bring on another fainting fit. Let us just speak plainly to one another, I'm tired of all this obfuscation." He gestured with the dripping knife, thus splattering the tablecloth with a multitude of orange blobs. "As gobblepricks go, I cannot say I was captivated by Mrs Cluett's talents. 'Tis said she was once famed for the bliss she afforded a fellow by sucking his sugar-stick, but I fear her talents are lost with her youth. I was not risen to a stand, and therefore I will not be availing myself of her company again."

Jane's cheeks bloomed red over his coarseness. "You won't?" she asked, dubiously.

"No."

She regarded him thoughtfully, as he chewed and swallowed, and washed the repast down with a long swallow of tea. "I'm not rightly sure I understand you."

"You understand me." He threw her a foxy grin. "My use of flash language does not make me so incomprehensible.

Jane sat. "But you refuse to send her away."

Linfield started on another slice of bread. "Best damn marmalade ever. Love it, I do. Mama's best..." He chewed and swallowed. "Janie, George is an old friend, and the weather is awful inclement. It wouldn't be very Christian of me to turn them out into the cold now, would it? Particularly as they have no place to go, and we're only weeks away from the Christmas season. I'm sure you don't wish to see them dead in a dell because we couldn't find it in our hearts to be forgiving. I think you're not such an unkind a woman as that."

Lord, but he was a manipulative devil.

"Shall we speak of other things? I thought I might attend you tonight."

"Tonight!"

"Yes. You are, of course, rightly aggrieved by my neglect of you. So, I will attend you in your chamber."

"My chamber. Linfield my room is blackened, the bed burned down to cinders."

"Well... whatever chamber you please. There are rooms aplenty in this place, either move yourself or Miss Wakefield to another of them."

"But I should wish to be close by her," Jane protested.

Linfield prevaricated by producing a kerchief and daubing his lips clean. "Janie, it need only be for one night, then you may bunk together if it pleases you. I can understand these things. How one might seek companionship during the night. It is something I'm partial to myself. Which I suppose brings me to another delicate topic. Suppose we speak about the arrangements in more detail."

"Detail?"

"Yes, dearest." He washed the words down with another swallow of tea. "I realise that you might not be terribly informed.... Might be best if I readied your mind for the occasion."

"My mind?"

Jane was clearly either so befuddled or angered by him that her voice had been almost stolen from her.

"In case you have a preformed notion of how things should proceed, based on what you have heard, or been told, by..."

"By?"

"Your mother? She might have hinted at what to expect... in the marriage bed."

"No," Jane said. "No, she did not.... Well, perhaps a little." It was obvious to Eliza that Jane added the latter realising that her knowledge of the marital act must be seen to have come from somewhere. If Linfield was at all acquainted with Jane's mother, he would not have proposed or ever believed her a source of such wisdom, Mrs Morley being as hard and brittle as an old broom handle, a sour spendthrift, and not the sort to spare an anxious bride some kindly, or even informative words.

"Well, dismiss whatever nonsense you've been told. It won't be like that."

"It won't?"

Poor Jane, she was clearly addled to her core.

"No. Well, perhaps a little. But, not really. That is to say, our," —here Linfield made a strange arrangement with his fingers— "our bodily parts will still come together." His complexion became increasingly peaky as he spoke. "However—"

"Are you trying to ask me to do what that woman was doing to you?" Jane blurted.

Linfield rose to his feet. "Hen's teeth, woman! Good God, no." He smashed his cup down onto its saucer, so that it made an appalling clatter. "I would never. Gracious..." He seemed most overcome, one hand flying to his hair and combing through the unruly strands of it, and the other forming a death grip around the handle of the cup he'd likely just cracked. "It's not the sort of thing one asks from one's wife.... Not at all. I'm not a monster, you know."

He backed away from her, as if she were some kind of hereto unidentified beast.

"Oh," Jane remarked, a tad more brightly than

one might have expected given the rather tumultuous nature of their conversation and prior relationship. "Only if it was, then—"

He cut her off with the slash of his hand. "Madam." He shook his head most insistently. "I intend to have my goujat attend me while at the task. That is all I am trying to say."

"Your goujat?" Jane repeated dubiously, her confusion now mirroring Eliza's own. She had never heard of such a thing. Well, not outside of whispered stories of the olden days when the marital act was to be witnessed so that all parties knew the couple were truly man and wife, but then all were invited in to observe, not merely one figure.

Jane followed her husband's agitated waddle across the hearth rug with her nose screwed up in perplexity. "Linfield, do you mean to say you wish a servant to witness us?"

"Witness? No. He will attend me. And no, not a servant. Why the devil would I wish that?"

"But you said your valet."

"I did not." He turned and reared, positively aggrieved, then stared down his nose at her, lips aquiver, while two ruby spots bloomed on his cheeks. "Perish the thought. My valet, indeed. That would hardly inspire anyone to the act. Be like doing it with your father watching." He shuddered. "No, Mr Whistler will attend me."

It was all Eliza could do to stop herself blurting out Jem's name as Jane did.

"Mr Whistler!" she cried, her whole-body forced into stillness from the shock of it. "Linfield, you cannot seriously mean that. I do not understand. Why should it be necessary for him to watch us?"

Eliza could no more fathom a reason than Jane. If Linfield had perhaps said he wished Doctor Bell to observe them... Well, it would still have been most strange, but might be ascribed to some medical matter he did not wish to reveal, but Jem? To have Jem present made no sense at all. Why?

Meanwhile, Linfield gave a taciturn sniff, as if Jane's reticence were the confounding part and not his intentions. "He shan't be lingering about like some twit at the opera," he said. As if that were a foremost concern. "He'll participate."

If it were possible for someone to look more aghast, Eliza could not imagine it, although perhaps seeing her own reflection might have countered that notion.

"Not that he'll touch you. No, of course not. That would be entirely unacceptable. He'll be my *aide de chambre*."

Jane worried her head from side to side. "Forgive me, husband, but I do not understand."

That made two of them, unless Linfield was really so hopeless, he couldn't manage to find his own cock well enough to put it in his wife's cunny and actually needed someone to do it for him. In which case, surely, he could have simply asked Jane to help line them up.

"It's entirely normal," Linfield said in such a reedy voice as to make it obvious he was lying. "Just isn't talked about. Trifle awkward. Not the subject for polite circles."

Eliza did not understand why he was insisting on this, or why he was lying to Jane's face to convince her of its convention. Why on earth would Linfield wish Jem to attend him while he was bedding his wife? Did Jem know? Had he agreed to it? There was no rationality to it. None. Except...

She reeled back in horror and clapped her hand to her mouth to stop herself from blurting a reaction to her thoughts. Following the incident of Pennerley being shot in the leg, certain rumours had circulated, many of which persisted even now Bella and Pennerley were wed, about the nature of the marquis's attachment to Lord Marlinscar. Of course, men formed fast friendships. Plenty idled away days together engaged in gentlemanly pursuits, but for some, it was suggested, the attachment was deeper than one of platonic love. That they did things that they really ought only to have been done with a member of the opposite sex when connected by the bounds of marriage. Was this demand of Linfield's thus a declaration of such an attachment between him and Jem?

Surely not... She could not believe it to be so. Not when Jem had made such declarations of love to her.

Yet, she could also hear him as clearly as if he were standing by her now insisting, *I'm not the man you suppose me to be.* Was he in truth bound to Linfield faster and in more ways than she'd supposed? That they were—dare she even think it— lovers? Lovers in the way that she and Jane had stupidly supposed Linfield and Henrietta to be.

Had they got everything hopelessly wrong?

Was this the reason for Linfield's reluctance to bed his wife? He was in love with another... with Jem? Her Jem?

-22-

Eliza

Her agitation was too great for Eliza to remain to hear out the remainder of Jane and Linfield's discourse. She slipped from the little room via the other exit, and thus back through the various rooms and chambers she and Jane had passed through to avoid the hallway. Her mind was awhirl, and no doubt Jane would need her. She would wish to discuss this development, for Eliza to state opinions, and alleviate her mind. To say, yes, I've heard tell of such a thing, it's nothing to be alarmed by. Not that it would matter either way. Jane would not refuse Linfield's demands, no matter how strange or unconventional they were. She would go along with practically anything at this point to ensure, rightly or wrongly, that Linfield believed the child she was carrying to be his.

Eliza, though... She could not find any bright sparks in this request. Indeed, she wished she could cut what she'd overheard from her memory. She'd been so sure of Jem's affections. So certain of him.

Surely it was not possible that Linfield had concocted this plan without Jem's accord. Linfield would not tell Jane he intended to bring another man into their bed without the other fellow being aware of and amenable to the prospect.

Would he?

The obvious thing to do was to seek Jem out and ask him straight out what he knew of the matter. Yet, how would she even broach the topic?

Jem, I've overheard the most curious thing. Linfield and Jane were talking, and I'm not rightly sure how to even ask this, but is it true you are to attend him while he...while he tups his wife?

How would she compose herself if he said yes? Would he even be truthful about the matter? How could she trust anything he said?

Jem, damn you, why would you agree to such a thing?

He was no licentious rakehell. Not the sort to thrive on merriment and mayhem. Unless her judgement of him was seriously awry. Had she misread the signs?

She was not sure where she would find him. Perhaps in Doctor Bell's surgery again. Yet she shied from returning there, and her feet took her upstairs instead, along corridors, and through deserted rooms, until she stumbled on a narrow spiral staircase within a spindly tower. This she followed to a hexagonal room at its summit, where she found George on a narrow balcony overlooking the misty world beyond Cedarton's borders.

"Miss Wakefield," he greeted her, raising a

bottle, of what she surmised to be port from the stains on his lips, in her direction.

"Sir, I did not realise the room was occupied."

"Aye, and I suppose my company is too distasteful to contemplate. Might tarnish your reputation, being seen to associate with the son of a whore, but I'll not be leaving. His chit can rattle and squawk all she wishes; Linfield knows the stakes."

And what were they, she couldn't help but wonder? Exposure, of some sort? The proliferation of rumours?

George grinned at her and patted his pocket.

"Staying, are ye?" George seemed as surprised as her that she hadn't already about turned, but having climbed the stairs, and now felt the breeze on her face, Eliza was in no hurry to flee. Besides, she wanted answers, and being as well into his cups as he was, maybe George could provide them. She moved over to the balcony and stood shoulder to shoulder with him. The tower stood high enough to have lifted them above the mist, so that some of their surroundings could even be seen. Rolling green fields, stone walls and denuded trees, mist clinging to the valleys like drifts of snow. She could just about make out the steeple of the village church, though the base of the tower in which they stood was wholly obscured.

George offered her the bottle. "A tipple? The vintage is not the best, but the taste grows on one after the first few swallows."

It struck Eliza that she had dabbled in enough substances that meddled with the mind for one day, nor did she desire such anodyne oblivion, merely explanations and the truth. "Is your quarrel with our host settled now?" One assumed it, given the Cluetts continued presence.

"Ah," George replied, sagely stroking his bare chin. Seeing that she wasn't about to accept his offering, he took a long swallow instead. "I suppose you might call it more of a stalemate."

"What you mean is that you have some hold over him." She could not get the memories of him creeping about Linfield's study from her mind. She might not have thought of it again if it weren't for the mention of Jane. She would not have her friend threatened. It was bad enough she was tied to Linfield and forced to endure his whims.

George snorted, then turned so that he could take in her profile. "How forthright you are! And how poorly you think of us all. Tell me, Miss Wakefield, are my actions truly so ghastly? What have I done, besides requesting recompense for certain slights?"

"Your mother was willing."

"Who said we were speaking of my mother? Though I shall not deny he deserves a beating for his actions this afternoon. That he should so take advantage of her... The man is a fiend." He swallowed hard. His grip whitening his knuckles. "But we shall not speak of that. It is by and by. We each know what the other wants, and I have given him until dinner to provide it. It is more than ample time."

"And if he does not?" Eliza asked.

Again, George's focus tightened on her, creating

a furrow at the apex of his nose and a fat dimple in his chin. He blew over the rim of the bottle, making it whistle. "That is hardly your concern."

Except that it was, insomuch as that she felt certain it would affect Jane.

"Lady Linfield wishes you gone."

"Lady Linfield can rot in hell. I will not depart empty-handed and condemn my mother to the gutter or whatever bogles occupy the hellscape beyond these walls. It was Linfield who created this woe. Why should I suffer for his mistakes? No, restitution is due. He will see reason; else he'll be made to."

"And if he does not?"

George gave a nasty laugh. "Then we will see what the gossips have to say of the matter. If he's any sense..." His mouth formed the sort of gurn that'd sour milk. "Well, I ask for so little. Only a fool would baulk at giving it."

"Blackmail," she muttered, turning away from him in disgust. "He is your host, and your friend."

"He's a pompous turd, a rat's arse of a man, and hardly an innocent. We all do what we must, Miss Wakefield. Your brother would tell you that."

"I'm sure I have no idea what you mean." Nor was she aware of Mr Cluett being an acquaintance of her brother, Frederick.

His laugh became even more hateful. "Oh, come now. Weren't he the army man who married an orphaned heiress who promptly croaked abroad?"

Outraged, she reared away from him. "Freddy loved Louisa." She had seen them before they departed for India, so desperately, desperately in love, and she'd seen the shell of a man who'd returned, broken, and with a babe in his arms.

"Of course, he did." George waggled the bottle before him in a meaningful sort of way that made his disbelief all too apparent. "Or perhaps it was convenient for you to believe that, given how you and your sisters have benefited from the funds she poured into his accounts. No need for you all to become paid companions and governesses anymore, or to dress in hand-me-downs from the last century. You didn't learn those healing skills for fun, now did you, dear? I'm sure they paid more regularly than having to sing or embroider for one's supper, although perhaps not so handsomely as if you'd opened your legs."

Eliza slapped him, causing him to lose his grip on the bottle as he reached to relieve the sting in his face. It fell, crashing and shattering against the castle wall as it tumbled.

"Dammit, woman. There was still a half bottle left. 'Tweren't worth sacrificing because you're oversensitive to the truth."

"You don't know a thing about my family." Nothing of Freddy and poor Louisa, and how her brother still mourned her passing.

"I know enough," he said. "You wouldn't be so fired up if my words didn't hit so true, and it's clear enough what you are. You can dress yourself up, but you're no simpering society miss who's never known hardship and thinks the worst fate that might befall someone is to have to wear the same dress twice in a row or miss the Aldershot's ball."

"Who are the Aldershot's?"

He waved away the remark. "I don't know. It doesn't matter. Only that they might have a ball, and that one might be forced to miss it. You've shivered and starved. Tell me truthfully that isn't so. You know plain enough that love doesn't fill your belly or stave off the winter frost. Only the flush and our giddy, glorious poets bind themselves for love, and idolise impoverishment. You are more practical. You are like the rest of us gathered here, eager to prove your worth, but the truth is that we're all just pawns... playthings, here for his entertainment and nothing more."

Angered, Eliza retreated from him. "Sir, I don't know what you mean to achieve by lecturing me like this, but I shan't stand idle and listen to it. I should think after today, you might value a sympathetic ally, and not be so ready with your vitriol."

"Is it vitriolic of me to state the truth?" He cast her aside with a turn of his now empty hand. "Linfield will see you gone afore long. 'Tis only because he seeks to keep his wife sweet that you've remained this far. Once he has what he wants from her, then... then I should watch out for yourself, Miss Wakefield. Linfield is jealous of his pets, and you've been playing far too greedily with his favourite."

~Җ~

Eliza returned to her chamber, and from there to the soot-stained ruin of Jane's room. The ceiling and walls were blackened, and the old bedframe burned through in the middle so that the two ends leaned together like two wraiths clutching one another's spindly limbs. She no more understood George's venom towards her than she did Jem's motives, or the cause of the fire that had almost consumed her friend, yet she felt certain that they were in some way connected. That all the mysteries of Cedarton were somehow linked, and if she could only fathom the common thread, then everything would make sense again.

The little maid Edith arrived not long after. "I'm t' fetch Lady Linfield's things, Miss. Mrs Honeyfield says she's t' be moved in ta old mistress's suite afore dinner's done. Master's orders. Like there ain't enough for us all t' do what wi serving dinner, and of course, none of us much wants ta go in there. There's a chill in tha' room, Miss, I'll tell ya. Freeze's ya reet down t' marrow it does. But I suppose it's only habitable room left. Canna say as I'd much fancy sleepin' there."

"Where is this room?" Eliza asked, refusing to buy in to the maid superstitious nonsense which had no doubt reached her ears by way of Betsy's tongue.

"Why 'tis in t' Lady's Tower, miss."

"I thought that was no more than a burned shell."

"Aye, mostly 'tis, but not alls of it. Gordy, t' gardener, Miss, has quarters there and there's a few rooms at top what escaped the blaze, like." She began to busy herself, collecting Jane's few undamaged things into baskets to be moved, allowing Eliza a moment to ruminate on the matter. Had Jane truly agreed to this move? What motivated it? And of all the chambers she might move to, was old Lady Cedarton's room truly where she meant to rest her head? But then, perhaps she did not mean to sleep there, only to entertain Linfield's husbandly demands.

It soured Eliza's mind to think of it, and Jem's role in what ought purely to be a matter of man and wife. Perhaps that was the reasoning behind the odd choice of chamber. The unconventional arrangement would not be seen or overheard. The thought left an even sourer taste on her tongue.

"Mrs Honeyfield's in ever so much pain," Edith was saying. She seemed most determined to fill the silence, rattling on regardless of whether Eliza was paying her any heed.

Which, indeed, she had not been.

"Cookie's had her rinse 'er mouth out wi' a gargle a lemon juice an' salt water, but she looks ever such a state. The whole reet side of 'er jaw's swollen exactly like me sister's bairn when 'e 'ad t' mumps. All cockeyed, she is. Ah thought ya tooth powder was sure t' sort 'er, but it dun't seem ta 'ave done a thing."

"She'll have to have it pulled," Eliza remarked offhandedly. Presently, there wasn't space in her thoughts for the dilemmas of others. She would have to speak to Jem. Tell him what she'd overheard and listen to his side of the matter, but the dinner bell sounded at that very moment, and she realised there wasn't time to see him before the meal. Would there be an opportunity afterward? Knowing Linfield, he'd march them all off to their beds the moment the last fork touched a plate.

"Oh, it can't be tha' time already," Edith complained. "I need another four hands ta deal with all this, and t'mistress'll need changin', and you t'—"

"I can attend to my own attire," Eliza reassured her. She left the maid, retrieving what could be retrieved from the wreckage of Jane's former room, and slipped through the little dressing room to her own chamber. Jane was already present.

"Eliza, wherever did you go? I thought you were only next door, but once Linfield had gone, I looked for you, and you'd vanished." She took hold of Eliza's hands and guided her to the bed so that they might sit facing one another. "You'll be pleased to learn that all is to be well between Linfield and me. An assignation has been arranged for tonight. The details of it are a little strange, but I can't tell you how relieved I am." She stroked a hand over her belly.

"I'm glad for you." Eliza leapt up at once and busied herself with her attire. She repinned her hair and changed her long-sleeved day dress for an evening dress and gloves. She knew Jane wanted to discuss the details of what had passed between her and Linfield, but she couldn't. She just couldn't hear it and not feel every word of it as a personal attack. Jem was hers. She was his. They hadn't stated it like that. In fact, she'd probably made him think that she wanted nothing more than a passing affair. Had perhaps even implied that she only considered him worthy of that...

Had she done that? Made him feel small, unvalued in some way. Oh, but he had been less than candid with her. This... this whatever it was that existed between him and Lord Linfield, it wasn't new. She felt certain of that, and while he had not lied to her, he had, she was certain, been circumspect with the truth.

"I'm going to head down. It'll give you space to change without us tripping over one another," she insisted, relieved that Edith waddled through from the adjoining room at that moment, for Jane was hovering around her, desperate to find an opening to step in and engage her about her husband's odd demands. "I'm glad for you, Jane." She squeezed her hands. "Truly, I'm glad that all is mended between you and that all will be well. You know I dearly wish you to be happy."

Jane followed her to the door, but she wouldn't speak in front of the maid, and so Eliza was able to slip away. Out in the corridor, the tears that she'd been holding back erupted in a sob. This was all too much. This house. Its inhabitants. Hope she hadn't realised she harboured now muddled her thoughts.

It seemed apparent that the connection between her and Jem had been so much less of a bond than she'd thought. She'd let herself be bowled over by physical pleasure, and then equated it to love.

But he wasn't in love with her. Not truly. Not if he meant to attend the Linfields.

She'd fallen for the oldest trick in the book. Show a woman a little affection, and she'll think you a prince right out of a faerie tale. Lord, she was a gullible as every other unwed girl in the land.

Eliza had to remain in the corridor for several minutes, swallowing down the bitter lump lodged in her throat before she could pull herself together enough to descend.

She was here in this damned castle for Jane's sake and would remain, but presently, she longed dearly for her shared room and shared bed in Bluebell Lane, and the comfort of her sisters' embraces.

-23-

Jem

"The arrangements are made?"

"Aye, with Bell's assistance I've managed to isolate Davy's gas, and the balloons are filled."

It was clear from the way Linfield peered at Jem down the length of his slender aristocratic nose that what Jem had taken to be a question had in fact been a statement, and one with an unexpected bite.

"But..." he blurted, at once enraged and agitated to the point of smashing the back of his hand against the sideboard. His knuckles stung, but rather than rub them, he stuffed his hands into his pockets. Safest place for them, else he might use them to throttle the life out of his host. "You agreed to try it. You promised that you would."

"And I will." Linfield's grin was all teeth and malice. "Shall you uphold your promises too, Jamie dearest?" He reached out to Jem, prompting him to flinch away.

"Don't touch me."

Linfield only laughed in the mean way of school yard bullies, but then Linfield was exactly the sort of spiteful miscreant to sneer down his nose at people and make their lives living hell. It was exactly what he was doing. He bore no real affection for Jem. He merely revelled in the control he had over him. Also, why did he insist on that pet name? Jem had never been Jamie, always Jem. Even Linfield had called him that until recently. Now suddenly it was Jamie this and Jamie that in an increasingly wheedling voice.

"Lady Linfield has agreed to your proposal?" he asked. Excuse him for questioning the likelihood of that considering how distraught the lady had been after catching Linfield *in flagrante*. It seemed highly illogical that she'd create such a fuss over a man fornicating with his mistress to being agreeable to him bringing his male lover into their marriage bed. One could only assume that Linfield had been deliberately vague over the particulars.

"What exactly has she agreed to? What did you tell her?"

"That I require your presence. That it is no way negotiable, but that you will not touch her or address her, and that the matter can be conducted in the dark so as not to offend anyone's sensibilities."

So, exactly as he'd expected, vague. No doubt the spiteful turd was relying on the fact that his pizzle would already be seated in his lady's garden to hide the fact that he needed to be simultaneously buggered in order to spend to pass unnoticed, or at least unremarked on until after the fact. And if Jane objected then, well, it was done, and who gave a shit? The seed was sewn, and if God was in any way merciful, well and truly planted. None of them would have to go through the deplorable experience again. The earl would get his grandson, and he'd put as much distance as he was able between himself and Linfield for the rest of his goddamned days. Not that it would matter, for the damage would already be done. Jane was bound to tell Eliza what had occurred, wasn't she?

Or might she hold her tongue for fear of the scandal it would cause if word were to get out?

"You'd better use the bloody gas, and you'll make a damn good show of it before I agree to come anywhere near you," Jem insisted through gritted teeth.

Linfield produced a child-like pout. "Jamie...Jamie, always so cross, when you used to be such fun." He ticked Jem on the cheek, making him flinch away. "Haven't I already said I'll breathe your vapours? I do hope they won't snuff me like a canary. That would be most unfortunate for us both. I'm sure you don't want to hang, Jamie mine."

"I'm not yours."

"You're mine if I say you're mine. And I do." Linfield caged him against the wainscotting to prove the point. "Best be mindful of the repercussions if you're about to contradict me."

Lord God, he hated him.

He hated every foul inch.

Hated himself too, for ever allowing himself to become ensnared in Linfield's sticky web.

In the whole of their blasted acquaintance, he'd never wanted to punch the supercilious sneer from Linfield's face more. He hoped all of Bell's leeches escaped and feasted on his tenderest flesh. That the Cedarton ghost scared him out of his wits and set his fucking bed alight so that he fried to a toasty crisp. That his goddamn cock shrivelled up and dropped off and he never managed to sire another dim-witted, blue-blooded, small-minded nob like himself. That, dammit, the bastard expired right here and now before Jem was forced to do something he absolutely did not want to do.

The nitrous oxide wasn't the answer.

They both knew how the night would end. He'd perform, like the trained monkey he was because the alternative would be so much worse. But worst of all, he knew he would do it because some impossible, nonsensical part of him was actually enthused by the idea.

It was a sickness. He probably needed locking away. Bedding Linfield and his lady wife was no substitute for the man and woman he wanted to take to bed. But that was never happening.

Linfield continued to regard him like he was a bug he was considering squashing, but then something shifted in his visage, and his hand dropped from where it had rested by the side of Jem's head to lie on Jem's hip.

"You want it."

"I most certainly do not."

Linfield's smile only broadened. "Such lies you tell. To me. To her. To yourself. If you're so sure you don't want it, then if I reach across, I won't find you stiff as a ramrod beneath your falls. Except," he wetted his lips, "we both know that you are." He leaned closer, so his lips caressed Jem's ear as he spoke. "Aren't you, my Jamie? What is it about the notion of buggering me while I'm inside a woman that makes you so cockish?"

"I'm not your Jamie. Stop calling me that." Jem brought his arms up fast to knock Linfield's out of the way. Unfortunately, instead of freeing himself from Linfield's caging embrace, he wound up with the whole of his lordship's body pressed fast to his.

"Oh, my. That is... It's a lot of excitement." Linfield made matters considerably worse by wedging his hand inside the fall of Jem's breeches and giving his irascible member an encouraging squeeze. "You're more than up to snuff. I do hope it's thoughts of my arse enveloping you that's causing that stand and not excitement over my wife."

"I'm not the slightest bit interested in your wife." He wasn't interested in Linfield either, but he was wise enough not to provoke him further by saying that. It just happened that he had particular fantasies about certain acts that his body reacted to, and that and when someone was stroking your cock, it tended to rise to the occasion regardless of what you thought of them.

"No, I'll concede that point. It's not my wife's cunny you wish to dip your wick into, it's Miss Wakefield's."

He was also wise enough to neither deny nor confirm that fact.

"The question is, whose arsehole is it you wish to plunder? Or are you imagining yourself as the piggy in the middle?"

"No. There's no one." Even as he said it, he knew it was pointless. Linfield was jealous enough to never believe him.

"Who is he? George? Bell?" It was so like Linfield to only consider what was present in the here and now. At least that meant he didn't have to obfuscate.

"No. There's no man here I wish to fuck."

Linfield made a noise as if he'd been struck. Then his slender fingers caught Jem around the throat and squeezed. "You jest, of course. Ah, Jamie, always such a joker." He gave Jem a squeeze lower down too, which naturally his traitorous cock responded to by further filling out. "Have I been too demanding of you? Have I not shown you enough affection? If the problem here is that you're full of pent-up need, I can see about rectifying that."

"Let go of me."

That merely prompted Linfield to put more pressure on the pulse points in Jem's throat, which left him uncomfortably lightheaded.

"Clearly you need a release, tutor mine." The bastard began circling the head of Jem's cock with his thumb, spreading the beads of arousal already gathered there and making him whimper despite his annoyance.

The problem was that Linfield knew what he liked and being teased into submission just happened to be one of those things that excited him, even when he really didn't want that to be the case.

The lack of blood flow to his brain wasn't helping.

"Stop it."

"I'll stop when you spend for me, and not before."

Linfield was tossing him now with rough and heady strokes, and no amount of hissing through his gritted teeth slowed him.

"For God's sake, we're about to dine. Your guests, your wife will be along any moment. Do you really want your perversions broadcast to the nation?"

The monster dug his teeth into his lower lip, mouth still stretched into a malicious smile. "Best let it happen quickly, then, or there are going to be an awful lot of questions asked. Imagine if your preferences became known outside of these walls."

"You're the one with his hand inside another man's breeches."

"Aye, but you're the one about to spend because of it."

He could already hear the tale Linfield would concoct to explain his part in it. Nothing sordid, and even if people questioned the truth of his words, he wouldn't suffer the same ignominy Jem would. No, Linfield would use his station, and laugh it off exactly as he'd laughed off a woman's death due to his driving. He'd parade his new bride around a few ballrooms, spin a tale of jealousy and obsession and his tutor's unnatural desires. *Had to dismiss the poor misguided fellow. Always knew there was something untoward about him. Mind you, I never imagined he'd do anything so disgraceful as that."*

There were footsteps approaching from the hall. The twitter of voices some distance away.

Jem wriggled and tried to shove Linfield off, but there was no moving him. He'd planted himself with roots as firm as a willow tree. Even raking his nails across his bare skin didn't budge him.

"Do that again, and I'll turn you about and fuck you, tutor, and I won't give a damn who sees it, in fact I'll line them up to watch. Perhaps you think otherwise, but I'll remind you, there's not a soul in this household who won't do exactly as they're told if I command it. Everyone has their weaknesses, Jem. I know yours. I know George's... Miss Wakefield's... Even Bell's. So, stop with your squirming, and come in my damned hand."

-24-

Eliza

There was such a thing as arriving in the wrong place at the wrong time. Caught up in her thoughts and determined to demand the truth of Jem the moment an opportunity to do so arose, Eliza didn't notice the two figures in the antechamber to the dining room until she was already through the double doors to that room. Then, for a moment she wasn't sure what she was witnessing, a disagreement, a fight? Linfield had Jem pinned. Jem's utterances made it clear. She had heard him make similar sounds thrice now.

She ought never to have trusted him for a moment.

He was not the man she'd hoped and believed him to be, nay, but every bit the one she'd prayed he was not.

"Look lively, Whistler, the company's arrived." Linfield turned, a smirk on his aristocratic features, while Jem remained sunk low in the shadow behind him. "You've made a dire mess of me, Jamie."

Horrified, Eliza watched as Linfield raised his hand to his mouth and licked his palm and fingers clean.

What a goddamned fool she was.

What a preposterous, ridiculous fool.

"I'm afraid you caught us in the heat of an exchange," Linfield crowed. "But we're all done now." He held his hand out to her. "Shall we go into dinner?"

For a moment, she thought she might be sick. Another woman would surely have fainted, but Eliza was no delicate society flower. She was of hardy Yorkshire stock. A woman who'd helped birth babies and who'd dug a pistol ball from a marquis's leg. She could be disgusted and still maintain her poise. Though she barely managed to nod her head.

The Cluetts entered behind her at that moment, followed swiftly by Doctor Bell, then Jane. Her friend linked arms with her, and danced her forward a couple of paces, merry as a spring lamb who'd learned he wasn't for the dinner table.

"What's the matter?"

"Nothing."

Dammit, even Jane had betrayed her. She'd agreed to Linfield's ridiculous proposition. Had barely even protested the inclusion of Jem in her bedding, even when she knew Eliza was soft on him.

All she cared for was her own security.

Never mind if her friend's heart got broken. It'd mend. After all, Eliza was hardy. Eliza never allowed her emotions to get in the way of sensibility.

But they'd been on the cusp of something. She'd

started to let herself believe she could have something meaningful on her terms.

"Eliza, shall we go in?" Jane tugged gently on her arm.

"You know, I'm not actually hungry."

How could she possibly sit at a table and do something as ordinary as break bread with these people?

"Oh, but you must eat."

Jem shot her a glance that one might describe as pleading, but she was done with being played for a fool. He was as untrustworthy and unreliable as the rest. There was not a single man in the world who could be trusted to do the right thing. What an idiot she had been to have forgotten that?

She would not allow herself to be so blindsided again.

"Eliza?" Jane tugged on her sleeve. "Are you unwell?"

She shook herself. "No. I'm well, thank you. Do go ahead. I'll be there in a moment."

-25-

Jem

Of course, it had been Linfield's intention all along to sever the growing ties between him and Eliza. That they had already been down to the last few hours of him being blessed by her regard was of no consequence.

Linfield had maintained his position before Jem until he'd had his clothing back in place, but it didn't matter. It was damned obvious what had gone on. Perhaps to the Cluetts, to Bell, even Lady Linfield, their proximity was only the sign of an intimate chat. But Eliza knew. She knew. He could see it in her face. And then Linfield addressed her and made it damned obvious by sucking his fingers clean.

He watched the light in her eyes die. The smile fall from her pink lips.

"Eliza?" he said, reaching out, but she pulled her arms tight to herself and looked straight through him, as if he were as insubstantial as the ghost rumoured to walk these halls.

"I'm sorry," he tried.

"Sorry?" That won her attention. "What is it you're sorry for, Jem?"

Through the open doorway to the dining room, he could see Linfield smirking.

"Could you be referring to the fact that you mean to spend the night in my best friend's bed chamber alongside her and her husband, or that... that you've been his...his catamite all along and you're only sorry that I got to observe that fact with my own eyes?"

He couldn't deny the truth of either accusation.

"Yes," he mumbled. "Eliza, truly, I'm sorry. I tried... you don't understand."

"Oh, I understand perfectly. You're a liar, James Whistler. I thought... I thought I could trust you, that perhaps..." She bowed her head.

He wanted her to continue, to finish that sentence in the manner he wished it to end, with the possibility of a future for them both, but that dream, if it had ever existed, was over. She couldn't even formulate the words to express her outrage with sufficient derision.

"Pray don't speak to me again."

He bowed, and allowed her to pass, knowing his cause was already lost, and that Linfield was still watching him, making sure the wind had turned in the direction he'd commanded it. "Happy now?" He mouthed to that miscreant.

Linfield's grin was enough to make it clear the answer was deliriously so.

"Stop dithering, Whistler. Let Miss Wakefield pass, so we may eat."

He had no desire to sit at the table and eat, but

nor would Linfield allow him to leave. No matter that he wanted to flee and throw himself into a ditch where he could wallow in the inkpot of his own misery.

"Don't get any crazy ideas now."

Crazy? Like perhaps throwing himself from one of Cedarton's lofty towers?

He was wounded not mad.

A vision hit him then, of himself hurrying away across the misty moors, and Linfield chasing after him with his dogs. He didn't have any dogs, but that was hardly the point. The point was that there was no sense in running because he'd just get hauled back here. The more Jem resisted; the harder Linfield would fight to hold on to him. He knew then that only when Linfield tired of him would he win his actual freedom.

This evening's spread consisted of broiled mackerel, roast beef, coxcomb skewers, asparagus, and shallots, along with some manner of fruit trifle the cook had clearly tried to dress up with a few beheaded winter pansies. He could summon no appetite for anything bar the sherry, and following that, the wine.

Linfield chattered. The rest of them were dour to a soul—Eliza, the Cluetts, Bell always looked like he'd just been winkled from a coffin, and as for their hostess... Actually, Lady Linfield bore more colour than she had in recent days. Was she? Merciful lord, she couldn't be excited by the prospect of what was to come later this evening? That thought horrified him almost as much as being expected to rise to the occasion.

It mattered not that Eliza now despised him. The threat of Linfield orchestrating some slight to her reputation remained real. Thus, he would do as he was bid.

Eliza, he noted, speared a single asparagus stalk, but did no more than cut it into narrow slices, none of which passed her lips.

"I can explain," he wanted to say to her. They were seated much too far apart to attempt actual conversation, a fact he could likely attribute to Linfield's manipulation. *"I know how it looks, but I don't want you to think—"*

"Are you, or aren't you accompanying Lord and Lady Linfield to her bedchamber this evening?"

"I am, but—" He tugged at the knot of his cravat. The damn thing was strangling him. "Only because there's no other choice. I'm a fool, Eliza, I readily admit that. I've handled everything badly, and now I've brought this down on our heads. I can't let him ruin you. I can't. And he will. I'm sorry. Truly, I'm sorry. If there were any other way."

As long as Linfield lived, he'd never be free.

"I love you, Eliza. I want you to know that's real despite all the rest. I wish I knew how to make things right. I wish it didn't have to end like this. I wish you'd never had to see this part of me."

He wished it were still August, and they were back at Stags Fell. That the brief moments of bliss they'd found in the gardens at Lauwine hadn't drifted by so quickly. That Joshua wasn't Joshua, and he wasn't himself. That he didn't find himself as attracted to men as he was to women. That he hadn't been a gentleman and had fucked her when he'd had the chance. At least he had the memory of her taste on his tongue, and the soft warmth of her within his arms to look back on.

From his right, Linfield shot out a hand and clamped it fast about Jem's wrist as if he could hear Jem's thoughts and sought to show his disapproval of them. Jem swung his gaze to him as he fought to withdraw his hand, but stilled at the look on Linfield's face. From across the table, Lady Linfield gave an alarmed cry and shoved back her chair, which toppled a glassful of wine all over her plate.

"Linfield," she gasped, bending to him like a flower to the sun.

Jem could not quite explain it, but there was certainly a bilious glow to his lordship's features, particularly around the mouth. He looked...he looked... stricken. Agonised. As if some foul wyrm were gnawing on him from the inside. He made a choking sound, his free hand rising to his throat.

"Good God, help him," George insisted, pushing back his chair. "He must have a fishbone stuck."

Linfield's grip only tightened as Jem rose to his feet. He had to peel back Linfield's fingers to release his grip. He raised his hand to strike between his lordship's shoulders, but before the heel of his hand could connect, Linfield spewed copious amounts of scarlet blood over the table linens.

The remaining two gentlemen stood at once. Eliza too was half out of her chair. Henrietta fell into a swoon.

"Bell!" Jane cried, seizing up her napkin to offer Linfield it, only to then use it to wipe the splatter from her face. Linfield seemed blind to their reactions.

The physician had hardly moved a foot when Linfield disgorged a second gout of blood.

"What's happening to him?" Jem still stood with his hands raised, uncertain as to where to put them. "Ulcer?"

The doctor shook his head, as if afraid to make his diagnosis. His brows were drawn into deep furrows, and he seemed as bewildered as the rest of them over what to do. "I think he's been…" He shook his head again, as if he couldn't equate what was happening before him with what his mind was telling him. Jem didn't want to fill in what he suspected Bell had been about to say either, but the evidence was there before them. The scarlet splatter was too bright against the table linen. Linfield's bilious hue, the haze of wrongness around him.

Jane howled and clutched her belly as if she too were about to cast up her assets. "No, no. This can't be."

As if awaiting the cue of her cry, Linfield buckled at the knees. Both Jem and Bell failed to catch him. Instead, they watched horrified as he bounced off both the table and his chair before landing with a thud, dragging the table linens with him. Only Eliza had the presence of mind to grasp the cloth as it slithered away, jostling the bone China and all the dishes into an ear-splitting clatter.

Bell followed his patient down to the floor.

Jem too, bent to his knees, "Tell me what I can do? There must be something... Will a drink help?"

Bell cut him off with a succinct shake of the head. "It's too late." He withdrew his hand from his patient's pulse point in his throat. "He's gone."

"What?" That could not be so. It could not be... "Are you sure?" he blurted. A nonsensical question. Bell knew his art, and he could see there was no breath left in Linfield's chest, which left him staring at his former patron's slumped and bloodied corpse uncomprehending, until Jane shoved him aside. A sob erupted violently from her mouth.

"No. No, he cannot be. He cannot. Doctor, you must do something. How can he be dead? He was well just two minutes ago." Her tears began to spill thick and fast. "Do something." She clutched at Bell's coat front and the ends of his periwig, but there was nothing to be done. Linfield was already past help.

"I'm sorry. Lady Linfield, please," Bell attempted, his atrocious bedside manner failing to rise to the occasion. To be fair, he looked almost as distraught as Jane, and every bit as addled as Jem felt. He did manage to free himself of her insistent grip and straighten his hair. "Madam, there's no remedy I can give. I'm sorry, but your husband is with his God now."

She howled. Howled like a banshee. Like the old Lady Cedarton was rumoured to have done before she leapt from the wreckage of the Lady's Tower. A moment later, she was risen to her full height and spitting red-eyed ire at them all as the shock melted away her usual meekness. "Who has done this?

Which of you has taken him from me?"

Heads swivelled in her direction, each of the stares more wild-eyed than the last. Jem saw only shock in their faces. If one among them was guilty, then they were hiding it well. George slapped his own cheeks as if to rouse himself from a daze. Bell uneasily shifted his weight from one sole to the other, Eliza stood too still, and Henrietta, having roused from her faint of her own accord, perhaps having realised she was no one's centre of attention, turned her bottle of smelling salts between her fingers as if she anticipated needing them again promptly.

"One of you has done this. You have tormented me and poisoned him. Drugged his food, his wine..."

"I cannot think what you mean to imply." Henrietta set her hand firmly on her son's forearm. Jem suspected she did it to prove to herself that her offspring remained alive and vital, but the touch served to single him out.

"You," Jane accused.

"Not I," he insisted. "'Tis one of you. Level your accusatory stares elsewhere."

"You did quarrel most vociferously, George. It's natural that would make people suspicious."

"Let go of me, mother." George shook off her grip. "That matter was settled between us. We'd reached an accord, and I am hardly the only one among us with whom he had a quarrel. Who among us had not felt the lash of his spite? Perhaps, madam," his gaze settled firmly on Jane, "you considered the slight of his afternoon activities too great to tolerate and chose to show your displeasure. You are right at his hand, in a prime position to taint his drink, after all, and likewise, Mr Whistler, who has done nothing but scowl at him since we sat down to dine."

Jem couldn't deny it was so, all too conscious of the malicious thoughts he'd been entertaining. Thoughts borne of anger, but which he'd never have acted on. And thoughts didn't kill people, only deeds did that, and looking around at them, they all had motive, each and every one of them.

Jane retaliated with further accusations of her own, and she and George got into a spat.

"Stop this," Bell called over them. "A man has died. Can we not manage a little decorum?" They continued to lob accusations around him. "Lord Bellingbrook must be informed, and the magistrate summoned." He rang for a servant, and Mrs Honeyfield answered, her jaw swollen out of all proportion. "The master is dead." Bell informed her. "Please instruct his valet. Word must be sent to Bellingbrook at once, and who is the justice of the peace in these parts? The coroner?"

No one paying any attention seemed certain.

"Which is the nearest large estate? Send someone there, they will surely know. Meanwhile, I will preserve the body."

Now the initial shock was done, Bell seemed to have found his feet and spun into the same sort of efficiency he'd done after that fateful day of the carriage race. Jem too vividly remembered the bend of the woman's neck and his own longing to correct all that lay askew. Linfield's body lay blood splattered, his mouth open and scarlet ringed. He reached for a napkin, meaning to wipe away the mess, but Bell stayed him with a hand to his shoulder.

"Don't."

He relinquished. It didn't seem right that his tormentor could be gone. He kept expecting him to blink or break into a twistical grin, and roar with laughter over their alarm. Instead, he remained still. Jem formed his fingers around Linfield's. Their warmth was already leaving them.

Above him, Jane continued to spit accusations. "Snakes. Maggots. Leeches. Why are you here?" she cried, wound into hysteria. Tears scored her cheeks. "Who among you has deprived my son of his father?"

The hair across Jem's body rose at her words. Bell too became rigid. It was Cluetts though who bleated the incomprehensibility they all felt.

"Your son? But it can't be. You can't be." Henreitta spluttered.

A statement Jem swore every person gathered was also thinking. If Jane was already swelling with Linfield's child, then the leeches, his torment, Davy's gas, Henrietta on her knees, Linfield's fight with George; none of it had been necessary. Either Linfield had played them all for utter fools, or his wife was a liar...or deluded...? Perhaps it was wishful thinking, like a woman facing the noose, eagerly making a plea of her belly to spare herself that dreadful fate.

"'Tain't legitimately his," George declared,

shaking his sandy head. "Even supposing he sired it, which—"

"How dare you? What are you accusing me of?" Jane wrapped her arms protectively around herself. "Of course, it is his. I have never been unfaithful to my husband. I can't believe you would accuse me of such... We've only been wed eight weeks."

Jem was damned certain Linfield wouldn't have borne leeches on his prick if the deed was done. Perhaps Jane was merely inexperienced enough that she believed the act accomplished. Whatever the case, this did not seem the moment to tease forth the truth. Linfield was not yet cold. Better they spent a few moments reflecting on the fragility of existence and considering what was important.

Eliza appeared before him. She must have crawled under the table. She was curiously composed as she double-checked Linfield's pulse and confirmed Bell's diagnosis of death for herself. Jem covered his mouth with his hand, still struggling to comprehend that the man was gone. For all his faults, his blackmail attempts, and manipulations, there had been good times back before the carriage race, before his marriage, when Jem had been far less reticent about their loving. When it had all been a grand lark, and there weren't ties and expectations binding them. When he'd been only too happy to escape his memories of this woman who he knew he couldn't have.

He felt a splash against his hand and was startled to find that he was weeping. A hole seemed burned through his chest. Eliza leaned over the body and whispered something. He wasn't sure what she said, but she pressed a kerchief into his fist.

Then she rose. "Quiet, all of you." The sharp bark of her voice won her the silence of the other guests. "Is this any way to behave? His lordship is dead, and you are screeching at one another like crows at a feast. Save your speculations and accusations for the coroner and his jurors. There will be a time for such things, but right now, we should afford him some dignity. Doctor Bell, you among us are most familiar with death. Is it best to leave him here or remove him to his bedchamber, perhaps?"

Bell twitched with unease. This was no natural death, and if it was murder, then the body ought to be left in place to be examined by those summoned to see justice done, but Bell was also a practical man. Not the sort to hand over the investigation of an aristocrat's death to a dozen or so of the parish's finest, and whose discretion was definitely not guaranteed. The earl would be ill disposed to the family being embroiled in a scandal, and that man was now their direct paymaster. Moreover, if the actual culprit were to be found, Bell was far more likely to find him with his science than a few local well to dos sniffing around and mulling their findings in the back room of the local ale house.

To that effect, Bell drew a cloak of humility about his person. "It would seem that Lord Linfield has suffered an acute malaise of the alimentary tract.

Every ear in the room strained in his direction. Every head turned.

Bell kept his head bowed.

Jane squinted sceptically at him, then down at her husband's blood splattered corpse. "A malaise of the alimentary tract?"

"Yes, or a tumour. Or an ulcer. Mayhaps, even a malady of the liver. If you grant me permission, then I can definitively determine which of those things it is."

"The old crow wants to carve him up," George chortled.

Jane paled and bit her lips. "I'm not sure... I don't think the earl would like to hear that his son had been dismembered."

"The earl will be pleased to know what has caused the death, and I think we can all agree that it is in our best interests to determine that quickly, without outside interference. I can assure you, Lady Linfield, that your husband will be treated with the uttermost care and dignity, and suitably preserved for his casket."

"Yes, I suppose." The meek, marrowless incarnation of Jane had returned. Her fire drained now that the possibility of murder had been cast aside. "What you say, does make sense."

Bell bowed rather stiffly. "I humbly request that I be allowed to move Lord Linfield's body to my surgery. It is much cooler in that part of the house, and hence better suited to the task of preservation, and I can better fulfil my investigations there."

She nodded, before sagging into a chair.

The Cluetts too, both slumped. George grasped the sherry decanter. Bell summoned the male servants and had them set about the task of improvising a stretcher.

"Jane?" Eliza came to her friend on her knees. "You must write to the earl. Shall I assist you?"

"Please. Yes," she replied soggily.

"Then, let us go to the library and use the desk there."

Eliza turned her head to Bell on the threshold. "I'll see she gets to bed afterwards, and I'll stay with her." She might as well have said that she didn't trust any of the castle's other inhabitants, Jem among them, but if she had to put her faith in someone, then the doctor was it.

The Cluetts lingered after the two women left. George watching the proceedings with sharp eyes as Linfield was lifted onto the stretcher and borne away.

"Perhaps best not to touch the remaining victuals," Bell remarked to the servants, which prompted George to set the sherry decanter he was in the act of pouring from down with a thud. He gave Bell a shrewd squint.

"A malaise?"

"Yes."

"Caused by?"

Bell chewed over the question but didn't supply an answer.

"I'll find an alternative." George galloped toward the exit, round face flushed and a pinch betwixt his brows that concertinaed the flesh. Henrietta trailed after him.

"'Tis no doubt the work of that horrid ghost," Jem overheard her saying. "He ought to have heeded the warnings. We'd be wise to all of us heed the warnings. The old mistress doesn't approve of us invading her domain and is determined to drive us out."

"Do curb your tongue, mother. I wish you wouldn't prattle on so with the maids. Drive us out!" He huffed. "Where would you have us go? The exchange was to be made this evening. All is not yet well and may never be well if we don't secure that—"

"I am perfectly apprised of the situation, George, and whose fault it is."

"Mother," George turned about sharply to face her, bringing the plump dove to an abrupt halt. "Cease, please. I don't wish to spend Christmastide in a cell. Neither for debt nor murder."

"The doctor said it was a problem with his gut."

"Aye, and he also claims that bloodletting can't possibly cure a headache, meat is bad for you, and that human beings do not contain a soul."

Suitably outraged, she huffed and strutted off towards the hall.

"Poison?" Jem ventured once there was only the two of them left. "You may have removed the onus on us to preserve the scene and provide testaments by refusing to speak your suspicions, but it's what you actually believe, isn't it?"

"Walk with me, Whistler." Ludlow led them out and to the stairs to his basement lair. "There's only one way to prove the matter. And—"

"You can spare me the explanation. I know perfectly well why you called off the hounds."

Bell nodded, and the two of them followed the body down to his surgery, where Bell instructed the servants to rest him on the table in the back room, where a sheet was draped over his still form. Jem collapsed onto the chaise in the main room. The skeletal remnants of his chemistry remained half-assembled on the table; the silk balloons gathered in a wooden crate beside them. He was tempted to stick his head into one and let the gas snuff him into insensibility.

Bell dropped to one knee before him and felt his pulse, before turning to his shelf of ingredients. He returned a moment later with a glass of amber liquid. "Drink this."

"What is it?"

"Cognac. One of the poor sod's best."

Jem took the glass. "What have you dissolved in it?"

Bell shook his head. "Not a goddamned thing. I need you lucid. God knows, you've reasons aplenty to be responsible for this, but it doesn't make sense that it would be you."

A sob erupted from his body, causing him to clap a hand over his mouth. Bell nodded at the glass, and Jem swallowed the contents. If Bell was drugging him, then there was no taste of it in the smooth liquid as it heated his throat.

"Better?"

"Not in the slightest. If not me, then who is it you think has done this?"

Bell steepled his long fingers and tapped them to his lips. "I don't know. Nor am I sure it will serve us any purpose to speculate at this point, not until I'm confident as to the cause of death."

"So, you do mean to cut him open?"

"I'd make for a very poor anatomist if I did not, and time is not on my side at this point."

"What do you mean by that?"

"I mean that if he is dead by virtue of something other than ill fortune, he is dead for a reason, and that as I do not know that reason, it's impossible to say whether the person who meted out such justice is satisfied with the result. They may strike again. Also, I feel it is of note that it is Lord and not Lady Linfield who lies next door, whereas all the ghastly visitations that have occurred since we arrived here have been targeted at her."

"I'm not sure what you're suggesting." Jem nevertheless felt that Bell was scratching at a scab. Nay, not a scab, more like a festering sore. "Are you suggesting that perhaps Linfield wasn't the intended target?"

Bell did not reply, though both his brows raised in a meaningful sort of way.

"But wait... Wasn't Linfield our chief suspect for orchestrating his wife's misery? He would hardly deliberately poison himself, and while I agree the man lacked wits, he was not so dumb as to be lackadaisical about drinking from a poisoned chalice, or whatever means by which you presume the substance was delivered." Indeed, Linfield had exhibited a talent for self-preservation, frequently at the expense of others. His entire philosophy was founded on the principle of putting himself first and not giving a damn about everyone else.

"Jem, I'm not suggesting anything, merely noting the deviation from the sequence. No doubt you can provide me with the statistical probability of that anomaly."

On another day at another time, perhaps. Currently, he couldn't fathom how one and one even made two.

"Please tell me this isn't some harebrained jape."

"His death is not a ruse, Jem. He is not about to spring up and shout 'Surprise!'"

"You would say that, even if he were, so as not to spoil the punchline."

Bell bowed his head and nodded at his chest. "Go next door and confirm it for yourself if you need to. I assure you; he's gone. Maybe you need a few moments before I set to work, to say whatever you need to say to him."

He wasn't sure he had anything to say to the man, nevertheless Jem left Bell in favour of the body in the inner sanctum.

-26-

Eliza

Jane did not settle to her task when they reached the library but took to pacing back and forth instead. While she wore a hole in the hearth rug, Eliza set about finding paper and pen so that when she was ready Jane could compose her thoughts and write to the earl. This necessitated a quick rummage through the desk to secure parchment and ink.

"What am I to do, Eliza? I don't know what to think or feel or anything." Jane's wan features were horridly blotchy, and her lips red from being bitten. The moment of anger she'd summoned following Linfield's demise had faded into a simmering sort of indecisiveness. "It's all so horribly sudden. It doesn't make any sense. We'd finally seen eye to eye and now... now he is no more. I want to be sad about it, but don't feel much of anything. Not even relief. I should feel something, shouldn't I?"

"Perhaps it is still sinking in," Eliza suggested as steadily as she was able. God's blood, she had no love for Lord Linfield, he had struck her as a snake from the start, and he hadn't shown his wife any great care. In fact, she'd wondered multiple times if he was trying to relieve his new bride of her wits. And... and he'd made that display before dinner purely to spite her, she was sure. On the other hand, he had not deserved such an abrupt and violent end. Nor to be deprived of his life in his own home. And for what? That was the part she could not fathom. What did anyone gain from his demise? The reasons and possibilities seemed endless and hopelessly theoretical. Not a single avenue of any substance stood out.

She drew out the chair for Jane to take and handed her the pen.

"What should I say?" her friend asked, settling uneasily on the edge of the seat.

Heavens, could she not manage one dratted thing for herself? Could she not comprehend that Eliza's mind was in as much of a whirl as her own?

"Say that you're not sure of the cause, but that he has passed away. That Doctor Bell is taking care of matters, and you'll await the earl's instructions as to funeral arrangements. They may wish him to be interred on the family estate. I would not mention the baby yet. Perhaps save those tidings for a missive to his mother once this news has had time to settle."

"Yes." She set ink to paper, writing the required words swiftly and sanding them dry. "Eliza, I have no black clothes."

"They can be procured. The servants will see to the mirrors being covered and other household arrangements. Really, there's nothing you can do, Jane, save hold yourself together as best you are able."

"Yes, of course, but shouldn't I attempt to find out what has happened?"

"I should leave that to Doctor Bell."

Jane levelled her with a surprisingly astute glare. "Truly? Where is my friend, Eliza Wakefield? What have you done with her?"

There were times to challenge the patriarchy, and this wasn't one of them.

"You think we should stand back and allow Doctor Bell to investigate?"

"He's the best qualified to determined how Linfield died. If it was a burst ulcer, he will tell us so, and if it was something else… that too." Although she sincerely hoped he'd spare Jane the details. She was far too tender and squeamish for a forensic discourse on the state of her husband's innards.

"Well, that's assuming we can trust him, and he isn't the one responsible."

"Responsible?" Bell was the least likely murderer among them. He was the only one of them she couldn't attribute a motive to.

Jane vacated her seat at the desk and began her pacing once more. It made Eliza weary watching her, so she folded the letter and set about locating some sealing wax. "I honestly trust him more than any other here."

"More than me?" Jane challenged, then bowed her head when Eliza met her gaze, for, yes, she did trust Bell more. There was something about him, something steadfast and reliable. He wasn't one to be easily swayed, and while his manner was frequently atrocious, it was equally atrocious regardless of whom he was speaking to.

"I thought we were friends, Eliza Wakefield. How can you suspect me of that? How could you think that I—"

"Do not challenge me on the grounds of friendship. You're the one who meant to spend the night with another man in your bed. A man you knew I particularly liked."

"Only because Linfield demanded it."

"And you didn't object. You didn't spare a single thought for how it might affect me."

"I had no notion that you were that enamoured of him."

"You knew it. You just chose not to acknowledge it when it mattered. In any case, do you not see how that plays into this? If it weren't for your condition, then you might not have been so ready to do his bidding, and you might have fathomed the truth of what manner of man you'd married."

Jane's mouth rounded into an angry O. She crossed her arms and set to rubbing their uppers. "He did ask that of me, and I did agree for exactly the reason you state. Why would I not? It was to be one occasion. Mr Whistler wasn't going to touch me. And really, Eliza, I know everyone believes me simple, but I thought you knew better. It's obvious that Mr Whistler is of the same inclinations as my husband, so it's not as if anything would come of your affection for him, anyway."

"You don't know that."

Jane sighed wearily. "I realise it's a shock to find out that he's... well, that he's unnatural, but do you really mean to punish me for that?"

"I'm not punishing anyone."

She'd been ready to give everyone involved the benefit of the doubt, right up until the point where she'd witnessed them fornicating outside the dining room. Keeping her head held high had been one of the toughest things she'd ever had to do. Looking at that beloved face, and seeing his guilt painted right across his features; it'd near hollowed her out completely. She'd wanted to shriek at him. To stamp her foot and succumb to the sort of rage her sister Maria would have displayed.

Only, she wasn't Maria. Nor was she Caroline, who would have swooned for definite, and then fallen into the deepest most desperate despair. Or, Joanna—stoic, loyal Joanna, who only ever cried on the inside. She was Eliza Wakefield. The sensible one. The practical one. The backbone of the family. The one everyone turned to. The one who stood firm when others faltered. She'd come here to support Jane in her new life as a member of the nobility, and that was what she would continue to do.

"I had no inkling of Linfield's inclinations until this afternoon," Jane confessed. She was worrying her skirts into knots, making alarming creases in the sheer fabrics. "If I'd had even the smallest notion of it, then I would never have agreed the match."

Of course she would not. Marrying had served a single purpose for Jane. Security for herself and the baby another man had planted in her belly. A man she still refused to name.

"You ought to be relieved, Eliza, that you shan't now be fooled in the same way. Not that you would have been. You're too clever for that."

She had only a sigh to give in response. "It's not important now."

"I'm sorry, Eliza. You're right, I allowed myself to be extremely selfish. I did know you liked him, and I ought to have stood up to Linfield and insisted he do his husbandly duties without assistance."

What did it matter? It wouldn't even happen anymore, and she ought to be pleased that she'd discovered Jem's deceit before their lovemaking had progressed any further. In truth, it was only his restraint that allowed her to say that. She'd been only too willing to play the silly fool and have him thrust himself inside her.

"He's not the man I thought him to be. He's just another scoundrel like all the rest."

Jane sighed and rested her hand on Eliza's cheek. "We're both dunces, and I, silly fool that I am, have let everyone know I'm with child when it would have been wiser not to do so."

"You did rather blurt it out."

"I did, didn't I? As I said, I'm a thorough ninny."

Eliza swallowed the hard lump in her throat. "You're not. Not really. You'd had a shock. We all had. Everyone's humours were up."

Eager for whatever manner of accord they could come to, Jane nodded eagerly. "Do you believe what Doctor Bell said, that some undiagnosed malady took him?"

Eliza swayed her head. "No," she admitted. "I think he said that to make sure the magistrate wasn't summoned. I think his first suspicion was likely the same one the rest of us formed—"

"Poison?"

"Poison."

"So, there's a murderer amongst us?"

"Perhaps," Eliza agreed. "Is it discomforting that I find that notion easier to reconcile than Cedarton having a genuine white lady walking its halls?"

"A little, perhaps. Eliza, do you think we might agree that neither of us did him in? Only, it will make our continued friendship a good deal easier to manage if we do."

"It will, and very well. Do you wish to shake hands on it?"

Jane offered up hers, and they sealed their pact like gentlemen.

"I don't recall anyone tampering with his glass, but I was at the other end of the table, and not inclined to pay him attention."

"I don't understand it," Jane said, worrying her lips. "Weren't we all drinking the same stuff? I swear my glass was filled from the same bottle, and Mr Whistler's too, and perhaps Mr Cluett's. He was drinking a lot. In fact, I think everyone was. Surely if something had been added to one of the bottles, then we would all have been affected."

"Not a lot of the food got eaten," Eliza observed. "So, it seems unlikely to have been something in that." She'd had no appetite, Bell never touched meat, and Jem had spooned a few things onto his plate, but she couldn't say for definite whether he'd eaten them or not. And surely poisoning the food indeterminately was far too risky, also one would have had to have access to it before it reached the table. That meant going down to the kitchens or intercepting it en route, something that would easily be determined with only a quick interview with Cedarton's handful of servants. But they'd all gone in to dine at the same time. She'd sat down last, and she couldn't recall anyone leaving to use the chamber pot.

"The Cluetts both ate heartily, but then if it was one of them, you'd think they'd be more circumspect about what they touched, and I think George had a bit of everything. I do think it was most likely them though. Don't you, Eliza? Didn't you see how quickly George was to defend himself and accuse me? But then that doesn't make sense. They wouldn't risk poisoning themselves, would they?"

"Maybe it wasn't anything on the table."

"You mean someone could have got to him earlier? Oh, yes!" Jane's eyes gleamed with sudden fervour. "Then I bet it was Henrietta. I bet she rouged her lips with it and then when she—"

"That is rather fanciful. It would hurt her as much as him if she put something on her lips."

"But just because it is fanciful does not mean it's not possible."

True enough. Jane seemed very taken with the idea, but perhaps that was down to her still harbouring ill-feelings over catching Henrietta with her mouth around Linfield's prick.

"What if it's all connected?"

"If all what is connected?" Jane asked.

"Everything. The ghosts, the bed fire, the quarrels, Linfield's death." Too many inexplicable things had occurred for them not to be related.

Jane nudged her arm. "I know that expression, you're cogitating again. Share your thoughts with me."

"I have nothing to share. I don't have any answers, Jane, nor even a working theory. I just think it's all related, Old Lady Cedarton appearing to you, your bed inexplicably burning, Linfield's death, even maybe the reason why you came to Cedarton to begin with."

"Are you suggesting this is all to do with..." She spread her fingers across her stomach. "It can't be. Nobody knows, and nobody ever will."

That was not what she had meant, rather Linfield's reason to sojourn in the Yorkshire countryside in a half-ruined castle cut off from its neighbours by frost and mist.

Then again, who was to say those two things weren't also connected? Matters felt so jumbled, it wouldn't surprise her at all to discover they were.

George lurched into the room at that moment, causing Jane to cry out, and Eliza to place herself between Mr Cluett and her friend. "Is there something you wish to say to Lady Linfield, Mr Cluett?" She was forced to put a hand to his chest to keep him from bowling her over. Now far beyond the stage of maudlin drunkenness he'd displayed earlier,

George's eyes blazed with tyrannical menace.

"Lady Linfield my arse," he blasphemed, shoving his blotchy red face up close to Eliza in a manner that caused her eyes to water as a result of the alcohol fumes on his breath. "'Tain't a legitimate marriage. You might have sworn it afore the Lord, but that doesn't change matters. Happens his lordship was already bound. I know. I've seen the record. Might be that he tore it from the parish record book, but it still happened. Was still witnessed and officiated."

"That's a hideous thing to say. You're lying," Jane protested. "He's only been gone a moment. I can't believe you're being this horrid."

"Good riddance," George snarled. "I hope the Devil has him dangling on the prongs of his pitchfork."

"What is it you want?" Eliza asked, both curious and determined to temper the level of drama occurring. "Or have you simply come to create mischief?"

"I've come for what's mine, and I'll have it, if you don't want the world to know your marriage is a phoney one." He nodded his head at Jane as he spoke.

"Don't heed him, Jane. Your marriage is valid. He means only to menace you, the same as all drunks."

"Happens I may have had a tipple or two." George rocked on his heels, before making a swipe in Jane's direction that fell far short of his target. "It don't change the facts. She ain't really Lady Linfield.

Can't be. He weren't free to have her. Yer can dispute it all you wish; I have the paper what says it plain. Married he was, last spring, to Janie Faintree, not Jane Morley, recorded by Thomas Jenkins, curate, in the presence of two witness all appropriately documented with their marks."

Eliza shoved him back from her person.

"That cannot be so. I don't believe you. Eliza, it can't be," poor Jane sang.

Worryingly, she feared it might be.

"Where is your proof, Mr Cluett?"

George patted his coat front, appraising them of an inside pocket. "Right where it's safe, that's where. If you want it from me, and for me to hold my tongue, then I'll make you the same offer I made him. The deeds to the Berkley Square property that he swindled from me, in exchange for my silence." He made a turning motion before his lips, then cast away the imaginary key. "Otherwise, I'll ruin you as surely as he's ruined me. Everyone who matters will know that you're a fraud, and that he was a bigamist. Your brat will be baseborn. The bastard brat of a dead bigamist. I'm sure he'll grow into a fine and respected citizen." His grin was entirely made of spite.

"What have I done to you?" Jane pleaded. The answer was nothing.

A fact George readily admitted. "You're even quite sweet in the insipid, useless way of proper society ladies. That's why I'm giving you the chance to buy my silence."

"But I don't know anything about a house on

Berkley Square, nor have I any notion where Linfield would keep the deeds to it. Would they not be with his man of business, or even the earl?"

"You had better hope they are not."

"Mr Cluett, I believe you said earlier that you and he were to make amends this evening," Eliza hugged Jane to her as she spoke. "Surely then the deed must be here at Cedarton, perhaps even on his person. That is, as you've already rightly pointed out, a very safe location."

"It is at that."

Jane gave an alarmed burp of protest. "You cannot mean for me to rifle through my dead husband's pockets."

That set George off into a cackle. "Frightened his ghost will rise and protest the theft? He probably will. He's just the sort of spiteful soul who'd linger to cause additional pain."

The pallor of Jane's face rather suggested she feared exactly that. Nor was it such a surprise, given the recent visitations she'd experienced. Coupled with the fact that Jane had always been the squeamish sort, it was perfectly obvious why she wouldn't wish to touch Linfield's corpse.

Jane wrung her hands together. "Doctor Bell has taken charge of the body. He's going to think it most peculiar if I rifle through Linfield's pockets." Particularly when she wouldn't wish to describe what she was seeking, for then there would be another person privy to George's claims.

"That's your concern, not mine. You'd better get to him quickly, otherwise the skinny quack will have him cut open and all his organs hanging out."

"Jane!" Eliza held her fast as she felt her friend's leg's sag. "He's saying these things merely to be cruel."

Finding her strength, though she continued to hold fast to Eliza for support, Jane straightened her spine. "Perhaps you ought to worry about what Doctor Bell might find instead of harassing me. After all, Linfield is dead, and you and he had a dreadful fight earlier today."

"I see you're accusing me again."

"Does that worry you, Mr Cluett?" Eliza met his angry gaze and didn't flinch. "It ought to."

"I've not killed him. If he was done in, it wasn't by my hand, and I won't be framed for it. Get me those deeds, unless you want your fraudulent marriage made public, Miss Morley. You have until breakfast."

Jane sank to her knees before the hearth once George had left and put her head in her hands. "It's not true is it, Eliza? It can't be true. 'Tis bad enough that in life, he couldn't give me the one thing I needed from him, but now I shall be damned for that very thing, for my virginity is gone, and the marriage is a lie. They will condemn me, even though I was deceived. It is always the woman's fault, even when she had no hand in it at all."

"You are not condemned yet." Eliza knelt before her and managed to coax Jane to raise her head. They embraced, Jane resting her head on Eliza's shoulder and wetting her skin with the snuffles she made.

"I know I am not blameless. I've been a fool a dozen times over. This is now my punishment for dishonesty."

"Jane, embracing this piteous state will not help anything. We must at least attempt to find the deeds George wants. Even if you decide not to hand them over, it will still put us in a better bargaining position. I doubt he or Henrietta have taken to their beds. They will be tearing the place apart searching for those papers. Moreover, he could be bluffing. Using your perceived greenness against you to swindle you."

"I don't care about a house, Eliza. At least not as much as I care about this child I'm growing. George can have the deeds if we can find them." She dried her eyes and set about searching through the desk drawers where Eliza had already looked. The remainder of the room was quickly examined too. There were a lot of books, but little furniture. If Linfield had hidden the deed in one of those, then it would take hours upon hours to find it. It made more sense to rule out other locations first.

"If you examine his person, I will go to his chamber," Jane proposed. "I cannot look at him again, not if Bell has begun his work."

Eliza squeezed her hand. "I doubt he has done so yet. A proper examination requires decent light."

"You mean he'll wait until morning?"

She shrugged. As a matter of fact, she didn't. Bell didn't strike her as one to put off what could be seen to now, but Linfield had barely been dead an hour; even if Bell believed urgency of the essence, he was unlikely to have begun yet. While she had not attended the theatre hosted by the anatomists after hangings, she had read accounts of such proceedings. The corpses were cleaned with camphor and spirits, and cuts were often made to determine death had actually occurred and the deceased wouldn't suddenly wake up. "I don't like the idea of you wandering about alone, Jane."

"I will be extra cautious, and no one will expect me to go to Linfield's room. They'll look for me in your room, or perhaps the new chamber I was to move to in the Lady's Tower. Do you suppose he could have left something there?"

Anything was possible.

"We'll meet back in my chamber," Eliza said. She waited for Jane to leave, then used the secret passageway that ran between the upper part of the library down to the rear of Bell's surgery. That was where they were most likely to have lain Linfield to rest, and perhaps she could slip in and out without anyone being the wiser to her presence.

-27-

Jem

The servants had covered Linfield with a sheet, which Jem turned down, mostly to prove to himself it was his former employer and tormenter lying still on the doctor's slab. Someone had balanced pennies on his eyelids and cleaned the blood splatter away, for which he muttered a silent thanks, uncertain he could have borne the sight of an empty stare and blood-ringed lips. His shoulders cramped as he stood gazing down at the still and silent form. It hardly seemed possible that a face that had been so animated only a short time ago was now frozen never to laugh or scowl or demand again. Jem determined to leave once Bell set about his work. He couldn't stay for that. To see a man who he'd made love to rendered into a piece of meat and carved open so that his viscera could be inspected. Much as he'd curse him, and it would put him right back into the early pickle in which he'd existed, he longed for Linfield's brows to crease, a clownish smile to stretch his cheeks and for him to sit and laugh at Jem for being fooled by his theatrics.

Alas, this was no make-believe. Two people he trusted in this matter had both confirmed it, and he knew it in his soul too. There was a stillness, an absence that came with death, a sort of primal revulsion for the thing that was no more even while enduring the pain of their loss and desiring to cling to what had been. He'd been too young when his parents had died to experience death in such proximity. He'd despaired over the inability to say goodbye. Now... now he was pleased he hadn't been given the opportunity to witness their silence.

Anon he retreated to the corner and the confines of the saggy wingback chair. "I wish I could say you didn't deserve this and truly mean it," he said into the palms of his hands before peering over his fingertips at the corpse as if in expectation of a reply. "You were rarely kind, and you've been a bastard since the day we came to Cedarton. Not just to me. To your wife, to George, to all of us. Watching Bell assault you with his leeches was one of the few highlights of being here. I realise that makes me sound horrid, but... it's the truth. You were an arse. I hated you more frequently than I liked you." Especially after all the business with Eliza.

Eliza whom he'd now lost for good, and for no good reason, since the whole bedding debacle was irrelevant now.

Then again, perhaps, much as it hurt, that was for the best. She'd have learned what manner of man he was eventually. Better now than later.

"We had some fun though, didn't we?" He

addressed Linfield again. "I wish I knew what you'd done to make someone... Who was it? Who's done this? I keep thinking you must have done something really foul, because you never pushed me that far, even at your worst, and you did some deplorable things. Then again, I suppose we all have different limits.

"Whoever it was, I'm not condoning what they've done. I'm just pointing out that you probably provoked them. That's if you were the intended target. You must have been. There's no reason for anyone to attack Lady Linfield." She was a sweetling. Then again, someone had been attempting to scare her witless. "I thought that was you. Doesn't make sense, now for that to be the case. None of this does. Were you trying to murder her and accidentally killed yourself?"

Was one supposed to laugh or cry over such a notion?

The door creaked in the room beyond. "Mrs Honeyfield..." he heard Bell say. "What is it? Ah, this isn't a good moment for a consultation, I'm rather—"

The housekeeper's replies were too quiet to discern, her voice reaching him only as a higher-pitched susurration.

"Very well, I agree. Now isn't the moment to be absent from your duties."

Had she finally consented to having her troublesome tooth pulled? Bell's voice continued to drift to him in snatches. She'd presumably come to him because Linfield's valet was currently riding south to Bellingbrook.

There'd be no merry making in that great house this Christmastide.

A sudden draft curled around Jem's knees, tugging his attention away from the surgery to the door he and Eliza had found onto the secret stairwell, and it was she who peeped around the jamb of that camouflaged portal now.

"I know you are there, so you may as well step in."

Never one to prevaricate, Eliza emerged from the darkness shielding a candle flame. She set the candleholder on the nearest bare surface, before taking in his pensive squat position on the chair, then Linfield's draped body.

Jem regarded her over the fingers that covered his lower face even though it wrenched his heart to do so. So much loss and for so little gain. Her hair, simply knotted at the back of her neck, was coming unwound from its coil. He recalled the floral smell of it, the tickle of those strands against his body earlier, and it caused a cry to wriggle free of his throat. "Why've you come?" he asked.

"Hm." The vocalisation was accompanied by the tilting of her head towards one shoulder, which didn't provide any enlightenment. Her tongue ticked against her eye-tooth. Perhaps she was determined not to speak to him. Had probably only spoken to him earlier due to the shock of the events.

Then, "I'm sorry for your loss," she said, upending that theory. She crossed to gaze at Linfield's frozen face.

"Mine? He wasn't mine to lose." Never had been and never would be, and more importantly he hadn't desired him to be. Linfield was not the love of his life snatched away from him too young, leaving him behind to suffer the devastation. This tragedy was not that. Truth told; Linfield's death had delivered Jem's freedom.

To think, it'd all started as merrymaking. A lark to take his mind off other matters…

He held Eliza's elegant form fast in his field of vision.

…to make him forget what he couldn't have.

Oh, the hilarity, that those actions were now the thing that had torn her from him.

"Eliza, whatever you imagine you know about…" His voice cracked, preventing him from saying Linfield's name. "About me and him, it's wrong… It's more complicated… thornier."

She drifted closer to the corpse in a purposeful sort of way that compelled him onto his feet.

"You were lovers," she said. It was not a question.

He gave her a nod. There was no sense in denying it. Yes, he and Linfield had been lovers. Yes, despite everything he was hurt by Linfield's death. An ongoing relationship with Linfield might not have been something he wanted, but this was not the way it ought to have ended. The fool was too young to have been snuffed out of existence. "I ought to have told you the truth, though I imagine you can deduce for yourself why I didn't."

Her head whipped towards him. "I'm not sure

that I can, Jem. I feel you've led me a merry dance, but then if one doesn't offer forever, one cannot expect to receive it, and I guess I did not demand your fidelity either."

"Eliza." It tore at the cavity inside his chest to hear her so choked. "I'd gladly commit to you forever. What you saw between Linfield and me earlier, it was not something I sought."

She gave a disbelieving tut, then shushed him with the raising of her hand. He supposed this was hardly the moment for a declaration, while standing vigil at his former lover's side. At best it would make him seem guilty... Not to mention heartless, fickle, and insincere. "I didn't set out to deceive you. It was already over between us—Linfield and I—leastways on my part."

"Was it, Jem? Was it truly? So, I didn't watch him lick your spendings from his fingers, and you weren't set for his bedchamber this evening... or rather his wife's?"

He heartily wished he could answer in the negative. "It's complicated." Although this hardly seemed the moment to get into the wherewithal of how he'd been cajoled into compliance. "You have to understand what he was like, Eliza. Possessive, spiteful... entitled. Lord, so damned entitled. There was never a damn thing he wanted he didn't get."

"Yet, you loved him."

Is that what she believed?

Jem vigorously shook his head. "Love? Lord, no. We made merry with one another for a time, but I was never in love with him. It was just... physical between us. Lust, I suppose. Foolishness. It ought never to have lasted more than a few..." Shags, was the word he refrained from saying aloud. "But he had his ways. He could be very charming, very persuasive." His shoulders slumped, feeling the sudden weight of all the promises of funding he'd put faith in, but had yet to materialise. "I wanted no part of the business with his wife. If you believe nothing else, please believe that. I was eager to be free of him."

"Free?" she echoed.

"Aye." The realisation how his words might be understood dawned. "But not like... you can't think," —he glanced at the body— "that I did this or even desired it. I didn't want him dead. I just no longer wanted the level of intimacy between us that formerly existed. This...This is..."

He hadn't the words to express the magnitude of his horror. It roiled within his belly and bile wormed its way up his throat and filled his mouth with a sickly acidic tang.

"'Tis a nightmare," she concluded for him. Her hand curled around his forearm, bringing a sensation of warmth even through the layers of his clothing. The knots in his innards loosened. They stayed posed thus for a long while, until Eliza broke the contact, and moved to the opposite side of the table on which Linfield was laid out.

"You are too shocked by this for me to believe you did away with him, Jem, but you are not the man I supposed you to be, so perhaps my judgement is suspect." He could see the shivers of anxiety racing through her limbs now, making her quake. She met his gaze for the briefest of moments, digging her teeth into her plump lower lip. "I ought to know better than to put my faith in a man. You'd think I'd have learned by now. Men can only be relied on to do the wrong thing. Always. That is always the outcome. My father and brother have both proved that a thousand times over. Why the devil I imagined you'd be different, I don't know. While you may not be a murderer, Jem Whistler, I can't see there's any future for us. I thought I could trust you, but you've been lying and misleading me from the start. I thought there was... Well, I believed..." Her limbs trembled with what he interpreted as barely contained rage. "It's of no matter. Our arrangement is done. Pray forget it ever occurred."

Forget that she had ever been in his arms, that he had tasted her, loved her. He could not. All he wanted was to be able to worship her, be with her. He had only ever hidden the truth from her so as not to drive her away, and he could not even say now that had been the wrong thing to do, given that it was his poxy relationship with Linfield that was stealing her from him now.

He ought to have admitted the truth of how he'd felt instead of agreeing to a grand passion and then concealing how vehemently he loved her. Had a man ever been so folious?

If he'd pursued her following their first meeting, instead of crawling away like a snivelling worm, then he'd never have fallen under Linfield's spell, and at least he'd have given her some agency over the matter. Instead, he'd shuttered his heart away in a box, and salved his wounds with the sort of sins that got men hanged.

"Why could you not have been honest with me, Jem?" she demanded, throwing up her hands in frustration. "If you'd admitted your attachment to Linfield, and your preferences—"

"My preferences!" He laughed, voice creaking with the strain. "Eliza, if I have any preferences, they are for you. I love you. What existed between Linfield and me was… It was… about physical pleasure, not genuine affection, and I have found it difficult enough to explain how I feel about you as it is, so that other conversation would have been nigh on impossible."

Addressing it now was every bit as traumatic as he'd ever envisaged it, but he refused to let her concoct an idyllic picture of boundless love between him and Linfield. There had never been anything even remotely romantic about it.

"You could have tried."

"Could I? And what should I have said? That it so happens that sometimes I whore myself to other men. That they ask me to fuck them, and I oblige, or horror upon horror, they fuck me. And, by the way, my current beau is none other than your dear friend's husband. But don't worry about it, I don't much care for him, and eventually he'll tire of me. It's you I want, really. Would that have made anything better? Of course, it would not. You would just have despised and been revolted by me sooner."

Tears burned his eyes by the culmination of his

speech, so he snapped them closed and bowed his head. Twin rivulets escaped, nonetheless. He wiped them away hastily.

"It would have been honest."

"Shit!" he swore, nerves so wrought he couldn't help but give in to further vulgarities.

Then, "I'm not revolted by you, Jem."

That would be why her hands were curled into tight fists, and her lips into a grimace.

"I'm revolted by me," he spat, and marched himself off to the darkest corner of the room.

"What I am is hurt, and perplexed as to why you never trusted me, nor gave any hint that you felt—"

Given no hint! Good God, he had made love to her, did she imagine his passion for her faked?

Irritably, he stared at the wisps of tattered cobwebs, and the corpses of spiders shrivelled down to husks caught among those threads. Damp had lifted the paint off the walls in patches, leaving behind concentric rings of feathery flakes. Jem clawed at the front of his hair; he'd do anything to be outside of his own skin at present.

"Eliza, if you want the truth from me, then I will tell you it." Why conceal it anymore. He'd already ruined even the infinitesimal chance he'd had with her. "I've loved you from the moment we were made acquainted at Stag's Fell, but I knew there was no chance that I could win you. I thought for sure that Joshua Rushdale would, and what am I compared to the brother-in-law of a Marquis?"

"He's just a man the same as any other."

"Nothing, that's what. A near penniless dreamer

who lives off his uncle's graces, who tutors idiot lords to pass exams they deserve to fail. And who isn't even much good at that." He'd spent more time fornicating with Linfield than he ever had teaching him how to conjugate Latin verbs. "I'm a sinner and a sodomite and I don't deserve you, Eliza. I'm so sorry that I'm not the man you hoped me to be, but know this, I would wed you in a heartbeat if you would have me. I know that is not the future you wish, you made that plain enough, and I would never try to gainsay your pursuit of learning, but it is the truth of how I feel."

He heard her gulp but dared not turn around.

If she wished to leave, he prayed only that she did so and spared him the look of revulsion on her face. He heard her move, then a gentle hand pressed against the centre of his back.

Warily, he turned. "Eliza?"

Her pretty face sat anguished, eyes ablaze with heat and watery with emotion. "I want to believe that all you say is truthful and sincerely meant, but—"

"I understand," he said. It was no more than he expected or deserved.

"I'm not sure you do. I'm not sure I do. Your actions and words don't map out."

Bell barrelled through the door at that moment, almost colliding with them both. He didn't seem the least bit startled to find two persons standing in his cadaver laboratory gawping at him. "I need a scalpel, the lancet's not enough." He slid sideways over to the cupboard and pulled open a drawerful of instruments. "I daren't use the pliers, I'm likely to extract half her jaw along with the tooth. There's so much pus and decay in there it's near impossible to see what I'm doing, let alone get a grip on the devil. The abscess needs to be drained first, then I can perform the extraction."

They both stared at him.

"You're extracting Mrs Honeyfield's tooth?" Eliza said. "But you're a physician!"

"Got you!" He held aloft the desired instrument. "I'll admit, Miss Wakefield, that dentistry isn't my forte. Nor do I wish it to be, but the state of matters is decidedly poor. I've seen corpses twelve month rotted with better gnashers." He clacked his teeth together for emphasis. "But there's been a death, and the servants are already stretched thin. The household simply cannot do without its housekeeper." He about turned towards the door again.

"Would it help if I assisted?" Eliza offered.

Bell levelled her with a look of intense haughtiness over his shoulder. "Draining an abscess, I can manage alone, Miss Wakefield, but if you stay right there then there's something you can help me with. Jem here is a glorious note taker, but I think unsuited to pathology."

Indeed, Jem paled and clutched the cupboard for support at the mere suggestion. "I can't stay for that."

Bell blessed him the sort of benevolent smile one would give a child before his attention fastened upon Eliza. "Given your history of extracting pistol balls from marquis's legs, one presumes—"

"I can assist, yes."

"Very good, Miss Wakefield. Very good. On this occasion I will overlook your sex."

"And I yours," she replied.

"I'm sorry," Jem muttered once Bell had returned to the other room. "I just can't."

"It's perfectly understandable."

"Is it? Bell seems to have no qualms—"

"Was Bell his lover?"

Jem swallowed hard. "No," he croaked. "No, I don't believe so. Point taken. Not that it's really about that. I doubt I could stomach it even it wasn't someone I knew. I much prefer numbers, potions at a push, but not viscera. I've seen one amputation, and that was more than enough."

"'Tis Bell's profession."

"Aye," he agreed, head still bowed. "Aye, that's true. And yours too."

She shrugged. "Not quite, but I do what I can."

A sharp trill came from next door, which they both took to mean the dentistry was done.

Bell barrelled back in, wearing a splatter of blood, which he wiped as best as he could from his waistcoat and cravat. "Gory business. I'm not a devotee." He cast a pair of stained gloves into a laundry pail. "That is by far one of the most putrid things I've done in my career. I've handled corpses in better health." His gaze strayed to the table, and he sucked his lips into a pucker on seeing them standing so close and face to face. "Whistler. Miss Wakefield. I realise that you are embroiled in making yourselves miserable with a torrid love affair, but if you could perhaps take time out of that mission, I intend to determine the cause of Lord Linfield's death now and will be needing this area to do that."

He turned to the drawer he'd left open before and began assembling a tray of instruments.

"Is Mrs Honeyfield all right?" Eliza asked, turning away from Jem to give Bell her attention, as if she hadn't been about to shatter Jem's heart into even smaller smithereens.

"Down a trio of teeth, but alive and about her business. I've prescribed a garlic-salt rinse, followed by a compress of thyme and cloves. And a tincture of opium for the pain. Necessary, I think. Despite what you think Miss Wakefield, I don't routinely dose my patients with opiates. Have I performed to your approval?"

"I'm sure Mrs Honeyfield is exceedingly grateful to you for such care."

He snorted. "Cursing and grumbling over my insensitivity and what I've prescribed, I imagine. She's some knowledge, I'll admit, but her thoughts are antiquated. Whistler, you may wish to leave, unless you mean to assist in undressing him."

"No." Jem curled his knuckles to his mouth. "Sorry, but no. I'll go next door. I don't want the vision of him laid out for you in my head," and it would be. It'd stick as a reminder of what was to come, and the images his mind conjured were gruelling enough. He glanced at Eliza, but she'd already turned away ready to assist Bell.

"Have you an apron I can borrow, Doctor Bell?"

She was still in the gown she'd worn to dinner. It was wool rather than satin, muslin, or whatever confounded thing dresses were made of, and devoid of excessive broidery, but comely nonetheless, and not something she would want ruined.

The last thing he saw as Jem hastened away was a streamer of pale cloth flying in Eliza's direction.

-28-

Eliza

Bell had Eliza gather lanterns and candles to bathe the area in light while he disrobed and inspected the body, but the room remained thoroughly gloomy. He noted her stares once she'd returned to the table and flicked a bemused glance in her direction. "This is not the first time you've seen a man disrobed I think."

She shook herself. It was not. Nor was Linfield the only male corpse she'd seen. "Why is his... Why is he so bruised about his nethers?" She cast a swift nervy glance at the door separating them from the surgery, while scraping her teeth against her lower lip. Not at all certain what to make of the contusions.

"Nothing to do with Jem, if that's what you're thinking," Bell remarked, demonstrating more insight into matters than she'd thought him privy to. Then again, he was more intelligent than most of the physicians she'd met, most of whom were too busy masquerading as gentlemen to notice anything that wasn't biting them on the nose. "My fault. I set my pets on him." He nodded to the bell jar full of leeches on the countertop at the foot end of the table.

"Why?"

Bell's eyes lit with mirth as he sought out Linfield's sternum and brandished his scalpel. "For the same reason your man Whistler produced that blasted gas. I'm guessing he didn't get into the details of why he was making it with you."

The laughing gas? All those bladders of it remained next door, ready for a party that would never come. "He was making it for Lord Linfield." Curious how it choked her to say that, while looking at his naked corpse.

"More like out of desperation. He needed to get himself out of a bind and he thought the gas might do it."

"I don't understand."

"Do you not?"

"Pray just speak to me as the idiot you consider me."

Bell grinned. "His lordship here needed to sire an heir but couldn't manage to maintain a stand robust enough to prick his wife with. He was getting desperate, the wedding was over two months gone, and the earl's impatient. He was ready to try anything: leeches, experimental gasses, inviting another man into bed alongside his wife, and likely a dozen other things. Daft really, given it wasn't a matter of impotence, merely preference."

"I see." She was not entirely sure that she did, but it was something to cogitate later. Jem had said the situation was more complicated than she wanted to believe. He'd hinted at coercion, but she'd seen them together. It hadn't looked that way. Or maybe, her heart was still too dented to genuinely accept that possibility.

She chewed that over as she watched Bell work. He raised a line of blood as he pushed the scalpel through the dead man's flesh.

At least Bell's words confirmed it wasn't anything Jane had done that had kept her husband from her bed. "Yet, Jane is with child," she said after a moment.

Bell flashed her a toothsome smile. "Did I imply that I thought otherwise? Swab, please, Miss Wakefield."

She obliged.

"We both know that the one thing is not dependant on the other."

"Will you say it is not his?" That would destroy Jane's reputation as surely as any threat posed by Mr Cluett. At least he might be bought, but Bell... She did not think he could be so easily swayed by money. Or maybe he could. She truly didn't know him at all.

"Why would I do that, Miss Wakefield, hm? They are wed. Of course it is his. Half the peerage is sired by someone other than the man acknowledged to be their father, and we should likely all be grateful for it or none of them would possess a chin or brains, and there's few enough of either to go between them all as it is."

"But you just said—"

"No one beyond Cedarton is aware of his issue, Miss Wakefield, and no one here besides you, me, and Mr Whistler. I shan't be slurring a dead man's name. How would that benefit me? Will you? And while I'm sure you have your quarrels with Mr Whistler right now, do not doubt his integrity. He will not share the intimacies Linfield confided in him, after all, he didn't share them with you, even when it would have benefitted him to do so."

"I don't see how announcing his lordship's impotence would have helped matters."

"No?" He shrugged. "Perhaps not. Perhaps one truly does need to consider the whole picture."

In actuality, she was more hurt by the deception than the notion of him having been intimate with another man. If two people loved one another, then it was for God to judge them, not their fellow man. Except, Jem had been quite adamant that love had not been a part of it.

Then again, she hadn't asked for his love either, when she'd asked him to sin with her.

"Wait, what do you mean the whole picture?"

She took Bell's silence as a refusal to elaborate. "I..." She sniffed hard and pulled her shoulders back. "I don't care for being deceived, Doctor Bell."

"I don't much care for lady doctors, but sometimes one simply has to get over oneself."

She bristled. "They are hardly the same things."

"They both involve things we love, Miss Wakefield." He challenged her with cocked brow. "Swab."

Eliza huffed. She had no intention of getting any further into the meat of the matter with him. Thus, when he opened his mouth again, she blurted, "What of Mr Cluett?" to divert him.

Bell stared at her bemused. "What of him?"

"Do you think him responsible? Trustworthy? Do you think he did,"—she peered down at the dead man—"this?"

"Trustworthy. George? Hell, no!" He laughed. "As to whether he's responsible, until I determine the cause of death, let's not be too hasty with the accusations. Poison doesn't strike me as his style though. It requires forethought and planning, and George is... Well, you saw the pair of them this afternoon chasing about. Now, if Linfield had been run through with a sword, or had a pistol ball lodged between his ears, then I would point the finger at George. The truth of the matter is though, Miss Wakefield, is that there's not a soul among us who didn't have a reason to want him dead, you included, so shall we concentrate on the task at hand and see what we might uncover?"

He completed the cut he was making so that it ran from sternum to pubic bone, then two more from each shoulder to the sternum so that the two lines formed a Y-shape. "You will find other anatomists tackle things in different ways, but this is my preference. And now, we will determine your true mettle, Miss Wakefield. These cuts traverse both the skin and abdominal wall, but to reach the organs it is first necessary to remove the ribs. For that we use—"

"A saw?" She reached for the tray ready to pass it, recalling the accounts of the surgeons' theatres she'd scoured in the past for insights.

"Pliers." He corrected her, reaching for them. "I prefer pliers. I find them more efficient. First, we need to ensure these flaps stay out of the way." He drew the top flap back over Linfield's face first, then peeled back the two sides, only to pause. "What in the name of hell?"

Eliza too gave a gasp. She was made of stern stuff, though her desire for knowledge was currently warring with her emotions. This was the man she'd only recently dined with, and with whom Jem had embroiled himself. The smell of offal and garlic assaulted her nostrils, prompting her to pinch them closed, but it was the sickly green glow emanating from within the cavity of his opened torso that prompted her to make an unladylike exclamation not dissimilar to Bell's. "That... that is not—" She looked to Bell for confirmation. "—normal?"

The physician stood with his arms raised, pliers at the ready. "No." His tongue swept his dry lips. "No. Not normal at all." He stretched out and snuffed a couple of the nearby candle flames, which made the glow increasingly apparent. It ran through many, but not all the exposed organs.

"It's concentrated in his alimentary canal." Bell gestured with the pliers, pointing out Linfield's stomach, and then both intestines. The glow was most pronounced in the upper regions. "This is certainly what did for him." The pliers clattered against the metal tray as he dropped them. "Never in all my days. That's..." He bolted through the door to the adjoining room.

"Doctor!" Eliza scurried after him. The hairs on

her own arms were raised. There was something particularly ghastly about the quality of the light spilling from Linfield's body. It filled the mind with unease, sucked at her sense of reality, so that all her hairs stood on end. "We cannot leave him exposed like this for the mice and rats to nibble on." Such a grotesque fate she wouldn't wish on a commoner, and absolutely wouldn't do for the son of an earl. It was not that one was more deserving of dignity than the other, rather a matter of decency. "Doctor Bell!"

"A moment, Miss Wakefield."

Jem hastened from the chaise as the pair crossed the threshold. "Are you done so soon? Does this mean... Is it as you feared? Poison."

Eliza froze, assaulted by memories forged earlier that day, of lying in Jem's arms, contented and merry, giddy with the possibilities that lay ahead. She hadn't dreamed of forever with him—well, maybe a little—but she had revelled in the pleasure of his company. What she wouldn't give to be back in that pleasant daydream. She noted that Jem was twirling one of the gas-containing balloons in his fingers. He let it go, and it sank to the floor, before being blown into a corner by Bell's swift pacing.

The doctor ignored them both. He bowed his head over the old bucket sink as if he thought he might vomit but uncurled to his usual height a moment later. "I'm not done, no. Barely begun, but yes, I think we might conclude poison the cause. Poison or the touch of whatever spectre roams this place."

"Spectre?" Jem's brows wrinkled in turn. "Eliza?

Whatever? What nonsense is this?"

"It's..." She raised a hand, while the other she pressed to her waist. "It's..."

Bell's agile fingers set to tapping against his troubled mouth. "I like none of this. It is distinctly wrong in every regard. Gentleman, Lady, I am not one given to theatrics, and while I enjoy novelty, this is... it's..." He rubbed his nose.

"It's what?" Jem asked, his eyes flashing with his frustration at the both of them.

"Peculiar," Eliza ventured. "I'd suggest you look for yourself, but perhaps don't." He turned almost the same sickly shade as the light in Linfield's guts at the mere suggestion. "The thing is Linfield's innards are... Well, they're glowing."

"I beg your pardon."

Bereft of an explanation, Eliza simply raised her shoulders.

"Glowing? Like a lantern?"

"What she says is true." Bell straightened the set of his wig, then gave a shudder as if to cast off his unease. "There's a spectral cast to his organs, an incandescence. Good Lord, I've lost count of the number of corpses I've examined. Young, old, rich, poor, bodies that had decades in the ground and those fresh from the gallows. I've dissected them all, but never once have I witnessed such as this, nor heard mention of such lambent light as part of the process of decomposition. It's eerie. It sends a shiver down the spine."

Such a reaction gripped him at that very moment.

To Eliza, the fact that Bell was shaken made the occurrence more disturbing. Panic was not part of his usual demeanour, nor any hint of fragility. He continued making staccato bursts of movement, clasping and unclasping his hands, and taking long-legged strides that took him nowhere in particular, but left his cheeks increasingly ruddy, while Jem scratched his chin.

"Eliza?"

"It's like pixy-light," she began uncertainly, quite as baffled by it as Bell. "I don't think the cause supernatural, though. It's probably caused by a chemical reaction related to decomposition."

"Nonsense." Bell slashed a hand through the air. "Have I not just said it is not that? This is not a normal occurrence. It is true, that there are spurious reports of bones glimmering in the dark, but not the soft tissues. Never the tissues. Man does not glow. He is neither firefly nor fungi. The bowels do not create light."

"Fungi glow in the dark?" Jem muttered.

Eliza levelled him with a look. Perhaps he was unfamiliar with foxfire. In any case, there'd been no mushrooms served at dinner.

Bell continued his agitated rambling. It recalled to Eliza Jane's back and forth march before the dining room fireplace earlier. Could she be entirely certain about her friend? They'd agreed to trust one another, but what if Jane were behind this? She was not without knowledge of toxins. They had nurtured the same kitchen garden during their stay at Miss Hardacre's School, learned its plants names and uses by rote, but naught among them glowed like Linfield's bowels were doing.

"Ludlow, I think you might agree that this is not a typical situation," Jem began, attempting to engage the physician in some reasoned discourse. "If Linfield has been poisoned by a substance it would usually be inadvisable to eat, then might that not cause the phenomenon you've just witnessed?"

They both waited while Bell thoughtfully scratched his clean-shaven jaw. "It is possible, one supposes. I guess it is the hypothesis we have. Pray, give me a moment, and I will resume my examination. But I do not anticipate finding mushrooms in his bowels." He idled by the skeletal remains of Jem's chemistry apparatus.

"There are other poisons besides toadstools," Eliza said. "Might we consider them?"

Jem nodded. "Bell?"

"What?"

"Other toxins?"

"Yes."

Eliza wasn't certain he was taking the words in.

Jem reached for a clean vessel and poured brandy into it. He then pressed the flat-bottomed flask on the doctor. "Drink." The two men shared a moment of mutual grim humour, before Bell downed the spirit in one. Fortified, he wiped his mouth with his coat sleeve and returned to his workspace. They both followed, but Eliza stayed Jem at the door. "Don't if you'll regret it."

"I'll stay on the threshold. I can't sit idle while the two of you investigate. Something or someone has killed him, and I mean to determine who and bring them to justice. He was a bastard, Eliza, a scoundrel, but he didn't deserve this."

She nodded, then returned to her former position on the opposite side of the operating table to Bell, whose face remained grimly shadowed and drawn. Linfield's inners still glowed with that same eerie light. She watched studiously as Bell cracked his lordship's ribs, then removed his innards, placing them on a tray and removing them to a clear surface on which to examine them.

Eliza relit the candles he'd snuffed and moved them closer to the organs.

"There's evidence of tissue damage consistent with chemical burns, but otherwise he seems entirely healthy. No obvious liver cirrhosis. No ulcers. No fungi. I can examine the brain, once I'm done with the intestines—"

"Is that entirely necessary?" Jem asked. "Surely the answer is staring you in the face. He was poisoned by whatever is causing that ghastly gleam."

"It's dimming slightly, I think," Eliza wafted the air before her up towards her nose. "The smell is dispersing too. Not the offal smell, I mean the other one. The garlic scent."

"I hadn't noticed," the doctor replied. "But, aye, you may be right about the glow."

"That would be consistent with something reacting with the air," Jem said. "I mightn't be the most competent chemist, but I know that. Oxidation of some sorts."

"Aye, perhaps," Bell muttered as he sliced open

his lordship's heart. "Though don't ask me what manner of poison could do this." He continued with his neat cuts and even smeared some samples onto slides to view beneath his microscope.

Vexed by the matter, Eliza rubbed her temple. Most of the poisons she was familiar with were plant extracts. "Hemlock, nightshade, aconite, foxgloves… They all caused nausea and vomiting, some, arrhythmia, but—"

"Not glowing intestines," Bell finished for her. "I've seen victims of all of those."

"I suppose there's arsenic and strychnine to consider."

"Do you intend to list every poison you can think of Miss Wakefield? For the record, I don't think it either of those. The latter especially we can rule out. There's many a cheap tavern that uses strychnine in their watered beer. Even fools aplenty who are happy to suffer its ill effects for the kick to the head and visions it brings on. I am well acquainted with strychnine poisoning."

She raised a hand to her throat. "Fools."

"Probably no worse for them than the gin."

"Cyanide?" Jem suggested.

"What's that?" Eliza and Bell both asked.

"Something my cousin Pip has mentioned a time or two. I assume it a recent discovery since neither of you appear familiar with it. Transmutation is his passion, not mine. The more dangerous the better. I only dabble. Numbers are infinitely less volatile. But there must be chemicals, medicines that phosphoresce, surely."

"Like phosphorous, you mean," Eliza said, brows raised. She also was no chemist, but she was familiar with Robert Kerr's translation of Lavoisier's work describing the elements. How her sisters had decried her over the purchase of that volume in place of *The Castle of Wolfenbach*, which they had to wait on the travelling library to provide.

"You'll not find that on my shelves," Bell insisted, as both Eliza and Jem scurried in that direction. "Fools. I'm an anatomist, not a chemist. Phosphorous is of no practical use to me."

"Mayhaps not, Ludlow, but your shelves are as well stocked as any apothecary's."

Also, he was wrong.

-29-

Eliza

octor Bell could claim there was no phosphorus on his shelves all he liked, but Eliza knew differently. She hurriedly searched along the rows of bottles and tightly packed drawers in Bell's surgery, with Jem beside her, trying to lend a hand, but seeming bewildered over what precisely they were looking for.

"Kunckel's pills," she informed him. "I swear they were here. They're usually prescribed for colic or gout, not that they work, but nor do half the things most quacks recommend."

"I heard that."

Despite his spurious use of leeches, she was prepared to accept Bell wasn't a typical quacksalver. He mostly knew what he was talking about and endeavoured to back up his practice with evidence. This matter clearly had him shaken though.

"Where are you?" Eliza tore several bottles from the shelves in case the jar had been jostled to the back. "I know it was here. You definitely had some," she called to Bell. "I remember seeing them, and they're phosphorous based. Coated in something. Silver, I think."

"If they're not there, I'm sure I haven't the faintest idea," he called back, before following them both through, with what she thought might be a kidney still in his hands. "I think it's worth noting that our poisoner must be in possession of some degree of specialised knowledge and intelligence if they're apprised of the composition of various medicines and remedies."

"That rules Cluett out, he's a fool," Jem huffed. "His mother too. Have you considered it might be Jane behind this, Eliza?"

She had, but a handful of minutes gone. "It is not unless she has become a particularly adept actress. Besides she was always a mediocre herbalist, and I'm sure she didn't set her own bed alight." Nor did it make sense for her to have done so. Linfield's death had left her in a pickle. Although, she hadn't known George Cluett was going to assault her with the possibility of her marriage being unsound.

"It weren't Lady Linfield who I was thinking of," Bell remarked, his gaunt features pulled into a thoughtful pucker. "It's interesting how familiar you are with the contents of my shelves, Miss Wakefield."

"Ludlow!"

"I'm observant, and Mrs Honeyfield needed a remedy, which is why I'm acquainted with your shelves. Yes, I came in here and mixed it. A fact I'm sure you already knew. Besides, what motive have I?

I've only known him a handful of days."

Bell gave her a tight smile. "Perhaps he was annoying enough that a few days were more than plenty? And as to reasons, there are two rather obvious ones. Perhaps you felt you needed to protect Lady Linfield. He was beastly to her, and you don't believe for a moment those attacks on her were caused by a ghost. And secondly, one could certainly argue that jealousy might prompt your hand. Anger at being played for a fool, not to mention that he was blackmailing your beloved into fornicating with him."

The doctor had obviously overheard every damned word of their earlier conversation while he'd been at work on Mrs Honeyfield's tooth.

"Perhaps you thought that if you removed Linfield, it would free Jem of his burden of protecting you."

"Ludlow!" Jem snapped, ahead of burying his head in his hands.

"What? Are we pretending you weren't going to bugger the bastard to preserve her reputation?"

A shiver of horror ran through Eliza's slender frame as she repeated the repulsive word under her breath. Her gaze shot to Jem's face as he peeped over his fingertips. "The noose he was holding over you was your relationship with me?"

Jem chewed his tongue, then covered his face again, clearly unable to face her. "You might have held your tongue, Ludlow."

"Jem, tell me." She pulled his hands away from his face.

"I'd wriggled free of him, but then he saw how I looked at you, and that was enough for him to know he could demand my compliance. Eliza, the truth of the matter was irrelevant. He knew only of my infatuation. That I cared for you. All he had to do was make a few remarks in a select few ears and you'd have been stripped of your reputation... ostracised. Your sisters too. I couldn't allow that to happen."

"And why did you not appraise me of this threat?"

"Because as we have already established, I am a fool. I meant to come clean about my situation and how I felt when I followed you down here the other morning, but then you said what you said, and I agreed to what I agreed. Eliza, I meant to do whatever I could to make you happy. I was not about to ask you to wed me, the only way I could actually have protected you, when you'd just explicitly stated you never wanted to be shackled by wedding vows."

"You meant to ask for my hand?" Her incredulity made her voice turn shrill. "But aren't you just a penniless tutor dependent on his uncle's goodwill?"

"Yes, but I wondered if maybe that didn't matter. That perhaps you were willing to overlook it, given that you hadn't wed Joshua Rushdale, when I was positive that you would have done, and he has all the funds you could want. I'd like to clarify, that I didn't expect you to accept. I was ready to be let down. Resigned to it even."

"So, when I offered an alternative, of course you grasped it. But then that enabled Linfield to get his clutches on you."

He bowed his head and nodded. "You said it, we men always muck things up."

"Ahem," Bell cleared his throat. "I believe we were discussing poisons and murder. If you're both done proclaiming, might we get back to that?"

They both levelled him with their glares.

Jem tugged on his cuffs. "Perhaps don't blurt out facts that are irrelevant to the investigation if you don't wish us to discuss them."

"And we're not done," Eliza snapped. "Did you really mean to propose?"

"I know. I know I'm a fool, and it's not the future you want."

"But you truly meant to ask?"

"Oh, good grief and damnation!" Bell resumed Eliza's search of his shelves. "Kunckel's pills, right? Evidently as elusive as brains in the sight of love. They're not here."

"Well, they were. I saw them." Eliza shadowed Bell's traversing of the shelves.

"Maybe you're mistaken."

"I'm not. I clearly saw them. It was when I came down to mix the remedy, and Mrs Honeyfield... Wait! That's it, she picked the bottle off the shelf, and I told her it wouldn't relieve her toothache, but she was loathe to relinquish them. Do you remember, Jem?"

"I don't think I saw any bottle," he said, semi-choked on emotion, and evidently still stuck on their possible futures.

He tried to catch her eye, but Eliza refused to be drawn in by a soulful plea. Now wasn't the moment;

they had to concentrate on the task at hand.

"I do recall you speaking to her, but I couldn't say for certain what about."

That was right, he'd stayed hidden in the other room, while she'd stepped through to speak to the housekeeper, lest they were witnessed together, and rumours arose. They may as well not have bothered since everyone seemed perfectly apprised of their attachment.

"She must have come back and taken them."

"Wait, you're proposing the housekeeper's responsible?" Bell scoffed. "Why the devil would his housekeeper wish him dead?"

She didn't have the faintest clue. "Did you not say just a few minutes ago that everyone in this house likely had a motive to murder him?"

Bell confirmed his words with a tilt of his head. "I did say that, but I was referring to the guests, not the servants. They're irrelevant. Only Linfield's valet has been with him any length of time, and he is well compensated for his troubles. The rest are recent additions to the household. You may as well say some rogue ventured in off the moors and did for him, or the elusive Cedarton white lady."

"Why should the length of service matter? And how can you declare them irrelevant? They are here among us when others refused to be."

"Perhaps they're just not so given to superstitious twaddle," Bell suggested.

"Betsy spouts superstitious twaddle every time she opens her mouth," Eliza countered.

"Apart from when she's just plain surly," Jem

added.

"Or they valued a decent wage," Bell continued. "One thing I think Whistler and I can both attest to is that Linfield was generous in that regard."

"Perhaps they knew one another previously."

"No!" Both men adamantly asserted.

"Eliza, he had no inclinations of that sort. Not for maids."

"Well, perhaps she made an advance, and he spurned her."

Bell rolled his eyes, clearly not persuaded. "Would one really poison someone for that? I should think she'd be relieved he didn't dismiss her on the spot."

Well, they might both claim Linfield had no interest in the fairer sex, but that didn't explain the nonsense with Henrietta. Jane certainly hadn't been mistaken about what she'd witnessed. Linfield's cock had certainly been inside that woman's mouth. She made the point with passion, which won her a response of, "Desperation," from both men.

"He was willing to try anything, and you realise she was a bawd," Bell said.

Jem nodded. "T'was once said she was the lady to see if one wanted that particular service, especially if you had a reluctant member. It's what he told me, anyway. Even showed me the entry in Grose's almanack. George pretends he doesn't know about it, but he knows. He doesn't know who his father is, mind. Poor sod."

"Lots of rumours though," Bell added. "One of which starts with B—"

"Linfield's father is also Cluett's?" Eliza gaped at the physician.

"'Tis but a rumour, Miss Wakefield. Now, if we're through with the gossip, I propose returning to conversing with the corpse. It's more likely to yield something sound instead of a lot of speculation about nothing."

While Bell took himself off, Jem reached for her.

"Don't." Eliza smacked Jem's hands away.

Resigned, he let his hands fall to his sides. Eliza made another quick survey of the shelves, to make sure she hadn't missed the bottle. It was definitely missing, and while she admitted, stealing a bottle of medicine was hardly a solid basis for a declaration of guilt, there remained enough of a tickle in her mind for her to refuse to let the notion go.

Truthfully, she was mad at Jem too, mad at having been deceived, and madder still knowing she'd been in possession of his affections and somehow lost them. It rankled to learn his compliance to Linfield's wishes had been won using her as leverage. And Doctor Bell had known and not done a thing about it.

"The rest of us have rather more valid motives for putting him in the ground," Jem said gently.

"Mayhaps, she does too."

The bruised parts of her soul certainly agreed.

"I'm right about the phosphorus."

"Aye," Jem agreed. "That you can't dispute."

"And she's the one who had it, and she'd likely know something of its properties. She told me her husband was an apothecary."

Bell, on the threshold of the other room, about turned. "Mrs Honeyfield told you that?"

"Yes, what of it?"

The colour had drained from the doctor's face. He remained eerily still for a moment, then the ringlets of his wig quivered as a shiver ran through his wiry body. He set aside the gristly lump of meat he still carried, scalpel too, and steepled his blood-stained fingers before him, though whether that was in prayer or thought, Eliza couldn't determine.

"Ludlow, what is it?" Jem cautiously approached.

"Nothing, most likely. In fact, it's almost certainly nothing. A coincidence. But... then again if it's not..."

He looked to Eliza, then Jem. "Jesus, I warned him at the time there'd be repercussions. Would he listen? Of course not. It was a miracle enough that he even had the sense to vacate town for a while, the blind fool."

"You're not making a great deal of sense, Ludlow, my friend." Jem remarked, echoing Eliza's thoughts as they both drew level with him. "Maybe you could explain whatever it is that's got you in its grip. A theory of some manner. What is it you warned him about? You're referring to Linfield, right?"

"It's not a matter I wish to get into. Not without consulting the earl."

"The earl ain't here, but a murderer is. For heaven's sake, man, tell us what you know."

Eliza encouraged him with a nod too, desperate

to hear. "Please. You look as if you've seen a ghost. A thought has clearly occurred to you."

"It's apt you should mention ghosts at this point, Miss Wakefield, for it's not so long ago that I saw one. Not the white lady that roams this accursed castle but a face out of my past in unexpected circumstances." He stumbled a few paces then and fell heavily on to the chaise longue. "I should not speak of this. He would curse me for it, and not just dock me pennies, but likely throw me out. I swore an oath of silence." His gaze snapped to the open doorway. Through that portal, Eliza could just make out the outline of Linfield's body, and the sickly green glow of his exposed organs.

"He's no longer in a position to punish you, nor is he about to rise from eternal slumber to do so. The dead don't walk, Doctor."

Bell nodded appreciative of her sensibility. "It was still an oath."

"But if it relates to his murder..." Jem interjected, both brows raised encouragingly.

"It can't be. Surely."

"Ludlow, for the love of Christ, what do you know? Are we still talking about Mrs Honeyfield, or something else?"

"Perhaps," he muttered, confusingly. "Did she ever happen to mention her husband's name?"

"Lord, I don't know," Eliza cried, her frustration with the physician flanking Jem's. "Why is it important?"

"Because I fear Linfield was entirely responsible for his demise."

"What?" She rocked back on her heels.

"You had better explain what you mean," Jem said.

The pair of them tilted forward onto their toes in readiness of hearing him.

Bell waved for more liquor, which he swallowed without delay. "Jem, you'll recall that ridiculous carriage race."

"All too vividly," he replied, shoulders hitching towards his ears. "But that was a woman who died—"

Bell made a noise in his throat that rather suggested Jem was mistaken.

"The newspaper reported it was a woman too," Eliza added. "I read about it before I ever came here and found it to show to Jane. She wanted to know what had necessitated the move to Cedarton for Linfield had never told her, merely insisted on it."

"It was definitely a woman," Jem confirmed. "I had a rather closer view of her than I cared to if you recall, Ludlow. I took notes for you, before you had her carted off to your address to do whatever you needed to do. There were plenty of witnesses to that race and the accident. One hardly needed the services of a professional to determine the cause of death."

"That was not the reason I whisked the body away. I was preserving Linfield's reputation, not to mention making sure an old friend wasn't made the subject of the scandal sheets in perpetuity. At least what reports reached the newspapers recorded the passing in a way that would've pleased him. As much as any report of a tragedy could."

The darks of his eyes reflected their eager faces when he looked up. "What you saw, Jem, was precisely what the person wished you to see. However, if you had peeled back the layers of their disguise, then the body you uncovered would have revealed a different tale. The woman who died, Janie Faintree, was not born with that name. I knew them first as John. John Faintree. We met while I was attached to St Thomas's Hospital, and he was working as a dresser. A good one too. Knew his stuff. Very nimble with his hands. Dainty for a man, but he made up for it with wit."

"A cross dresser," Eliza gasped.

Bell nodded. "It's not as uncommon as you might suppose."

"I did not suppose any such thing. I have eyes and I read. I'm aware there are mollies in every town."

"Aye, indeed, there are."

"Don't look at me," Jem decried. "I've never knowingly set foot inside such an establishment."

Bell looked sheepish. Eliza couldn't help some measure of scepticism from bleeding into her expression. Still, Bell returned to his tale. "We lost touch when I moved on from St Thomas's, but I heard through a mutual acquaintance, that John had passed the apothecaries exam and determined to set up practice rather than complete another year to become a physician. One supposed he'd done it for love. He'd married when he was barely old enough to do so, and gossip suggested she wished them to set up home together. She'd remained in the countryside in service while he trained, so I was given to understand, but the family for whom she worked had learned of her marriage and dismissed her in favour of an unwed girl."

"God forbid that a married woman earns her way," Eliza muttered. When Bell glared at her over the interruption, she waved him to continue.

"Our paths crossed again this last summer when I was brought into the employ of the Earl of Bellingbrook. I will not describe the circumstances of that meeting other than to say he, or rather she, was in the company of Lord Linfield, and I'd been tasked by the earl to locate his errant son and encourage him back to his studies."

"Lovers," Jem muttered under his breath.

"Rather more than that. They were cohabiting as man and wife."

"Was Linfield a molly too?" Eliza asked.

Bell ignored her.

"If you mean, did he dress in women's clothes, then not so far as I know," Jem said out of the corner of his mouth. "But if you mean, did he prefer to take a man over a mistress, then you already know the answer to that, and he liked to be taken as if he were... No matter, never mind. It's hardly relevant to the point of all this."

It seemed to Eliza it was very much the point of all this.

"Linfield, as you can imagine, was resistant to his father's request." Bell gave an expressive sniff, which conjured visions of many a long argument, and objects being thrown about, followed by arduous strained silences. "In the end, I was obliged to ride away and report my failure. Though, as it turned out, Linfield returned to Oxford of his own accord not long after. I believe there'd been a quarrel between the two lovers that led to a parting of ways. Back at Oxford, Linfield fell straight into his old roistering ways, and soon found himself some new sport," he nodded in Jem's direction. "Janie, or rather, John, returned to his wife and shop though he did not settle there long. I had to see him off at Linfield's request more than a few times. I suspect whatever the pair of them shared during those months together wasn't so easily put aside for the other party as they were for Linfield. It's my belief that's what prompted the appearance at the carriage race. Alas, the heartfelt plea resulted in tragedy."

Jem snorted. "A fine yarn, Ludlow, except the ending is over kind. I witnessed that race. Linfield never even tried to swerve to avoid the collision. He rode her down, and while he bleated about having had no time to react, I never quite believed it. I'd seen him weave his phaeton between obstacles a steeplechaser might decry over."

"Nevertheless, I don't think his intention was murder, more that, in the spur of the moment, he chose not to act as swiftly as he might. Perhaps that was out of surprise, perhaps a form of self-preservation. We'll never truly know."

"The only thing it makes clear to me is what that *Jamie* nonsense was about," Jem retorted. "I have never in my life been Jamie, until these last few days when he was all glib-tongued and determined to cajole me into doing his bidding. I think he hadn't so completely moved on from his past love as you'd have us believe, Bell. Wasn't it Janie or Jamie he cried out for in his last moments too? I don't think any of us believe it was his wife he was calling for."

The physician shrugged. "His mind and counsel were his own. We did not speak of the matter. Ever. I arranged the burial and such like so that no questions might be asked. As for his relations with his wife, I'm afraid Lady Linfield's finer qualities were largely lost on him."

"Well, I still don't know that I am rightly following all this." Eliza perfectly understood the part about John and Janie being the same person, but it was its relevance to the current case she was woolly over. "Are you suggesting that Mrs Honeyfield is the wife Faintree abandoned in the countryside so that he might live in sin with Lord Linfield?"

"Possibly," the physician replied uncertainly. "You'll admit it's a motive—the theft of her husband and her dignity. And not forgetting her livelihood. The shop would have to close if there was no longer a licenced practitioner attached to it."

"Aye." Jem nodded sagely. "No matter her knowledge."

"Never mind, aye." Eliza swore, batting him with her elbow. "If this is what you suspect, why are we all sat here like three limp noodles? The magistrate must be called, and she detained." Her words propelled Bell onto his feet again, but he did not hasten into action.

"It is simply a hypothesis, Miss Wakefield. Are we so certain we wish to stir this hornets' nest."

Eliza gawped at him thoroughly aghast. "Don't tell me you are dithering over a confrontation, sir! She has murdered an earl's heir. I think confining her to her room is the very least of what we should do. Nor is there longer a question over sending for the magistrate. If neither of you two men will attend to it, then I will do so. She needs to be restrained before she takes it into her head to harm anyone else."

"Harm anyone else...?" Bell's eyebrows drew low over his beady eyes. "Why the devil would she? Her revenge, if she is even guilty of the crime, and we have no proof of it, is already served. She cannot kill him twice over."

Lord save her from dim-witted men. Eliza slapped her brow. "No, she cannot, but she might seek to rid the world of his heir, and thus butcher the line."

If her mind had turned to such action, it would mean Jane was in peril. Jane, who had already been the target of untold ghastliness. It was she who had been haunted, and near burned alive, and whom Eliza had left alone far too long. Why she had only meant to be down here for a moment. To find the wretched papers that Mr Cluett demanded and return to Jane with them.

"Linfield deprived her of the opportunity to grow a family, might not she seek to deprive him of the same? Can you not see that? I know if I'd had the man I loved snatched from me, then I would wish to make those responsible pay."

The declaration earned her four raised eyebrows.

"I'm now positively afeared," Bell backed away from her warily. "What alarming creatures you women are, so driven to volatility."

"Did you even give the man a headstone?"

"Of course. Well, I gave Janie a decent burial and a proper marker. We had once been confreres. However, I think you a little hasty in your judgements. We cannot prove, nor reveal any of this. Also, you still haven't entirely dissuaded me that you're not equally likely the culprit. I think you have motives aplenty between Linfield's treatment of your friend, and him blackmailing Jem into questionable acts."

"Except that I was unaware of the latter, and I would never act in a manner that would harm Jane. Plus, disposing of Linfield would hardly help her current situation."

"With him gone, there is no one to contest her immaculate conception."

Jem pushed his way between them. "Ludlow, it's not her. You know it's not her. And your delaying makes me question your motives."

"It is fine, Jem." Eliza shoved him aside. "I am more than capable of fighting my own battles. If he wants to act like a fatuous old quack, then it is his prerogative." She tore open the knot in her borrowed apron and cast it aside. A whole hour must surely have passed since she and Jane parted ways in the library, and she hadn't yet retrieved the one thing she'd come here looking for. It was well past time she left. Thus, she hurried into the rear room and sought the clothing Bell had taken from his lordship's corpse.

"What the devil are you about, woman?" The doctor hollered on seeing her rummaging through the dead man's pockets.

"An unrelated matter." She plucked the folded parchment from a concealed inner pocket in Linfield's soiled coat. It appeared to be as George alleged: a deed to a London property.

"Eliza, I'm not sure you should give that to George," Jem insisted on seeing what she held. He remained in the doorway, as if an invisible barrier were set across it of the sort one marked out with salt to dissuade boggarts and other fae folk from entering your abode.

"'Tis Jane's decision, not mine."

"Why are you giving anything to George?" Bell loomed over her, blocking her route to the exit.

Eliza simply about turned, and opened the hidden door instead, startling a coarse exclamation from the leech's throat.

"Because Cluett is blackmailing her, and this is what he demanded in exchange for his silence regarding a certain matter of legitimacy," she explained.

"Whose legitimacy? Not the Hans in kelder's?"

"The marriage."

Eliza didn't wait for Bell's response to that. She'd lingered overlong already. "I'm going to find Jane, gentlemen. I shall appraise her of what we've learned, and then once I am assured, she is safe, I intend to send a man for the magistrate since it seems I cannot rely on either of you to do so."

"I didn't say that," Jem blurted, seeming quite put out by the accusation. "Eliza, take care." He was milling on the room's threshold but refused to cross it. "Are you sure you wouldn't prefer me to accompany you?"

"I am not at risk, Jane is, and only for so long as the guilty party walks free. If you want to be of use, then send for the magistrate, and put Mrs Honeyfield under lock and key."

"Bell?" Jem asked.

The last of their words she caught was a resigned sigh from the quacksalver. "'Tis your call. I intend to restore Lord Linfield's bowels to his body afore your beloved bluestocking brings the power of the law down on us. I fear the presence of my lord's glowing entrails on the countertop will not go over well with whatever local bumpkin arrives. Our murderer will walk free because they're too busy shackling me on the charge of desecrating his corpse."

-30-

Eliza

Eliza raced through the concealed passageways as though the devil—or at least a knife-wielding lunatic—were at her heels. She burst into her bedchamber through the armoire to find the room dark and entirely deserted. The fire that had burned bright earlier was now no more than white dusted coals. The charred remains of Jane's room were equally void of inhabitants. Her foray into Bell's domain had taken far too long. Jane should have been back here by now, wearing a groove in the already uneven floor with her nervous pacing.

"Where are you?" she huffed, hand to her mouth, her mind awhirl with all manner of ill-fated nonsense. She had to be practical... logical about this, not give in to fear and fantasy. Jane had been bound for Linfield's room. It seemed unlikely that she would still be there, but she had made mention too of her new chambers. She must surely be there. Though where that was, and how the room was reached she was far less certain about. Still, find it she must. Thus, Eliza tumbled into the corridor, tripping over her feet in her haste, to find a figure standing there. The maid, Betsy, idling, backlit by moonlight, in the looming maw of the hideous iron-pinned door.

"What in heavens?" Eliza asked, approaching cautiously. "Why is this door unlatched? Whatever are you doing?"

The sky outside was the black of coals, clouds so fearsome dark as to be almost indistinguishable from the heavens. The shell of the tower gleamed like the withered bones of a slumped giant, where a frosty rime clung to its remains.

"Begging your pardon, Miss, but... my mistress asked me t' keep watch."

"Your mistress? Whatever is there to keep watch for out there?"

"Oh, Miss, Old Lady Cedarton's ghost. Terrible, she is, and milord's death only proves it. She'll see us all into our graves if she can."

"Nonsense." Eliza dismissed the notion before the tale grew any longer. She had to wonder if Mrs Honeyfield hadn't a hand in raising that spectre. "What are you really about, girl?" There was something about outwardly bright and bonny Betsy that tickled in Eliza's mind and raised her suspicions. A certain slyness to her pale eyes. Something about the defiant tilt of her chin. It was then she saw the rope and her heart jumped right into her throat. Tied, it was, to a spoke on the lintel just beyond the door, and she feared at once what she would find dangling from that hempen horror. A fool may have rushed forward to determine what or who hung there, but Eliza had wits aplenty, and had no intention of placing herself in a position where she might be pushed. She remained well back from the ledge.

"What are you about?" she asked again.

This time visible wroth crossed Betsy's features before it was masked by a studied servitude. "Nowt that needs be any concern of yours," she snapped, before adding a reluctant, "Miss." She pushed the door to then, but didn't, Eliza observed, fasten any of the many bolts. "Does't need me for summat?"

"Yes," Eliza replied cautiously. "You can tell me where I might find your mistress"

At least the girl's gaze did not stray towards the end of that wretched rope.

"Went 'up ta 'er new chamber. Mrs Honeyfield showed 'er."

"How long ago?" Her heart was hammering, bile flooding her throat. If that monster had hurt her dearest Jane....

The maid's gaze went to the door again, but she fixed on a smile. "Need ta know where 'tis?"

"Yes."

Surprisingly, directions were provided in a swift and straightforward fashion. Eliza recited them back and received a nod in return. She did not like to leave another mystery behind her, but Jane had to remain her goal, and she had to believe that whatever mischief Betsy was about, it wasn't murder, but a lesser sin. Theft, perhaps. Was there more to her scaremongering tattle than a typical maid's delight for the macabre? Cedarton had stood empty for years. It wasn't far-fetched to believe it had attracted other inhabitants over that time. Folk for whom the ghostly rumours about the place made it an attractive proposition. Again, it was a riddle for another moment. She had to remain focused on reaching Jane.

Eliza's travel took her through portions of the castle as yet explored with swiftness that fast extinguished the candle she'd lit from the fireplace. Eliza left it abandoned on a window ledge. Through the glass she saw the groundsman's crooked form, pitched almost double as he wheeled a small barrow before him towards the tower. "Theft," she repeated to herself. It was almost a prayer. It was too horrid to think of her dear friend being taken from her. No, she would find her yet, and deliver her from the monster who'd dwelled beside them all.

Once again, she cursed Linfield for the wretched cur he'd been. What manner of man placed his wife's chambers this many acres away from all the other inhabitants?

One with secrets, that's whom. He'd meant to conduct his sinful business without fear of being observed or overheard, though with Cluett already in possession of that worrisome record of a previous marriage, 'twas a wonder he even bothered to try and hide the matter at all. For certain the drawing room tattletales would have decried his antics, but she did not suppose the bucks would have done so. Two men sharing a woman was hardly unheard of. Such possibilities had after all reached her tender ears. The scandal here was more to do with the woman in question being his wife. No one would imagine sodomy to be involved. And as for the possibility of him already been wed to another... Well, one might say he was only copying the Prince Regent.

When she found the room, the only one at the end of a tediously long corridor, and some very narrow stairs, she burst in without making any sort of knock. "Jane... Jane, are you there?"

A smoky fire burned in the grate, providing the main light source. Although twin candelabras were also lit and burned atop a chest of drawers. The hexagonal room, which seemed to occupy the whole top floor of this turret was far better appointed than Jane's previous room. It was warm and comfortable, draped all in red velvet and old fringed brocade. As for her friend, Eliza's heart leapt to find her curled beneath the eiderdown. She dived towards her crying, "Jane? My Jane."

Pale hair curled against a cheek that remained rosy. Relief seeped through Eliza's veins. Jane remained very much whole and hearty.

Released from her doze by Eliza's shaking, Jane roused with a sigh, then sat, and sleepily rubbed her eyes.

"Eliza." She blinked. "I'm sorry, I've found not a thing." She yawned again, only at the last remembering to cover her mouth. "I must have dozed off. What of you? You've been ever so long."

Eliza crushed her in a fierce embrace. "Jane, thank the Lord. You're well. When Betsy said Mrs

Honeyfield had showed you here—"

"She did, but she left right away. The poor woman is in the most dreadfully poor state, Eliza. She's only abroad so that she might help drape the mirrors. Is there not anything you can do for her?"

Eliza both nodded and shook her head. "Bell has extracted the problem tooth. But Jane, tell me, you haven't eaten or drunk anything? Especially nothing that Mrs Honeyfield has brought to you. Pray tell me that's so. Please, Jane. It is so, isn't it?" She looked around for evidence but spied neither crockery nor crumbs.

"Eliza?" Jane's brow crumpled in confusion. "Heavens, you're in a tither, and you're making very poor sense. Has something happened? Something more? Could you not find the deed?"

The document was forthwith pressed into her hands. "Hidden in his coat pocket. Jane, there is so much foulness afoot I hardly know where to begin, but you must not call for or accept anything from Mrs Honeyfield. In fact, if you've men at your command who can do it, she should be placed under lock and key."

"Mrs Honeyfield? Eliza, why? Whatever for? Wait, you can't think—" Scepticism twisted her bonny features.

"But Jane, I do, and there's evidence for it. Bell has performed his autopsy. I shan't burden you with the details of it, but it was... It was both ghastly and enlightening. There's no question that Linfield was poisoned. You must summon the magistrate and inform the earl at once that his son has been murdered."

Jane leapt up immediately, but she did not reach for the bell pull to summon anyone. "I cannot quite believe it, even if you are quite sure." She shook herself, and began to wring her hands, the very picture of indecision and distress. "Oh, what to do? Linfield's man has already departed for Bellingbrook with my letter, and I can hardly spare another to tear off after him. Unless one of the gentlemen were to go, but then what if you are wrong, and I am letting the culprit go free? You have to admit, they are each more likely to want Linfield dead than our housekeeper."

"I don't admit that."

"But Mrs Honeyfield? Truly?"

Why was it so hard a notion to grasp?

"What would even prompt her to such action? 'Tis more likely George, or Henrietta, or your Mr Whistler, or you or I than her."

"And yet it is her. Jane, I am certain of it. I don't know that I can rightly prove it to you, but there is cause, if all I've learned is true. Your husband was responsible for the death of hers. She is here for revenge, and I fear for your safety, and that of the bairn. I shouldn't wonder if you weren't in her sights from the beginning. Think Jane, someone has meant you ill from the moment you arrived here, and she has been here throughout, passing by without notice. I bet she used the pills to set your bed alight. It would be easily done. One would only have to seed them among the sheets or the curtains, and time would do the rest."

"Eliza?" Jane shook her head. "Truly? You are clever and beloved, but the bed fire was just as likely a result of an upset candle. Such things are easily done. Nor do I see how pills can cause a fire. Things don't spontaneously ignite."

Except that sometimes they did. Eliza wasn't in the mood to conduct a lesson. It would be daybreak before Jane likely wrapped her head around it. Not because she didn't have the mental capacity for science, rather she would interrupt and take them off along tangents so that the fundamental facts about phosphorus were entirely lost in amongst the sixteen other subjects they had conversed on while Eliza attempted to explain the basic chemistry of the matter.

"Explain away the ghost you saw, then," she challenged instead.

Her friend shook her head.

"The pills—" Eliza insisted.

"I didn't take any pi—"

"Or at least the phosphorus contained in them. It would account for the spectral glow, and I'm sure there are tricks with mirrors or glass that could be used to make it seem she was floating." If there was one thing her sister Caroline was good for, it was keeping her abreast of society's doings, or more specifically the Marchioness of Pennerley's doings. She'd heard all about Bella's first visit to her husband's home, and the phantasms he'd created to spright his guests. "Jane, please. What harm will it do to summon the magistrate? If I am wrong and look a fool, then I will accept that."

Again, her friend shook her head. "Who should I send, Eliza? Moreover, where should I send them? You have given me a means by which we could all have been tricked, and delivered the likely method of my husband's poisoning, but not a reason why Mrs Honeyfield should be behind it beyond some vague mumblings about a husband that I wasn't aware she had. I think I need more than that to rouse a man from his post-dinner tipple."

"A peer has been murdered; I should think he would be astonished that you had not sought to rouse him."

Truthfully, people had a habit of leaving things until morning, so he might not have thought over much of leaving things until daybreak, especially given the weather, but really Eliza had simply been trying to spare Jane all the gruesome details of her husband's actions and peculiarities. Now, it rather seemed she would have to recount them. Only when she tried, Jane swiftly cut her off.

"Eliza, stop. I don't wish to hear of Linfield's foibles or his sins. I'm abreast of enough of them to know my position is precarious. I can't help but feel that is where I must place my focus. If Mr Cluett's demands are not met..." She set to pacing and worrying her hands again. "Can you not see what a threat he is? Far more dangerous than a woman with chronic toothache. Eliza, society... my new family, must believe that I am carrying the Bellingbrook heir... Linfield's heir. I cannot have George cast the slightest doubt over that. Besides, if Mrs Honeyfield meant me ill, then she could easily have dealt with me. It was she who led me to this room faraway from everyone else, but instead, she was delighted to hear my news." She pressed her hands protectively to her belly, though there was no trace of any roundness there yet.

None of which made sense. Why would Mrs Honeyfield be pleased to know Jane was increasing with Linfield's brat? Unless it was mere guise. The woman had certainly proved herself talented in the art of deception.

"Where is she now?"

Jane wrang her hands. "About her tasks, I should imagine. Although, I hope she is resting, considering the pain she was in."

"Have you not heeded a word I have said? She is likely your husband's killer, and you are rattling on as if she is someone we ought to feel sorry for."

"Well, it is a rather spurious supposition. You've mentioned some pills and the bed fire, and her being married, but nothing more concrete. No reason why she'd do away with her master."

They hadn't got into the details because Jane kept insisting that she didn't want to hear them!

"Revenge," Eliza summarised.

"Eliza, I've more reason to suspect you on those grounds than my housekeeper. You're the one who feels slighted over the fact that Linfield meant to bring Mr Whistler into our marriage bed, and you have all this knowledge of things that others don't— chemicals and surgeonry, and how all manner of plants and poisons work on a body."

"I thought we agreed we weren't going to suspect

one another."

"I'm just saying that what others will, if you start finger pointing without any evidence to back the accusation up."

"There is evidence."

"You have these pills?"

Not yet, but she'd find them given the chance, and there was the evidence of Lord Linfield's body.

"Proof that Mrs Honeyfield is a wedded woman? You know that every housekeeper in the land is termed missus regardless of her actual matrimonial status?"

"Jane, I cannot believe you won't listen to me. You were there in the room when she told us her husband had recently passed."

"Was I? I don't recall. And, I am listening to you. I just can't... It seems so far-fetched... ridiculous. I think Mr Cluett is by far the more likely culprit. They fought only this afternoon."

With irritation now causing her nose to tingle, Eliza rubbed at it, then crossed her arms to suppress her vexation. "Jane, if you truly believe that, then why are you about to hand him the deeds to a property in London?"

"Because I know when I'm defeated, Eliza." Jane yelled at her, raising her arms above her head, then letting them drop like stones. "Do I like any of this? Of course not, but what else am I supposed to do? Should I risk what little I do have simply to see justice done? We've been wed little over two months, and now Linfield is dead. Nothing I do will change that. But I can at least give my new family—a family

I have not yet properly met—the heir they so desire. But only if George doesn't blab."

"So, your plan is to buy their affections with another man's child?"

"And now you are judging me because I was fool enough to fall in love."

"That is not what I am doing."

"It is exactly what you are doing. Just because you are so wise and inured to strong emotions—"

Eliza's jaw fell. "Is that what you think?"

"It is what I know. Oh, you are vexed about certain things, for sure, but do you feel them in here?" Jane clamped her hand fast to her breast, which in turn made Eliza's breast ache with all the things she had bottled up to deal with later, when there wasn't a man's death to investigate. "I dare say you like Mr Whistler, but you've no idea what it is to be in love, Eliza," Jane continued, oblivious to the pain she was causing.

She made Eliza sound about as warm and friendly as Doctor Bell, with a fraction of his qualifications, and hence reasons to be aloof. She wasn't nearly so cold or dispassionate. Not that Bell, once you got past the professional persona he presented, was either of those things either. His drollness had rather grown on her.

"You don't know how love feels. How it makes the heart sing and every waking breath sweeter. Eliza, I might be a ninny, but at least I felt something. At least I lived. I loved. And I wouldn't change that. I would do it all over again, even knowing where it has led."

"What you describe sounds very lopsided. Where is he now, Jane? This man who loved you so, and whom you so desperately adore? The truth is that he abandoned you. He did not love you. He used you. You were taken in by a rogue. If he'd loved you, if it'd been remotely real between you, he wouldn't have filled your belly and then run for the hills leaving you no choice but to marry another rapscallion to preserve your reputation."

Jane paled, and her lower lip began to wobble, but Eliza was not quite done. "And if you tell me now that he was unaware of your condition, then I shall think very poorly of you indeed for both your dishonesty, and not holding him to account."

"I can't... I can't believe how horrid you are being." Jane bit her lip, and snuffled, but soon wiped the tears from her cheeks and pulled herself together. "He did... He does know. I made him aware."

"And he left anyway."

Jane did not reply. She didn't have to. The story was an all too familiar one.

"Who is he, Jane?" They were getting further away from the matter that needed dealing with and deeper into murky waters, but the opportunity for such directness might not occur again. "I don't know why you won't say, unless you fear I would recognise him. What do you imagine I'll do? Challenge him?"

She very well might.

Jane stiffened her spine and pulled her shoulders back. Her head remained bowed as she sighed, then she looked Eliza straight in the eyes and said, "I've only ever known my husband carnally. It's a tragedy that our time together was so short."

Eliza gave a slow blink. So that's how things were going to be. "You'd best hope the bairn is born with Linfield's colouring. Tongues will certainly wag if the baby has black hair with Linfield and yourself so fair."

"Of course it'll be golden haired."

So, the father was blond also. That didn't narrow things down overly.

They stewed in uncomfortable silence for several minutes more, Jane pacing, Eliza noting details of the room like the fact it had doors in three of its six walls, each shooting the other uncomfortable glances but refusing to meet the other's gaze.

"Do you not think capturing your husband's killer might be beneficial?" Eliza eventually asked. Mrs Honeyfield could have packed her belongings and walked up onto the moors never to be seen again by now.

"I do," she said with teeth clenched. "But at the same time, I'm still unconvinced, and I realise this is going to sound heartless, but I never even liked Linfield overly much. Obviously, I'm shocked and horrified by what has happened, but..." She shrugged her narrow shoulders. "But maybe it's for the best. Maybe he even deserved it. Let us not pretend he was a nice man."

That was something they could agree on. "Nevertheless, no one deserves to have their life snatched from them like that."

Jane gave a modest snort. "Yes, I recall that

about you. You were always the one arguing for lesser punishments and rehabilitation for villains during our philosophical debates. What was it you would say? 'That it wasn't anyone's fault if they were born poor or unlovely, and that we oughtn't to punish them for it. That we are all equal in God's love and should be afforded the same dignity and respect.' Except Linfield never did a thing to earn my respect. Mostly he mocked and belittled me. Truly, Eliza, I cannot be sad. Dying is probably the best thing he could ever have done for me. I wasn't exactly relishing the mechanics of him finally bedding me."

"Jane, if you keep saying such things, then I'll begin to suspect you are at very least in collusion with Mrs Honeyfield."

"Perhaps you have been reading too many horrid novels if you think I conspired with my housekeeper to do away with my husband."

"It's always the men who are diabolical creatures in those books," Eliza pointed out.

Jane sat with a thump. She sagged forward from the shoulders and sighed into her hands as she covered her face. "I'm sorry. It is all just too much. Everything is buzzing around in my brain like a swarm of angry wasps. I am not used to being the one who must make decisions. It is not what I was bred for. Eliza, I'm not like you. I don't like puzzles or unravelling conundrums. I just want things to be simple, and nothing here feels that way. If I send for the magistrate, then the earl might see me as a meddling woman who has brought outside attention onto something he would rather handle in his own way. But, as you say, if I do nothing, then it makes me look unfeeling at best, and guilty at worst."

She flopped backwards so that she was looking at the canopy. Eliza sat alongside her, suddenly bone-tired of arguing. Sometimes, it was wiser to save your breath, and act alone, than exhaust yourself trying to win people to your cause.

"How soon do you mean to negotiate with George?"

"Soon."

"What if I went for the magistrate?"

Jane pushed herself up on her elbows. "Eliza Wakefield, you are not marching across the moors in the mist gone midnight."

"Frightened a boggart'll get me?"

"No," Jane confessed with a sad shake of her head. "I'm worried one might come for me if you're not here to see them off."

"Well," Eliza said, getting to her feet. "I can't sit and do nothing." She had to assume that neither Bell nor Jem had acted as she'd bid them do. "I mean to find Mrs Honeyfield and confine her to her quarters. Then, I shall see if I can track down a footman to send for the magistrate. I shan't mind in the slightest if the earl sees me as a meddlesome woman. This is of course assuming I can find any servant at all in this place, and they haven't all already departed with your silverware ahead of the Cedarton ghost eating their faces off."

"I don't think I should accompany you to do that."

"Then stay here and bolt the door behind me."

"Eliza, be careful," Jane said, as they lingered on the threshold. She hugged Eliza to her bosom, then let her go. Eliza paused until she heard the bolt slide into place, then trotted back down the narrow stairs again, her heart heavy in her chest. As the gloom pressed in around her, she felt the keenness of her loneliness. At home in Bluebell Lane, she eternally longed for solitude; now, she would like nothing more than her sisters about her, to share the burden of this adventure. At least them, she could rely on.

Jane was too tied up in her own shortsighted vision of the future, and Jem... How bitterly she felt the loss of his affections. The strings of her heart remained cut by his betrayal. She couldn't entirely forgive him the hurt, even knowing he'd acted to protect her.

He still ought to have confided in her.

Trusted her.

Treated her as the equal he claimed he considered her.

Instead, it was all ruined between them, and over something so utterly pointless. Yes, certainly, Linfield could have ruined her reputation, but such scandals were easily averted by means of a wedding ring. Marriage pacts aplenty were formed for similar reasons, and while she didn't want to be wed, that didn't mean she wouldn't have gone through with it if it'd become necessary to ensure her sisters' futures.

Sometimes things were bigger than your own wishes, and you were obliged to act accordingly.

Besides, as husbands went, Jem wouldn't have been such a bad one. They could have brewed potions and meddled with machinery together. Plus, the lovemaking part might have been fun. At least, so long as they could agree to avoid or at least postpone having children.

There were ways of doing that.

Ways she wished more women were acquainted with and didn't judge one another over.

If Jane had only confided in her the truth of what she was about in Scarborough much earlier, then she could have educated her in the ways of avoiding mishaps.

But, Lord, she was being as big of a ninny as Jane thinking of such things now. She needed to apply her mind to the matter at hand. Jane's bun was already buttered, and whatever she and Jem might have had was already lost.

She could forgive him his past lovers, was undaunted by the fact he loved other men, what she couldn't get past so easily was him not trusting her enough to confide the truth. In that regard, he was too much like every other man.

-31-

Jem

Jem tightened his hold on the doorframe when Eliza took off through the concealed passageway. If it weren't for Linfield's cadaver laid open on the table, he'd have gone straight after her. As it was, he stood paralysed. On feeling Bell's gaze on him, he winced, then met the doctor's unflinching gaze. Given that Bell was at work on Linfield's body, there was no option other than to keep his chin up if he wanted to avoid the gristly sight of his lover's remains, a nightmare that was sure to revisit him until the end of his days. Mercifully, the candlelight meant for poor visual acuity.

"The earl won't thank you for a scandal."

"He won't thank us for letting his son's murderer walk free either." There was a smear of viscera on Bell's cravat.

"I doubt that will be the outcome. Powerful men have their ways. However, I won't stand in your way, if you feel you need to act, for whatever reason. I'm just reminding you that any public investigation into the matter is going to unearth things both you and the family would rather stay buried."

He knew that. Knew it all too well. If Linfield were exposed as a molly, a sodomite, or both, then there would be serious repercussions. Attention would turn in his direction. His actions would be scrutinised. Conclusions reached. Did he want to face any of that? Of course he didn't.

"Need it all come out? They're unlikely to crack open Janie Faintree's grave to see if it's a man or a woman buried there. It'd cause too great a noration if they did so and found the grave already emptied by body thieves. They'll accept whatever your word is on the matter, and my relationship with him is hardly of relevance to the case. Why can I not simply be Linfield's tutor?"

"Because, Jem, people are motivated by hunger, for food, for gossip, and especially for scandal. It's the salacious gossip that always spreads the fastest, and when there's a scandal, everyone has their bit to contribute. Also, do you really think Mrs Honeyfield won't have her say before the judge? No one goes quietly to the gallows, and we all know that is the outcome for the one deemed responsible. She'll spill every sordid detail she can, and likely invent a score of embellishments. The crowd will be half in love with her by the end of it. Pamphlets and broad sheets will have been printed. Folks up and down the country will know the tale of the poor young housekeeper who was driven to desperate measures after a known rapscallion, a lord no less, stole her husband from her and swived him with gusto up his bumhole."

The crudity of the description certainly hammered home the potential breadth of the mire.

"Every associate of Linfield's will be scrutinised for similar signs of unnaturalness, and you, the scholarly bachelor, with no reputation for rakery of any kind, a man who's never set foot inside a brothel, will be found wanting."

"I have." Of course he'd been in a brothel, but Bell's point was made. He'd wind up tarnished. Investors would shy from backing his work into high-pressure engines, and he'd be stuck teaching idiots forever, except who would have him after such a scandal? Even other sodomites would shy from the stigma of associating with him in case they too were identified.

Still, he could not stand back and do nothing. There was a moral obligation to fulfil, and Eliza was depending on him. He could not let her down again, not after he'd already hurt her so very much.

"I've no notion of who the local magistrate is, do you?"

Bell, with a curved sailor's needle held between his teeth, took a moment to thread it. "Jem, I'm barely cognisant of my surroundings beyond the castle walls. I came here because Linfield waved a substantial purse of coins in my direction and agreed to me cutting up corpses in his basement. I don't even know where *here* is, let alone where the nearest big house is. Hell, I'm not sure I could even find my way to the village. Could you?"

On a clear day, perhaps, but when was the last time they'd enjoyed one of those? The weather had been miserable since they'd arrived.

"I can't stand here and do nothing, Bell." He bit his thumbnail. "It can't harm to have the woman confined to her chamber. Can it?"

"That depends on whether you want any breakfast."

"I'm not sure any of us need a breakfast that's been overseen by a poisoner."

Bell shrugged. "I'm fine. I only ever take tea with an egg anyway, and it's rather hard to adulterate an egg fresh from a hen's arse without breaking the shell. Also, who in their right mind would ever adulterate the tea!"

"Yes, that would be the sign of a deeply unsettled mind, because plotting murder is completely sane."

Bell shrugged, leaving Jem to curse beneath his breath. The more time he spent around Bell, the more he'd become acquainted with his inglorious sense of humour.

Jem was not usually one for wearing grooves in the floorboards, not being one of those who required motion to think, but he was restless now. And torn. Deeply torn. Thus, he paced to combat the sense of inertia.

"I think I ought to have gone with her."

"Then go. I'm not holding you here."

"You agree, then, that I should have accompanied her?"

"I think you should be wherever you'll feel most effective and do whatever you deem best. There's nothing I need you for. You're a passable secretary, but a godawful surgical assistant. Miss Wakefield is far more gifted in that regard, and I hope you realise how grudgingly I part with that observation."

"I fear she'll challenge Mrs Honeyfield on her own."

"A most likely possibility."

"Do not say that!" He came to an abrupt standstill, gruesome visions of Eliza being hurt flooding his mind. What if his lingering meant she was already wounded?

"Fine," Bell conceded. "I imagine she's attempting to shepherd Lady Linfield into some manner of meaningful activity...and has likely already realised the futility of that at least in terms of apprehending a murderer, given Lady Linfield seems far more concerned by whatever nonsense George is about."

"The validity of the marriage."

"Yes, I heard her say that too. Utter pap, of course. Non-consummation doesn't invalidate anything."

"Assuming that's what he's claiming."

"What else would he claim? That Linfield has another wife somewhere? Oh, yes. Desperately likely. He's such a one for the ladies. Loves them, he does."

A pertinent point. Linfield was the last man on the planet who would enter a secret marriage. Had been... "Answer me one thing, Ludlow. Truthfully, do you think Eliza is right, and Mrs Honeyfield is responsible?"

The physician refused to look at him and focused on his work for several excruciating seconds. He was still stitching, and Jem was doing his best not to notice; still, he suspected he'd flinch every time he saw a lady at her embroidery from now on.

"What I think is that the idea has considerable merit. Poisoners are usually women, and while the evidence against the housekeeper is largely circumstantial, the only real alternative is that it was your Miss Wakefield who did the deed."

"Why would she, Ludlow? She knew nothing of Linfield and me. I think you are saying so just to incite my ire."

"Perhaps it was on behalf of her friend, who Linfield was treating abominably. You're not the centre of the universe, not even the centre of her world, I think."

"You're making my point for me," he muttered. He definitely wasn't the most important thing in Eliza's world. He was likely a peripheral distraction at best. In any case, murdering a man as retaliation for Linfield being a somewhat rubbish husband to her friend seemed far-fetched. If he'd been a violent tyrant, maybe... "I think Mrs Honeyfield avenging the loss of her husband a far more plausible narrative."

"As you say." Bell momentarily looked up from his needlework. "Jem... James, why are you still here?"

"I beg your pardon?"

"Fool...fool... My dear friend, I could draw you a perfect anatomical heart, but I freely confess, matters of love are not my forte. However, I can tell you with some certainty that while the odds are against you gaining Miss Wakefield's forgiveness, she most certainly won't do so if you're not there when she needs you. So, ask yourself, do you think she needs you? Is there a task she asked of you that you might perform?"

There was.

"Now, ask yourself, is the possibility of gaining her forgiveness worth the proverbial bricks you will no doubt bring down on your head by assisting her?"

For Eliza, he'd endure whatever ostracism society threw at him.

Bell's black wing eyebrows perked meaningfully. God damn him, the doctor was right. Maybe he couldn't undo the hurt he'd caused, but he could put Eliza's wishes before his own and help her, and believe in her, when no one else was ready to do so.

"Bell," he turned to say on reaching the surgery door. "It wasn't her. I don't care for you suggesting it was. Dammit, she's the only one among us who would never stoop to such measures, and I include both you and I in that judgement."

His friend snorted. "Go. Away with you. Go and earn your knightly spurs."

~Ж~

The kitchens were deserted. Jem knew there was a dearth of servants at Cedarton, but he couldn't account for the absence of them all. Someone ought to have been about below stairs. He poked his head into both the butler's pantry and the housekeeper's office. The former was home to a pair of black-eyed rats, the latter a few shabby cushions and some dried flowers in a vase. A little dish on the windowsill housed a few small amber stones, which he prodded with a fingertip. There was no sign of the Kunckel's pills Eliza insisted were the source of the phosphorous Linfield had somehow ingested, but nor had he expected to find them so obviously situated.

Thence, he headed up to the parlour, stopped by the study and library and the rest of the furnished rooms without stumbling on any signs of life.

Jem turned one of the little rocks he'd picked up between his fingers, perturbed by the quiet. Even with the pall of death looming over the property, he expected more evidence of habitation. It was too quiet. As if the house itself were holding its breath in expectation of trouble.

On the ground floor, only one of the mirrors had been covered, the largest one in the hall that reflected the main entrance. Unsure where to look next, Jem took to the stairs.

A distinct nip in the air set him rubbing warmth into his arms when he reached the third-floor landing. When he turned the corner onto the corridor that led to Eliza's room, the reason became apparent. The great iron-pinned door at the end of the corridor which had once connected this portion of the house to the Lady's Tower stood open onto the night sky. In its frame were a gaggle of four or five squat figures. Men with swaddled faces and hoods pulled low.

A small figure flew at him, sending him skittering back into the gloom. Betsy, the garrulous maid who'd openly spied on him and Eliza stuck her oval face right into his and growled. "Where's tha gawping at? Ain't nowt to see along here."

"Is that right?"

"Oh, just leave it be, will ya. Away ta ya room and stay outta sight like a nice fella. It'll be better for us all that way. Ya ain't been seen yet, and you ain't seen nowt either. That's reet ain't it, mister?"

It was, but he didn't think theft was something he ought to turn a blind eye to. He did, however, allow the maid to hound him back towards the stairs, so that they were entirely out of sight of the figures in the looming maw.

"What's going on—"

"Don't," she insisted, raising her fingers as if to silence him. "Like ah already said, tha ain't seen owt 'cept some folks moving some things what belongs t' them."

An unlikely story. He was sure his scepticism showed.

"Mister—I'm sorry, I forget ya name. This place's been empty for years. Nee one came here, due t' stories. How was we supposed t' know 'is lordship would show up reet afore Christmas when it were too late t' make other arrangements? Even a wee bit a notice would've done. We'd a up and shifted things, no harm done, like, but no, he just rides up unannounced, and says t' Gordy t' start seeing off anyone who's not invited wi' a gun. I mean who does that? Lordlings ah suppose. So, we've been waitin' for the reet time, an' t'night... I can see t' gettin' ya summat nice, if ya keep ya trap shut."

Jem frowned, not entirely sure what to make of the tale he was being spun. It was serving the purpose of keeping him out of sight and inactive, so on that score it was presumably working. Then again, he wasn't sure what the alternative would have been. He wasn't dumb enough to see off four grown men and a wily maid single-handedly. He did not possess a pistol, and he suspected the tallest fellow he'd seen was in fact the footman he'd been looking for to assist him in detaining Mrs Honeyfield, and whom he'd then intended to send for the magistrate. All in all, his options were thin.

"What is it they're collecting?" he asked.

Betsy's mouth twisted into a conflicted pucker.

"I'm going to assume they're making off with the silver if you don't convince me otherwise," he added reasonably.

"Fine. Victuals," she spat. "Victuals what folk hereabouts depend on, especially at turn o' year."

"Victuals," Jem repeated, beginning to see the lay of things. "But we're miles from the coast."

Her deadly glare continued.

Ah, that was the point. Cedarton was being used as a stopover point for smuggled goods shipped in from Holland to coves along the coast and then sent inland to York. Much easier to avoid the revenue men if you crossed the moors instead of taking the more established roads.

"Brandy," he said. "I'll be delighted to find a

bottle in my room."

Betsy grumbled. "Why not just take one of 'is lordships? It's not like he'll be needing it any longer, and Lady Linfield dun't know if there's four or forty in't cellar."

He couldn't fault her logic, even if she was advocating theft.

"Where's your mistress?"

"Gone t' bed."

Jane's room had been destroyed, and Eliza's stood nigh with the smuggling going on.

"Why?" Her gaze turned sly and suspicious. "What's tha planning? Are yer gonna offer comfort, like? Ain't it a bit soon? He's not even laid out proper yet."

"Watch your tongue, girl. That's not my intent. Nor is it any of your business why I wish to see your mistress. Just tell me how to find her."

"Fine, fine, I'll keep me neb out. 'appens, I recalls you're affatuated with tother one."

Jem gave her his meanest glare.

"Down a floor." She wafted him in that direction with her hands and the sway of her broad hips. "Go t' end of the hall past t' master's room, an' take backstairs. It's a bit twisty and turny, but if ya keep goin', you'll find it. Most of them parts are burned or boarded."

They were not the best of directions he'd ever had, but not quite as dire as the ones his cousin Sheridan had once given him for how to reach Hardraw Falls.

"Be off with ya then. Miss Wakefield did wi' the

same instructions and didn't linger."

So, Eliza was with Jane.

"Wait. I've another question first. Where are the other servants?"

Her scowl was enough to curdle cow's milk fresh from the teat. "Weren't tha supposed t' be the smart one? Or are ya trying t' get your head bashed in? Edith's in bed. Everyone else is about their business, and if yer've any sense you'll be about yers."

"Mrs Honeyfield... She's not involved in this?" He nodded his head towards the door.

Betsy's gawked at him like he'd suggested her mother was an aardvark. "She ain't' from here. Why would she know owt about owt? Ah don't know where she is, but you'll like as not smell 'er as not. Reeks a rot, she does."

"Betsy?" A man's voice called. "We're done? Where's tha?"

"Comin'." And off she went.

It seemed there were few, if any, of the servants in the castle he could trust. To that end, rather than pursuing Eliza up to Lady Linfield's room, he settled on saddling a horse and setting forth himself to fetch the magistrate. With luck, it would not be far to the neighbouring estate, and he could be back at Cedarton before anyone missed him.

Vexingly, the stables were as deserted of human occupants as Cedarton's interior had been. He'd held some hope of finding a stable lad to send off.

Jem walked a path between the stalls, prompting several horses to wicker and stick their noses over the stall doors. He was almost to the door of the tack room when he noted a curious swag of fabric trapped within the door jamb of the end most stall. Closer, it was clear that something lay within.

"Who's there? Name yourself."

A muffled thump sounded in reply.

Jem flung the door wide. On the floor in the gloom, bound and muffled, sat Linfield's valet. He blinked warily and flinched away when Jem reached for the gag around his mouth. "Clement, ain't it? I mean you no harm." He raised his lantern so Clement could better identify him. Then he uncovered his mouth and set to releasing the knots in the cords around his wrists and ankles too. "I thought you'd hastened away south hours gone."

"Mr Whistler.... Thank you." Wrists freed, the fellow pressed his fingers to the back of his head, then brought them into the light of Jem's lantern gingerly. They were clean of blood, but judging by the man's wince when he prodded a second time, there was a lump the size of a bird's egg on his noggin.

"I were supposed to be. I was all set to be off, just tightening the girth, and someone struck me from behind. They took my horse and cloak and left me trussed up here."

"Do you know who it was?"

The fellow shook his head, and promptly groaned. "Someone shorter than I, I think." He winced again. "Based on the angle from which I was hit. I suppose they meant to stop me reaching Bellingbrook." He stood and dusted off his coat and breeches. "I can saddle another mare now. She won't be as swift, but—"

"Do," Jem agreed. "I came here to do as much myself, but if you're able to take a message then all the better."

"You were heading to Bellingbrook?"

"Ah, no! Closer. We've need of the magistrate. You don't happen to know who that is? I'm afraid I don't have the lay of the land."

"I know where the nearest big house is. It's Sir Cyril Berkley's place. It's a couple of miles east of here. I could ride that way and then head south to Bellingbrook. That's assuming you still want me to do that?"

With a name like Sir Cyril, the man was sure to sit on the bench. "Yes. Yes, the earl needs to know. Go to Sir Cyril first and make sure you convey the urgency of the situation. Explain to him that Lord Linfield has left his mortal coil, and that Doctor Bell believes he's been poisoned."

The fellow's eyes widened. "That's ill news."

"See he sets off tonight and doesn't wait until daybreak."

"I will. I'll do that, sir."

Jem helped Clement saddle up and mount. He lent the fellow his lantern and watched him down the driveway as far as the mists allowed before turning back to the building. As he did, he caught a flash of light at the top of the fire-blackened Lady's Tower.

Now what mischief was afoot?

Two black silhouettes emerged onto the spindly balcony. He could not make out who they were, but they seemed to be both women from this distance. It was clear only a heartbeat later that trouble was afoot, when the second figure snatched at the first, and a blood-curdling cry split the night like lightning forking through the heavens.

-32-
Eliza

Eliza's feet didn't have to carry her far at all before she found the housekeeper. In fact, it was the smell of rot coupled with cloves that brought her to the woman's side. She was huddled in an alcove just a flight down from where Jane's room lay, a tray set with tea, thick cut bread, and bergamot marmalade balanced against her cocked hip.

The sight of the tea tray sent a shiver right through Eliza's body. It was set exactly like the one that had been delivered to Jane the previous afternoon, right before Linfield arrived and announced that he meant to have Jem join them in their matrimonial bed.

"Lady Linfield's sleeping, she won't be needing that," she said making her presence known. Something on that tray was laced with the phosphorus from those missing pills and had already stolen Linfield's life. There was no way she was letting Jane anywhere near it.

"Ey up, Miss Wakefield. I'll just take it up

anyway, in case. I've had trays sent t' all the guests' rooms as none of ya had a meal, what with how things happened. You're all sure to be hungry by now. Especially t' mistress. We don't want her skippin' meals in her condition."

"Really, do not. I'd prefer you don't disturb her."

"Ah, miss, ah heard ya," the woman hushed her in a motherly fashion that was all too convincing, and made Eliza wonder if she was wrong to be so suspicious. "I won't make a sound. Quiet as a mouse... Sh' won't even know that I'm there."

"No." Fear put a bark into Eliza's voice. She could not bear the thought of this woman near her friend, especially not bearing poisoned gifts. It had to be the marmalade. Hadn't someone said Linfield loved the stuff? While Jane had been bewildered as to why anyone would rejoice over something so bitter.

Could Jane hear them from above? Probably not. This part of the castle was old, and the walls thick enough to muffle sound. Likewise, no good would come of calling for help. No one would hear her, and it would only alert Mrs Honeyfield to her suspicions, assuming her scepticism had not already turned the tide of events. The woman had her head cocked and was now regarding her with narrowed eyes.

"I'll take it," Eliza offered, reaching for the tray.

The mistake was already made.

Instead of handing it over, the wretched woman flung it at her.

China flew and shattered. Scalding tea splashed

over Eliza's face and décolletage contributing to her cry of shock. Mrs Honeyfield seized the momentary distraction to fly past her and sprint up the stairs with her skirts held aloft.

"No!" Eliza frantically pulled the scalding hot fabric away from her skin and lunged after her, only to skid on a saucer that splintered beneath her foot, and sent her crashing into the stone steps, so that she jarred her knees and scraped raw both palms.

This time, she didn't let the shock slow her, but rose immediately, and took the stairs two at a time. She could not let that fiend near her friend.

Mrs Honeyfield proving herself both swift and nimble had already reached the chamber door. "Jane," she called, imitating Eliza's voice with alarming accuracy. "Jane, let me in. Be quick."

"Jane, no! Don't open the door."

Too late; she heard the bolt slide.

Mrs Honeyfield threw her weight against the wood, opening a gap just wide enough for her to slip through, then about turn and slam the door behind her. Eliza reached for the latch, but it was futile.

"Let me in. Open up." She drummed her hand against the barricade, but to no effect. "Jane, don't heed her. I'll find help. Be strong. Be brave."

She received no obvious reply, but with her ear pressed to the wood, she thought she heard Jane's voice, high-pitched and frantic. Was she praying? Pleading?

Oh, unbelievable fool that she was. She ought to have turned tail and returned to Jane's side the moment she caught sight of the wretched housekeeper. Nay, she ought never to have left her alone. Now what was she to do? It was too far to go to seek help, assuming anyone could be found to lend it. And who was to say if they would even get back in time. Mrs Honeyfield obviously meant mischief. And no amount of kicking or drumming would get her through the door. It'd been built to withstand armed invaders.

"Think, Eliza. Think."

There had been two other doors within that room. That meant potentially two other exits. As neither led onto this landing, it was reasonable to assume there was perhaps another, and a second stair. With no time to lose, she tore off in search of it, muttering a prayer under her breath as she ran.

-33-

Jem

Instinct sent Jem across the courtyard to the base of the Lady's Tower. He knew that whatever was occurring above him against the backdrop of the night sky, he would never get there in time if he followed the internal route Betsy had described.

At ground level, the tower seemed little more than a pitted ruin, an old gate the only barrier to his entry. It gave to a sound kick that set it clanging against the stonework. Within the shell of the east wing, the layout was confusing. The roof was missing in several places, and many of the floors had fallen through, meaning he could see through to the night sky. In a few areas, great supporting timbers slouched at alarming angles, as if likely to drop without notice and spear him through.

Interestingly, it was the upper portions that seemed to have survived best. The cap house at the top of the tallest tower seemed entirely sound. A fraction lower, he could see sections of corridor nestled between the foot thick stonework.

Beneath one such section, Jem found an open stairwell. The steps were cracked and weathered, slimy with moss, and infested with tenacious weeds that grew between the pointing. Still, it was a way up, and he took it as far as it would take him.

Three storeys up, the stairwell deposited him on a landing open to the elements. The wall of the tower stretched to the side of him, while an internal passageway petered out after a few feet. His only option seemed to be to backtrack or scale the outer wall like some mediaeval invader.

"Jem!"

He turned his head and found Eliza leaning out of a window arch, one leg already over the mantel. There was little more than a sheer drop below her. One could only assume she *did* mean to scale the walls.

"Go back," he urged, terrified by her fearlessness.

"The door's bolted on the inside. I can't get in, and Mrs Honeyfield has Jane. If I go up, I can shimmy in through that garderobe."

She was both insane and a genius. He adored her even as he despaired.

"It's too dangerous."

"I have to get to her," she retaliated.

Of course, no risk was too big.

"Then at least let me climb." He was better situated.

She drew her mouth into a mutinous pucker that only eased when he pointed out the lack of voluminous skirts to hamper his footing.

"Trust me, Eliza."

Of course, she didn't trust him with such a precious thing as her friend's safety. Men let her down, especially when it mattered. He'd let her down. And a second chance was merely a second chance of being disappointed.

"Look, can you get to there?" He pointed to a particular window. "You'll be able to guide my handholds from there."

"I don't know. I don't think... I don't like this."

Damn her, she was looking for toeholds.

Jem wasn't much for the prospect of climbing either, but he'd rather risk his neck than hers, and he definitely wasn't ready to stand back and watch her fall to her death.

"Please, Eliza. I'm closer." He was also taller, and likely a more experienced climber.

He took the fact she disappeared back inside as proof of her agreement.

Jem found purchase for his hands amidst the crumbling pointing. He did not look down. This was not the worst surface he'd ever climbed, though trees were his more usual choice. Thank God for the countless misspent summers spent tramping the countryside and scrumping apples with his cousins. It meant his muscles recalled how best to balance his weight, and his arms didn't scream too loudly over the effort of clinging on by his fingertips.

"Go right," Eliza yelled, leading him to assume she'd made it to the spot he'd indicated. He pointedly didn't turn his head to look. Her instruction was completely counterintuitive, as the balcony lay to his left.

"I can see them," he said, raising his left hand. Not very well, only as occasional glimpses between the crenulations and not enough to determine which silhouette was which.

"Right," she insisted again. "Jem, hurry."

Not, take care, just hurry. He'd have laughed if his situation weren't so perilous. He had a choice, follow his instincts, or put his faith in her directions. There was only one choice he could make. To act contrary to her wishes, would be to act as all the men who'd failed her before. If Jane perished, then she would forever hold him accountable for believing he knew better.

"Right?"

A stone slipped away beneath his hand and fell for far too long before he heard it smash.

"Eliza, are you sure?"

He could hear the women's voices now: Jane pleading, and the housekeeper repeating over and over that there was no getting around the fact that the brat couldn't be allowed to live.

The woman meant to kill Linfield's unborn son!

The realisation spurred him on. He scrambled sidewards; limbs spread spider-like as he stretched to find invisible handholds. Then, blessed relief when his efforts were rewarded as he climbed onto a window ledge that had been entirely invisible to him from his former position. He was a little east of the garderobe spout she'd initially pointed out as an entry point.

The dark arch in which he sat was wholly

without glass, and internal wooden shutters blocked the view of the room within. Jem applied his heel and secured himself entrance. From the smell of it, he'd landed in the former privy. The space was barely three feet wide and entirely comprised of grey stone. He found the stub of an unlit candle in a small cubbyhole, and from that intuited where the exit must be.

He blinked as he emerged into a well-appointed bed chamber. A hearty fire roared in the grate. This, he realised, was where Linfield had meant them to conduct their business far away from the rest of his guests.

To Jem's left, a woman laughed, the sound reminding him of screeching door hinges. One door stood bolted, the other a fraction ajar. He popped the bolt on the former, then tiptoed over to the latter.

Through the inch-wide gap, he could see Jane cowered against the wall, her head tucked low, and her skirts bundled around her feet. The silver of tear-tracks shone on her cheeks where the moonlight caressed her.

"Why are you doing all this? I don't understand," she sobbed.

"Why? Why?" Mrs Honeyfield's voice rose and fell in a sing-song fashion.

She remained out of Jem's field of vision, but he didn't want to charge out for fear of precipitating a reaction.

"Oh, should I tell you a story? I could do that, a story to send you to your eternal rest."

"Was I not kind enough? Did I not—"

"Kind enough? Aye, you were kindly enough. I've heard tell of far worse from folks that've served highborn ladies like yourself. You're not one t' pinch a body, or dock wages for things as trivial as a sneeze. It doesn't change matters though. I 'ave to end it, ya see. Make sure 'is villainy dun't continue. I'll nee 'ave his brat born."

Jane wailed. "You have already killed Linfield, why can't you let me alone?" She edged backward pushing herself further into the corner of the balcony.

"Killed him, aye, but not through design. It weren't suppos't t' be 'im, but you as ate those sandwiches. I brought you tha' pot especial like."

Her menacing shadow fell across Jane's form, who instantly winced away from her.

"His lordship was meant t' survive. T' suffer as I've suffered. Ah wanted him t' feel everything he made me endure. I'd take away 'is pretty little bride, and he'd know it. He'd feel the stab of 't reet 'ere." She thumped a fist to her heart. "Same as I felt when 'e stole me John away."

Jane raised her head a fraction, so she was peeping over the shield of her folded arms. "You were married?" she asked tremulously.

"Aye, love. I were wed t' me John when I were eleven and him fifteen. All those years and hardly any of 'em t'gether." Her tone turned nostalgic. "Years, I'd endured, wed in name but forced apart so 'e could better our lot. We finally got our shop. It twere our dream 'hat shop. I loved it, all polished wood, 'twere."

She breathed deeply, as if she could smell the scent of beeswax and herbs combined in the enclosed room full of apothecary shelves.

"Hours I'd spend watching him mixing his tinctures and powders. 'Ada m'love,' he'd say. It always gave me butterflies the way he'd say me name. 'Pass me this or that.' And I'd learned me letters, so I'd know reet away which drawer t' look in."

The longing in her voice tugged at Jem's heart strings; he felt the same melancholic loss when he thought of his parents. His mother smiling at him, ribbons in her hair. The shiny buttons of his father's coat, and how they were always fastened misaligned.

"What—what happened?" Jane ventured.

Yes, Jem silently encouraged. While the housekeeper was talking, she was not about anything more alarming. He sensed a stir in the air behind him and turned to find Eliza approaching with cat-like stealth.

"What—"

He raised a finger to his lips and shook his head, whereupon she quietened until she was right alongside him, and the warmth of her presence had him plucking at his collar and cravat. "What are you stalling for?" she said, leaning in close enough to stir the hairs above his ear.

He shivered, tried to control it, but ultimately failed. It was just what she did to him. "There's only one way in or out. I don't want to startle her into doing anything rash."

"We need a plan."

They did. He also wanted to listen to what Mrs Honeyfield had to say. It was likely stuff they could use when it came to trial, as proof of intent.

"Ah knew... Knew it t'minute he saw me John tha' he were trouble.

"That were the thing about 'im, John. He were different, see. The bonniest man you'd ever seen. Folks 'ud say his kin rowed over with t'Vikings on account of 'is fair hair. He were pretty as a maid. Delicate, reet. Like fine bone China. It weren't reet what Linfield did to 'im, having 'im dress up in frocks and paint 'is face like a strumpet.

"John, he says, 'Now lass, it's just a bit a fun between me and Lord Linfield like', but it weren't funny. And then off to 'em foreign parts he whisked 'im, without so much as a tarra and did who knows what to 'im while they were there. Well, I can tell ya, he weren't the same again afterwards, so it were obvious summat bad."

Her shadow trembled with the volatility of her feelings. Jem had far too clear a notion of what those times had encompassed: a great deal of fornication of the variety that the holy book condemned. His own sins in that regard make him even more hot around the collar. Why were the things that brought joy always tainted by Hell's shadow?

"Three months I waited, and then when he comes back, he came inta shop and put head in 'is hands. Well, of course I was reet pleased t' see 'im, but the moment he looks at me, I could see 'is soul had been ripped reet out of him. All the goodness, all the light, all gone due t' tha' devil.

"He weren't reet from then on. Couldn't focus. He'd always be off in some make-believe, or he'd disappear for days at time and there'd be no getting out of 'im where he'd been. Then, the next I know, I get word from t' Earl of Bellingbrook's man, who says, me John's gone for good, off t' 'is maker. 'Well, where's he buried?' I asked. 'It's only reet that a wife can lay a flower at 'er husband's grave.' But all I'd get was 'Be away wif ya. And stop ya beefin'.'"

No wonder the woman was aggrieved.

"Jem?" Eliza's hand rested between his shoulder blades. "Haven't we stalled long enough?"

He was sure it would be a mistake to dart out there without any certainty of what they were facing. "And if she's a knife, or a pistol?"

"She meant to poison Jane in the way she did Linfield. She'd brought up a tray."

"That doesn't mean she's unarmed."

"I still don't understand what this has to do with me," Jane's voice rang with fear.

"Then you ain't been listening," came the reply. "It's why I came 'ere. To do away with ya, t' take from 'im what he'd stolen from me, so he'd know the same agony like. An eye for an eye. Let's see how he likes it when I take 'is precious wife, I said."

"But he's dead."

"And so'll be 'is bairn. Because a course ya were blessed with a little 'un reet away, mind."

"But we weren't," Jane blurted, still cowering from the other woman. She raked her teeth over her trembling lower lip.

"Two months wed and one on t' way! Ya didn't

waste any time, love."

"But... It's not his."

Mrs Honeyfield cackled as if that were the grandest joke she'd ever heard. "D'you expect me t' believe ya? A fine lassie such as you, carrying a bun that ain't ya husband's? No! I'll not be persuaded by that. It's 'is all reet. A proper little lording with hair as white and fine as 'is."

"It isn't." Tears spilled down Jane's pale cheeks. "I was pregnant before we were wed. Before I even met him. He didn't know... Our fathers arranged the match. It's why I agreed to it. I didn't have to. I'm past twenty-one."

Mrs Honeyfield's shadow loomed larger. "Brussen, but unconvincing. Stand up now, Lady Linfield, be a love."

"No! Listen to me. It's not his. We never even consummated the marriage."

"That's wholly irrelevant," Jem muttered, but Eliza was done waiting. She wrenched the door wide, which smacked Jem square in the centre of his forehead when he failed to back up in time.

"Ow!" He teetered backwards, bringing his hand up to the point of impact and found a new groove in his brow.

Eliza barrelled straight onto the balcony. She grabbed Mrs Honeyfield by her scrawny shoulders and pushed her away from Jane so that she fell against the stone wall.

"You!" the housekeeper barked. She righted herself and swirled. "How'd you get in?"

The answer hardly mattered, and indeed, Eliza

didn't give one. Ignoring the woman, she stretched out a hand to her friend. "Jane, come to me. All will be fine."

It would not. Jem could see that already. There was no way Eliza could hold Mrs Honeyfield at bay and pull Jane to safety without making her back a target. He loomed in the doorway, strove to catch the housekeeper as she hurled herself at Eliza, only to yelp when in the confusion of the ensuing tussle his pocket set alight and then Jane punched into his side. She shrieked as her hands met the flames and pulled away, causing them both to fall back. Entwined, Eliza and Mrs Honeyfield fell hard against the crenulations. Alarmingly, several bricks fell away.

Jem staggered backwards. Now that he was out here, he could feel exactly how unstable the balcony was. It jutted out from the side of the tower supported below by fire-blackened beams. "Get inside," he yelled as he wrenched his arms free of his burning coat and cast it away from himself.

They were putting too much strain on the structure.

He knew his mathematics. Knew his engineering.

"Now!"

The stones and beams were already groaning in protest, providing a gravelly accompaniment to Mrs Honeyfield's shrieking rage.

Pain stretched all along Jem's left side, but he ignored it, stepping into the fray to grab Jane and haul her within. The moment she was over the threshold he about turned to reach for Eliza too.

His love was bound in a deadly struggle with the housekeeper. Her long hair was pulled loose from the knot into which it'd earlier been bound, and her assailant was using it like a tether to pull her closer and closer to the edge where the crenulations were broken.

"You, missy, you're always meddling. You couldn't just let 'er go quiet like." He supposed she meant that in reference to poisoning Jane's tea, or whatever it was on that tray Eliza said she'd brought up.

Eliza dipped, and strained. When that failed to free her, she drove her weight against her assailant's middle.

"No!"

Jem knew what was coming as if time were flashing before him out of sequence. The pair stumbled because of their collision and crashed against the crenulations. The mortar gave way. The wall cracked, then with a sound akin to a titan's hammer splitting a mountainside, the whole balcony parted ways with the tower.

Jem hung in the doorway. He caught a last, terrified glimpse of Eliza's face before she and Mrs Honeyfield fell into the darkness below.

A moan of utter despair wormed free of his throat. "Eliza!" It could not be so. The world could not be this cruel. He winced as timbers and stone collided with the earth below, sending tremors back up the tower. No one could survive such a fall. She was gone, taken from him before he'd had a chance to rectify any of his mistakes, before he'd had a chance properly to tell her how much he loved her, or how desperately he wanted a second chance to prove himself the man worthy of her affection.

He'd dreamed of sliding a ring on her finger one day, of the home they'd created. How he'd come in from the work shed after a long day, still smeared with oil and grease, and peep around the door of her workroom to spy on her lost in her own investigations into medicines and disease. Of how one day, maybe there'd be a child... A bonny bairn with her warmth and his nose. One he'd share an equal burden in raising.

Beside him, Jane's shrieking ceased; she fell into a faint. He felt sick to his core. His stomach roiled, pitching bile up his throat, while his legs collapsed beneath him, dropping him onto his knees.

Gone! He could not believe her gone. Eliza, who was so kind and brilliant, who was always so determined to help, who used her knowledge to aid others. She could have idled her days away living in luxury, but she hadn't. She'd been determined to make her mark on the world instead. She'd lived to better not just herself but the lives of others.

"Help!"

He truly believed he'd imagined it when the cry filtered through his numbed senses.

"Jem... Jem! Please help! I can't... I'm stuck."

He could not see her. "Eliza," he screamed again and again.

Her reply was faint. He couldn't see her, but beyond the door now lay a sheer drop.

Ignoring the pain in his side, he dropped to his belly to peer over the edge down past the broken timbers, down into the inky gloom and the shadows that pawed at the tower's sides. It was there he spied her, clinging to a beam trapped betwixt the stonework and one of those hanging supports he'd been so alarmed of when he'd observed them from below. She was wan with terror, but miraculously whole and alive.

"Don't move, I'm coming."

"I can't. Jem, please."

He stepped over Jane in his haste to act. She was breathing and in no imminent danger. Jem sprinted to the bed, where he tore down the curtains and gathered the linens into a heap. He'd learned knotting as boy, building rafts to ride along the River Ure. He worked quickly, fashioning the fabric into a makeshift rope that he secured both around the bedpost and his waist.

The climb down was utterly terrifying and seemingly endless. He had no choice but to look down to make certain of his footing, and each time he did, he glimpsed Ada Honeyfield's smashed body spread ragdoll like on the grass, broken timbers scattered around her like kindling.

Eliza's pale face was turned up towards him. Her hair danced wild around her, caught in the gusts of the evening wind that also pulled at his shirt. Her clothing was torn, and he could see the strain in her jaw from clenching her teeth.

"Hold on. I'm almost there."

Finally, he was able to straddle the support

beam and clasp her to his body. "I have you now. It's going to be all right."

He felt every tremble that shook her body as he loosened the makeshift rope and bound it fast around her waist instead.

"I think I may have broken my arm," she said, tears spilling.

"We can get Bell to splint it."

That made her splutter something approaching laughter. "Oh, Jem, I'm such a fool. You were right. I shouldn't have charged out there. I could have killed us all."

"You weren't to know it was unsound. None of us did."

"It's my fault Mrs Honeyfield..." She turned her head away from the shattered body, pushing her wet face into the crook of his shoulder. "I'm always so sure I'm right, I forget to listen."

"Eliza, it was not your fault." She peeped up at him with watery eyes. Jem pressed his hands to either side of her head and drank down the vision of her while his heart rioted inside his chest. They were in no position to be exchanging any sort of tendresses, but he pressed his lips to her brow, nonetheless. "I'm going to get you down from here. I think I've enough length to lower you to the parapet below. It was a mere ten feet or so, rather than the thirty he estimated the ground to be.

"Promise me your knots will hold."

"They'll hold," he promised, and pressed another desperate kiss to her brow.

She nodded her assent, and he gingerly began to

lower her. It was almost worse dangling her at the end of a line than making his arduous crawl down the tower wall. Ten feet had never felt so interminably far. When she finally landed, he gasped deep lungfuls of air. His heart was ready to burst right out of his chest.

Eliza freed herself of the rope, then still holding fast to the end, waved for him to follow.

"Perhaps I missed my calling as a sailor," he said when he was finally on a level with her again.

"Well, I'm glad that you didn't take to the sea, else we might never have met."

"It's good to have met you, too." He smiled, as did she, right before both their brows knit and their expressions crumbled into frowns.

"What now?" she asked, turning away.

Jem winced, feeling the rejection as keenly as the wound on his side.

Her head jerked towards him again. "You're injured."

"Some," he concurred. Neither of them had got away unscathed. He finally looked down at the damage. His shirt was stuck to his side, and the flesh there was red and bloody. "My coat caught alight. Jane's hands," he muttered recalling she'd fallen against him.

"How?" Eliza asked.

"I don't..." The little amber rock he'd picked up had been in his pocket. "I...I think I found one of the missing pills. It wasn't as I expected...I didn't recognise it as... I mean it didn't look like something you'd swallow, more like a speck of amber you might pick up off the beach. In the scuffle, it must have—"

"It's unstable in the air. It's why the pills are coated with silver, and generally stored in water."

"And you say that you're not a chemist!"

She winced as she snort-laughed. "I'm not. I've only read Lavoisier."

Jem shook his head, wearily bemused. "I should introduce you to my cousin Pip, he'd talk your ears off about the subject. He used to correspond with Lavoisier before... Well, before the revolution took its toll."

"I should like that." She blessed him with a smile. "I should like very much to do something as ordinary as drink tea and converse with your learned cousin, but first we should find a way down from here, and then you must get Doctor Bell to dress your wound."

"Shan't you do it?" he asked. He'd much rather her hands on him than Bell's. It wasn't that he didn't have faith in the former, only his bedside manner wasn't half so endearing. Plus, he was loath to part company with her so swiftly after so great a shock. His mind was still catching up with the fact she wasn't dead. He thought the image of her falling away from him would stay in his head forever.

"My arm," she reminded him. "And if it weren't so sore, my hands are not so steady at the moment."

She was shaking from head to foot, but he wasn't faring much better.

"Jem, someone needs to fetch the magistrate. Also, where is Jane? Is she all right? I didn't see her fall. She didn't, did she?"

He'd temporarily forgotten Lady Linfield. "Only into a faint. I'm sure she's roused by now. We can go to her." They were back at the top of the stairs he'd forced his way up earlier. They would take them down to the tower base, and from there wherever they wished. "You don't need to worry about summoning the magistrate either. I saw to it. I sent Linfield's man. Hopefully, Sir Cyril should be on his way."

She sighed as if a great weight had lifted to hear that was the case. "Then let us collect Jane and get our stories straight before they arrive, for there's a deal of explaining to do, and I expect some of the details—"

"—ought to be lost," Jem finished for her. For definite the precise details of Linfield's relationship with Ada Honeyfield's husband ought to be side-stepped, and nor would there be any suggestion of misconduct on Lady Linfield's part.

"Also, the Cluetts will need to be handled…"

Ah, yes. George's blackmailing scam.

Supporting one another, they hobbled their way into the house.

-34-

Eliza

After Bell had been dispatched to retrieve Jane and a suspicious pot of marmalade, and Edith, then Betsy, and finally Gordy to deal with Mrs Honeyfield's body, and various wounds had been dressed, and the matter of Jem's pocket fire and the earlier spontaneous ignition of Jane's bed-curtains been thoroughly discussed and pontificated on, and sensible conclusions drawn was Eliza free to go with Jane to address the Cluetts.

The mayhem of the evening seemed to have entirely passed them by, for neither mother nor son had left their rooms.

Henrietta, not George, opened the door to their shared sitting room when Eliza knocked. It struck Eliza how much more comfortable these rooms were compared to the ones Linfield had given his wife. Beast! She was finding it difficult to mourn his passing. At root, all the woe they'd suffered was down to him.

George sprang out of an armchair at their

arrival. He was in his shirtsleeves. His sandy hair damp at the front and curling, while his lips were port stained. "What is it? I hope you're not here to haggle over terms, for I made my part of this bargain entirely plain, and I won't move on it."

"Now, George," Henrietta chastened. "Don't be disagreeable. We are still Lady Linfield's guests, and she has suffered the appalling loss of her husband this evening. I think we'd do well to be civil."

"I'm not here to negotiate." Jane ignored the chair Henrietta offered in favour of remaining on her feet, though she clung to the back of it. Eliza could see the tremble of nervousness running through her. "I simply see no reason to delay matters. Tonight has been entirely too trying…. Well, never mind that."

"You have it?" George's eyes bulged in a greedy way, reminding Eliza of a moneylender on payday. It saddened her that her first perceptions of him were so lacking. She'd thought him a wastrel, but at least a good-natured one. In truth, he was as mean as the next man, and willing to do any awful thing imaginable if he believed it to his benefit. He was preying on Jane, when he ought to have been providing comfort and support as her husband's alleged best friend. "If you haven't, then we have nothing to say."

She heartily wished they were not so pressed for time, for then she might have counselled Jane against this exchange. Bell had laughed at the very notion that Linfield was already wed. Had flat out said it was impossible, as well as preposterous.

"I have it," Jane confirmed, her tone weary. "But

you'll forgive me if I don't altogether trust you. What assurance do I have that you won't spread your horrid tales, anyway?"

George gave her a studiously lazy shrug. "What would be the point in that? I'd have no evidence, for you will have that, and I imagine you'll destroy it. Nor do I wish to earn the wrath of the earl. I simply want what is mine."

Henrietta gave a cough.

"What is mine and my mother's returned to us. Once that's settled, there need not be any animosity between us. We'll be happy to leave as soon as the day breaks." At least he did not offer to stay and fake regard for Jane's welfare during her time of loss.

"You may wish to make it sooner," Eliza advised. "If you want to avoid dealings with the magistrate. I imagine he'll want to hear testimonies from everyone present."

She rather hoped that matter might be resolved with a simple presentation of the bodies. Victim, culprit, *et voilà*. The Cluetts need not feature in the narrative. Only the earl needed to hear the full details of his son's death. Bell would no doubt report them, hopefully minus the parts about Jane's cuckoo.

"Eliza? How should we manage this?" her friend asked.

"Give both papers to me." She extended her uninjured hand. "I will confirm they are what you each claim them to be, and then I shall pass them over simultaneously. Is that agreeable?"

George huffed and shook his head. "You are her

friend. What's to say you haven't concocted a plan to swindle me?"

"George," Henrietta chastened again. "I think you're forgetting who you are dealing with. They're two honest, god-fearing young ladies of decent upbringing, not the sharps you usually associate with."

Actually, two young ladies of dubious morality who had just dealt with a murderess, and now intended to white-lie to a magistrate.

"However, I will examine the papers too, as Miss Wakefield does. That will make things all fair and equal, will it not?"

Fair, perhaps, but it meant yet another person was privy to the knowledge that Linfield was already wed when he took Jane to wife. Although, likely enough George had already shared that gossip with his mother. "Jane?"

"I suppose."

George agreed with a grumble, and the papers were passed to Eliza for inspection, Henrietta observing them over her shoulder. They were both precisely as they were supposed to be. A deed for a London property, and the record of a marriage, signed by both parties and properly witnessed.

Eliza extended them to the requisite recipients. "If any mention of this gets out, we shall know the source, and make sure the earl does too."

"It won't." Henrietta snatched the deed from her son's hands, and the pair set about quarrelling over ownership of the paper. In comparison, Jane paled to the roots of her golden hair, prompting Eliza to catch her around the waist and hurry her from the room.

"Eliza, what am I to do? One only has to look at this to see that my marriage is void. He was already wed." She tore at the soft skin of her face, leaving scratch marks across her brow. "Oh, Lord! I am ruined."

"Burn it."

Jane's teary gaze met hers, and Eliza saw straight into the depths of her friend's soul. Saw all her fears and the swirling maelstrom of anxieties. The belief that her own sin and folly had led her here and that perhaps she was deserving of the misfortune.

"That will not suffice. People know of it. There are witnesses out there." Their names written in browning ink on the parchment she held onto so tightly. "There's the priest too. What if they come forward? The notice of Linfield's death is sure to appear in the newspapers, and they will see it and realise there is a story to be sold."

"Jane, they won't." She drew her friend along the corridor, and downstairs to the Lady's Parlour. The fire had burned out, but the room retained the heat. The curtains were drawn and someone had finally covered the mirror above the mantle.

Eliza urged Jane into a chair and settled on a footstool by her side. Ignoring the clamminess of Jane's hands, she gave them a reassuring squeeze. "None of that will come to pass—"

"It will."

"It won't, Jane. Look again at the certificate. Mr

Cluett may believe this a legitimate record, but it isn't. It can't be. The person here,"—she ran her finger under the woman's name—"doesn't exist. Never has, at least in accordance with the laws of the land. Janie Faintree is the name Mrs Honeyfield's husband took when he went off with Lord Linfield. It's therefore not a legal union, because two men can't be wed. And even supposing they could, Janie died before you ever married Linfield. It was in the newspapers if you recall."

Jane stopped her sobbing and wiped her face clean with the back of her hand. The palms were blistered. "I'm not going to pretend to understand all the revelations of this evening. Eliza, I couldn't take in the half of what Mrs Honeyfield was saying to me. I just want to know that this bairn's future is safe."

"It's safe, Jane. All is going to be well. Your marriage is legitimate, no one can say or prove otherwise, and while this paper if it got out certainly has the makings of a scandal, it's not going to get out, because I'm putting it on the fire now." She tugged it from Jane's fingers, and did just that, using the bellows to persuade some fresh bits of kindling to catch, then chew on the edges of the parchment.

They watched as the tiny flames crawled across the vellum, slowly devouring one inked word after another, until the little slice of history that had recorded the union of Lord Eustace, Viscount Linfield and a spinster named Miss Janie Faintree was no more.

"I cannot be sad that he is gone," Jane confessed, retreating from the hearth once the last curl of parchment had been consumed. "I realise that makes me seem horrid, but I was nothing but a nuisance to him. A yoke around his neck. I didn't love him, and he didn't love me. And the sort of love he didn't feel was sure to bring us to ruin eventually. I'll mourn him as society dictates, of course, and raise his son."

"And bring his killer to justice," Eliza prompted.

Jane kicked off her shoes and curled into the armchair as if she hadn't heard.

"I expect I'm too overwrought to meddle in such things. I'll leave that to Doctor Bell and my new father-in-law. Oh, don't put on so. It suits me to have him think I'm a pea-brained imbecile incapable of anything but birthing his grandson. Men like that. They enjoy playing the grand protector, and thinking is dreadfully tiring. I don't know why you're so enamoured of it."

"Because men are ninnies," she retorted reflexively.

Except, that wasn't entirely true. There was one, who for definite had his faults, but she wouldn't be here now if not for him.

"What will you do now?" she asked Jane, putting thoughts of Jem aside, so that she didn't give herself away with an involuntary grin.

"I'll go to Bellingbrook," Jane insisted, her pale bow-shaped lips barely moving to form the words. "Hopefully, they'll welcome me. Whatever happens, I shan't go back to my parents."

Eliza nodded. She could see why Jane had no desire to do that.

"And Cedarton?"

Jane glanced around at the walls and windows before her gaze settled on the hearth. "I'll see that it's shuttered and left to rot as it ought to have been in the first place."

"That might be for the best," Eliza agreed. Now probably wasn't the time to mention the castle happened to be the primary store of a local smuggling gang.

~Ж~

Sir Cyril arrived shortly after the Cluetts took their leave. They'd taken the hint about the prospect of having to provide testaments and relieved themselves of the bother of it. Dawn was still a long way off, but the dreadful mist that had swaddled Cedarton and its surroundings had finally lifted, leaving behind only a ghostly rime around the moon as the remainder of their party huddled together on the entryway steps to meet the magistrate.

Jane welcomed him and dropped a curtsey, but it was Doctor Bell who took charge of matters and imparted all the details of the case in his succinct and utterly dry way. The two men went off to examine the bodies of Lord Linfield and Mrs Honeyfield together, while the rest of them dallied in the hallway.

"I wonder if I might avail myself of your bed, Eliza," Jane said, in between swallowing yawns. "I can barely keep my eyes open any more, and a swarm of angry bees are buzzing in my head. I'm sure if Sir Cyril desires to interview me, he might wait until I'm risen again. I'm not sure I could count past five right now, let alone get all that has happened straight enough not to sound like a complete lunatic.

"Go. You should rest," Eliza encouraged. "Shall you need my help?"

Despite her sore palms, Jane shook her head. "I think I'd like a few minutes alone in which to collect myself, and this dress is easy enough to unpin."

Eliza pulled her into a quick embrace, then released her and watched her up the stairs. Jem was lingering by the solitary suit of mail when she finally turned away from the stairs.

"Will you join Doctor Bell and Sir Cyril?" she asked.

Jem shook his head. "I've had more than my fill of adventures for one night, and I've no desire to be tugged into a conversation over either body. I think I might follow in Lady Linfield's footsteps and see if I can catch forty winks before anyone asks me to relate what has happened. What about you, Eliza? Do you intend to go down and make sure that facts are being presented as you wish them?"

A part of her was certainly being tugged in that direction, but another was eager for a soft pillow and the respite offered by an eiderdown. "I should give Jane a few moments," she said, committing to neither. Of course, there were other beds in other rooms she might avail herself of, but that would feel like an imposition, even though Jane would never scold her for it. Besides, she wasn't certain she wanted to close her eyes, for she was sure to tumble headlong in memories of the balcony tipping beneath her feet and the ground rushing fast towards her. It was a wonder that she'd survived. Jem would probably be able to show her the mechanics of it. How her trajectory accounted for the fact she'd survived bruised but unbroken whereas Mrs Honeyfield had met with an undignified end, but she wasn't ready to relive it yet.

"I might pen a letter." It would help untangle her thoughts to have to pin them fast to the page, and it would entertain her sisters to hear of her adventures. Although, she would omit certain factors, and definitely miss seeing their reactions as they read. Would they believe it? She was sure she would not if she were presented with such an account. They would wince and laugh and clap their hands in delight though over the many twists and turns, and Maria would claim to have known from the start who was responsible. Her other sisters would nod, but not believe her, while Frederick would insist on voicing that fact, and then a squabble would break out and little Leesa would join in the tableau, her toddler voice out screeching them all.

All at once, she was dismally homesick for the familiar comforts of Bluebell Lane and her kin. Their warmth, their presence, and their fierce love for one another.

"Goodnight, then," Jem bowed his head to her, then took to the stairs. "Eliza?" He paused part way up, one hand clasped to his side, reminding her of his injury. None of them had survived the evening unscathed.

"Good night," she returned, allowing him to nod and depart.

She stood for some minutes looking at the step where he'd been, feeling like a piece had been cut from her reality, a certain sliver that was vitally important, and with that realisation she knew precisely where she wanted to be. It was not with Jane, or her family, nor with Bell in his basement surgery, but next to the man she loved. The man who had been there when she'd needed him to be. Who wasn't perfect in any way, but who was perhaps perfect for her.

She ran up the stairs and straight to his room. Nor did she wait after she wrapped her knuckles against the door, but brazenly barrelled right in. He stood stripped to his skin on top, candlelight painting bronze shadows over his creamy skin. A large section of his abdomen was bandaged, and he was as bruised and scraped as she knew herself to be, but he was also undeniable lovely, and she loved him.

"Eliza! Whatever's the matter?"

"Nothing." She laughed, moving the bottle of brandy that lay on his quilt to the bedside table. "It'll make the bed awful lumpy," she said by way of explanation.

"I don't... What are you doing here?"

She shrugged. "I just realised where I wanted to be, and it wasn't home, or with Jane. It wasn't even down in Bell's surgery or buried in the pages of a scientific treatise. It's with you. I love you too, Jem. I still don't know that I want to get married, but I do love you, and I want... I want at least this night."

"Just this one?" He'd found a smile too now, of the quick nervous variety as if he didn't quite dare believe in what he was hearing yet.

"Oh, I don't know. Shall we see what tomorrow brings? I mean, boggarts might assault us, or one of us might discover we're actually the heir to a far-flung realm...or I might discover you snore most horrifically and decide that Joshua Rushdale is by far a better prospect." She imitated a potential such sound.

"I do, exactly like that, and he definitely is."

But Joshua was also not gazing at her like she was a queen among maids, nor had he ever made her heart leap in quite the same way, or hinted he was prepared to hike across the globe with her, or stargaze, or mix noxious gases in a makeshift laboratory or recite mathematical equations to her in a husky tone that made her toes curl.

He was, more importantly, not here, and semi-naked, and he'd never made her heart leap in the way that Jem did when he leaned in close, and the scent of him caught in her nostrils, and his touch washed heat through her skin. He'd never fingered her until her heart felt like it would explode or pushed her to spend over his face.

"I'm glad to see you're considering it properly."

"Oh, I am," she agreed. "Perhaps we could convince him into being part of a triumvirate, like the Marquis of Pennerley and—"

"You know it's only speculated that he and Viscount Marlinscar—"

"Fie, I know the Marchioness. She and my sister Caroline exchange letters practically every other day. There are definitely three of them in that relationship. So, perhaps—"

"You'll recall Joshua shot the Marquis in the leg," Jem said.

"I do," she said, "But he could hardly let it go in front of such an audience, and he really was protesting to the fact he'd been flaunting her as his mistress and planted a penny in her pudding. It wouldn't be at all like that between us. We'd cajole him with iron filings and axle grease and belching pufferoos."

"I don't know what one of those is."

"Oh," she waved with her uninjured arm and hand. "Nor do I, I just thought of the word, but we could invent it together, or you could with Joshua, while I—"

"Dissect corpses, birth babies, and cure the morbid sore throat."

"Precisely." She nodded.

"Careful," he said. "I might start believing in this utopian future."

"It could be ours, Jem," she said, laying her hand against his bare chest, and grinning when the smattering of hairs there tickled her palm. "But for tonight, the only thing I want you to believe is that I want you as much as you ever wanted me, and that I don't mind if you've lain with other men, or other women, or both. And I won't mind if you still look on them and think they're lovely, because who doesn't look on lovely things and admire them."

"Eliza." He pressed a finger to her lips, quietening her. "You've already said all you ever needed to say." He put his hand over hers where it still lay against his chest. "I'm yours. You enchant me... And I'm very relieved I won't have to poke out my eyes with a stick, because the world is full of lovely things."

"Never on my account."

"I'll never belittle you, Eliza. You're the cleverest person I know."

Now he was making her blush. "I think you're cleverer."

He dipped his head and kissed her nose. "I'm really not, you know."

She kissed his jaw. "I intend to stay tonight." Then the side of his throat.

"Hm, scandalous. You know, I won't be clever at all if you keep pressing your lips to me."

"I don't want you clever, I want you hard. No. No... Actually, I want you both." She let her hand fall from where it rested, so that it traversed a line down to the falls of his breeches. "I think I have the essence of how to accomplish the one, which leaves you to handle the other."

"Proving my cleverness," he huffed. "You realise it's rather hard to think when you're touching me there."

"I bet you can still conjugate Latin verbs for me. No. No, wait. Explain to me Boyle's Law."

"Ah, yes," he began licking his lips, as Eliza licked something else entirely. "It's really quite simple. If you take a fixed mass of gas at a constant temperature, then the volume it inhabits is inversely proportional to…"

"Go on."

"Is inversely proportional to the pressure!" He near squeaked the last as she ran her tongue over the crown of his cock. "And that is quite enough of that. I think we should concentrate on some biological sciences for a while, don't you?"

Her mouth was too full to reply.

~Ж~

Thank you for accompanying me on this foray into gothic romance. If you're not ready to let go of Jem and Eliza, scan the code below to download a bonus scene.

The Wooing the Wakefield's series will continue exploring the relationships of the various Wakefield siblings. Also, as I've developed rather a soft spot for Ludlow Bell, I think you can be assured that he'll be back.

-ACKNOWLEDGEMENTS-

Dear Reader,

This book was never meant to be. The Wooing the Wakefield's series was supposed to begin with a different book. One about Jem, Eliza, and Joshua finding a happily ever after, but then I had a bright idea about writing a short prequel novella to pique readers interests. I think you can probably tell where this is going.

A Devilish Element was born, complete with its cast of characters and a murder mystery that obliged me to read numerous historical science texts. (I'm not complaining. I loved it.) The book became more gothic, more of a mystery and less of an erotic romance, and thus the whole series shifted a little. I hope you like what it's become. I've always loved the blending of eroticism, mystery and gothic aesthetics. I think anyone who knows me or has read any of my previous books is probably not surprised by this. Well, maybe if all you've read is Flugwhump & Betty.

But then, you might also imagine I'm a cat person.

I'm not.

Now for some thank yous.

 To Ren & Mandie, thanks once again for your diligence. To Mandie, I'm sorry that I write villains that make your blood pressure spike, but I do like my villains to be villainous.

To Dayna, for loving the weird and the wonderful as much as I do. Keep those book and film recommendations coming.

Finally, thanks to everyone who's read this far. You're appreciated so much.

Madelynne Ellis, April 2024.

-ABOUT THE AUTHOR-

Madelynne is a New York Times & USA Today bestselling author. She wrote her first novel after discovering Black Lace Books in the 1990s. After escaping the Hotel California, she dived into storytelling full time. Her books are filled with bisexual bad boys who like to get down and dirty, and stories so angst-filled you know they're going to hurt.

She lives in the UK near the Welsh border, where you can find her surrounded by books, drinking rapidly cooling decaf coffee, and listening to loud music.

Keep up with her by joining her email newsletter using the QR code below, or check out her website www.madelynne-ellis.com